CHAPTER ONE

MARRYING a man she didn't love was surprisingly easy, Jasmine Kouri thought as she handed her empty champagne flute to a passing waiter. Why had she wasted so much time struggling to be alone? She should have done this a year ago.

Her engagement party was in full force. All of Qusay's high society—everyone who'd once scorned her—was now milling beneath the white pavilion on the edge of the Mediterranean Sea, sipping Cristal in solid gold flutes as they toasted her engagement to the second richest man in Qusay.

Her fiancé had spared no expense. Jasmine's fifteen-carat diamond ring scattered prisms and rainbows of refracted sunlight every time she moved her left hand. It was also very heavy, and the pale green chiffon dress he'd chosen for her in Paris felt hot as her skirts swirled in the desert wind. Across the wide grassy vista, the turrets of his sprawling Italianate mansion flew red flags emblazoned with his personal crest.

Then again, Umar Hajjar never spared any expense—on anything. Everything he owned, from his world-class racehorses to his homes around the world, proclaimed his money and prestige. He'd pursued Jasmine for a year in New York, and yesterday, she'd suddenly accepted his proposal. This party was Umar's first step in making the people of Qusay forget her old scandal. He would shape Jasmine into his perfect bride, the same as he trained a promising colt into a winner: at any cost.

But that wasn't why Jasmine's heart was pounding as she looked anxiously through the crowds in the pavilion. She didn't care about money. She was after something far more precious.

Jewel-laden socialites pressed forward to congratulate her, including some whose vicious gossip had ruined her when she was young and defenseless. But it would be bad manners to remember that now, so Jasmine just thanked them and smiled until her cheeks hurt.

Then she caught her breath as she saw the people she'd been waiting for.

Her family.

The last time she'd seen them, Jasmine had been a scared sixteen-year-old girl, packed off into poverty and exile by her harsh, heartbroken father and quietly weeping mother. Now because of this marriage, no one would ever be able hurt Jasmine—or her family— ever again.

With a joyful cry, she held her arms wide, and her grown-up sisters ran to embrace her.

"I'm proud of you, my daughter," her father said gruffly, patting her on the shoulder. "At last you've done well."

The Royal
HOUSE OF KAREDES
Desert Throne

Jennie
LUCAS

Trish
MOREY

Annie
WEST

MILLS &
BOON

Published in Great Britain 2014
by Mills & Boon, an imprint of Harlequin (UK) Limited,
Eton House, 18-24 Paradise Road, Richmond, Surrey, TW9 1SR

THE ROYAL HOUSE OF KAREDES: THE DESERT THRONE
© 2014 Harlequin Books S.A.

Tamed: The Barbarian King © 2010 Harlequin Books S.A.
Forbidden: The Sheikh's Virgin © 2010 Harlequin Books S.A.
Scandal: His Majesty's Love-Child © 2010 Harlequin Books S.A.

Special thanks and acknowledgement are given to Jennie Lucas, Trish Morey and Annie West.

ISBN: 978 0 263 24597 4

027-0414

Printed and bound in Spain
by Blackprint CPI, Barcelona

Tamed: The Barbarian King

JENNIE LUCAS

Jennie Lucas grew up dreaming about faraway lands. At fifteen, hungry for experience beyond the borders of her small Idaho city, she went to a Connecticut boarding school on a scholarship. She took her first solo trip to Europe at sixteen, then put off college and travelled around the US, supporting herself with jobs as diverse as gas station cashier and newspaper advertising assistant.

At twenty-two she met the man who would be her husband. After their marriage, she graduated from Kent State with a degree in English. Seven years after she started writing, she got the magical call from London that turned her into a published author.

Since then life has been hectic, with a new writing career, a sexy husband and two babies under two, but she's having a wonderful (albeit sleepless) time. She loves immersing herself in dramatic, glamorous, passionate stories. Maybe she can't physically travel to Morocco or Spain right now, but for a few hours a day, while her children are sleeping, she can be there in her books.

Jennie loves to hear from her readers. You can visit her website at www.jennielucas.com, or drop her a note at jennie@jennielucas.com.

To my fellow authors of this series:
Carol Marinelli, Trish Morey and Annie West.
You girls rock!

Plus an extra heap of thanks to Trish Morey,
who's the one who got me into all this
trouble in the first place.

"Oh, my precious child." Her mother hugged her tearfully, kissing her cheek. "It's too long you've been away!"

Both her parents had grown older. Her proud father was stooped, her mother gray. The sisters Jasmine remembered as skinny children were now plump matrons with husbands and children of their own. As her family embraced her, the wind blew around Jasmine's ladylike dress, swirling around them all in waves of sea-foam chiffon.

It was all worth it, she thought in a rush of emotion. To be with her family again, to be back at home and have a place in the world, she would have given up a hundred careers in New York. She would have married Umar a thousand times.

"I missed you all so much," Jasmine whispered. But all too soon, she was forced to pull away from her family to greet other guests. Moments later, she felt Umar's hand on her arm.

He smiled down at her. "Happy, darling?"

"Yes," she replied, wiping away the streaks of her earlier tears. Umar hated to see her mussed. "But some of the guests are growing impatient for dinner. Who is this special guest of yours and why is he so late?"

"You'll see," he replied, leaning down to kiss her cheek. Tall and thin and in his late forties, Umar Hajjar was the type of man who wore a designer suit to his stables. His face was pale and wrinkle-free with the careful application of sunscreen; his dark gray hair was slicked back with gel. He tilted his head. "Listen."

Frowning, she listened, then gradually heard a

sound like thunder. She looked up, but as usual in the desert island kingdom, there were no clouds, just clear sky blending into sea in endless shades of blue. "What is that?"

"It's our guest." Umar's smile widened. "The king."

She sucked in her breath.

"The...king?" Sudden fear pinched her heart. "What king?"

He laughed. "There is only one king, darling."

As if in slow motion, she looked back across the wide grass.

Three men on horseback had just come through the massive wrought-iron front gate. The Hajjar security guards were bowing low, their noses almost to the ground, as the leader of the horsemen rode past, followed by two men in black robes.

They all had rifles and hard, glowering faces, but the leader was far taller and more broad-shouldered than the others. A ceremonial jeweled dagger at his hip proclaimed his status while the hard look in his blue eyes betrayed his ruthlessness. Beneath the hot Qusani sun, his robes were stark white against his deeply tanned skin as he leapt gracefully down from his black stallion.

Shaking in sudden panic, Jasmine looked at him, praying she was wrong. It couldn't be him. Couldn't!

But when she looked at his handsome, brutal face, she could not deny his identity. For thirteen years, she'd seen his face in her dreams.

Kareef Al'Ramiz, the barbarian prince of the desert.

The party guests recognized him with a low gasp that echoed her own.

Kareef. The man who'd seduced and deserted her to shame and exile. The man who'd caused the loneliness and grief of half her life. The man who'd made her pay so dearly for the crime of loving him.

And in a few days, Kareef Al'Ramiz would be crowned king of all Qusay.

Fierce hatred flashed through her, hatred so pure it nearly caused her to stagger. She clutched at Umar's arm. "What is he doing here?"

His thin lips curved in a smile. "The king is my friend. Are you impressed? It's part of my plan. Come."

He pulled her across the grass to greet the royal arrival. She tried to resist, but Umar kept dragging her forward in his thin, sinewy grip. The colors of white tent and green grass and blue sea seemed to blend and melt around her. Trying to catch her breath, to regain control, she twisted her engagement ring tightly around her finger. The enormous diamond felt hard and cold against her skin.

"Sire!" Hajjar called jovially across the lawn. "You do me great honor!"

"This had better be important, Umar," the other man growled. "Only for you would I return to the city in the middle of a ride."

At the sound of Kareef's voice—the deep, low timbre that had once sounded like music to her—the swirls of color started to spin faster. She started to fear she might faint at her own party. How would Umar react to that?

Marry me, Jasmine. Kareef's long-ago whisper echoed in her mind. He'd stroked her cheek, looking down at her with the deep hunger of desire. *Marry me.*

No! She couldn't face Kareef after all these years. Not now. *Not ever!*

Her heart pounded furiously in her chest. "I have to go," she croaked, pulling frantically away from Umar's grasp. "Excuse me—"

Startled by her strength, Umar abruptly let go. Knocked off balance, she stumbled forward and fell across the grass in an explosion of pale green chiffon.

She heard a low exclamation. Suddenly hands were on her, lifting her to her feet.

She felt the electricity of a rough touch, so masculine and strong, so different from Umar's cool, slender hands. She looked up.

Kareef's handsome, implacable face was silhouetted against the sun as he lifted her to her feet. His ruthless eyes were full of shadow. Blinding light cast a halo around his black hair against the unrelenting blue sky.

His hand was still wrapped over hers as their eyes locked. His pupils dilated.

"Jasmine," he breathed, his fingers tightening on hers.

She couldn't answer. Couldn't even breathe. She dimly heard the cry of the seagulls soaring over the nearby Mediterranean, heard the buzz of insects. She was barely aware of the two hundred highborn guests behind them, watching from the pavilion.

Time had stopped. There was only the two of them. She saw him. She felt his touch on her skin. Exactly as she'd dreamed every night for the last thirteen years, in dark unwilling dreams she'd had alone in her New York penthouse.

Umar stepped between them.

"Sire," the older man said, beaming. "Allow me to present Jasmine Kouri. My bride."

Kareef stared down at her beautiful face in shock.

He'd never thought he would see Jasmine Kouri again. Seeing her so unexpectedly—*touching* her—caused a blast of ice and fire to surge through his body, from his hair to his fingertips.

Against his will, his eyes devoured every detail of her face. Her long black eyelashes trembling against her creamy skin. The pink tip of her tongue darting out to lick the center of her full, red lips.

Jasmine's dark hair, once long and stick-straight, now was thickly layered past her shoulders, cascading over a flowy, diaphanous dress that seemed straight out of a 1930s Hollywood movie. The gown skimmed her full breasts and hips, tightly belted at her slim waist. Her graceful, slender arms could be seen through long sheer sleeves.

She was almost entirely covered from head to toe, showing bare skin only at the collarbone and hands, but the effect was devastating. She looked glamorous. *Untouchable.* He wanted to grab her shoulders, to touch and taste and feel her all over and know she was real. Just the mere contact of his fingers against hers burned his skin.

Then he realized what Umar Hajjar had said.

Jasmine—Hajjar's bride?

As if he'd been struck by a blow, Kareef abruptly released her. He glanced down at his fingers and was almost bewildered to find them whole. After the electricity he'd felt touching her hand, he'd half expected to find his fingers burned beyond recognition.

With a deep breath, he slowly looked up at her. "You—are married?"

Jasmine's dark eyes met his, stabbing into his soul as deeply as a blade. Licking her lips nervously, she didn't answer.

"Not yet," Umar purred beside her. "But we will be. Immediately following the Qais Cup."

Kareef continued to look at Jasmine, but she didn't speak. Not one word.

Once, she used to chatter away in his company— she'd cajoled away his bad moods, making him laugh in spite of himself. He'd found her easy conversation relaxing. Charming. Perhaps because it was so natural—so unguarded and real. She'd been shy at first, a bookish girl more comfortable with reading newspapers and studying charts than speaking to the son of a sheikh. But once he'd coaxed her out of her shell, she'd happily told him every thought in her head.

They'd both been so young then. So innocent.

Fire burned through him now as he looked at her. *Jasmine.* Her name was like a spell and he could barely stop himself from breathing it aloud. He had to force his face to remain expressionless, his body taut and implacable as if ready for battle.

To attack what? To defend what?

"I'm so pleased you could attend our party at such late notice," Umar continued, placing his hands on Jasmine's shoulders. "We await your permission to serve dinner, my king."

Kareef found himself staring at Umar's possessive

hands on her shoulders. He had the sudden urge to knock them away—to start a brawl with the man who had once saved his life!

But this wasn't just any woman. It was Jasmine. The girl he'd once asked to be his wife.

"Sire?"

"Yes. Dinner." Still clenching his jaw, Kareef motioned to his two bodyguards to attend to the horses. He glanced toward the white pavilion and all the eager waiting faces. Several of the bolder guests were already inching closer to him, trying to catch his eye, hoping to join the conversation. After so many years of solitude in the northern desert of Qais, Kareef was not known for his sociability. But somehow being inaccessible and cold had just made him more desirable to the elite Qusanis of Shafar. Everyone in this godforsaken city seemed desperate for the barbarian king's attention, his favor, his body or his soul.

He wasn't even crowned yet, but according to Qusani tradition they already called him king—and treated him almost like a god. The people of Qusay had seen what he'd done for the desert people of Qais, and wanted that same prosperity for themselves. So they worshipped him.

Kareef hated it. He'd never wanted to come back here. But a few weeks ago, shortly after the death of the old king in a plane crash, his cousin, the crown prince, had abruptly removed himself from the line of succession. Xavian—no, Zafir, Kareef corrected himself, so strange to suddenly call the man he had thought his cousin by a new name!—had learned he had not a single drop of Al'Ramiz blood in his veins, and he'd abdicated the throne. He'd left to jointly rule the nation of Haydar with his wife, Queen Layla.

Zafir's decision had been correct and honorable. Kareef would have approved his actions completely, except for one thing: it had forced him to accept the throne in his place.

And now—he would see Jasmine married to another man before his very eyes.

Or would he? Legally, morally, could he allow it?

He cursed beneath his breath.

"You honor us, sire." Umar Hajjar bowed. "If I may ask another favor…"

Kareef growled a reply.

"Will you do my future bride the honor of escorting her into the pavilion?"

He wanted Kareef to touch her? To take her by the hand? Just looking at Jasmine was torture. She'd once been an enchanting girl with big dark eyes and a willowy figure. Now she'd grown into her curves. She'd become a mature woman. Her expression held mystery and hidden sorrows. A man could look into that face for years and never discover all her secrets.

Jasmine Kouri was, quite simply, the most beautiful woman Kareef had ever seen in his life.

And she continued to look at him silently with her dark gaze, her eyes accusing him of everything her lips did not. Reminding him of everything he'd nearly killed himself to forget.

Kareef closed his eyes, briefly blocking her from his vision. He forced his body to be calm, his breathing to become steady and even. He discarded emotion from his body, brushing it from his soul like dirt off his skin. After so many years of practice, he knew exactly what to do.

Then he opened his eyes and discovered he'd learned nothing.

Looking at Jasmine, years of repressed desire dissolved his will into dust. Heat flashed through him, whipping through his skin like a sandstorm flaying the flesh off his living bones.

He wanted her. He always had. As he'd never wanted any woman.

"Sire?"

Unwillingly, Kareef held out his arm, a mark of the highest respect for another man's bride. When he spoke, his voice was utterly cold and controlled.

"Shall we go in to the banquet, Miss Kouri?"

She hesitated, then placed her hand on his arm. He could feel the heat of her light touch through the fabric of his sleeve. She tilted her head back to look up at him. Her beautiful brown eyes glittered. "You honor me, my king."

No one but Kareef could hear the bitter irony beneath her words.

The party guests stepped back with deep, reverent bows as he led Jasmine up on the dais, Umar following behind them. Once they were on the dais, Kareef dropped her hand. He picked up a gold flute from the table.

Instantly, the two hundred guests went silent, waiting breathlessly for their new king to speak.

"I wish to thank my honored host and friend, Umar Hajjar, for his gracious invitation." He gave his old friend a nod. In response, Umar bowed, elegant in his designer suit. "And I wish to welcome his future bride, Jasmine Kouri, back to her homeland. You grace our shores with your beauty, Miss Kouri." He held up the flute, looking at the guests with hard eyes as he intoned forcefully, "To the happy couple."

"To the happy couple," the guests repeated in awed unison.

Jasmine said nothing. But as they sat down, he could feel the glow of her hatred pushing against him in waves of palpable energy.

Dinner was served, a meal of limitless, endless courses of lamb and fish, of spiced rice and olives and baked aubergines stuffed with meat. Each dish was more elaborate than the last. And through it all, Kareef was aware of Jasmine sitting next to him. She barely ate, even when encouraged by her fiancé. She just gripped her fork and knife tightly. Like weapons.

"You should eat, my dear," Umar Hajjar chided her from the other side. "It would be unattractive for you to grow too thin."

Unattractive? *Jasmine?*

Kareef frowned. Thin or fat, naked or dressed in a burlap sack, any man would want her. He clenched his hands into fists upon the table. *He* wanted her. Right now. On this table.

No, he told himself fiercely. He wouldn't touch her. He'd sworn thirteen years ago to leave Jasmine in peace. And she was now engaged to another man—his friend.

Turning to Umar Hajjar, Kareef forced himself to speak normally. "I did not know you were friends."

"We met in New York last year." Umar gave her arm a friendly little squeeze. "After my poor wife died, I asked Jasmine many times to marry me. She finally accepted yesterday."

"Yesterday? And you plan to wed in a few days?" he said evenly. "A swift engagement. There are no…impediments?"

Jasmine looked at Kareef sharply, with an intake of breath. He did not meet her eyes.

Umar shrugged carelessly. "Any wedding can be arranged quickly, if a man does not care about the cost." He glanced down at Jasmine teasingly. "Beautiful women can be fickle. I'm not going to give this one a chance to change her mind."

Jasmine looked down at her full plate, her cheeks bright red. She ran tracks through her rice with her fork.

"I would have married her immediately, in New York," Umar continued, "but Jasmine wished to be reconciled with her family. After my horse wins the Qais Cup, we will move to America for half the year to pursue my next goal—the Triple Crown. And of course I will take over Jasmine's business in New York. Her only job will be as mother to my four sons. But her connections in America will be useful to me as I…"

He paused when one of his servants bent to whisper in his ear. Abruptly, Umar rose to his feet. "Excuse me. I must take a phone call. With your permission, sire…?"

Kareef gave him a single nod. After he left, as all the guests on the lower floor buzzed loudly with their own discussions, he lowered his head to speak in a low voice to Jasmine alone.

"Does he know?"

Her whole body became strangely still. "Don't even

think about it," she ground out. "It doesn't count. It meant nothing."

"You know you cannot marry him."

"Don't be ridiculous."

"Jasmine."

"No! I don't care if you're king, I won't let you ruin my life—again!" Her eyes flashed at him. "I won't let you ruin my family's hopes with this wedding—"

"Your family needs the wedding?" he interrupted.

Clenching her jaw, she shook her head. "I won't let them be crushed by my old scandal again, not when everyone's still buzzing about my sister!"

"Which sister?"

Staring at him, she exhaled. "You haven't heard? I thought everyone in Qusay knew." She gave a sudden humorless laugh. "My youngest sister Nima was at boarding school in Calista. She had a one-night stand with some sailor whose name she can't even remember. Now she's pregnant. Pregnant at sixteen."

The word *pregnant* floated between them like poisoned air.

Ripping his gaze away, Kareef glanced at her large family, now seated at a lower table. At Umar Hajjar crossing the grass near the tent. At all the guests watching the king surreptitiously beneath the white pavilion. Then he looked back at Jasmine, and it all faded away. He couldn't see anything but the beauty of her face—the endless darkness of her eyes.

"Nima's staying in New York now, living in my apartment, trying to wrap her head around the thought that she will soon be a mother." She blinked back tears. "My baby sister. When she showed up on my doorstep two days ago, I suddenly realized how much time I'd lost. Thirteen years without my family." Her voice cracked. "No money can replace that."

"So you got engaged to Umar Hajjar," he said quietly. He narrowed his eyes. "Do you love him?"

With a sigh, she rubbed her neck. "When my father sent me away thirteen years ago," she whispered, "he said not to bother coming home again. Not until I was a respectable married woman."

Kareef set his jaw, furious as he glared at her. "So that's why you got engaged?" he bit out. "To please your father?"

She looked up at him, hatred suddenly blazing in her eyes.

"What do you care? You washed your hands of me long ago. In a few days I'll be married and out of your life forever." She lifted her chin, and her eyes glittered. "So leave me alone. Go get yourself crowned. Sire."

In all the years he'd known Jasmine, he'd never heard that bitter tone from her lips. But could he blame her? What she'd gone through would make any woman's soul grow brittle. Her young spirit had been so happy and bright, but he'd crushed that long ago. His hands tightened as he leaned forward over the table.

"But Jasmine," he said in a low voice, "you have to know that I—"

"Forgive me," Umar Hajjar interrupted, his voice high and strained. They turned almost guiltily to find him standing behind them. "My children's nanny was on the phone. There is an emergency. I must go."

"Oh no!" Jasmine rose to her feet anxiously. "I will come with you."

Umar held up his hand. "I must go alone."

"What? Why? Please, Umar," she begged. "Let me come with you. You might need my help!"

"No," he said harshly. His eyes fell upon Kareef. "My king, I ask you to take Jasmine under your protection."

"No! Absolutely not!" she cried, too loudly. Guests turned to look.

"Jasmine," Umar cautioned in a low, hard voice, "do not create a scene."

She swallowed. "I won't," she choked out softly. Her dark eyes glimmered, pleading with him as they turned away from the crowd. "Just don't leave me with the king."

"Why?" her fiancé demanded.

She licked her lips, glancing at Kareef beneath trembling lashes. "Though he is king…he is also still a man."

"Don't be foolish, Jasmine. He's the king!" Umar said. "His word is unbreakable. His honor is respected across the world. He—"

"No, she is right," Kareef interrupted. He looked down at Jasmine with glittering eyes. "Though I am king," he said in a low, dangerous voice, "I am also still a man."

Her long, black eyelashes swept across her pale cheeks as she visibly trembled beneath his gaze.

"And I would trust you with my life," Umar said stoutly. "Please. You must take her, sire."

Kareef slowly turned to his old friend. Bring Jasmine back to the royal palace? Beneath the same roof? The gleaming palace already felt like a prison with its thick walls, when Kareef hungered for the wide freedom of the desert. He couldn't imagine being trapped in that gilded cage with the additional torture of Jasmine's company—under his protection as he waited for her to marry another man!

"No," he said coldly. "She cannot stay at the palace. It's impossible."

But even as Jasmine exhaled in relief, Umar pressed his lips together. "She cannot stay unchaperoned here until we are married. It would be improper. I have my children to consider."

"Send her home to her family."

"It will be far more useful if she stays at the palace, my king."

Ah, so this was about status. Kareef's lip twisted with scorn.

"For Jasmine's sake," the other man added in a low voice. "Your attention will go far to negate her old scandal. People will forget the whispers beneath the weight of your honor."

Staring at him, Kareef frowned in sudden indecision.

Umar lowered his head. "My king, if I have ever done anything worthy of your esteem, I beg you this one favor. Place my bride formally under your protection until the day of the Qais Cup, when I will return to marry her."

If he'd ever done anything worthy of Kareef's esteem?

He'd helped Kareef bring prosperity to the desert. Made him the godfather of two of his four young sons. And most of all—he'd found Kareef in the desert, half-mad and dying of thirst thirteen years ago. He'd brought him home, brought him back to health. He'd saved Kareef's life.

"Perhaps…" Kareef said grudgingly, and Umar pounced.

"Your mother is at the palace, is she not, sire? She will make a fine chaperone, if you are concerned about propriety."

"No," Jasmine whimpered softly. "I won't do it."

Umar ignored her. He kept staring at Kareef with hope—almost desperation.

If the bride had been any other woman, Kareef would have immediately agreed. But not *this* woman. He cursed beneath his breath. Damn it, didn't the man see the risk?

No, of course he did not. Umar had no idea Kareef was the one who'd taken her virginity and caused her accident in the desert thirteen years ago. No one knew Kareef was the man who'd been her lover, her partner in the scandal. Jasmine had made sure of that.

She still hated him. He saw it in her eyes. But he had no choice.

Slowly, Kareef rose to his feet. His voice was loud, ringing with authority beneath the white pavilion.

"As of this moment, and until the day of her marriage, Jasmine Kouri is under my protection."

Another buzz rose across the crowd. They stared at Jasmine with awe. Even her old father cracked an amazed smile.

If only he knew the truth, Kareef thought grimly.

Nodding in relief, Umar turned to go.

"Wait," Jasmine cried, grabbing her fiancé's slender wrist. "I still don't know what's happened! Are your children sick? Is it the baby?"

"The children are well. I cannot say more." The older man's eyes were narrow and tight. "I will call you if I can. Otherwise—I will see you at the race. On our wedding day."

And he was gone. Kareef and Jasmine sat alone on the dais, with two hundred pairs of eyes upon them.

Keeping his face impassive, Kareef threw down the linen napkin across his empty plate and glanced at Jasmine's untouched dinner and stricken, forlorn face. "Are you finished?"

"Yes," she whispered miserably, as if she were trying not to cry.

He held out his hand. "Then let us go."

She focused her eyes on him. "Forget it. I've been under my own *protection* for years. I do not need or want yours."

He continued to hold out his hand. "And yet you have it."

"I will go stay at my family's house."

"Your betrothed wishes otherwise."

"He is not the boss of me."

"Is he not?"

She tossed her head. "I will stay at a hotel."

She was trying her best to be insolent, making it clear she did not respect him. He should have been insulted, but as he watched the tip of her pink tongue dart out to lick her lips, he couldn't look away from the lush, sensual mouth he'd kissed long ago. It seemed like only yesterday. His lips tingled, remembering hers.

With a deep breath, he forced himself to look up. "You will find no available hotel room, anywhere on this island. All the world has come for my coronation." He tightened his jaw. "But that is not the point."

"And that is?"

"I gave my word to Hajjar," he ground out. "And I keep my promises."

"Do you?" Her eyes glinted at him sardonically. "A new skill?"

Anger flashed through him. But he held it back, dousing it with ice. He deserved the jibe. He would accept it from Jasmine as he would from no other person alive.

He would still prevail.

"Are you afraid to be near me?" he quietly taunted.

"Afraid of you?" Her voice shimmered with hatred like moonlight on water. "Why should I be?"

He held out his hand. "Then come."

Narrowing her eyes at him in fury, she pushed her hand into his. She never could resist a dare. But the same instant he knew he'd won, he felt the electric shock of her touch. And realized he was the one who should be afraid.

He, Kareef Al'Ramiz, the prince of the desert, soon to be absolute ruler of the kingdom of Qusay, should be afraid of what he'd do when left alone with this woman he craved. This woman he could not have. His friend's betrothed. Because Jasmine wasn't simply a woman to him.

She was the only woman.

CHAPTER TWO

TWILIGHT was falling over the gleaming towers and spires of the royal palace overlooking the city. Built over the ruins of a Byzantine citadel, the palace had been modernized in the last century and could be seen for miles across the Mediterranean, shining like a jewel.

So strange to be back here, Jasmine thought, in the place she'd grown up when her father had been the old king's favored counselor. Although this was the first time she'd ever been in this particular wing. The maid had left her in a shabby garret in the oldest wing of the palace, where the servants lived.

Jasmine looked out through the grimy window toward the garden. This room was smaller than the walk-in closet of her Park Avenue penthouse, but all she felt was relief to be alone.

Her knees were still weak with shock as she hefted her small rolling suitcase on the single bed. When Kareef had led her away from the white pavilion to his waiting limousine, she'd been half-terrified that he would take her straight to his bedroom in the palace. Would she have been able to resist—even hating him as she did?

The thought was still staggering. After so many years, she'd seen Kareef again. Heard his voice. Felt his touch.

The air in the room felt suddenly stifling. She punched buttons on the control panel of the air-conditioning, then gave up and tried to open the window, but the glass wouldn't budge.

Cursing aloud, she covered her face with her hands. Why had she ever come back to the palace? Because she was obeying Umar's orders? She'd survived on her own in New York City for thirteen years. She did not need or want Kareef's *protection*!

Or did she?

Against her will, she remembered the touch of Kareef's hand against her own and felt like she was burning up with a fever. Sweating, she yanked off the chiffon dress. She wrenched off her stockings and sandals. Standing in just her white bra and panties, she felt relief.

Until there was a hard knock and the door swung open.

"Jasmine—"

Kareef stood in the door. He sucked in his breath when he saw her in the middle of her bedroom, half-naked.

With a stifled scream, she grabbed the chiffon dress off the floor to cover herself. "What are you doing here?"

He stared at her, clenching his hands into fists at his sides. He was no longer in white robes, but more casually dressed in a long-sleeved white shirt and black pants. He looked more devastating than ever, and his towering body was taut. "I want…I want you to join me for a late supper."

"So call me on the phone and ask!" she cried. A servant passed by in the hallway, trying not to gawk. Frowning, Kareef stepped inside the room, closing the door behind him.

"You can't come in here!" she said, scandalized.

"I can't let anyone else see you like this."

"Anyone? What about *you*?"

Lifting a dark eyebrow, he looked her over slowly. "I've seen far more of you than this."

Her cheeks flamed red-hot—and she truly wanted to kill him! "We can't be alone in a closed bedroom! In some parts of the country, you would be required to marry me!"

He gave a low laugh. "It's a good thing we're in the city, then."

"Don't you dare! Don't you realize how gossip can spread?"

"My servants can be trusted."

She shook her head fiercely. "How do you know?"

"One servant betrayed us, Jasmine. One." His eyes glinted. "And I made him pay. Marwan—"

"I'm not going to argue with you!" she nearly shrieked, grabbing a pillow off her bed and lifting it over her head. The dress fell to the floor but she barely noticed. Modesty was inconsequential compared to the blaze of her fury. "Just get out!"

He looked at her body in the white cotton bra and panties. She felt his gaze upon her bare skin from her collarbone to the curve of her breasts, down her flat belly to her naked thighs. Her mouth went dry.

Then, slowly, he met her gaze. "You're threatening me with a pillow, Jasmine?"

Since he was a foot taller and probably eighty pounds heavier than her, she could see why that would seem like a joke. It only made her more angry. "Do you need a handwritten request? Get out!"

"When you agree to join me for dinner."

Staring at him, a jittery nervousness pulsed through her. The last time she'd seen Kareef, he'd been barely eighteen, the king's eldest nephew, slender and tall and fine. She'd been the bookish eldest daughter of the king's adviser; he'd been a wild, reckless horse racer with a vulnerable heart and joyful laugh.

But he'd changed since then. He was no longer a boy; he'd become a man. A dangerous one.

His once-friendly blue eyes were now ruthless; the formerly vibrant expression on his handsome, rugged face had become tightly controlled. His once-lanky frame had gained strength. Even the muscle of his body proclaimed him a king. He could probably pick up someone like Umar and toss him through the air like a javelin. She'd never seen any man on earth with shoulders like Kareef's.

But the biggest change was the grim darkness she now saw beneath his gaze. She could sense the cold warrior hidden beneath his deeply tanned skin. He had only the thinnest veneer of civilization left. The danger both attracted her…and frightened her.

It doesn't matter, she told herself desperately. In a few days she would become Umar's wife and she would never have to see Kareef again. If she could just make it to her wedding…

"So you'll join me?" he said coldly.

"I'm not hungry."

"Come anyway. We have…something to discuss."

"No," she said desperately. "We don't."

He lowered a dark eyebrow. "Do I really have to say it?"

She swallowed. No. She knew exactly what he was talking about. She'd just told herself many times that it didn't matter, that it didn't count, that it had just been a few whispered words between kisses.

The pillow dropped from her hands. She wrapped her arms around her body, glancing toward the deepening shadows of the garden. She whispered, "It's all in the past."

"The past is always with us." Out of the corner of her eye, she saw him take a single step toward her. "You know you cannot marry him."

Oh my God, Kareef was going to touch her! If he did—if he reached out and took her hand—she was afraid of how her body would react. Only her anger was keeping her hands wrapped around her own waist, when some uncivilized part of her longed to stroke the dark curl of his hair, the roughness of his jawline, to touch the hard muscles and discover the man he had become….

With a harsh intake of breath, she held up her hand sharply, keeping him at a distance.

"All right!" she bit out. "I'll join you for your fancy dinner if you'll just leave!"

His blue eyes held hers. "It won't be fancy. Simple and quiet."

"Right." She didn't believe him for a second. She'd never seen any Al'Ramiz king dine with fewer than fifty people and ten courses of meat and fish and fruit.

"The blue room." He looked her over, and she felt

that same flush of heat as his gaze touched her naked skin. "Ten minutes."

The blue room? Now she knew he was lying. The blue room was for entertaining heads of state! But she'd worry about that later—when she wasn't naked and confined with him in such a small space! Unwillingly, her eyes fell on the tiny bed between them.

He followed her gaze.

Suddenly, her heart was pounding so loud she could almost hear it. Then he turned toward the door.

"See you at dinner."

"Yes." She could suddenly breathe again.

He paused, as his large frame filled the doorway. "It's good to see you, Jasmine." And he closed the door behind him.

Good to see her?

As soon as he was gone, she dug frantically through her suitcase and found nothing at all to wear. She lifted up the crumpled green chiffon dress from the floor only to discover a stain on the bodice.

Why was Kareef doing this to her? Why couldn't they just ignore the past? Why couldn't they just pretend it did not exist?

You know you cannot marry him.

She took a deep breath. They'd share one meal. He would speak a few careful words, and it would be done. They could both go on with their lives.

She grabbed a white sundress, fresh and pretty with a modest neckline. It wasn't nearly fancy enough for a fifty-person banquet in the blue room with the king, but it would just have to do. She added sandals and a string of pearls. All sweet and simple, and *hers*. Not selected for her by Umar from a designer boutique. She brushed her long hair, and looked at herself in the mirror.

Bewildered brown eyes looked back at her. She looked young and insecure, nothing like the powerful woman she'd become in New York. Being close to Kareef made her feel vulnerable again. As if she were sixteen.

Her feet dragged as she left her room and headed toward the east wing. The hallways were oddly quiet but she passed two women as she made her way to the blue room—the Sheikha, Kareef's mother, and her much younger companion trailing behind in her black abaya. The Sheikha saw Jasmine and her wrinkled, kindly face lifted into a vague, benevolent smile. She probably didn't remember who Jasmine was. Jasmine bowed deeply.

When she looked up, she saw the Sheikha's companion smiling down at her. It was Sera, her childhood friend! But the Sheikha was in a hurry. Sera had only time to whisper, "Glad you're back," before she had to quickly follow her employer down the hall.

A surprised smile rose on Jasmine's face as she stared after her old friend. Sera still remembered her after all these years? A surge of happiness went through Jasmine, then she turned back to hurry down the hall. The palace seemed strangely silent, almost desolate. Had the big fancy dinner been canceled? Was she late? With a deep breath, Jasmine pushed open the double doors.

The long dining table, big enough to seat forty-eight, was lit by long-tapered candles. Only one person was seated there.

"Jasmine." Kareef rose to his feet with a short, formal bow. He moved to the place beside his at the table, standing behind her chair. "Please."

Shocked, she looked right and left. "Where is everyone else?"

"There is no one else."

"Oh."

"I told you. Simple and quiet."

She was having dinner with Kareef…alone? Feeling like she was in a surreal dream, she walked toward the table. The candles flickered light and shadow upon the white wainscoting and pale blue walls of the cavernous room. She swallowed, then lowered herself into her chair. He pushed it forward for her. As if they were on a date.

No—she couldn't think that way! This was the *opposite* of a date!

Kareef sat down in the chair beside her, then nodded regally at two servants who appeared from the shadows. She jumped as they took silver lids off trays to serve two exquisite meals of cool salad, cucumbers, exquisite fruits, bread and cheeses. They opened a bottle of sparkling water, then a bottle of expensive French wine. After serving the trays, they backed away with a bow and disappeared, closing the double doors softly behind them.

They were alone. And Jasmine felt it. She licked her lips nervously. "What is all this?"

Kareef leaned forward to pour her a glass of wine. "You didn't eat at your engagement party. You must be hungry." His sensual lips quirked. "I allow no one to starve while under my protection."

She watched him, involuntarily noticing the way the candlelight cast shadows across the astonishing masculine beauty of his face.

He looked up, and his blue eyes sizzled through hers with the intensity of his gaze. "Are you?"

"Am I what?" she stammered.

"Are. You. Hungry," he said with slow deliberation, and she found herself looking at his lips and remembering the last time he'd kissed her. So long ago. Or was it? It seemed like it was yesterday, and all the long years since had just been a dream. "Jasmine."

With an intake of breath, she looked up. "Starving," she whispered.

He smiled, then indicated her plate. "One of the few perks of being king," he said. "A world-class chef at my beck and call. A far cry from what I'm used to at my home in Qais."

She took a bite of the food and noticed it was indeed delicious, and she was indeed starving. But as she ate, she couldn't look away from Kareef's face.

Oh, this was dangerous. She couldn't trust him. He'd betrayed her! Ruined her! But her body didn't seem to care. Every time he looked at her, she trembled from within.

She set down her fork. "Kareef. I don't want to be here with you, any more than you want me here. So if you'll just do what must be done—"

"Later," he interrupted. He pushed the crystal goblet full of ruby-colored wine toward her. "We have all night."

All night. Trembling, she took a bracing gulp of wine and wiped her mouth. "But with your coronation in a few days," she stammered, "you must have many demands on your time. I heard something about fireworks tonight, given by the city council in your honor—"

"Nothing is more important—" he refilled her wine-glass "—than this."

Why was he stretching this out? Why? What possible reason could he have?

Helplessly, she took another sip of wine. Silence fell in the shadows of flickering candlelight as they ate.

He glanced at her enormous diamond ring, heavy as a paperweight on her hand. "An expensive trinket, even for a billionaire," he said. "Hajjar values you high."

Embarrassed heat flooded her cheeks. "I'm not marrying him for his money, if that's what you think!"

Something like a smile passed briefly over Kareef's face. "No," he said. "I know you are not."

What was that smile hiding? Some private joke?

Once, she'd known him so well. The boy she'd loved had hidden nothing from her. But she did not know this man.

She watched him take a sip of wine. There was something sensual about watching his lips on the crystal glass, his tongue tasting the red Bordeaux. She could almost imagine those lips, that tongue, upon her body.

No! she ordered herself desperately. *Stop it!*

But every inch of her skin shivered with awareness that she was sitting beside the only man she'd ever loved.

The only man she'd ever hated.

"Do you like New York?" he asked, taking a bite of fruit.

"Yes," she said, watching his sharp teeth crunch the flesh of the apple. "I did."

"But you're eager to leave it."

She looked away. "I missed Qusay. I missed my family."

"But you must have made many friends in New York."

There was something strange beneath his tone. She looked back at him. "Of course."

His tone was light, even as his hand tightened around the neck of the goblet. "Such an exciting city. You must have enjoyed the nightlife frequently with many ardent…friends."

Was that an oblique way of asking if she'd taken lovers? With a deep breath, she took another sip of wine. She wasn't going to tell him he'd been her only lover. It would be too pathetic to admit she'd spent the best years of her life alone, dreaming of him against her will. Especially since she knew he'd replaced her the instant he'd left her. She wouldn't give Kareef the satisfaction of knowing he'd been not just her first—but her only!

Taking a bite of salad, so delicious with its herbs and spices and multicolored tomatoes, she deliberately changed the subject. "What's your home like?"

He snorted. "The palace? It has not changed. A rich and luxurious prison."

"I mean your house in the desert. In Qais."

Taking another sip of wine, he blinked then shrugged. "Comfortable. A few servants, but they're mostly for the horses. I like to take care of myself. I don't like people hovering."

She nearly laughed. "You must love being king."

"No." His voice was flat. "But it is my duty."

Duty, she thought with sudden fury. Where had his

sense of duty been thirteen years ago, when she'd
needed him so desperately and he'd abandoned her?

Anger pulsed through her, making her hands shake
as she held her knife and fork. But it wasn't just anger,
she realized. It was bewilderment and pain. How could
he have done it? How?

Placing her hands in her lap, she turned her head
away, blinking fast.

"Jasmine, what is it?"

"Nothing," she said hoarsely. She would die before
she let Kareef Al'Ramiz see her weep. She'd learned
to be strong. She'd had no other choice. "I just
remember you once dreamed of a house in the desert.
Now you have it."

"Yes." His voice suddenly hardened. "And I will be
your neighbor. My home is but thirty kilometers from
Umar Hajjar's estate."

She turned with an intake of breath at mention of
her fiancé's name. Oh God, how could she have already forgotten Umar? She was an engaged woman!
She shouldn't be looking at another man's lips!

But she could not stop herself. Not when the man
was Kareef, the only man she'd ever loved. The only
man she'd ever taken to her bed. And until yesterday—the only man she'd ever kissed.

Umar had kissed her for the first time only after
she'd accepted his marriage proposal. His kiss had
been businesslike and official, a pledge to seal the deal
when a handshake wouldn't do. He did not seem particularly keen to sweep her immediately into bed,
which was just fine with Jasmine. Their marriage
would be based on something far more important:

family. And she wasn't just getting back her parents and sisters. She would finally be a mother. She would help to raise his young sons, aged two to fourteen.

"Do you know his children?" she asked thickly.

He nodded. "I am godfather to his two eldest—Fadi and Bishr. They are good children. Respectful."

Respectful? They hadn't seemed that way when she'd met them last year in New York—at least not respectful to Jasmine. The four boys had glared at her, clinging to their father and their French nanny, Léa, as if Jasmine were the enemy. She sighed. But who could blame them for being upset, when their mother had just died?

"I hope they're all right," she whispered. "I met them only once. His poor children. They've had a hard time. Especially the baby," she added, looking away.

"They need a mother," Kareef said softly. "You will be good to them."

She looked at him with an intake of breath. He leaned across the table, his gaze intense in the candlelight. He was already so close, his knee just inches from hers.

"Thank you," she said softly. Sadness settled around her heart as unspoken memories stretched between them.

"Didn't you know she was pregnant, my lord?" the doctor's voice echoed in her ears, from the dark cave long ago. *"She'll live, but never be able to conceive again...."*

Remembering, Jasmine dropped her silver fork with a clatter against her china plate. Clasping her hands tightly in her lap, she tried to close off the memories from her mind.

"You've always wanted children," Kareef said. There was a grim set to his jaw. "And now you're to be married to Umar Hajjar. A fine match by any measure. Your father must be proud."

"Yes. Now," she whispered. She shook her head. "He's never cared about my success in New York. He even refused the money I've tried to send the family, as his fortunes have faltered while mine have grown." She lifted her gaze. "But I've always believed some corner of his heart wanted to forgive me. My success in large part came from him!"

Kareef shifted in his chair.

She continued. "When I first arrived in New York at sixteen, I had nothing. No money. My only friend there was an elderly great-aunt, and she was ill. Not just ill—dying. In a rat-infested apartment."

"I heard," he said quietly. "Later."

She narrowed her eyes at him, feeling a surge of bitterness. "I worked three jobs to support us both. Then," she whispered, "out of the blue the month before she died, I got a check from my father for fifty thousand dollars. It saved us. I invested every penny, and gradually it paid off. But if not for him," she said softly, "I might still be an office cleaner working sixteen hours a day."

He picked up his glass, taking a sip of wine.

Jasmine frowned, tilting her head. "But when I tried to thank my father for that money today, he claimed not to know anything about it."

Kareef stared idly at the ruby-colored wine, swirling it in the candlelight.

And suddenly, she knew.

"My father never sent that money, did he?"

He didn't answer.

She sucked in her breath. "It was you," she whispered. "You sent me that money ten years ago. Not my father. It was you."

Pressing his lips together, he set down the glass. He gave a single hard nod.

"The letter said it was from my father."

"I didn't think you would accept it from me."

"You're right!"

"So I lied."

"You…lied. Just like that?"

"I intended to send you more every year, but you never needed it." Kareef's voice held a tinge of pride as he looked at her. "You turned that first small amount into a fortune."

"Why did you do it, Kareef?"

He turned to look at her. "Don't you know?"

She shook her head.

Reaching over the table, he took her hand in his own. Turning it over, he kissed her palm.

A tremor racked her body, coursing through her like an electric current, lit up by the caress of his lips against her skin.

He looked up at her. His blue eyes were endless, like the sea in the flickering light. "Because you're my wife, Jasmine."

Silence filled the blue room, broken by sudden booms of fireworks outside, rattling the windowpanes.

She snatched back her hand. "No, I'm not!"

"You spoke the words," he said evenly. "So did I."

"It wasn't legal. There were no witnesses."

"It doesn't matter, not according to the laws of Qais."

"It would never hold up in the civil courts of Qusay."

"We are married."

Through the high arched windows, she saw fireworks lighting the dark sky. Struggling to collect her thoughts, she shook her head. "Abandonment could be considered reason for divorce—"

He looked at her. "Your abandonment?" he said quietly. "Or mine?"

She sucked in her breath. "I was forced to leave Qusay! It was never of my free will!"

He looked at her. "I had cause to leave you as well."

Yeah. Right. Her eyes glittered at him. "We were barely more than children. We didn't know what we were doing."

As the explosions continued to spiral across the night sky, booming like thunder, he leaned forward and stroked her face.

"I knew," he said in a low voice. "And so did you."

The tension altered, humming with a hot awareness that coiled and stretched between them.

Her cheek sizzled where he stroked her. His gaze dropped to her mouth. She felt her body tighten. Her breasts suddenly ached, her nipples taut with longing.

No!

"If we once were married," she choked out, "speak the words to undo it now. All I care about now…is my family."

"And what of you?" he said, cupping her face in his strong hands. "What do you want for yourself?"

She wanted him to kiss her. Wanted it with every ounce of her blood and beat of her heart.

But she wouldn't allow this insane desire to destroy the life that was finally within reach, the family life she hungered to have. She lifted her dark lashes to look into his eyes. "I want a home." Her voice was as quiet as the whisper of memory. "A family. I want a husband and children of my own."

A loud crash boomed in the night sky outside them, shaking the palace.

Kareef looked down at her, his eyes suddenly dark as a midnight sea. He dropped his hands from her face. "Umar Hajjar loves his children, his horses and his money—in that order," he said harshly. "As his wife, you will be valued a distant fourth on his list."

"He values my connections in America. He thinks I will be the perfect wife—the perfect hostess. That is enough."

"Not enough for him."

"What else could he want from me?"

He looked at her.

"You're a beautiful woman," he said thickly. "No man could resist you."

She stared up at him for several heartbeats, then turned away, hiding her face.

"That's not true," she said in a low voice. "One man has had no trouble resisting me, Kareef." She looked up. "You."

He grabbed her wrist on the table. His fingers tightened on her skin. "You think I don't want you?"

His voice was dangerous. Low. She felt tension snapping between them, rippling through her body, sharp against every nerve.

Her heart beat frantically in her chest. As he leaned toward her, she breathed in his masculine scent, laced with the flavor of wine and spice. His body, in all its strength and power, was so close to hers. She yearned to lean across the table, to lose everything in one moment of sweet madness and press her mouth against his….

Another loud boom exploded outside. It broke the spell. Made her realize she was perilously close to doing something unforgivable.

Rising to her feet, she stumbled back from the table.

"Divorce me," she whispered. "If you've ever cared about me, Kareef, if I was ever more than a warm body in the night to you…divorce me tonight."

He stared at her, his jaw tight. Then he shook his head. Tears rose to her eyes and she fought them with all her might.

"You bastard," she choked out. "You cold-hearted bastard. I've known for years you had no heart, but I never thought you could…never thought you would—"

But the tears were starting to fall from her lashes. Turning before he could see them, she shoved open the double doors. They banged loudly against the walls as she fled down the hallway.

"Jasmine! Stop!"

But she didn't obey. She just ran.

Fireworks boomed outside the tall windows as she raced past the corner where she'd first crashed into Kareef—literally—by sliding on the marble floors in her socks, playing with her sisters. When she slid too fast around the corner, he'd grasped her wrists, catching her before she could fall. His blue eyes had smiled down at her with the warmth of spring's first sun. She'd loved him from that first day.

Now, after thirteen years of trying to forget Kareef's existence, this one day had brought it all back, times ten. A single word from his deep voice, a single look from his handsome face, and he'd caught up Jasmine's soul like a fish in his net.

Racing down the hall, she pushed open the first door on her left and ran down the wooden stairs into the courtyard. Cloaked in darkness, she took deep rattling gasps of the warm desert air. She stood beneath the swaying dark palm trees of the garden, beside the dark water shimmering in the silvery moonlight, and wrapped her arms over her thin cotton sundress. She could not allow herself to cry. She could not allow herself to collapse.

Because this time, if she fell, there would be no prince to catch her.

CHAPTER THREE

KAREEF nearly staggered in shock as Jasmine fled the dining room. Jasmine thought he didn't want her? *Didn't she know her power?*

When he heard the double doors bang behind her, he leapt to his feet. With an intake of breath, he pursued her. He saw her disappear through a wooden door in the hallway. The door to the royal garden, forbidden to all but the king's family. He followed her outside.

He stopped at the foot of the stairs, turning his face up to the night sky. He heard an owl's distant echoing cry. He felt the warm desert wind against his face, blowing open his white shirt.

He was on the hunt. He no longer felt like a king, constrained by the rigid boundaries of duty and appearance. Suddenly, he felt wild. Uncontrolled. For the first time since he'd returned to the palace in Shafar, he felt like himself again.

No. It had been longer than that since he'd truly felt like himself. Far longer…

Where was she? He looked to the right and left, searching across the dark shadows of trees and shimmering pools of water like a Qusani hawk seeking his prey. Had she disappeared into the night? Did she truly exist only in dreams?

The moonlight cast a silvery glow on the swaying palm trees. He could hear the wind through the leaves, hear the burbling water of the fountain. In the distance, he could hear the Mediterranean pounding beneath the cliffs.

Booms like cannons ricocheted with increasing vigor across the sky. Explosions spiraled like pale flowers of smoke across the night—fireworks provided by the city of Shafar to celebrate his coming coronation. He knew he should be thanking the city council right now, instead of pursuing this ghost from his past— this woman who'd given herself freely to another man.

But not yet. She was still his. *She was still his.*

He saw a sudden flash of white. He saw her lithe body cross the garden, darting and shimmering between the dark shadows. Silvery moonlight twisted through her onyx hair, causing her short, filmy white gown to glow. She was a creature of seduction, a faerie creature of the night, illuminating it like any man's fantasy.

Jasmine. How long had he hungered for her? How long had he thirsted, like a man crossing oceans of hot sand?

He stood still, watching her in the moonlight. Afraid to breathe, lest the dream disappear.

His expression hardened as he moved forward.

Too many years of hunger. Too many years of denied desire.

She wished to have her freedom. He would give it to her. But not yet.

Tonight, she was still his.

For this night, she was his to possess.

As he caught up with her, he saw her long dark hair tumbling down her pale, bare shoulders in the moonlight. Shoulders now shaking with silent sobs.

A branch snapped into the grass beneath his foot as he stopped abruptly.

She didn't turn around, but he knew she'd heard him by the sudden stiffening of her posture.

"I know I shouldn't be here." Her voice was sodden, muffled. "Have you come to kick me out?"

Grabbing her shoulder, he turned her around. "This garden is forbidden to all but the royal family."

"I know—"

"And you are my wife."

She looked up at him with a gasp. Her eyes were wide and dark, her tears glimmering in the moonlight like endless pools. "But I can't be," she choked out. "You are the king. And I must marry—"

"I know." His eyes searched hers. "I will give you your divorce, Jasmine."

"You will?"

"Yes," he said in a low voice. "But not yet."

"What do you want from me?" she whispered.

His hand tightened on her bare shoulder. What did he want?

He wanted to strip the flimsy dress off her body and lay her down beneath him in the moist, cool grass. He wanted to close his eyes and feel her wholly in his grasp, to feel the beat of her heart and warmth of her skin.

He wanted to kiss her senseless, to lick and suckle every inch of her naked body, from that slender, delicate neck to her full breasts, down her tiny waist to the wide sweep of her hips.

He wanted to dip his tongue into every crevice of her, to taste and bite every delicious curve. To savor the spicy sweetness of her skin until he could bear it no longer, while he plunged himself into her so hard and deeply that he would never resurface again.

Part of him—the civilized part—knew it was wrong. Jasmine was another man's betrothed. And she was under his protection.

But as he held her in his arms…Kareef was no longer a civilized man.

"You," he growled in reply. "I want you."

"No," she gasped. Her brown eyes shimmered with fear. "We can't!"

He breathed in her scent of spice and blood oranges and something more, something distinctly her, the intoxicating feminine warmth of her skin. He smelled the fragrant night-blooming jasmine, and he didn't bother to answer. He just lowered his head to kiss her.

With a jagged intake of breath, she turned her head away, toward the darkness of the trees.

He put his hand on her cheek. "Look at me, Jasmine." She stubbornly refused.

"Look at me!" He twisted his hands into her hair, forcing her compliance. He lifted her chin, looking down into her face. "You are my wife. You cannot refuse what we both desire."

She took a deep breath, then closed her eyes. Moonlight illuminated a trail of tears streaking down her pale skin.

"No," she whispered, trembling in his hands. "I cannot deny what you say."

He felt her surrender. Gloried in it. His calloused hand stroked her bare arm. Her skin felt soft, so soft beneath his fingertips. Just touching her face, as he breathed in her delicious scent, caused a sizzle like fire to spread through his veins. He felt her shudder beneath his touch.

Kareef was king of the land, but there was one thing that had always been beyond his control. One thing that had always been more powerful than his own strength.

His desire for her.

She made his blood boil with longing. Her memory had driven him half-mad with the unsatisfied desire of thirteen years.

And now…she was in his arms.

He looked down at Jasmine's beautiful face with a shudder of longing. Holding her close, he cupped her chin. Lowering his head, he kissed her closed eyelids with a feather-light brush of his lips.

Then, with a hunger he could barely control, he slowly lowered his mouth toward hers. He paused, his lips inches from her own. Then he ruthlessly kissed her, searing her lips with his.

Jasmine gasped as he kissed her.

The hot dark pleasure of his embrace was beyond every fantasy of her endless lonely nights. As his lips crushed hers, she felt herself slide beneath the waves of her longing. Even as she knew it was wrong, she felt herself drowning in desire.

Kareef. Her husband. She could not resist him. She

could not deny him. Body and soul, she felt herself pulled down, down, down into the consuming passion of his savage embrace.

His lips plundered hers with power and skill. As his tongue swept her mouth, entwining with hers, she sagged in his arms, shaking with explosive need. Her knees were weak, but every other part of her was taut and tense. Her nipples tightened painfully, her breasts aching and heavy. Nerve endings sizzled down her body, coiling low in her belly.

She was breathless, helpless with desire. He possessed her as no man ever had.

Then his kiss somehow changed. His lips gentled against hers, and she wasn't just submitting to his power. She was kissing him back. His sensual mouth moved against hers in a languorous dance, and every part of her body beneath her thin dress felt on fire where he pressed against her. She was fragile against the hardness of his chest, and the muscles of his thighs strained against her own. He held her so tightly she no longer knew where she ended and he began, and she realized she'd wrapped her arms around his neck.

A soft cry came from deep inside her, a gasp for breath. Her head fell back, exposing her neck. He pressed small intense kisses along her throat, sending sparks up and down her body. He caressed her body, whispering words of tenderness in the ancient dialect of Qais before suckling the tender flesh of her earlobes. His hands moved against her bare arms, cupping the full breasts that strained toward him beneath the fabric.

How long had she desired this? How long had she told herself she would never feel this way again—that at twenty-nine she was too old, too used-up, too numb to ever feel such pleasure? How long had she told herself she should settle for being useful, for earning money, for trying to be a good daughter, a good sister, a good wife?

Hands in her hair, Kareef whispered ancient words of longing and tenderness against her skin. Around them, she was dimly aware of dappled moonlight through the dark waving silhouettes of palm trees, of the stars scattered across the violet night. They were entwined in each other.

Kareef. The only one who'd ever made her feel such explosive joy. The only one who'd made her feel the night was magic, and life as infinite as the stars above her.

Opening her eyes, she stared at him. She saw the new tiny crinkles at his eyes, the way his shoulders had broadened with muscle. He'd grown into his full strength, with a warrior's posture and brutal power.

But his smile hadn't changed. His voice hadn't changed.

His kiss hadn't changed.

As he lowered his mouth to hers, every inch of her skin sparked with awareness, as if there were a magnetic attraction between them. Pulling them together. Forcing them apart.

Everything else might have altered in their lives, but somehow in his embrace, time stood still. She was sixteen again. They were in love, in longing, full of faith for the future.

That feeling was the most dangerous thing of all.

She shuddered, and with all her strength, she pushed him away.

"I can't," she choked out. Above them, she could hear only the waving palm fronds, the sigh of the wind, the plaintive cries of night birds. "I'm sorry."

"Sorry?" Kareef's voice was barely more than a growl in the darkness. "I am the one to blame. I wanted you then." Reaching down, he caressed her cheek and whispered, "I want you now."

The timbre of his low voice, sharp and deep, caused a seismic shift inside her, breaking her apart in bits like the emeralds hacked from Qusani mines beneath the earth. Gleaming facets and chinks of her soul scattered beneath his touch.

She closed her eyes as she felt his rough fingertips against her cheek. She felt his thumb slide lightly across her sensitive lower lip. Her mouth parted, her body ached, from her nipples down her belly and lower still.

"I will make you a wife, Jasmine," he whispered, stroking her cheek. "I will make you a mother."

Her eyes flew open. He was looking down at her with intensity, his face so boyishly handsome it took her breath away. As teenagers, they'd had many innocent trysts in this very garden so long ago, in another life. But here in the warmth of the desert night, with the spice of the air sifting the salt from the sea, anything seemed possible.

"What do you mean?" she said in shock, searching his eyes.

"If Umar Hajjar is the man you want to marry," he said, "I will not stop you. I will give you away at the wedding myself."

A lump of pain rose in her throat. Oh. "You will?"

His sensual lips spread into a half smile, his eyes heavy with desire. "But not yet."

She trembled.

From a distance she heard a servant calling for the king. She tried to pull her hand away. "I have to go."

The cell phone in his hip pocket started to buzz. Even here in the forbidden garden, they were not completely alone. But he ignored it. As she tried to pull away, he tightened his hand on hers. "Come with me where no one can reach us. Come with me to the desert."

She shook her head desperately. "I have no reason to go anywhere with you!"

He pulled her close against his chest, looking down at her. His face was inches from her own and suddenly she couldn't breathe. He looked down at her, brushing tendrils of hair off her face.

"Are you sure?" he said in a low voice. "Absolutely no reason to be alone with me?"

"Yes," she breathed, hardly able to know what she was saying. "No."

He suddenly leaned back on his hip. "Surely you're not afraid?"

Terrified was more like it, but she would never admit that in a million years. "I'm not afraid of you. I've never been afraid of you!"

"So there's no reason to refuse. We'll leave tomorrow."

When he touched her, she had a difficult time concentrating. "Why—why would you take me to the desert?"

He gave her a slow-rising smile. "You're under my…protection. I take you as my duty."

She stared at that sensual smile. How could he be so cruel? Didn't he realize how desire tormented her?

No, how could he? His bed was likely filled with a new woman every night.

As he stroked her cheek, she looked up at him with pleading eyes. "No," she choked out. "I won't go."

"I can't divorce you unless we go to the desert," he said quietly, looking down at her. "The jewel is there."

She blinked. The emerald. Of course they needed that for their divorce.

And to think she'd actually imagined he was going to whisk her off to the desert for some kind of seduction. Ridiculous. Even if Kareef wanted her, he wouldn't take a long journey across the country just to seduce the woman he'd abandoned years ago. Not when half the women of this city were eagerly begging for the new king to sample their charms!

She truly had lost her mind to think she'd be that special to him. But still—the idea of being alone with him frightened her. "You have so many diplomatic duties here for your coming coronation," she said. "Surely you can send someone to get it?"

"There are some things a man prefers to do himself," he said evenly. "Even if he is king." He raised a dark eyebrow. "And I'm taking you with me."

She licked her lips. "All…all right."

She couldn't leave any question mark that might cast doubt on the legality of her new marriage to Umar. What choice did she have?

A slightly hysterical bubble of laughter escaped her. She could just imagine her father's face if he found out that she was married to the king!

"What is making you smile?" Kareef demanded.

"I was just imagining my father's face if I told him we'd been married for the last thirteen years. Do you think he'd find that respectable enough?"

Kareef paused, then laughed with her in a deep baritone, his eyes bright. "And Hajjar would find a way to incorporate the royal Qusani coat of arms onto his flag, or at least his business card."

For a moment, they grinned at each other.

Then Jasmine's smile faded. "Except no one must ever know I've been your wife."

His eyes darkened. "Because?"

"There must be no scandal against the new king's name. Not after the grief of your uncle's death—the shock of your cousin's abdication." She shook her head. "The people of Qusay have been through enough in the last few weeks to last a lifetime." She took a deep breath, raising her eyes to his. "And you must think of your bride."

He frowned. "My bride? What bride?"

"The bride you will soon take, in your duty as king."

He stared at her, clenching his jaw.

"A royal princess," she said. "With a perfect reputation."

He looked away.

"A beautiful virgin to give you children," she continued, plumbing every depth of her own misery. "To be your queen and give you heirs. You will marry her, give her plump-cheeked, blue-eyed babies, and the whole country will rejoice."

He jerked his head back to look at her, and his blue eyes seemed to glitter in the moonlight.

"Yes, Jasmine. Is that what you want to hear? Yes. I must take a royal virgin to be my queen. She will give me heirs. It is required of me as king. The Al'Ramiz lineage goes back a thousand years. I must have children of my own bloodline. I *will* have them. Does that satisfy you?"

Her heart pounded painfully in her throat.

"Yes," she choked out. "It's exactly what I wanted to hear."

Exactly what she needed: the finally crushing blow to any glimmer of hope. The brief illusion of being young again, of going back to the time they were in love, was gone.

Kareef wasn't hers anymore. Married or not, he had never truly been hers.

A night breeze cut through the courtyard, causing her hair to whip darkly across her face. She heard the plaintive call of owls in the shadowy darkness. The spice and warmth of the air whirled around Jasmine. The memory of his touch a moment ago still burned her cheek.

She heard servants calling his name, louder this time. Any moment now, the servants would find them.

With a deep breath, Kareef stepped toward her.

"But the day of my marriage is far away," he said, tucking her hair gently behind her ear. "And we will take the time we have. Tomorrow, I will take you to the desert."

She shivered at his touch. "And there you will divorce me?"

He smiled, and the dark hunger in his eyes made her tremble. "Good night, my jewel." Lowering his head, he kissed her cheek. "Until tomorrow."

"Yes," she whispered, pulling away. As the servants found Kareef, exclaiming excitedly that his brother, Tahir, had been found, she hurried back to her tiny room in the servants' wing. She ran until she was out of breath.

But even as she collapsed on her small bed, she could still feel Kareef behind her, still feel his lips on hers.

She knew what awaited her tomorrow. She knew it by the dark hunger she'd seen in his eyes. He meant to take her in the desert. *To take her in his bed.*

No! She would not—would *not*—surrender!

CHAPTER FOUR

IT WAS high noon the next day when Kareef arrived at Qusay International Airport.

He'd spent the whole morning in meetings with advisers and undersecretaries, signing papers and discussing upcoming treaties. But he'd smiled all morning. He couldn't stop anticipating the pleasure that was to come.

Tonight, he would finally have Jasmine in his bed.

Kissing her last night had been incredible. If his servants hadn't come out into the garden to find him—something he could not fault them for, since he'd ordered them to tell him if they ever got his youngest brother, Tahir, on the phone—Kareef would have thrown Jasmine over his shoulder and taken her straight to the royal bedchamber.

But this way would be much better. They would have privacy in Qais. And if there was one thing he hungered for almost as much as Jasmine in his bed, it was the freedom of the desert.

Jasmine was right. Their paths lay elsewhere. He would allow her to follow the path she'd chosen for herself. He would give Jasmine her divorce.

But not yet.

For now, Kareef had only one desire. One need. To satisfy this all-consuming hunger of thirteen years.

For her.

Was she sleeping now in that little bed of hers in the palace? Was she naked? Was she dreaming? He closed his eyes, imagining her hair tousled, her soft body warm beneath the blankets. He growled. Every moment away from her seemed wasted.

But at least this particular royal appointment was one he'd looked forward to. As his chauffeur opened the door of the silver limousine, Kareef climbed out, the wind whirling his ceremonial white robes around his ankles as he glanced around him on the tarmac.

Behind him was the second limousine of his motorcade; to the left were four uniformed motorcyclists and his own Bentley, with flags bearing the royal insignia of Qusay whipping in the wind. Directly in front of him he saw his brother's Gulfstream jet, newly arrived from Australia.

His spirits rose still higher.

A perfect day, he thought. Jasmine would soon be in his bed. Rafiq had just returned to Qusay, and even Tahir, who'd been in self-imposed exile for so many years, was on the way. Kareef's heart suddenly felt as bright as the Qusani sun shimmering heat against his white robes.

Rafiq appeared at the door of his airplane. At thirty, there were faint lines at his brother's narrowed eyes, a ruthless set of his jaw that hadn't been there before. Years building a worldwide business empire had changed Rafiq every bit as much as Kareef's years in the desert had changed him.

But as his brother came down the steps to the tarmac, looking every inch the sleek, sharp tycoon in his gray Armani suit, Kareef took one look at him and grinned. "Rafiq!"

"It is good to see you, big brother," Rafiq replied, taking Kareef by the arm. Pulling him close, he slapped him on the back, then teased, "Or should I call you 'sire'?"

With a snort, Kareef waved the joke aside. He ushered his brother into the cool interior of the waiting limousine and the chauffeur closed the door solidly behind them. The motorcade pulled away, motorcycle lights flashing as they left the airport. "It's good you could come at such short notice."

"You think I would miss your coronation?"

"You almost missed Xavian's wedding. How long were you here? Three? Four hours at most."

"It is true," Rafiq conceded. "Although as it turns out, he wasn't Xavian, our cousin after all. But there was no way I was not coming for your coronation. And if there is one thing I am sure of, Kareef, it's that you are indeed my brother." They exchanged a grin, their eyes the same shade of blue, each with the same chiselled jawline. "Speaking of brothers, where is Tahir? Is our wayward brother to grace us with his presence this time?"

Kareef frowned. "I spoke with him…." Name of God, was it only last night, after he'd left Jasmine in the garden? It seemed far longer than that. He'd spent all night dreaming of Jasmine—and all morning dealing with Akmal, his vizier, who was furious at Kareef's plans to leave for the desert. He smiled broadly. "I spoke with him yesterday."

"I don't believe it!"

"It's true. Though it wasn't easy to track him down in Monte Carlo, he's coming to the coronation."

"All three of us, back here at the same time?" his brother said in amazement.

"It's been too long," Kareef agreed.

Rafiq suddenly gave him a sharp look. "That's quite a smile."

He blinked. "Of course I would smile. You're here and Tahir is on his way."

His brother narrowed his eyes, looking at him keenly. "You're smiling with your whole face," he observed. "I haven't seen you do that for years. Care to explain?"

"You'll know everything soon enough." And he feared it was true. Rafiq had always been the sharpest—the most ruthless—of the brothers. To change the subject, Kareef leaned forward and slapped his hands on his thighs. "But you are here and that, my brother, is a good thing. I hear your business goes from strength to strength. Tell me more."

The journey through the city was swift as traffic halted for the king's motorcade. Kareef tried to pay attention to the details of the new emporiums Rafiq had just opened in Auckland and Perth, but his mind kept wandering to the woman who waited for him at the palace. And the night that awaited them in the desert.

Jasmine would resist him. He knew that. He also knew she would fall. She would be in his bed—tonight. Tomorrow. And the day after that, if he still wanted her. He would make love to her until they were both utterly spent.

Then, and only then he would speak the words that would part them forever. And let her go on to her marriage.

His smile faltered. The motorcade went past the palace gate and stopped beneath a portico. A turbaned footman opened his door. As they went up the sweeping steps, Kareef glanced back at his brother. Rafiq seemed dazed as he stared up at the turrets and domes reaching into the sky, glowing like a pearl beneath the noonday sun.

Kareef stopped, taking his brother by the arm. "Here I must leave you, my brother. So if you will excuse me…"

Rafiq cocked a suspicious eyebrow. "Off to place a bet on the Qais Cup?"

Kareef laughed. "I haven't gambled on a horse race in years."

"Then it's being crowned king," he guessed. "All that raw power." He winked. "I'm almost envious, my brother."

"No." That definitely wasn't it. "Excuse me."

"Then what is it?" his brother called after him. "What's got you so damned *happy*?"

Kareef didn't answer. He hurried down the stone cloister of ancient Byzantine arches around the courtyard. Servants stopped to bow as he rushed past them, his white robes whipping around his ankles. In the courtyard, the sun shone bright and hot. A warm breeze blew through the palm trees, rich with the fragrance of spice and oranges.

Her scent.

He glanced at the bright blue sky, hearing birdsong

from the garden. It was after noon, and he hadn't yet eaten. But he hungered for only one thing.

He found Jasmine waiting in her small bedroom in the servants' wing, sitting on the bed reading a paperback book, her packed suitcase at her feet. When he opened the door, she looked up, her expression grave and pale.

"Finally, I am ready." He glanced around the tiny, shabby room, noticing it for the first time. He cleared his throat. "I regret this was the only room available in the palace...."

"That's quite all right," she said quietly, marking her place and tucking her book in her suitcase. "This room has suited me very well." She rose to her feet. "Shall we go?"

Her wide eyes looked up at him, the color of sepia fringed in black. She was wearing a short modern dress in pink silk. Her dark hair was pulled back in a chignon beneath a little felt hat. Her look was retro, modern and with a quirky style all her own.

She looked sixteen still. The same pale, olive-hued skin. The same full black lashes, sweeping over high cheekbones. The same full, luscious lips, bare of makeup. The color of roses.

He longed to kiss those lips.

He was already hard for her.

No wonder. He'd been celibate for... He didn't like to think about that. He'd thought he was too busy for women, or simply uninterested in the particular succession of gold diggers who threw themselves at royalty on a daily basis, even if he had been only minor royalty until recently.

Now he knew the truth. His body had hungered for only one woman. The woman in front of him now.

He could hardly wait to satiate himself with her. It was a journey of several hours to the desert. His eyes fell upon her tiny bed. He was not sure he could wait that long....

But even as he considered the size of her bed, she'd already left the room, dragging her tiny suitcase behind her. He caught up with her, lifting up the suitcase on his shoulder.

"Thank you," she said gravely.

"It weighs almost nothing." And it truly did. He carried it easily with one hand. "Why did you pack so little?"

"Um." Her lips turned upward at the corners. "To avoid baggage fees at the airport?"

He snorted a laugh. "Hajjar has his own plane." He shook his head. "You always enjoyed dress-up as a girl, always had your own style different from the rest." He smiled. "Has so much changed for you? You're too busy to worry about clothes, now that you run your own multimillion dollar company in New York?"

"Ah. Well." Her eyes shifted away uneasily. "Umar has already picked out the clothes he thinks appropriate for me. They will arrive from Paris in a few days. So he didn't—I mean, *I* didn't—see much point in bringing my own clothes from New York, especially since we'll only be in Qusay until we're married."

"I see." He was suddenly irritated by the thought of anyone telling Jasmine what to wear. He tried to shrug it off. If Jasmine didn't care, why should he? Her relationship with Umar was none of his business. In fact,

Kareef was determined to make them both forget his existence for the next few days.

Outside the palace, a bodyguard hefted the small suitcase from Kareef and carried it to the bottom of the sweeping stairs. Another assistant packed it in the front SUV of the motorcade.

Jasmine looked at the SUV and limousine behind it, and all the many bodyguards and servants bustling around the motorcade, with palpable relief. "I see we're not traveling alone."

"Don't get too excited. I travel as the king of Qusay." He gave her a sudden wicked grin. "But in the desert, that will change. As you said, in the desert I'll be just a man. Like any other…"

He let his voice trail off suggestively and saw her shiver in the sunlight. As his chauffeur opened the door, she was very careful not to touch Kareef as she scooted past him into the backseat of the Rolls-Royce.

Sitting beside her, Kareef leaned back, glancing at her out of the corner of his eye as the motorcade drove out the palace gate. She was clinging to the farthest side of the car. It almost amused him. Did she really think she would get out of this without falling into his bed?

Well, let her continue to think so. He loved nothing more than a challenge.

And she had nothing to feel guilty about. Not in this case. Nor in the other—

Memory trembled on the edge of his consciousness, threatening to darken his sunshine. He pushed the troubling memory away. He wouldn't think of what they'd lost in the past—what he'd caused her to lose. Today would be about one thing only: pleasure.

The motorcade moved swiftly out of the city, heading northeast along the coast. But with Jasmine sitting against the opposite window, doing her level best not to touch him, every mile seemed to stretch out to eternity.

He should have listened to Akmal Al'Sayr, he thought grimly. His vizier had tried to convince him to use one of his royal helicopters or planes currently shuttling foreign dignitaries to Qusay, rather than waste time traveling by car. Now Kareef wished he'd taken that advice. Coddling diplomats suddenly seemed a much lower priority than getting Jasmine into his bed.

Kareef glanced at her. She refused to look in his direction, continuing instead to stare stonily out the darkly tinted window. Behind her, he could see the bright turquoise sea shining beyond the smooth, modern highway.

Neither of them moved, but tension hummed between them.

He wanted her. Wanted to take her right here and now in the backseat of this limousine. But was that the private, discreet affair he wanted? Tossing her like a whore in the backseat of a Rolls-Royce, with bodyguards surely able to guess what went on behind darkened windows?

Kareef cursed beneath his breath. He would just have to wait.

But as they approached a fork in the road, he suddenly leaned forward.

"Turn here," he ordered.

"Sire?" His chauffeur looked back in surprise.

"Take the old desert road," he commanded in a voice that did not brook opposition. As his bodyguard communicated the order over a walkie-talkie to the SUV in front of the motorcade, his chauffeur switched lanes on the modern highway, heading toward the exit that would lead straight north through the sands and rock, toward the desert of Qais.

He sat back. He might have to be patient, but he'd be damned if he wouldn't get it over with as soon as possible, by taking the most direct route.

The modern highway of Qusay stretched around the circumference of the island, a new way to travel north to the principality of Qais, a harsh landscape of desert sands and cragged, desolate mountains. Only two years ago, Kareef, as Prince of Qais, had finished the highway with the new influx of money brought by his developments, including the blossoming sport of horse racing. Qais was now second only to Dubai as the emerging hotspot on the thoroughbred racing circuit.

Ironic, Kareef thought, that after personally giving up the sport, the thing he'd once loved the most in the world, he'd turned it into a thriving industry for others.

Although that wasn't entirely true. There had once been something he'd loved even more than horse racing.

He glanced at Jasmine. Her beautiful face was wan. Dark circles were beneath her eyes, hollows beneath her cheeks.

Damn it all to hell.

Why was she trying to resist what they both wanted?

He turned back to the window. Rolling dunes sifted scattered sand onto the road, brushed by wind beneath the hot sun. The road was very old, dating to his grandfather's time. During sandstorms this road could disappear altogether.

Disappear. As he'd tried to do thirteen years ago.

He'd wanted to die rather than face the accusation in her eyes. He'd fled into the desert, praying to be sucked beneath a grave of sand.

Instead, Umar Hajjar had found him and brought him home. Unable to die, Kareef had thrown himself into a life of sacrifice and duty. The nomadic people of the desert had eventually looked to him for leadership, turning his family's honorary title of Prince of Qais into a real one.

Against his will, Kareef had been brutally sentenced—to live.

He rubbed the back of his tense neck, giving Jasmine a sideways glance. He would never be able to make amends to her for what he'd done.

But should he try?

He wanted her. But did that mean he had the right to take her? Should he try to do one last unselfish thing…by letting her go?

One man has had no trouble resisting me, Kareef. You.

He suppressed a harsh laugh. He, who'd shown such perfect control with women, lost all self-control around her. Prickles of heat went through his body just sitting beside her.

Any man would be attracted to Jasmine. Even if he were blind. Even if she were wrapped in veils from head to toe. Any man would seek her warmth. Her scent, a tantalizing mix of citrus and clove. Her seductive shape, with that tiny waist setting off her delectable breasts and the wide curve of her hips. The perfect backside for any man's hands. The heartbreaking sweetness of her glance. Of her soul.

No, he would not think of her soul. He would think only of her body.

"We're not going to stop, are we?" she suddenly whispered. Her voice sounded tortured. "We're not going to stop on the way?"

He turned to her. Her beautiful brown eyes were shimmering with light.

"Do you wish to stop?" he asked in a low voice.

She shook her head. "I want to drive through the mountains as quickly as possible."

"Are you afraid?"

This time, she had no bravado in her.

"Yes," she whispered. "You know what I fear. I see it in my nightmares. Don't you?"

Kareef's throat closed. He gave a single unsteady nod.

Here on the old desert road, they would drive right past the riding school and the red rock mountains beyond. The cliffs. The hidden cave. The place where he hadn't protected her, where he hadn't protected the child neither of them had known she was carrying. Where Jasmine had nearly died of fever because he'd given the ridiculous promise not to tell after the horse-riding accident. As if love alone could save them.

He'd been helpless. Useless. He'd failed at the most basic test of any man. Jagged pain cracked his throat, making his voice husky as he said, "We will not stop."

He saw her take a deep, grateful breath. "Thank you."

He nodded, not trusting himself to speak. Long ago, they'd escaped the prying eyes of the palace at the riding school. Her friend Sera had distracted the girls' aged chaperone so Kareef and Jasmine could have some precious time together—alone.

The remote school, surrounded by paddocks and stables, had been where Kareef felt most truly alive, the place he'd loved to race his black stallion, Razul. He'd loved to feel Jasmine's eyes on him as he showed off for her.

"Ride with me, Jasmine," he'd begged, adding with a grin, *"You're not afraid, are you?"* And one day— she'd finally agreed.

They'd thought themselves so clever, to evade the restrictions set by her parents and find a way to be together. But in the end, fate had punished them all— even her strict but well-meaning parents whose only crime had been trying to protect Jasmine from a man who might bring destruction and shame to her loving, innocent soul and fairy-tale beauty. *A man like him.*

As their motorcade traveled through the desert, he stared out at the sharp light of the sun reflecting against the sand. Scattered clouds like yin and yang symbols of darkness and light moved swiftly against the bright blue sky. He wondered if a storm was coming.

Then he felt her small hand on his arm and knew the storm was already here. Inside him.

"Thank you," Jasmine whispered again. Her fingers tightened on his arm. "Umar is a kind man, he tries to be good to me, but I did not wish to face this for the first time beside him, traveling through the desert on my wedding day." She shook her head, lifting her luminous eyes to his. "He can't understand. You do."

At the light touch of her fingers, he shuddered.

If he were a civilized man, he thought suddenly,

he'd set her free right now. He would divorce her immediately and let her go untouched to the man she wished to marry. His friend. But the thought of her with any other man was as sharp as a razor blade inside him.

Kareef wanted her for himself.

Wanted? Was that even close to the right word? His body craved her, like it craved food or water or air.

Wanted?

He wanted her so much that she made his body shake with need. It was an inhuman test of will that he should be so close to her, trapped in the back of a Rolls-Royce but unable to touch her.

With a shuddering intake of breath, he looked down at her hand on his arm, fighting to control himself when all he wanted to do was seize her in his arms and crush her lips against his own.

But after all his time living unselfishly to serve others, could he really allow himself to take what he needed, what he wanted most?

What would it cost her if he did?

Kareef heard the intake of Jasmine's breath, felt her body move against his, and he knew she'd just seen the riding school on the other side of the road. He put his arm around her. He felt her body tremble. She stared out at the school as they passed, her face stricken, her brown eyes swimming with tears like an ocean of memories.

And in that instant he forgot about his own needs.

He forgot the heat of his own desire.

All he knew was that it was Jasmine in his arms, Jasmine who was afraid—and that he had to protect her. Holding her against his chest, he leaned forward urgently and barked out an order to his chauffeur. "Drive faster."

The man nodded and pressed on the gas.

The riding school passed by in a blur of color. He saw the place where they'd first whispered words of love. The place where he'd drawn her into a quiet glade of trees behind the farthest paddock, and on a soft blanket beside a cool brook—the place he'd first made love to her, virgins both, pledging hushed, breathless, eternal devotion.

"*I marry you,*" she'd whispered three times.

"*I marry you,*" he'd answered once, holding her hands tightly between his own.

Kareef took a deep breath.

He would be unselfish—one last time.

In the old days, the king's will in Qusay had been absolute. No one could deny the king the woman he wanted, under pain of death. He would have taken possession of Jasmine like a barbarian. He would have thrown her into his harem, locked the door behind them and not come out again until he was satisfied. He would have taken her on a bed, against a wall, on the soft carpets in front of the fire. He would have lifted her against him, the firelight gleaming off the sweat of her silken skin, until he made her gasp and scream his name.

But Kareef was not that barbarian king. He couldn't be. Not when Jasmine trembled with fear in his arms.

"The memories can't hurt us anymore," he murmured, holding her tight as he stroked her hair. "It all happened long ago."

"I know that. In my mind," she whispered, her voice barely loud enough to hear. "But in my heart, it happened yesterday."

They stared out the window as the motorcade flew past the humble outbuildings of the riding school, its paddocks and fields and stables.

The intimacy of being so physically close as they shared the same exact memories made him taut with an emotion he didn't want to feel. His muscles shook from the effort of just holding her, of just offering comfort—thirteen years too late.

Then they were past it. The school disappeared behind them. Their limousine flew down the bumpy old road through the red rock canyon toward Qais.

He felt Jasmine relax in his arms. Closing his eyes, he breathed in the scent of her hair. She leaned against his chest. For long moments of silence, he held her. Just the two of them. Like long ago.

Then Kareef heard the cough of his bodyguard in the front seat, heard his chauffeur shift position. And he forced himself to pull away from their compromising position.

He looked down at her, gently lifting her chin.

"You're all right then?" he said softly, offering her a smile.

Her eyes shone back at him with unshed tears.

"I was wrong," she whispered. Her dark eyelashes trembled against her pale cheeks. "I see that now. I was wrong to hate you," she said softly, reaching out to hold his hand. "Thank you for holding me. I couldn't have faced that alone."

He stared at her incredulously.

She was forgiving him? For one brief moment of sympathy, the kind any stranger might have offered to a grieving woman, she was willing to overlook what he'd done?

He looked away, his jaw tense. "Forget it."

"But you—"

"It was nothing," he bit out, ripping his hand from her grasp.

He would let her go, he told himself fiercely. His only way of making amends. Honor and duty were all he had left. He would not seduce her. He wouldn't even touch her. As soon as they arrived at his home, he would immediately divorce her and send her on her way. He would leave her to her happiness.

His jaw clenched as he stared out at the sun.

For thirteen years, he'd buried himself so deeply in duty that he couldn't breathe or think. He'd immolated himself like some mad desert hermit buried neck-deep in hot sand. But being near Jasmine had brought his body and soul alive in a way he hadn't felt in a long time. In a way he'd never thought he'd feel again.

But he would let her go. No matter how he wanted her. *He owed her.* He would let her disappear from his life, and this time it would be forever. Umar Hajjar would guard her covetously, like the treasure she was.

Kareef would be unselfish one last time. Even if it killed him. He almost hoped it would.

The shadows of the red rock mountains moved in mottled patterns over their motorcade as they passed out of the canyon. As they went through the mountains into the wide sweep of the desert of Qais, he saw the wind picking up, swirling little spirals of sand, twisting them up into the sky.

Kareef felt the same way every time he looked at her. Tangled up in her.

He felt her dark head nestle on his shoulder. Looking down at her in surprise, he saw her eyes were closed. She was sleeping against him. His gaze roamed her face.

God, he wanted to kiss her.

More than kiss. He wanted to strip her naked and feast on every inch of her supple flesh. He wanted to explore the mountains of her breasts and valley between. The low flat plain of her belly and hot citadel between her thighs. He wanted to devour her like a conqueror seizing a kingdom for his own use, beneath his hands, beneath his control.

But the old days were over.

He was king of Qusay, yet unable to have the one thing he most desired. No strength could take her. No brutality could force her. He couldn't act on his desire. Not at the expense of her happiness.

His muscles hurt with the effort it took to feel her against him, but not touch her. Clenching his jaw, he turned back out the window. He could see his house in the distance. In just a few minutes, they would be done. He would go inside, find the emerald and speak the simple words to set her free. And after today, he would make sure he never saw Jasmine again—

His thoughts were interrupted when he heard a sudden squeal, the sickening sound of metal grating against the road.

As if in a dream, he looked up to see the SUV at the

front of the motorcade slam hard to the right, then smash against the rock wall along the road.

He heard his own bodyguard shout, saw his chauffeur frantically try to turn the wheel. But it was too late. Kareef barely had time to think before he felt the Rolls-Royce hit against the SUV, felt his body jack-knife forward.

As their limousine flew up, rolling violently through the air, he looked down at Jasmine. His last image was her wide-open, terrified eyes—his last sound, her scream.

CHAPTER FIVE

JASMINE opened her eyes.

She was lying on a blanket, amid the cool shadows of green trees. Nearby, she heard a burbling brook and horses racing in the paddocks of the riding school. She felt the soft desert wind against her face. And the greatest miracle of all: the boy she loved was beside her, smiling with his whole face, love shining from his electric blue eyes.

He pulled her down against him on the blanket, reaching to tuck her hair behind her ear. Dappled golden light caressed his black hair as he rolled over her body with sudden urgency, his eyes gazing fiercely down into hers.

"I have no right to ask you this," he whispered. "But I will regret it forever if I do not." He cupped her face in his hands. "Marry me, Jasmine. Marry me."

"Yes," she gasped. He smiled, then with agonizing slowness he lowered his lips toward hers. He kissed her. Then, for the first time, they did far more than just kiss….

"Jasmine!"

His sudden harsh shout was jarring. She heard the

panic in his voice, but couldn't answer. Something was choking her. Slowly, blearily she opened her eyes.

And realized she wasn't on the blanket by the stream.

She was strapped into a car upside down. Her knees were hanging against her chest and she could see the blue sky through the window at her feet. The seat belt felt so tight that she couldn't breathe. Something warm and liquid dripped across her lashes.

"I'm bleeding," she whispered aloud.

She heard Kareef's curse and suddenly the passenger door was wrenched open, causing scattered pieces of broken glass to clatter from the window to the road. Suddenly, the seat belt was gone and she was in Kareef's arms, sitting on his knees in the dusty road.

She felt his hands move over her head, her arms, her body. "Nothing's broken," he breathed. He held her tightly against his chest, kissing her hair, whispering, "You're safe. You're safe."

She closed her eyes in the shelter of his arms. She pressed her cheek against the warmth of his neck.

Time felt as mixed and confused as the smashed, upside-down cars in the road. For the space of a dream, she'd been sixteen again, with her whole life ahead of her, certain of Kareef's devotion and his strong arms around her.

Those same arms were around her now, even more powerful and muscled than they'd been before. What had happened?

"Get a doctor!" Kareef turned and thundered.

She was dimly aware of bodyguards rushing around them, shouting into cell phones, but they all seemed far away. She and Kareef were at the eye of the storm.

She looked at him and saw the blood on his clothes, the tears in the white fabric of his shirt, and a chill went through her. Trembling, she reached her hand toward his face, toward the thin lines of red streaking his chiseled cheekbone. "You're bleeding."

He jerked his head away. "It's nothing."

He didn't want her to touch him. That much was absolutely clear. She felt her cheeks go hot as she put her hand down. She pressed her lips together, wanting to cry. So much had changed since the time of her beautiful dream. "But—you should see a doctor."

He rose to his feet, holding her. "Unnecessary. But for you…" He looked down at Jasmine. "Can you stand alone?"

"Yes." Her head was pounding, but she would not try to lean against him. She would not make him push her away. If he did not want her to touch him, she would stand alone on her own two feet if it killed her.

Releasing her hand, he brushed dirt off the shoulders of her pink blouson minidress. "Your hat is gone," he muttered.

She looked up at him in a daze. "It doesn't matter."

"We'll have someone find it." Taking a damp towel from a bodyguard, Kareef wiped her forehead, then paused. "You've got a small cut on your scalp," he said matter-of-factly, his voice calm, as if trying not to scare her. He turned back to his bodyguard. "We must take Miss Kouri back to the hospital."

Miss Kouri. So he'd reverted to that. He was already keeping his distance, as if he'd already divorced her.

The bodyguard shook his head at Kareef. "The cars

are totaled, your highness." His voice grew bitter, angry. "That mare escaped into the road again. Youssef had to swerve to avoid her."

Kareef looked past the smashed, upside-down Rolls-Royce toward the black horse still standing in the road. "Ah, Bara'ah. Even put out to pasture," he murmured softly, "you're up to your old tricks."

Jasmine followed his gaze. The slender black mare, chewing lone wisps of grass that had grown through the cracks of the pavement, looked back with placid amusement.

"Get her back in her paddock," Kareef said. "Get a new car from my garage."

His garage?

Jasmine looked down the road and saw a wide, low-slung ranch house of brown wood, surrounded by paddocks and palm trees.

Comfortable and peaceful, without any of Umar's gilded, lavish ostentatiousness, Kareef's home was a green oasis in the vast wasteland of the desert.

He'd done it. He'd created the house he'd once promised her. But he'd done it alone....

Her hands tightened. And Kareef wanted to take her away. He wanted to take her back to the city, to leave her in some sterile, beeping hospital room—alone. Perhaps he intended to run inside and get the emerald, and divorce her on the way?

It was what she'd thought she wanted—a quick divorce without seduction, without entanglements. But now, she suddenly felt like crying.

"I don't want to go to the hospital."

At the sound of her voice, Kareef and the bodyguard turned to her in surprise, as if they'd forgotten she was there.

"But Jasmine," Kareef replied gently and slowly, as if speaking to a recalcitrant child, "you need to see a doctor."

"No hospital." Dark hair blew in her eyes from her collapsing chignon. Pushing back her hair, she saw blood on her hands. Looking down, she saw drops of blood on the pink silk of her dress.

Just like the last time she'd been in an accident. The last time she'd seen her own blood. After the accident—before the scandal…

She suddenly couldn't get enough air.

She couldn't breathe.

Panicking, she put her hands on her head as she tried to get air in her lungs. More dark tendrils tumbled from her chignon as the world started to spin around her.

Kareef's eyes narrowed. "Jasmine?"

Her breath came in short, shallow gasps as she backed away from him. Everything was a blur, going in circles faster and faster. No matter which way she looked, she saw something that trapped her. The home of her dreams. The man of her dreams. The blood on her dress…

Kareef grabbed her before she could fall. His intense blue eyes stared down at her. She dimly heard him shouting. She saw his men rushing to obey.

She saw Kareef's lips moving, saw the concern in his blue eyes, but couldn't hear what he was saying. She could only hear the ragged pant of her own breathing, the frantic pounding of her own heart.

Colors continued to spin around her as her knees started to slide. In the distance she saw the black mare staring back at her. Black like the horse who'd thrown her long ago. Black like the accident that had caused her to lose everything.

Black.

Black.

Black…

Suddenly, Kareef's worried face came into sharp focus.

"You're awake," he said in a low voice. "Do you know who I am?"

Jasmine discovered that she was lying on her back in a bedroom she didn't recognize. Her head was pounding; her throat was dry.

She tried to sit up. "Where—where am I?"

"Don't try to move," he said, pushing her back gently on the bed. "My own doctor's on the way."

Her head was flat on the pillow as she looked slowly around the bedroom. It was large, rustic and comfortable, with a king-sized bed and spartan furnishings. It was very masculine, smelling of leather and wood. She looked at the small fireplace made out of hewn rock. "I'm in your bedroom?"

"So you know who I am," Kareef said, sounding relieved.

Jasmine gave a derisive snort. "The illustrious king of Qusay, the adored and revered prince of Qais, the delight of all harem girls everywhere, the…"

"How hard did that glass hit your head?" he demanded, but his mouth quirked up into a smile. He'd been worried, she realized. Very worried.

"Did I faint?" She tried to sit up, to show them both she was all right.

"Don't move!"

"I feel fine!"

"The doctor will be the judge of that."

"You said I have a small cut on my scalp. That doesn't require a team of specialists. Stick a bandage on my head."

"And you fainted," he reminded her.

Her cheeks went hot with embarrassment. She felt sure her fainting had nothing to do with the bump on her head and had been instead some kind of panic attack—but how could she explain that without bringing up the long-ago accident she absolutely, positively did not want to talk about?

She didn't need to bring it up. His next words proved that.

"What is it about you and doctors?" he said softly, looking down at her. "Why do you refuse to let me take decent care of you?"

Their eyes locked, and she sucked in her breath. She knew what he was thinking about.

After the horse-riding accident, he'd pleaded to fetch a doctor. But she'd refused. She been desperate to keep her shame a secret, to protect her family. *Please, Kareef, just hold me, I'll be fine,* she'd cried. But when she'd started shaking with fever, he'd broken his word. He'd returned with a doctor and two servants he thought he could trust.

One of the servants had been Marwan, who'd betrayed them the instant Kareef disappeared into the desert. Her family had been devastated, nearly destroyed. *Because of her.*

Blinking fast, she turned her head away.

Kareef leaned over the bed. With the prison of his arms on the mattress around her, she slowly looked up into his face.

Their faces was inches apart. Tension coiled between them.

"Here," he muttered, looking away. "Let me fix this."

He reached behind her and rearranged the pillows. He lifted her, and she closed her eyes, relishing the warmth and strength of his arms. Then he gently pushed her back against the pillows, into a sitting position. He stroked her hair.

"Better?" he said in a low voice.

His mouth was inches from her own. She felt the warmth of his breath against her skin. It made her shiver from her mouth to her earlobes to her nipples and neck. Even her supposedly injured scalp tingled with a feeling that had nothing to do with pain and everything to do with—

She cut off the thought. With Kareef so close to her, she was having difficulty thinking straight. What question had he asked her? She licked her lips. "I'm much…much better…."

"The doctor will be here soon," he said hoarsely. The hard muscles of his body seemed strained, almost shaking, as if he were struggling to hold himself in check. "Any moment, he will be here…."

He started to pull away. And suddenly Jasmine couldn't bear to lose his arms around her. Not after she'd been so cold for so long. Not when they were this close, this man she'd tried to hate, this man she'd never stopped craving.

Leaning up, she pressed her mouth to his.

It was a short kiss. A peck. Just enough to feel the roughness of his lips, his masculine power and strength. But it caused a hot fever to spread through her body.

Kareef looked down at her in shock. She heard his hoarse, ragged breath as his hands gripped her shoulders. Then, with a growl, he pushed her back against the pillow as the simmering conflagration exploded into fire. He kissed her, hard and deep. His kiss was hungry. Brutal.

He kissed her as if he'd been starving for her half his life.

His arms wrapped around her, pressing Jasmine back against the pillows. He enfolded her small body with his larger one. His mouth was rough and savage against hers, bruising her lips even as his hands caressed the back of her head, holding her like a fragile rose.

The hot demand of his kiss seared her, sending sparks down her body. Her breasts felt heavy, her nipples tightening to painful intensity. An ache of longing coiled low in her belly, curling lower, lower still, between her thighs.

His mouth never left hers as he stroked down the front of her body, from the smooth curve of her collarbone to her flat belly, seeing her with his fingertips. His feather-light touch against the smooth pink silk of her blouson dress caused exquisite agony of sensation. His kiss deepened, became more demanding. He gripped her bare arms, her shoulders, holding her down.

How many nights had she dreamed of this? Of feeling his hands on her skin, of being in his bed?

She was dreaming. She had to be. And she prayed she would never wake.

His large hands splayed across her silken belly in the bright sunlight of the windows. He plundered her lips, spreading her mouth wide to accept his tongue.

A soft moan escaped her. She wrapped her hands around his neck to hold his body against her. Their tongues intertwined, mingled, fought. His lips bruised hers—or was it the other way around? She no longer knew. Neither of them could hold thirteen years of desire in check. They barely kept themselves from causing injury to the other beneath the weight of their mutual, insatiable hunger.

It was better than it had been at sixteen. Now, at twenty-nine, she knew how rare this fire truly was.

She reached her hands beneath his shirt and felt the heat of his skin, the hard knots of his muscles and taut belly. Felt the soft coarse hair between the hard nubs of his nipples. With an intake of breath, he pulled back, grabbing her wrists.

"Tonight, you are mine. Whatever the cost." His voice was low and dark, as if ripped from the depths of his soul. "I will make you forget all the others."

Their eyes locked in a moment that seemed to stretch out to infinity. She swallowed.

"There have been no others," she whispered. "Only you. How could I give my body to another, when I am still your wife?"

Her cheeks went hot, and she couldn't meet his eyes. Would he mock her pathetic fidelity? Would he laugh at her?

Then she heard his harsh intake of breath. *"Jasmine."*

Suddenly, his hands were in her long tangled hair, his body pressed against hers. His blue eyes were dark and hungry as he tilted back her head, exposing her throat.

"Jasmine. My first," he breathed. "My only."

Her heartbeat tripled. Could he mean…?

No! It wasn't possible. He was a handsome, powerful sheikh, the king of Qusay. He couldn't have spent the last thirteen years as she had done—with a lonely bed and an aching heart!

But as Kareef's eyes burned through hers, she felt the truth. He stroked down her cheek, tracing his thumb against her bottom lip. Trembling, she closed her eyes as he touched her. This couldn't be happening…couldn't be…

Cupping her chin in his hands, he kissed her fiercely. His kiss was so deep and pure that she was reborn in the blaze, fired in the crucible of their desire. His hands moved beneath the pink dress, pressing rough and raw against her skin. He ripped the silk off her body, and she felt his hands everywhere. On the skin of her back as he undid her bra in a single swift movement. On her belly and hips as he pulled her white panties off, ripping them down over her long legs.

And suddenly, she was naked and spread across his bed.

Rising abruptly from the bed, he pinned her with his hot gaze as he slowly unbuttoned his tattered white shirt and cuffs. He dropped the shirt to the ground, then kicked off his black shoes and pants. From where she lay, naked on his white bedspread, she looked up at him and drew in her breath.

His tanned body was magnificent in the brilliant,

blinding sunlight from the windows, casting a halo over him like a dark angel. Shadows flickered over his well-built chest and downward, against a line of black hair that stretched past his taut belly to the thick length of him, so hard for her, jutted and proud in its unyielding, brutal masculine demand.

A cry caught in her throat as she looked at him. He knelt over her on the bed, his muscular thighs stretching over hers as he ran his broad hands down the length of her flat belly.

His fingers, once rough, became tantalizingly light. His fingertips barely made contact with her skin as he traced her hips and thighs. He cupped her breasts, feeling their weight, worshipping them. Kneeling over her, he kissed her neck, then her mouth.

He kissed her with reverence that seared her to the ends of her soul. His hands caressed her heavy, aching breasts and she closed her eyes. She nearly protested as his lips left hers. Then she felt him move down her body as he lowered his mouth to her breast. Feeling his lips suckle her aching nipple, his tongue swirling against her and his teeth creating a pleasure almost like pain, she gasped, arching her back.

Whatever it cost her, she didn't want him to stop.

His lips and tongue were pure fire against her skin as he tasted her, sucking and biting each breast until her breath came in short little gasps and she cried out. His hands cupped her, squeezing the full flesh with increasing intensity until her breasts lifted of their own accord to meet his mouth. She felt the warmth of the bright sun against her skin, heard her own gasps as if from a distance. His hard body moved against hers, and desire swept her up with the intensity of need, suspending her breathless in midair.

He kissed down the soft length of her belly, pressing her breasts together to lick the deep crevice between them.

She felt the coarse hair of his muscular thighs move against her legs as he moved farther down her body. She felt the hard jut of his erection press against her, demanding attention, jerking hard when it brushed briefly against her skin. But he didn't position himself between her legs. Instead, she felt his hands caress her hips, between her thighs.

With a growl, he spread her legs apart.

She squeezed her eyes shut, blocking out the light. If she opened her eyes and saw his head between her thighs, she feared she'd lose control.

His jawline was rough and scratchy against her tender skin. She felt the heat of his breath against her thighs as, stretching her wide with his fingers, he took a long, languorous taste of her.

She cried out, arching her back violently. The back of her head sank into the soft piles of pillows as she shook beneath the shocking, unendurable waves of bliss.

The pleasure, oh God, the pleasure! Tension twisted and coiled inside her, sending her higher with every sweep of his tongue, with every tiny curling flick of his tip against her wet body. Her chin tilted back higher as her eyes closed, almost rolling back in her head. Her breaths came in increasingly desperate pants as his powerful tongue worked against her, widely lapping one moment, the next moment swirling light circles against the painfully taut center of her longing.

Reaching up his hands to feel her breasts, he continued to lick her. His tongue was a wet, hard column of heat and he slowly thrust it inside her.

New trembling started deep inside Jasmine. She put her hands up against the headboard to brace herself. She felt dizzy, her body spinning out of control.

He thrust his tongue farther inside her, stroking her hard nub softly with his thumb. Then he moved his tongue upward to her most sensitive spot and suckled her there, swirling her with his tongue as he pushed a thick finger inside her.

Then two fingers. Then—three.

Oh God.... She couldn't take this, she couldn't...

Her body shook as if by an earthquake traveling hundreds of miles an hour. Harder, higher, faster... Her body and soul opened to him like cracks in the desert rock, letting in the sun and wind. She felt him move up her body to kiss her neck, positioning his hard, wide length between her thighs. His hands grasped her wrists against the headboard, holding her fast. Holding her down.

But she was already caught. She looked up at him above her.

No man had ever been so beautiful. His eyes were a brilliant blue, searing her with his need and hunger. His jawline was taut and dark with new stubble. Sharp cheekbones cast shadows on his Roman nose, below the black slash of his eyebrows. He was her dark angel. Her husband. Jasmine's heart rose to her throat.

His returning gaze whipped through her soul. Made her lose all sense of place and time. All sense of where she ended and he began. They were one.

Staring into her eyes, he slowly thrust himself inside her. Ruthlessly, he watched her face as he pushed himself to the hilt, right to her heart.

She gasped at the feeling of him inside her. The size of him hurt her. Pleasure and pain together rolled over her body in waves before she stretched to accommodate him.

He drew back and pushed inside her again, so hard and deep—with such force—that another new wave of pleasure hit her, knocking her over and sucking her beneath the waves. Slowly, he rode her, pushing deeper with each thrust, until the pleasure was too much, too much, beyond thought or reason.

Gripping his shoulders in her hands, she cried out, exploding like a fire scattering embers in the night. And as she shattered into a million pieces like stars across the sky, she dimly heard her voice gasping his name, crying words of love as she fell.

CHAPTER SIX

WHEN Kareef heard her gasp with joy, when he felt her tremble and shake around him, it was almost too much. His first thrust was nearly his last.

But he was no longer an eighteen-year-old boy. He took a slow, shuddering breath, holding back his raging desire, regaining control. He held himself in ferocious check as he pushed inside her. It took every bit of will that he possessed to hold himself back.

It was bliss.

It was hell.

It was everything he'd dreamed and more.

He looked down and saw Jasmine's luscious body spread out beneath him, saw the afternoon sunlight against her full breasts, casting her pink, taut nipples in a warm glow as she arched her back. Her beautiful face was lost in an expression of fierce, agonized joy as he rode her. She triumphed in her possession of him, as he gloried in taking her.

The bright desert sunlight touched everywhere on her skin, like curling fingers. Her image washed over him like a wave of cool water. How long had he desired her? How long had he thirsted, like a perishing man for an oasis? How long had dreams of Jasmine Kouri tormented him, body and soul?

His hands shook as he gripped her shoulders, fighting to hold himself back from the thrust that would make him pour his seed into her.

He was no selfish boy, to take her quickly at his own pleasure. He would make it last. He'd brought her to fulfillment several times but it still wasn't enough. He wanted to give her more—to make her feel more. He wanted to make love to her all day, all night until she could bear no more.

"Jasmine," he whispered. His voice was raw even to his own ears.

He heard her soft, kittenish gasp in reply.

God, she was beautiful. He stared down into her face. The beautiful, beautiful face of the only woman he'd ever desired.

Lowering his head, he kissed her. She twisted beneath him, reaching her arms around his back, holding him down against her. He tightened in sweet agony.

Jasmine. He whispered her name soundlessly as he stroked up her naked body to her soft cheek. She was his, only his. There'd been no other lovers in her bed. He was the only man who'd ever possessed her.

The thought caused a surge to rush through his blood. Beads of sweat broke out on his forehead from the effort it took to hold back his own climax.

There was no need to hurry, he told himself. No need to rush. He had all the time in the world.

Pulling back, he slowly moved inside her. She

arched her back with a gasp, whispering rapturous words he could not hear.

With iron self-control, he thrust inside her again, riding her with increasing depth and speed. Their bodies became sweaty, sliding against each other as he pushed inside her with increasing roughness and force, almost impaling her as his muscled chest slid against the soft bounce of her breasts.

He couldn't hold back much longer...couldn't—

He felt her start to tighten again around him. Saw her hold her breath, then gasp, slowly letting out the air in a hiss through her full, reddened, bruised lips.

Suddenly, her nails gripped into his naked back. Screaming incomprehensible words, she twisted her hips, thrashing back and forth beneath him and he could hold back no longer. She screamed out his name, and he finally lost all control.

With a groan, he thrust inside her so deeply that almost at once, the orgasm hit him like a blow, with joy so intense he blacked out for several seconds.

It could have been minutes or hours later when he finally resurfaced. Kareef found himself naked on the bed, still holding her to his chest, with a sheet twisted haphazardly around them.

His heartbeat still hadn't returned to normal as he looked down at her beautiful, exhausted face. Tenderly, he bent his head to kiss her dirty, smudged forehead.

Her eyelashes fluttered open, and she looked up at him without speaking. He heard the ragged pant of her breath. For a moment, he just cradled her in his arms and they looked at each other silently in the roseate glow of twilight.

Then he heard a knock, heard the door push open.

"Sire, forgive me, I was assisting at a difficult labor, but now I'm ready to see the— Oh."

His trusted personal doctor, an elderly Qusani who'd been loyal to the Al'Ramiz family for generations, had peeked his head around the door, and clearly he'd had a shock. The physician's cheeks burned red as he backed away. "Er—I'll wait outside 'til you're ready, and until then, leave the patient in your… er…capable hands."

The man left, discreetly closing the door behind him.

Kareef and Jasmine looked at each other, still naked and sprawled across the bed, with only the twisted sheet like a rope over them.

And to his surprise, she burst into laughter.

"So much for discretion," she said, wiping her eyes.

Kareef's eyes couldn't look away from her face as she laughed. Her sparkling eyes, her white teeth, the sound of her laugh. "He will never tell," he promised. But he couldn't stop smiling at her.

He'd never heard anything more beautiful in his life than her laugh. He'd never thought he'd hear it again.

Many hours later, after the doctor had given her scalp two stitches, bandaged her other cuts and pronounced her well, they made love several times more before they lay sleeping in each other's arms. Or rather, Kareef held her as she slept.

He couldn't stop looking at her.

Now, outside the window of his bedroom, he could see dawn rising over the desert, and his stomach growled. Time for breakfast, his body insisted. He realized he hadn't eaten at all yesterday. He smiled down at Jasmine sleeping in his arms and softly caressed her cheek. He'd been distracted.

He could hardly believe he already wanted her again. They'd barely slept at all last night. They'd made love at least four times, possibly four and a half, depending on what counted and what did not.

He should just hold her and sleep. He closed his eyes. Jasmine was the only woman he'd ever wanted close like this. He suddenly realized she was the only woman he'd ever slept with, in any sense of the word.

His arms tightened around her. Then his stomach growled again, louder this time. He glanced at her, surprised the sound hadn't startled her.

Kareef gave a resigned sigh. Careful not to wake her, he moved his arm from beneath her head and quietly dressed before he left her.

When she woke, he would surprise her. First with breakfast. He allowed himself a wicked smile. Then with dessert.

He went down the hallway to his modern kitchen and turned on the gas stove. Pulling pans off their hooks, he prepared eggs scrambled with meat, then toast and fruit. He got two plates from a cupboard and arranged them on a tray. As an afterthought, he went outside and picked a flower from the small pot of roses beside the front door.

When he came back into the house, he found Jasmine standing in the middle of the gleaming kitchen, wearing only an oversized T-shirt emblazoned with the name of some 1980s rock band.

"I couldn't find you," she said accusingly.

Leaning forward, he placed the rose in her hair,

tucking it behind her ear as he leaned forward to kiss her cheek. "I was hungry."

She smiled, looking somehow like a fairy princess in the large T-shirt with the flower in her mussed hair. "You're hungry an awful lot," she murmured.

Giving her a sensual grin, Kareef lifted a dark eyebrow. "You bring it out in me."

Her forehead furrowed as she searched his gaze. Then with an intake of breath she looked down at the tray. Her voice was soft, almost impossible to hear. "It looks delicious. Who made it?"

"I did."

She laughed, looking around the kitchen as if she expected to find three sous chefs hidden behind the huge refrigerator. "No. Really. Who made it?"

"I have no live-in staff here, Jasmine," he said. "I told you. I don't like being fussed over."

She looked at him skeptically, wrinkling her nose. "You mean to tell me—" she indicated the spotless, sparkling tile floor "—you mopped that yourself?"

"I'm independent—not insane," he said with a laugh. "I do have a housekeeper, as well as gardeners and my veterinary staff and stable workers. But they have their own cottages on the edge of my land. I live in this house alone. I prefer it that way."

"Oh."

"Let's go outside." Taking two cups of steaming Turkish coffee, he placed them on the tray beside the breakfast plates. Holding the patio door open with his shoulder, he carried the tray in one hand. "We can watch the sun rise."

She followed him out to the wooden deck behind the

kitchen. Leaning against the railing, she looked out at the vast expanse of desert stretching beyond the valley.

"You said you someday wanted to build a house out here," she whispered. "But I never imagined anything so beautiful as this."

Setting the tray down on the table, he looked at the dark, curvy silhouette of her body in front of the vast wide desert now glowing pink in the sunrise.

"Beautiful indeed," he said quietly.

She turned to face him. "It must be hard for you to leave this all behind."

A dull throb went through his head, in the back of his skull. "Yes."

He'd briefly forgotten the royal palace, forgotten the endless, unsatisfied crowds of people hemming him in, making demands of their king. Forgotten the fact that in just a few days, he would formally and forever renounce all right to be a private citizen with his own selfish desires. He would be king, sacrificing himself forever for the good of his people.

He took a deep breath. But today at least, he was home. He was free. He looked up at Jasmine, so impossibly beautiful in the old T-shirt that stretched over her breasts and barely covered her thighs. *Today at least he was with her.*

"Here, we can forget you are the king," she said softly. She turned back to lean against the railing, watching the pink sun peeking slowly over the violet mountains. "And I can forget I will be soon married."

Staring out blindly across the desert, she shivered in the cool morning.

Taking two cups of steaming coffee, he walked

across the deck to stand behind her. Handing her a mug, he wrapped one arm around her and pulled her back against his chest. He held her close as they watched the sun rise across the desert, filling the land with warmth and color like rose gold, as they both sipped coffee in silence.

She glanced back at him with a sudden embarrassed laugh. "You said you come here to be alone. Do you want me to go?"

He held her against his chest.

"No," he said quietly. "I want you to stay."

She didn't interrupt his solitude, he realized. She improved it. The quiet intimacy she offered him enriched everything, even the sunrise.

Looking out at the vast desert, he realized he was holding the only person on earth he'd ever wanted to be close to him. Not just in his bed, but in his life.

It couldn't last. He knew that. In just a few days, they would return to the city. Kareef would again become the king; Jasmine would become another man's wife. The magic would end.

But staring out at the streaks of orange sunlight now streaking across the brightening blue sky, Kareef told himself they had time. They had days left, hours and hours stretching ahead of them.

And surely, in this magical place, those days could last forever.

Two days later, Jasmine was floating on her back in the swimming pool, staring up at the bluest, widest sky on earth, when she felt Kareef rise up in the water beneath her, pulling her into his arms.

"Good morning," he growled. Rivulets of water trickled down the hard, tanned muscles of his chest as held her against him. "Why did you get up so early?" he whispered, nuzzling her neck. "You should have stayed in bed."

Looking down, she realized he was naked. And that there was something specific that he wanted from her.

"Early?" she teased, clinging to his shoulders and pretending to kick her feet in protest. "It's noon!"

"You kept me up 'til dawn, so it's your fault," he said, then all talk ceased as he kissed her. A few minutes later, still entwined in a kiss, he walked out of the pool with Jasmine's legs wrapped around his waist. Carrying her across the back patio, he laid her on the cushioned lounge bed beneath a loggia. There, he pulled off her string bikini and slowly made love to her in the open air, beneath the hot desert sun.

Afterward, Jasmine must have slept briefly in his arms, for when she opened her eyes, the sun had moved in the sky. But she no longer could recognize the line between sleeping and waking. How could she tell when she was sleeping, when everything she'd imagined in her heart's deepest dreams had become real, flesh and blood in her arms?

Her days here at Kareef's desert home had been drenched with laughter and tenderness and passion; her short stay here had been so full of color and life, they'd made the thirteen long years before seem nothing more than a lonely gray dream.

If only she could stay here forever.

Staring out at the reflected sunlight of the turquoise pool, she tried to push the thought from her mind. She had only one day left here. She should enjoy it. To-morrow morning, Kareef had to be back in the city. His diplomatic engagements could no longer be kept waiting; nor could he put off the royal banquet, which would be attended by the foreign dignitaries who'd come for his coronation.

Tonight, the dream would end.

Stop thinking about it, she tried to tell herself. *You'll only ruin the precious hours you have left.* But she couldn't stop herself. Even when she'd been in bed that morning, cuddled in Kareef's arms as he slept beside her, she'd stared up at the ceiling of his bed-room and wished with all her heart that she could stay here forever.

In his bed. In his arms.

She'd wished she could remain his wife.

The wish had been so powerful it had nearly choked her. And so she'd fled the bedroom and thrown herself into the pool, to stare up at the sky, to let the water and chlorine and hot sun dissolve her tears.

But now, as she held him on the lounge bed beneath the loggia beside the pool, she was almost tempted to ask him if there were any chance. Any chance at all. The words were trembling on her lips. Even though she already knew the answer.

"Kareef?" she whispered, then stopped.

"Hmm?" His face was pressed against hers, his body still naked beneath the sun. He didn't open his eyes. The sun had already half-dried the dark wave of his hair.

She took a deep breath. "I was…I was wondering…"

Then a sparkle caught her eye. She looked out by the pool and saw the pants he'd discarded carelessly before he'd jumped into the water. Something had tumbled out of the pocket, now glistening green in the light.

The emerald.

The tiny heart-shaped emerald on a gold chain her parents had given her for her sixteenth birthday. She'd been wearing it when Kareef had asked her to marry him that day in the thicket of trees behind the riding school. According to the ancient Qusani ritual, she'd been required to give a token as pledge of her faith. So she'd pulled the gold chain off her neck, and placed it in his hand as she'd tearfully spoken the words that would bind them.

And now, after thirteen years, he was carelessly carrying the necklace around in his pants pocket, awaiting the moment he would divorce her.

Staring at the emerald glinting in the sun, she blinked hard as all her dreams came crashing around her.

Kareef lifted his head. "What is it?" he said lazily, his hand lingering on her breast. He sighed. "Don't tell me. Do you already want more?" He yawned, but was already smiling as he reached for her. "You tire me out, woman...."

She closed her eyes. She *did* want more. More of him. More of everything. And she suddenly couldn't allow him to touch her—not when she felt like crying, thrashing, wailing like a child for what she could never have.

He stopped. "Jasmine?"

"It's nothing," she whispered. "I'm just—" her voice broke *"—happy."*

"As am I." Kareef's hand suddenly tightened on her own. "But you know our time cannot last."

Her eyes flew open. Already? She wasn't ready for

him to speak the words. Her eyes fell upon the emerald necklace hanging out of his pocket in the shorts crumpled by the pool. She wasn't ready! Not yet!

With a nimbleness born of fear, she leapt to her feet, backing away. "It's a beautiful day. Shall we go for a ride?"

The way his jaw dropped would have been comical, if her heart weren't breaking.

"A ride?" he repeated in shock.

"Horse riding," she explained succinctly.

Frowning in bewilderment, he rubbed the back of his head. "But you hate riding. You…hate it."

Was he remembering the same thing she was, of their long-ago horse ride in the desert? Of how he'd found her, thrown on the rocks after his horse Razul had been spooked by a snake? Kareef had fallen to his knees before her, his eyes dark with fear, his face pale and streaked with dirt beneath the red twilight. *"Hold on, Jasmine,"* he'd whispered as he'd carried her to the cave. *"Just hold on.…"*

Lifting her chin, she swallowed, pushing the memory away. "I don't hate riding," she said flatly.

"Since when?"

Her eyes flashed at him. "I've been gone a long time."

"Have you changed so much?"

"How about we race, and see?"

"You—race against me?" He laughed. "You're kidding, right?"

"Are you scared?" she taunted in reply.

His face grew serious. He rose to his feet. Standing naked in front of her, beneath the shadows of the loggia, he cupped her face in his hands.

"You don't have to do this, Jasmine." His tender blue gaze, endless as the desert sky, whispered through her soul. "You don't have anything to prove."

"I know." In his arms, beneath the deep intensity of his glance, she could feel her heart break with yearning to be his wife. Not just today, but forever. With a sharp intake of breath, she forced herself to pull away. "Race you to the stables!"

She hurried to their bedroom and ransacked the bottom of her suitcase. *I'll just enjoy this last day,* she vowed to herself. *I'll emblazon it forever on my heart.* Throwing on underwear beneath a long white cotton dress of eyelet lace, she quickly ran a brush through her long dark hair and ran out of the house.

A few minutes later, when Kareef appeared at the stables dressed in black pants and a white shirt, she'd already climbed into the saddle. When Kareef saw the horse she'd chosen, he stopped in his tracks.

"Not that one."

"She's the one I want," Jasmine replied steadily.

Kareef glowered down at the wizened old horse master with skin like tanned leather who'd assisted her into the saddle.

"Bara'ah is the one she chose, sire," the Qusani said with a shrug, his raspy voice tinged with the ancient dialect of Qais. "Give your lady the freedom of your house, you said. Obey her every whim, you said."

Caught by his own command, Kareef scowled at them both.

Jasmine beamed back at him. She was determined to show them both how much she'd changed over the last thirteen years. She was strong. Independent. She didn't need him to protect her as she once had, and she would prove that. *To both of them.*

Kareef stepped toward her, looking up. "Not this mare, Jasmine. Bara'ah is full of tricks. You saw how she escaped her paddock—she caused the car accident."

"She didn't do it on purpose." She patted the horse's neck sympathetically. "She was just tired of being trapped behind walls."

"Jasmine—"

"You're already losing the race," she said, and lightly kicked the black mare's sides. The horse sprung forward, flying out of the stable, leaving Kareef cursing behind her.

He caught up with her five minutes later across the flatlands, when she slowed the mare down to a controlled trot.

"You *do* know how to ride," he said grudgingly. "Where did you learn?"

She gave him a sweet smile. "New York."

She'd taken lessons in Westchester County, spending her free time riding in Central Park. She'd learned to ride English style, Western style, even Qusani bareback. She'd hoped it would stop her nightmares, stop her from dreams where she hit the ground and woke up with the taste of blood in her mouth.

It hadn't. But at least she had learned a new skill. It gave her great pleasure now to ride beside Kareef as his equal, with confidence and skill. Especially in this beautiful place.

Qais was so stark and savage, she thought, looking around her. Some might have found the vast open landscape bleak, but she felt freedom. She no longer felt hemmed in by skyscrapers that blocked her vision, that blocked the sun.

Here, in every direction, Jasmine could see a horizon. *She felt free.*

"Come on," she said playfully, turning her reins in a new direction. She had no idea where she was going, but she loved not knowing. "On the mark…get set…*go*!"

She took off at a gallop into the desert, and Kareef pursued her.

Jasmine was ahead of him for about three seconds before his stallion whooshed past her. She followed, clinging to Bara'ah's back with every ounce of her determination. But Kareef had been a horse racer since childhood, and he was on a bigger, faster horse; her ten years of practice could not compete with his glorious fearless speed.

Whirling around, he pulled in front of her with a grin. "I win."

"Yes," she sighed. "You win."

"And so I take my prize." Drawing his horse beside hers, he leaned over and kissed her in the saddle. It was a hard, demanding kiss that left her aching for more.

When he pulled away, she stared at him in shock.

Here in the desert, the sun burned away all lies. As she stared at his beautiful, strong, arrogant face, everything suddenly became clear.

She loved him.

She always had, and she always would.

Jasmine gripped the pommel of her saddle, blinking, staggered by the realization.

Smiling, Kareef reached out to stroke her cheek.

"You kiss like you ride. Like a wanton," he murmured appreciatively. He looked down at her intently. "Jasmine," he said in a low voice, "you have to know that I…"

Then his eyes suddenly focused on something in the distance behind her. His hand dropped from her cheek. He sat back stiffly in his saddle.

"What is it?" she whispered, staring at him.

Clenching his jaw, he nodded to a spot behind her. "The house where you will live. Hajjar's house."

She twisted in the saddle and gasped. Far on the horizon, she saw an enormous monstrosity of a mansion, a red stone castle with red flags flying from the turrets. She blinked at it in horror.

"He's not there," he said quietly behind her. "They're not at home."

"So where are they?" she whispered. "Where did they go?"

Kareef exhaled, hissing through his teeth. She heard him shift in the saddle. "Don't like the look of those clouds," he said. "See them?"

Desert sandstorms were the subject of scary tales told to Qusani children, so Jasmine looked sharply at the horizon. The sky had indeed darkened to a deep gray-brown; but she could barely look past Umar's hideous red castle to see the clouds. Comparing the hideous red edifice to Kareef's simple home in the oasis, she wanted to weep. But she wouldn't let Kareef see her cry. Couldn't!

"Jasmine, we should go back," Kareef said quietly behind her. "Then we need to talk."

She whirled back in the saddle. She saw his hand already reaching in his pocket. She sucked in her breath. In another moment, he'd pull out the emerald necklace. He only needed to hand it to her and speak three words to separate them forever.

Irony. The same hour she'd realized she loved him, he would divorce her.

She would marry Umar and be his trophy wife, caged in this monstrous red castle and other sprawling mansions just like it in luxurious locations around the world.

She would have respectability. She would have a family.

But at the price of her soul.

Kareef's eyes narrowed as he again stared past her toward the horizon. "We must hurry. Come now."

With a low whistle, he whirled his horse around and tore into a gallop, clearly expecting her to follow.

She watched him for one instant.

"No," she whispered. "I won't."

She turned her reins in the opposite direction. With a sharp voice in the mare's ear, she leaned forward, pushing her heels hard against the mare's sides. With a snort, the horse flew.

"Jasmine!" Kareef shouted behind her. "What are you doing? Come back!"

But she wouldn't. She couldn't even look back. Love was burning her like acid, bubbling away her soul.

Tightening her knees, she held her body low and tight against the horse's back, riding up the red canyon. Riding for her life.

CHAPTER SEVEN

KAREEF gasped as he saw Jasmine leap her horse across a juniper bush, sweeping across the sagebrush. She'd once been terrified of horses. Now she rode with the grace and natural ease of a Qusani nomad.

He stared in shock at the cloud of her dust crossing the desert.

But she didn't know that devious mare like he did. There was a reason Bara'ah wasn't north at the stadium, training to race in the Qais Cup in two days' time. She'd left one jockey in a body cast last year. Full of malicious tricks, she liked nothing more than to throw her riders.

He had the sudden image of Jasmine half-smashed on the rock, crumpled and bleeding, as he'd found her thirteen years ago....

"Jasmine! Stop!"

He saw her goad her mare into greater speed.

Fear rushed through him as he glanced back again at the distant horizon and saw scattered brown clouds moving fast, much too fast. A sandstorm could cross the desert in seconds, decimating everything in its path.

A shudder went through his body. He turned back. With iron control, he clicked his heels on the stallion's flanks. Huffing with a flare of nostril, the animal raced forward. But Jasmine was already far ahead.

Kareef hadn't expected her to disobey him. No one had disobeyed him for years.

He should have expected it of her.

As he pursued her, he cast another glance behind him. The clouds were beginning to gather with force across the width of the desert. The sky was turning dark. There could no longer be any doubt. Holding the reins with one hand, he reached into his pocket and discovered his cell phone was lost, fallen in the rough speed of their race. But he still had Jasmine's necklace.

His eyes narrowed as he watched her race her horse headlong into the canyon. No help could come for them before the storm.

So be it. He would save her alone.

As long as she stayed hidden, as long as she didn't climb up out of the canyon, she would live.

If she rode onto the plateau, the coming sandstorm would eat her alive.

Hoofbeats pounded in rhythm with Kareef's thoughts as he raced after Jasmine into the dark shadowed canyon.

He had to find her.

He *would* find her.

Clamping his thigh muscles over the saddle, he leaned forward and urged his horse faster. He'd spent his youth in these canyons. He was again a reckless horse racer who feared nothing...but losing her.

He raced fast. Faster. His stallion kicked up dust,

scattering it to the four winds. He raced beneath the sharp arches and towering cliffs of the canyon.

Within minutes, he'd caught up with her. Leaning forward, he shouted Jasmine's name over the pounding hoofbeats of their horses.

She glanced back and a shadow of fear crossed her face. He heard the panic in her voice as she urged her mare faster.

But Kareef gained ground with every second. He reached out his hand to pluck her off the mare's back—

His hand suddenly grasped air as she veered off the road. She'd abruptly turned the mare west through a break in the red rock, climbing the slope up out of the canyon.

"No!" he shouted. "The storm!"

But his words were lost in the rising blur of the wind, beneath the pounding hooves of her mare's wild, joyful, reckless climb.

He could feel, rather than hear, the approaching storm behind him. The first edges of dark cloud pushed around them, turning blue sky to a sickening brown-gray. The crags were turning dark and hidden in deep shadows.

Cursing her, cursing himself, he veered his horse up to pursue her. She was fast, but he was faster. For the first time in thirteen years, he was again Kareef Al'Ramiz, the reckless horse racer. Unstoppable. Unbreakable.

He would die rather than lose this race.

"Sandstorm!" he shouted over the rising wind.

At the top of the plateau, Jasmine turned back to him sharply. But at the same moment, he saw her mare draw to a sudden skidding stop as she suddenly grew tired of the race and deliberately, almost playfully, threw her rider. For a long, horrible instant, Kareef watched Jasmine fly through the air.

Sniffing, the mare jumped delicately in the other direction, then turned to run back the way she'd come, toward the stables and oats that awaited her.

Jasmine hit the ground and crumpled into the dust. Kareef's heart was in his throat as all the memories of the past ripped through him. He flung himself off his stallion, falling to his knees before her.

"Jasmine," he whispered, his heart in his throat as he touched her still face. "Jasmine!"

Like a miracle, she coughed in his arms. Her beautiful, dark-lashed eyes stared up at him. She swallowed, tried to speak.

"Don't talk," he ordered. Relief made his body weak as he lifted her in his arms. He held her tightly, never wanting to let her go. How had he spent so many years without her? How could he have known she was alive…without tracking her to the last corner of the earth?

He heard the distant rattle of sand and thunder, heard the wail of the wind.

"I have to get you out of here." He whistled to the horse. "We don't have much time."

He glanced behind them. The safe part of the canyon was too far away. They'd never make it.

Jasmine followed his glance and instantly went pale when she saw the dark wall of cloud. "I thought—" her voice choked off "—I thought it was a trick."

She'd grown up in Qusay. She knew what a sandstorm could do. He shook his head grimly, clenching his jaw. "We have to find shelter." His eyes met hers. "The closest shelter."

Her chocolate-brown eyes instantly went wide with panic. "No," she gasped. "Not there, Kareef. I'd rather die!"

He felt the first scattered bits of sand hit his face.

"If I don't get you to safety right now," he said grimly, "you *will* die."

Whimpering, she shook her head. But he knew she had to see the darkness swiftly overtaking the sun, had to feel the shards of sand whipping against her skin. If they didn't find shelter, they'd soon be breathing sand. It would rip off their skin, then bury them alive.

"No!" she screamed, kicking and struggling as, holding her with one arm, he lifted them both into the saddle. "I can't go back!"

"I can't leave you to die," he ground out, turning the horse's reins toward the nearby cliff.

"I died a long time ago." Her eyes were wet, her voice hoarse as she stared at the dark jagged hole, hollowed and hidden in the red rock. "I died in that cave."

The pain he heard in her voice was insidious, like a twisting cloud of smoke. He breathed in her grief, felt it infect his own body.

Jasmine Kouri. Once his life. Once his *everything*.

Then his eyes hardened. "I can't let you die."

She twisted around in the saddle, wrapping her arms around his neck as she looked up at his face pleadingly. "Please," she whispered, her eyes shimmering with tears. "If you ever loved me—if you ever loved me at all—don't take me there."

He looked down at her beautiful face, and his heart stopped in his chest.

If he'd ever loved her?

He'd loved her more than a man should ever love any woman. More than a man should love anything he couldn't bear to lose. Looking down at her now, he would have given her anything, his own life, to make her stop weeping.

Then he saw a drop of blood appear on the pale skin of her cheek, like a red rose springing from the earth. First blood.

A growl ripped from his throat. His own life he would give. But not hers. *Not hers.*

Ignoring her cries, he grimly urged the black stallion toward the plateau to the red rock cliff. The sounds of her wailing blended with the howls of the wind. He felt prickles of sand start to abrade his skin with tiny cuts.

He held her against his chest, protecting her with his own body as he rode straight for the one place he never wanted to see again. The place where they'd both lost everything thirteen years ago. His own private hell.

Hardening his heart to granite, he rode straight for the cave.

"No!" Jasmine screamed in his arms, struggling to jump off the horse's back. But Kareef wouldn't let her go.

She felt the bone-jarring pounding of the stallion's gallop beneath her. She felt the heat of Kareef's chest at her back, felt his strong arms protecting her as the flecks of sand began to snarl around them with deadly force.

The howl of the wind grew louder. Her dark hair

flew wildly around her face. She closed her eyes, fighting the rising tide of fear. He was taking her to the cave. The place that had terrified her beyond reason for a thousand nightmares.

"We'll make it," Kareef said harshly, as if he could make it true by the sheer force of his will. His shout was a whisper above the wail of the storm.

Looking back, she saw a wall of sand pouring like a massive dark cloud behind them, a black blizzard sweeping across the wide plateau, leaving nothing in its wake.

They reached the cave just in time. He pulled her off the horse, yanking them back some distance inside the darkness. Stumbling, she watched the huge wave of wind and sand pass the mouth of the cave, leaving them coughing in a cloud of dust.

Staggering back, she looked blindly behind her into the black maw of the cave. And against her will…

She saw the spot where she'd lost their baby.

Pain racked through her, pummeling her like a torrent of blows. Anguish broke over her, as devastating as the wall of sand outside, crushing her soul beneath the weight.

As Kareef turned to calm the stallion, tying his reins to a nearby rock, Jasmine's trembling legs gave way beneath her. She fell back against the red stone walls, sliding down to the ground, unable to look away from the spot of earth where she'd nearly died.

Where she *had* died.

Across the cave, she saw Kareef gently calm the stallion, whispering words in ancient Qusani as he removed the pack from the horse's haunches. He offered the horse water and food then brushed down the horse in long strokes. The sound of the brushing filled the silence of the cave. She stared at him.

Kareef always took care of everything he loved. What a father he would make.

But they could never share a child.

Not a day went by that Jasmine didn't think about the baby she'd lost in the riding accident before she'd even known she was pregnant. Their child would have been twelve now. A little boy with his father's blue eyes? A little girl with plump cheeks and a sweet smile?

As Kareef started a fire in the fire pit with wood left recently by Qusani nomads, a sob rose from deep inside her.

"I'm sorry," she whispered, looking up as tears spilled down her cheeks. "It's my fault I lost our baby."

She heard his harsh intake of breath, and suddenly his arms were around her. Sitting against the wall of the cave, he lifted her into his lap, holding her against his chest as tenderly as a child.

"It was never your fault. Never," he said in a low voice. "I am the only one who was to blame—"

His voice choked off as the small fire flickered light into the depths of the cave, casting red shadows over the earth. She looked up at him slowly. His face was blurry in the firelight.

She blinked, and the pain in his eyes overwhelmed her. She could hear the roar of the wind and hoarse rattle of the sand against rock outside. Instinctively, she reached out to stroke the dark hair of his bowed head. Then she stopped herself.

"You broke your promise to me, Kareef," she said hoarsely. "You brought a doctor to this cave, after you gave your word to tell no one. Though we both knew it was too late!"

"You were dying, Jasmine!" He looked up fiercely. "I was a fool to make that promise, a fool to think I could take care of you alone, a fool to think that love alone could save you!"

"But when I lost your child and the ability to ever conceive," she said numbly, "you couldn't get away from me fast enough."

His hands suddenly clenched around her shoulders. The dark rage in his eyes frightened her.

"I left to die," he ground out. With a hoarse, ragged intake of breath, he released her, clawing his hand through his black hair. "I failed you. I couldn't bear to see the blame and grief in your eyes. *I went out to the desert to die.*"

His voice echoed in the cool darkness of the cave.

He'd tried to die—the strong, powerful, fearless boy she'd loved? The barbarian king she'd once thought to be indestructible?

"No," she said, "you wouldn't."

"One more thing I failed to do."

Bewildered, she looked up at his handsome face, half-hidden by the shadows. "But…it wasn't your fault."

"I was the one who saddled Razul for you! I was the one who taunted you into climbing on his back! I wanted so badly to race with you." He gave a bitter laugh. "I thought I could keep you safe."

"Kareef." Her voice was a sob. "Stop."

But he was beyond hearing. "After the accident, I

let you stay here in the cave for days, injured, without a doctor's care. You nearly died from the infection."

"I was trying to protect my family from the shame—"

"I brought the doctor too late, and never thought to worry about his assistant." He gave a bitter laugh— brittle, like dead leaves blowing in the wind. "Afterward, when I disappeared into the desert, I left you believing you'd be happier without me, safe and protected by your family. It never occurred to me that the scandal could break and you'd be sent into exile. You'd already been in New York for three years before I even heard you'd left Qusay!" He leaned forward, his jaw tight. His eyes were dark in the flickering fire. "But I made him pay for what he did to you."

Her full, pink lips trembled. "Who?"

"Marwan. When I discovered he was the one who'd started the rumors, I stripped him of everything he owned. I sent him into exile."

A small sound escaped her lips. A rush, like a shuddering sigh. "Thank you," she whispered. "Did you know he blackmailed me?"

"What?"

"On my journey back to the city, when I still had a fever, he threatened to tell everyone about my miscarriage. He said he'd claim I did it deliberately to rid myself of the baby. He'd say I'd had endless nameless lovers and couldn't guess the father. He said he would ruin me." She took a deep breath, forcing her eyes to meet his. "He would do this—unless I took him as my lover."

Kareef sucked in his breath.

"What?" he exploded.

"He was afraid of you," she said softly, wiping her eyes hard. "But he wasn't afraid of me. When I wouldn't do it, he carried through with his threat. Within days, the scandal cost my father his job at the palace. It gave his enemies the weapon they needed. If my father couldn't control his own family, they said, how could he advise the king? So everything that happened, it's my fault, you see." She took a deep, shuddering breath. "All my fault."

She looked back at Kareef.

And almost didn't recognize him.

Rage such as she'd never seen before was on his face. Rage that frightened her.

"I will kill him," he ground out. Clenching his hands, he rose to his feet. "Wherever that man is hiding in the world, I will make him feel such pain as he cannot imagine—"

"No," she gasped, grabbing his hand. "Please. It's all over." She pressed his hand against her forehead, closing her eyes. "Please, I just want to forget."

His hand tightened, then relaxed. Slowly, he sank beside her. Kneeling, he took both her hands in his own.

"By the time I found out you were in exile…it was too late to do more than send money to New York." His voice was ragged. "But every day since then, I've tried to find absolution." He turned away. "But I know now I will never find that, no matter how hard I try."

"Kareef," she whispered, tears in her eyes. "It wasn't your fault. It was… It was…" Putting her hand on his shoulder, she stared at the smooth rock wall of the cave and the truth dawned on her. "It was an accident."

His back slowly straightened. "What did you say?"

"An accident." She looked at him, and it was as if the sun had broken through dark clouds, bringing light, bringing peace. Tears fell down her cheeks as she breathed, "I was barely pregnant. We didn't know. The accident was no one's fault. No one is to blame. We'll never forget we almost had a child. But we need to forgive—both of us. It wasn't your fault."

His voice was low and thick with grief as he said, "I wish I could believe that." He looked down at her hands. "You're shivering."

She was, but not with cold.

Rising to his feet, he crossed the cave. Digging through the horse's pack, he found a red woven blanket and unfolded it near the fire. Jasmine watched his face in the flickering shadows, her heart aching.

All these years, she thought he'd blamed her—and he'd thought the same.

For her, it had been thirteen years of exile.

For him, it had been a living death.

"Here," he said in a low voice. "You can rest here, where it is warm." He turned away. "I will stay awake and keep watch until the storm is over."

Trembling, Jasmine rose to her feet. She slowly walked toward him. Reaching up, she placed a hand on his cheek and forced him to look at her.

"It was an accident, Kareef," she said, looking straight into his eyes. "You were not to blame!"

He gave a hoarse intake of breath. "Is it possible you could forgive me?" he whispered, searching her gaze. His blue eyes were deep and endless as the sea.

She stroked his cheek with her hand. Tears filled her eyes. "How could I blame you? You were…have always been—" *my only love*, her voice choked "—my dearest friend."

She heard his ragged breath, felt the pounding of his heart against hers. His body was hot. His skin smelled of musk and sun and sand.

He looked down at her, and his gaze suddenly burned through her, stretching every nerve from her fingertips to her toes in taut anticipation as she heard the howl of the darkness outside. "And you are mine."

Lowering his head, he kissed her.

Hidden in this cave, hidden far from the outside world and protected from the outside storm, he kissed her as if nothing and no one else existed. He pressed her against the smooth red rock wall of the cave, and she kissed him back fervently, her heart on her lips.

He abruptly pulled away from her. She blinked at him in the flickering firelight, dazed. His eyes were dark with need. Her lips felt swollen and bruised from the ferocity of his kisses—almost as bruised as her healing heart.

With a growl, he lifted her up into his arms, holding her against his hard chest as if she weighed nothing at all. She stared up at him, breathless, mesmerized by his brutal strength. She could hear the howl of the wind whipping sand outside, hear the whinny of the stallion. The small fire flickered shadowy firelight against the smooth red rock of the cave.

They were safe here. They were warm. They were together.

He lowered her gently to the blanket, then pulled off his white shirt and black pants and shoes. She gazed at his naked body in wonder as he stood before her. The muscles of his tanned body glistened in the twisting firelight.

Kneeling in front of her on the blanket, he slowly pulled off her panties beneath her dress, drawing them down her legs.

Then, with a wicked half smile, he tossed them into the fire.

"What?" she spluttered, staring at the white cotton fabric now burning beside the charred wood. "What did you do that for?"

He lifted a black eyebrow, giving her a dark look that curled her toes. "We needed fuel for the fire," he whispered.

But a fire was already burning inside Jasmine, burning right through her, consuming her whole. He pulled her down into his lap, pulling her white skirt up to her hips. She was naked against him as he slid his hardness against her, rocking back and forth against her wet core. He leaned up to kiss her.

Hot. *Hot.* She was burning up, turning to ash and flame.

"Take off my dress," she whispered. "Take it off."

"You," he repeated approvingly, sliding his hands over her breasts as he nipped little kisses up her neck, "are a wanton."

With a tug, he pulled the white cotton dress up and over her shoulders and threw it down on the earth. She sat in his lap, her legs wrapped around his waist. She looked down at their naked intertwined bodies in the firelight. As he started to move against her, the soft sound of her gasps soon matched the cries of the wind outside.

The tension coiled low in her belly as he slid over

her. Pleasure built inside her and then, suddenly, he lifted her up and impaled her with a single deep thrust. She gasped at the depth of his penetration.

He hadn't just filled her body. He filled her soul.

She gripped his shoulders and let the ecstasy build inside her, higher and higher. Even when the euphoria finally ripped her to shreds, exploding her into pieces, she kept her secret hidden inside.

I love you.

I will always love you.

She couldn't speak the words. She knew they changed nothing.

CHAPTER EIGHT

FOR an instant Kareef was afraid he'd hurt her. Then she moaned, swaying against him, tightening her legs around his waist as he filled her.

He gasped at that movement, at the way her full breasts brushed against his chest. Then he pushed her down again, thrusting inside her, filling her so deeply a growl escaped the back of his throat.

Firelight cast shadows over her beautiful face, her full, swollen lips, and the long dark eyelashes tightly closed in an expression of joy. Watching her, he held his breath with the effort it took to hold himself back.

He was inside her, but she was the one who filled him.

Jasmine. Her beauty. Her boundless sensuality. She swayed against him with the decadent grace of a houri. Beads of sweat were like clear pearls on her white, swanlike neck as she leaned back, gasping. The veil of her dark, glossy hair cascaded down her back, swinging back and forth as she kept her eyes closed, panting for breath.

Lifting her head with his hand, he kissed her. She gasped her pleasure against his mouth, gripping his shoulders, biting into his flesh with her fingernails, marking him in her own act of possession.

The force of his taking was primal—unstoppable. He heard her cry out and could hold back no longer. He gripped her against his body as he poured himself into her with a shout.

He collapsed back on the red blanket, holding her against him. He did not know when he woke. She was still sleeping in his arms.

They were both naked. The fire was dying. The night was growing cold, the darkness growing around them.

He felt her shiver. He looked down at her face. She was sleeping, her cheek pressed against his chest. Her beauty went beyond her dark hair or perfect pink lips. It went deeper than her pale skin with roses in her cheeks.

Even after all the times he'd made love to her, he did not feel satiated. And he was starting to fear he never would be.

He did not want to divorce her.

Silently, Kareef withdrew himself from beneath her body and rose to his feet. Crossing the cave, he pulled a second blanket from the horse's pack. Crawling back beside her, he covered them both with it, wrapping her in his arms. He knew, even in sleep, he would not let her go.

Growing drowsy, he looked down at her sleeping against him. He wanted her like this every night. In his bed. At his table. On his arm. Charming diplomats with her beauty. Dancing in his arms.

With her beauty and gentle grace, Jasmine would be the perfect queen. But…

His jaw tightened as he stared at the dying fire.

He still had to divorce her. He had to provide an heir of the blood. The Al'Ramizes had reigned Qusay for a thousand years. His cousin Xavian had given up the throne when he'd learned he was a changeling, a substitute for a lost Al'Ramiz child.

Blood meant everything. It gave the Al'Ramiz men the right to rule. Not just the right—the obligation. And Jasmine could never become pregnant with his child.

His throat became tight. He looked away, staring at the bumps and rocks of scattered earth illuminated by the fading embers of the fire. Outside, he could hear the rattle of the sand against the solid rocks of the cliffs, hear the wind wailing in disappointed fury as it slowly died.

He slept fitfully, holding her tight.

"Kareef." Her naked body stirred in his arms. "Are you awake?"

Her voice was like a dream, full of sweet warmth, offering such peace. He slowly opened his eyes.

At the mouth of the cave, above the piles of new sand, he saw the gray light of dawn creeping over the western mountains. The wind had died down. The desert was calm. He could hear the plaintive sound of morning birds, hear the soft whinny of the stallion hungry for breakfast.

It was morning. The storm was over.

Their time was over.

Unwillingly, he turned to Jasmine. Her face was like cool water, a balm to his spirit. Her brown eyes reflected deep pools of light. But it only made the pain worse.

He did not want to let her go.

"It's barely dawn," he lied softly. His arms tightened around her. "Go back to sleep."

For a moment, she rested against him, and silence fell in the cool darkness of the cave. Then she shifted in his arms and her head popped up to look down at him. "Do you think your men are looking for us?"

"Yes," he said. "They will be here soon."

He heard her intake of breath, felt her pull away from him on the blanket. When she spoke, her voice was curiously flat. "Then it's time."

"Time?"

"Time for you to divorce me."

He looked up at her. Her expression had turned to stone, the pools of light shuttered and gone. She glanced over at the black fabric now crumpled on the other side of the cave.

"I know you have the emerald," she whispered.

"Yes," he said, his jaw tight. "I brought it with me."

"So eager to be rid of me?"

"I promised to set you free."

She lifted her chin, her expression a mixture of bravado and pain. "So do it."

Kareef's hands tightened into fists.

Jasmine was right. It was time. The storm was over, and his men were no doubt grimly combing the desert. Soon, they'd be found, and Kareef would return to Shafar. Back to the royal palace, back to his endless duties. He would be hosting a royal banquet tonight.

Then, tomorrow, he would attend the Qais Cup. And witness the wedding of Jasmine Kouri to Umar Hajjar.

It was dawn. The magic was over.

"Kareef?" Jasmine looked at him, her eyes swimming with misery.

She felt the same as he did, he realized. She did not want this divorce.

The knowledge flooded him with sudden strength.

So he would not give her up. Not yet. *He wasn't done with her yet.*

"No," he growled. "I won't speak the words yet."

"But Kareef," she choked out, "you know you must!"

"Must?" He sat up. His shoulders straightened as his whole body became as unyielding as steel. He looked down at her, as selfish and ruthless and harsh as any ancient sultan.

"There is no *must*," he growled, lifting his chin as his eyes glittered down at her. "I'm the king of Qusay. And until I release you, *you belong to me.*"

You belong to me.

Jasmine shivered at the words. She could not deny them. She did belong to Kareef. She always had, body and soul.

But he was king of Qusay. He could not keep a barren woman as his bride. And she couldn't openly remain his mistress. Such a scandal would make the one thirteen years ago seem like nothing.

Jasmine closed her eyes with a shuddering breath. She'd returned to Qusay to help her family, not ruin them again! And how could she stab Umar in the heart with such a public humiliation, after everything he'd done for her?

They had to divorce. They had to part. There was no other way. If she allowed herself to be with Kareef as she wished—if she allowed herself to be *selfish*—it would destroy everyone she loved. She looked up at Kareef.

Already, a team of his bodyguards was searching, no doubt panicked that their king had disappeared in the sandstorm.

Was that a helicopter she heard in the distance now?

No, she told herself frantically. *Not yet!*

But she had to face the hard truth. Their sweet, stolen time was over.

Pushing away from Kareef's warmth, she rose numbly to her feet. It was too late for her panties—they'd been annihilated in the fire—but she pulled on her white cotton bra, which she found on the floor of the cave.

"You don't need that," Kareef said, lying back against the blanket. "We have hours yet. It's barely dawn."

She didn't answer.

Kareef pushed himself up on one elbow. "Jasmine."

She didn't look back. She was afraid if she looked into the basilisk intensity of his gaze, she would be caught by his magic once again and lose her own ability to do what must be done. Even now, her body shook with the effort of defying him—and worse, defying her own deepest longings.

She found the white cotton dress, now dirty and with tiny rips in the eyelet lace, crumpled behind a rock. It seemed eons since he'd pulled it off her body.

So much had happened since then. Entire worlds had changed.

She felt his gaze, but wouldn't turn to meet his eyes.

Naked, he sprang lightly to his feet, like a warrior. Taking her in his arms, he forced her to turn around and meet his gaze. "What is it? What's wrong?"

She swallowed. "Thank you for these beautiful days in the desert," she whispered, feeling like her heart was splitting, bleeding in her chest. "I will never forget them."

"Our time is not over."

Trembling, Jasmine closed her eyes. It would be easier to say this if she didn't have to look at his beautifully masculine face, at his sensual mouth, at his eyes of endless blue. He took her heart apart in his gaze.

"It is over," she whispered. "We are over."

She felt his shock. Felt his hands go slack before he tightened his grip painfully around her. "Look at me."

She wouldn't.

"Look at me!"

Compelled to obey, she opened her eyes.

His face was dark with fury.

"You are mine, Jasmine. For as long as I want you."

Her throat went dry. How she wished it could be true, wished she could be his forever—or for even one more night!

"How?" she replied hoarsely. "How can I be yours, Kareef?"

His eyes darkened and cooled until they were like a thousand storms over the Arctic Sea. "You bound yourself to me long ago."

"Kareef—"

"You will not marry him tomorrow. It is too soon!"

Her tortured eyes flickered up at him. "What would you have me do, then? Desert Umar at the altar? Be your mistress? Leave my family to their ruin?"

His jaw clenched. "We could keep our affair a secret—"

"There's no such thing at the palace!" she cried.

"Here in the desert, perhaps, with only your trusted servants, we could keep it quiet for a short while. But you know as well as I do that there are no secrets at the royal palace. There's likely gossip about us already. I've already caused my family so much pain, and now my little sister is pregnant. How could my parents ever hold up their heads in the street, if I let myself be branded as your whore?"

Air hissed through his teeth.

"No one would call you that," he raged. "You would be respected as my…as my—"

"As your what? As your wife? We cannot remain married. You know we cannot!"

His eyes glittered down at her. "I can do as I please. I am the king."

She heard a distant helicopter, a deep *flick-flick-flick* high above the desert, and this time there could be no doubt. Shaking her head, she gave a harsh laugh.

"For a man with your sense of honor," she said, fighting back tears, "that makes you less free than the lowliest servant in your palace."

"Jasmine…"

"No!" she shouted. "I cannot back out of my engagement. Umar would be humiliated. My family's reputation would be destroyed. First my scandal, then Nima's pregnancy—my parents would never be able to leave their house again!"

"Why do you even care, after the way they've treated you?"

"Because I love them. Because—" she lifted her head as tears filled her eyes "—they are the only family I'll ever have. They, and Umar and his children. I cannot be the cause of their ruin by becoming your whore!"

"Don't use that word! I would kill any man who called you that!"

"All of them?" Her throat tightened as a hoarse laugh escaped her. "You would kill your own subjects for speaking the truth?"

His hands clenched her shoulders. "It's not the truth, and you know it!"

She briefly closed her eyes, trying to regain her strength, to catch her breath. "What else would you call an engaged woman who's done what I've done with you?"

"You've done nothing wrong. You're my wife."

"Let me go, Kareef," she whispered. "Set me free."

He looked down at her, his eyes full of an impetuous mixture of autocratic male possessiveness and emotion that struck her to the heart. "I can protect you, Jasmine."

"How?" she whispered, then shook her head. "Even you cannot work miracles—"

"It's a miracle you're here with me now." Cupping her face, he looked down at her. "And I will not let you go. Not yet."

She felt his rough fingertips against her skin. Felt his naked body, so warm and hard and fierce against hers. Felt how much he desired her. Felt the power of his savage strength as he lowered his mouth to hers.

His lips moved against hers with deep, exquisite tenderness. Persuading her. Mastering her, not just with his sensual power, but with the ache of her own body and heart.

When he finally released her, a low sigh rose from

her throat. She gazed up at him, this man she loved, feeling dazed and warm, drenched by the soft sunlight of his nearness.

His kiss had conquered her as a thousand words could not.

Exhaling, he pulled her back against his bare chest, stroking her hair as he felt her surrender. "You're mine, Jasmine," he murmured into her hair, almost too softly for her to hear. "As I am yours."

Distantly, a voice cried inside her that he wasn't hers—that he could never be hers, not anymore. And that by going back to Shafar with him as his secret mistress, she'd be risking everything she held precious—everyone she loved.

But she could not let him go. Not yet. Not yet!

She closed her eyes as he held her in her arms. *Let the future come as it will*, she thought. Somehow, they could find a way to be together just for a little while longer without hurting anyone. Couldn't they?

The helicopter was very loud now. She saw the swirl of sand outside the cave turn by the force of its rotor blades as it landed on the nearby plateau.

Jasmine pulled back with sudden alarm. "Get dressed. We can't let your men find you naked...alone with me!"

He snorted a laugh. "That would be a most unexpected sight for them, wouldn't it?"

Picking up his clothes from the ground, she shoved them into his arms. "Get dressed!"

He smiled down at her, and she couldn't help smiling back. For one instant time hung between them, breathless with the anticipation of endless future joys.

Then she heard his men shouting, heard the pounding

of machines against the earth. Heard a rush of heavy footsteps coming toward the cave, growing louder.

Sighing beneath her anxious, pleading gaze, he moved with rapid military precision, stepping into his boxers and black pants. As he pulled on his shirt, she peeked one last look at his handsome physique and marveled that she was the only woman who'd ever experienced the incredible pleasure of being in his bed. How was it possible? How was she so blessed?

She thought again of the reverent, hot, tender way he'd touched her in the night. And in the day...

"Sire? Sire!"

Kareef's chief bodyguard peered over the piled sand at the mouth of the cave, then fell to his knee in gratitude and relief. Behind him were a dozen men, geared up as if for battle. "God be praised! That blasted mare returned riderless right before the storm hit the house. We thought... We feared..."

Buttoning his ragged white shirt, Kareef stood before them, tall and proud. He looked every inch a king.

"We are safe, Faruq. Miss Kouri and I were riding when we were caught in the storm and took shelter here. Thank you for finding us." He gestured at the black stallion tied to the rock. "Please see Tayyib is cared for. He bore us well."

"Yes, sire."

"And my people? My home?"

"No injuries," the bodyguard replied. "Little damage. A great deal of sand. We brought a doctor for you just in case."

"I am unhurt. He will check Miss Kouri for injury."

Faruq glanced at her uneasily, then bowed and

backed away. She felt the other bodyguards giving her sideways glances, and her face grew hot.

"The helicopter will return us to the royal palace immediately," Kareef said. He turned to her, holding out his hand. "Miss Kouri?"

As Kareef escorted her out of the dark cave, lifting her back into the hot white sun, he smiled down at her. And all her sudden anxiety disappeared as if it had never been.

He led her to the waiting helicopter, and she smiled at him, trying to ignore the grim-faced bodyguards trailing behind. They would manage to keep their affair secret for one more day. One more precious day before Kareef would be forced to realize he had no choice but to divorce her, and they each parted to face the separate lives that fate had decreed for them.

One more day, she thought desperately. No one would be hurt by one more selfish day. A single day could feel like a lifetime.

Kareef would find a way to keep it secret. She'd never seen a secret kept at the palace, but he could find a way. He was magic. He was power.

He was king.

Kareef's shoulders were tight as he stormed through the corridors of the royal palace, scattering assistants in his wake.

Every minute of his schedule since his return to the city had been meticulously dictated by five different assistants and undersecretaries working in conjunction, overseen by the vizier. The king's duties were endless. Treaties to negotiate. False smiles under cloak of courtesy. Diplomacy. Politics. Saying one thing and meaning another. What did Kareef know of those?

He growled to himself. He was already learning far more than he'd ever wished.

He despised keeping Jasmine a secret.

She'd slept against his shoulder on the helicopter journey from the desert. He could still feel her, somehow still smell her intoxicating scent of oranges and cloves against his body, though he'd showered and changed out of his clothes and into white robes at the royal palace.

The moment he'd set foot back at the palace, he'd wanted to take her to his bedchamber; but she'd demurred, glancing at the endless secretaries and assistants waiting for him in the hallways. "Later," she'd whispered, and with a sigh, he'd let her go. He'd told himself he'd be able to cut his meetings short and return soon to her little room in the servants' wing.

That was ten hours ago. His elderly vizier, Akmal Al'Sayr, was still tearing his beard out at the days Kareef had missed. It seemed even being lost and half-presumed dead in the desert wasn't enough to excuse a monarch from his duty.

It was now twilight, and he hadn't seen Jasmine since they'd arrived at the palace. His entire day had been wasted. A day devoted to cold duty in a palace full of hidden corridors and sly whispers of gossip.

His hands tightened. He hated all this secrecy. He had to convince her to give up the marriage. He would smooth things over with Hajjar somehow. Once she agreed to call off her wedding, Kareef would be willing to divorce her. When she agreed to be his long-term mistress.

How could my parents ever hold up their heads in the street, if I let myself be branded as your whore?

The word made him flinch. No. Damn it, no! If any man dared insult her, Kareef would throw him into the Byzantine dungeon beneath the palace. He would exile him to the desert without food or water. He would—

You would kill your own subjects for speaking the truth? He heard the echo of Jasmine's whisper in the cave. *Let me go. Set me free.*

Clenching his jaw, he pushed the thought firmly from his mind. He would keep her as long as he desired her—whether that took ten years or fifty. He was young yet, only thirty-one. He would keep her for himself, and put off his own marriage as long as he could.

He quickened his pace down the hall, growling at any servant who dared to look his way.

Was Jasmine awake yet? he wondered. Was she naked beneath the sheets, with her dark hair mussed across the pillow? He felt rock-hard, aching for her. He went faster, almost breaking into a run.

"Sire, a word?"

In the hallway near the royal offices, he saw his vizier hovering in the doorway.

"Later," he ground out, not stopping.

"Of course, my king," the vizier said silkily. "I just wanted you to know I've begun negotiations for your marriage. You needn't worry about it. I will present your bride to you in a few weeks."

Stopping dead in the hallway, Kareef whirled into the reception room and closed the door behind them.

"You will arrange nothing," he said coldly. "I have no interest in marriage."

"But sire, these things take time. And you are not getting any younger...."

"I'm thirty-one!"

"After all the chaos caused by your cousin's abdication, your subjects need the comfort and security of seeing the line of succession continue. A royal wedding. A royal family." He pulled on his graying beard. "It might be difficult to find the right bride, a young virgin with the correct lineage and a perfect, unsullied reputation—"

"Why must she be a virgin?" Kareef demanded.

"So no one can ever doubt that your children are yours," he replied, sounding surprised. "You must have an undisputed heir."

Kareef clenched his jaw. "You will not negotiate a bride for me. I forbid it."

The vizier returned his look with gleaming, canny eyes. "Because your interests are elsewhere?"

Kareef looked at him narrowly, wondering how much he already knew. The vizier's spies were everywhere. He cared so obsessively about the security of the country, personal privacy meant nothing to the man. "What do you mean?"

His dark eyes affixed on Kareef. "It would be a grave mistake to insult Umar Hajjar, my king," he said quietly. "I've heard he is returning from Paris tonight."

Paris. So Kareef's suspicions had been right. Hajjar had been spending time with his French mistress.

And Kareef was expected to give up Jasmine to a man who did not even care enough to be loyal to her?

Too angry to be fair, he clenched his hands. "I have no intention of insulting Hajjar. He is my friend. He saved my life."

"Yes. Quite." The older man cleared his throat. "The royal banquet begins soon, sire. Ambassadors and foreign princes have come from all over the world to celebrate your impending coronation. You will not wish to be late."

Kareef ground his teeth. Making small talk with people he didn't care about? "I will attend in my own time."

The vizier tugged his beard. "It's just a pity you don't have your future bride on your arm for such a social event," he sighed, then brightened. "Princess Lara du Plessis is attending with her father. She is a possibility as well. She's very beautiful—"

"No marriage," Kareef barked out. His mind already on Jasmine, he turned to go.

"You will find her in the royal garden," the vizier called sourly behind him. "Where she does not deserve to be."

Kareef whirled to face him.

Jasmine was right. There were no secrets in the palace. Akmal Al'Sayr knew them all.

Except one.

He did not know Kareef was already married.

"You will call off your spies," he said grimly. "Leave her in peace."

Akmal's mouth twisted sharply downward, his lips disappearing into his long gray beard as he fell into dutiful silence.

"And find her a place at the banquet."

The vizier looked unhappier still, his slender body

drooping like a frown. But he hung his head beneath his sovereign's decree. "Yes, sire." He looked up, his beady eyes glittering. "But she can never be more to you than a mistress. The people would never accept such a woman as your wife, a woman who's had so many lovers she threw herself from a horse to lose her nameless, ill-gotten child—"

Red covered Kareef's gaze. In two strides, he'd grabbed the other man's throat.

"It was an accident," he hissed. "*An accident*. And as for her many lovers, she's had only one. Me. Do you understand, Al'Sayr? I was her lover. The only one."

The older man's eyes started to bulge before Kareef regained control. He let him go. The vizier leaned over, holding his throat and coughing.

"Never speak of her that way again," he spat out. With a growl still on his lips, Kareef whirled away in murderous fury, striding down the hall in his robes.

His heart was still pounding with rage when he found Jasmine in the royal garden in the twilight, sleeping on a cushioned seat in a shady, quiet bower. A book was folded upside down unheeded in her lap. He stopped, staring down at her, marveling again at her beauty.

She slept peacefully, like a child. The wind blew softly through the trees, rattling the leaves, brushing loose tendrils of dark hair across her face. She was wearing a fitted black sweater over a high-necked white shirt and a long black skirt. And below that—red canvas sneakers.

Her lovely face was bare of makeup, and beautiful in its natural simplicity. Modest, simple, like a maid. She looked the part of a perfect wife and mother—the perfect heart of any man's home. *Of his home.*

He took a deep breath, calming down beneath the influence of her sweet purity, of her innocence. He smiled down at her. Then his gaze fell upon her hand, and he saw she still wore Hajjar's diamond upon her finger.

Jasmine's dark brown eyes fluttered open. A smile lit up her face when she saw him. Her smile struck through his soul.

"Kareef." The sweet lilt of her voice washed over him like a wave of water. "Oh, how I've missed you today!"

He sat next to her, taking her hands in his own. "I thought the day would never end."

"And once again, you've caught me in the royal garden." Her expression became bashful, apologetic. "Where I should not be."

"The garden is yours," he said roughly. "You have the right."

She tried to smile at him, but her expression faltered. She looked down at her hand, twisting the ring on her finger. "For now."

A spasm of unexpected jealousy went through him as he looked at that ring, the physical mark of another man's ownership. "Take that off."

She looked at him in surprise. "Why?"

"Take it off."

"No."

"You're not going to marry him tomorrow."

Her expression became mutinous. "I am." She rose to her feet. "And if you can't accept that—"

"We won't talk about it now, then." He caught her wrist. "Just come to the royal banquet with me tonight."

She looked down at his hand on her wrist.

"This is how we would be discreet?" she said. "Beside each other at the banquet, as lovers for all the world to see?" She shook her head. He saw tears in her eyes. "Admit I was right," she whispered. "The palace separates us already. Let's end this cleanly. We must part."

He looked at her with a heavy heart. How could he change her mind, when he himself could feel the truth of her words?

But taking a deep breath, he shook his head. "One more night."

"It won't change anything."

"Attend the banquet with me. Give me one last chance to change your mind, to convince you not to marry him. One last night." He set his jaw. "Then, if you still wish to wed him—I will say farewell."

He watched her face as her expression struggled visibly between desire and pain. "You will divorce me?"

"Yes."

"On your honor?"

"Yes," he bit out.

She gave him a slow nod. "Very well." She reached out to caress his cheek, then hesitated. She glanced wryly at her red high-top sneakers. "I will go get dressed." She bowed her head, then looked up. Tears glistened in her eyes. "Until tonight, my king."

A half hour later, Kareef arrived alone to thunderous applause at the grand ballroom. Five hundred illustrious guests clamored for his attention, clamored for his gaze—and he still hadn't thought of a way to convince Jasmine to remain his mistress. Because there wasn't a solution.

Jasmine wanted respectability. She wanted a family of her own. She wanted children.

As king, what could he offer her—except disgrace?

Greeting his honored guests, Kareef walked to the end of the long table, looking for one beautiful face. Where was she? Where had the vizier placed her? Without her calming presence, he felt like a trapped tiger in a cage, half-mad in captivity. He prayed to find her beside him at the table.

But when he reached his place, he stopped.

Seated on his left he saw the elderly king of a neighboring nation.

Seated on his right was a beautiful blonde of no more than eighteen, bedecked in diamonds and giggling behind her hand as she stared up at him with big blue eyes. He instantly knew who she must be: Princess Lara du Plessis.

Silently cursing his vizier, Kareef sat down. His hands clenched on the fine linen tablecloth of the table. He stared dismally at his plate setting of 24-karat gold-patterned china and crystal stemware filled with champagne. Where was Jasmine?

As the meal was served, the elderly king on his left complained at length about some unfair customs tax between Qusay and his own country, and it was all Kareef could do to keep from turning his ceremonial dagger on himself, like a wolf chewing off his own paw to escape a trap.

Then he felt the prickles rise on the back of his neck. And he looked up.

Jasmine looked at him from the other side of the ballroom, as far away as she could possibly be. She'd been seated beside some plain woman dressed in brown and the fat, balding secretary of the Minister of the Treasury. No doubt a location that the vizier had arranged for her personally.

She tried to give him an encouraging smile, but her eyes were sad. The shadows of the darkening ballroom beneath the candlelit chandeliers made everyone else disappear.

She was so beautiful. And so far away.

His heart turned over in his chest. Was this all it was to be, then? Was this all he could offer her? To be his secret mistress, fit only for clandestine trysts in his bedroom—instead of be the honored companion by his side?

Kareef ate quickly and spoke in monosyllables to the elderly king and the giggling young princess when they forced a direct question upon him. The instant the musicians and fire dancers arrived in the ballroom, signaling the end of the banquet, the candles were put out to highlight the magic of the performance.

Kareef threw his linen napkin on his plate and went to her.

The shadows were dark and deep as he made his way through the ballroom. All the audience was mesmerized by the intricacies of a dance with flames and swords, set to the haunting melody of the *jowza* and *santur*. Kareef was invisible in the darkness. He passed many whispered conversations that he knew would never be spoken before the king.

"…Jasmine Kouri," he heard a woman hiss, and in spite of himself, he slowed to listen. "Spending every day with him at the palace—and nights, too, I wager.

The king's a good, honorable man but when a woman is so determined to spread her legs…"

"And her an engaged woman!" came the spiteful reply. "She's made a fool out of Umar Hajjar for wanting to marry her. You remember that scandal when she was young? She was bad from the start."

"She'll get her comeuppance. Wait and see…."

Hands clenched, Kareef whirled to see who was speaking, but the women's voices faded and blended into the rest of the crowd. He saw only moving shadows.

Oh God, give him an honest fight! A fight where he could face his enemy—not the whisper of spiteful gossips in the dark!

He was still trembling with fury when he reached the lower tables of the ballroom. He whispered Jasmine's name silently. He craved her touch, yearned to have her in his arms. He yearned to keep her safe, to somehow give her shelter from the cruel words.

But when he reached for her chair, it was empty.

The instant the musicians entered the ballroom with their guitars, dulcimers and flutes in an eerie, haunting accompaniment to dancing swords of fire in the abruptly darkened ballroom, Jasmine bolted from her seat.

The banquet had been hell. She'd heard whispers and caught stares in her direction—some curious, some envious, a few hateful. It was clear that in spite of the fact that she and Kareef had neither kissed nor slept in the same bed since they'd returned to the palace, everyone already believed she was his lover. And they blamed her—*only her*—for that sin.

On her right side at the table, a fat, balding man had

leered at her throughout the meal. On her left, a plain woman had stiffened in her mousy brown suit and pointedly ignored her for a solid hour.

Jasmine had watched Kareef across the ballroom. He was clearly adored and praised by his subjects, and he accepted their attention carelessly, as his due.

Kareef didn't need her in his life, whatever he might say. He was surrounded by people begging for his attention, including the virginal blonde princess seated beside him. She was the type of woman he no doubt would marry—very soon.

She'd fled as soon as the ballroom went dark. She'd been desperate to escape before anyone could see her tears. But as soon as she was in the hallway, she felt a hand on her shoulder and whirled around, her hands tightened into fists.

Then her hands grew lax. Her body went numb.

"Father," she whispered. "What are you doing here?"

Yazid Kouri seemed to have aged in just the last few days, his once-powerful frame grown stooped and thin. He looked her over from her careful chignon to the black formal dress she'd borrowed from her old friend Sera for the occasion.

He gave a harsh laugh. "Why did you come back here?"

"You know why—"

"I thought you'd at last become a respectable, dutiful girl." He shook his head, his black eyes suspiciously bright. "Why would you agree to marry a respectable man, only to betray him with the king before you have even spoken your vows?"

She shook her head. "You don't understand!"

"Tell me you've never lain with the king," he said. "Tell me it's just an ugly rumor, and I'll believe you."

Blinking fast, she looked away. Her father's disappointment hurt her so badly she could hardly bear it. "I've betrayed no one except myself. There is no shame if I am with the king, not when he…not when we…"

Not when we're married. But the words caught at her throat. She couldn't reveal their secret. The king's word of honor was admired around the world. How could she reveal that he'd hidden such a secret for thirteen years?

As a girl, she'd remained silent to protect him.

As a woman, she still would.

"You see nothing wrong in sleeping with a man who is not your husband?" her father continued, his voice sodden with grief. "That sort of behavior might be acceptable in the modern world, but not in our family. Your sister needs you. Marry Umar. Return to New York with your new husband and family. Help Nima raise her child!"

Jasmine's jaw dropped. "You've spoken to her?"

"She called us two hours ago." He looked away, his jaw clenching. "She says she doesn't know how to be a mother. She's threatening to give the child to strangers when it's born! She's scared. She's so young."

Fury suddenly raced through Jasmine, fury she could not control. She raised her head.

"Just as I was!" she cried. "I was sixteen when you threw me out of our family, out of our country!"

"I was angry," he whispered. Tears filled his bleary eyes. "I had different expectations of you, Jasmine. You were my eldest. You had such intelligence, such strength. I took so much pride in you. Then…it all fell apart."

Her heart turned over in her chest.

"Go back to New York as a married woman. Steady Nima with your strength." His eyes glistened with unshed tears. "Tomorrow, I will be in Qais, expecting to see a wedding."

Turning to leave, he stopped when he saw Kareef standing behind them, his body tense in the ceremonial white robes.

Her father's face went almost purple. Distraught, he raised his fists against the much taller, stronger man. "I should kill you for the way you've shamed my daughter!"

Kareef didn't move. He didn't flinch. He just stood there, waiting to accept the blow.

Her father dropped his fists. Tears streaked down his wrinkled face.

"You're no king," he said hoarsely, his voice shaking with grief. "You're not even a man."

Turning on his heel, he stumbled down the palace hallway.

Jasmine watched him. When he was gone, she crumpled. Kareef pulled her into his arms and held her fast as she cried.

Softly stroking her head, he looked down at her, cupping her face with his hands. His eyes were deep and dark as he wiped the tears from her cheeks with his thumbs. He took a deep breath. Then his shoulders fell in resignation.

"Come with me," he whispered.

In the ballroom behind them, she could still hear the eerie music and shouts of the performers behind the closed doors. But Kareef led her down the dark hallway, passing several servants who pretended not to notice, who pretended not to see that the king had left his own banquet with a woman who belonged to another.

Kareef took her down the hallway into the east wing, into his bedchamber. Closing the door behind them, he set her down on the enormous bed.

Sitting on the bed beside her, he leaned over and kissed her. Tears streamed unchecked down her face as she kissed him back with all her heart. Everything she felt for him, all the tenderness of a young girl's dreams and the fire of a woman's desire, came through in her kiss.

His enormous gilded bedroom was dark. The balcony window was open, and a hot desert wind blew in from the garden, along with the noise, sudden explosions of laughter and applause from the ballroom on the floor below. But they were a world apart.

Gently, tenderly, he lay her back against his bed and made love to her one last time. The ecstasy of her body was as sharp as the pain in her heart.

I love you, her soul cried. *I love you.* But she knew her love changed nothing.

When he brought her to aching, gasping fulfillment, she wept. For a moment, he held her tightly against his chest, in his arms, as if he never wanted to let her go.

Then he slowly rose from the bed. He put on his clothes. Without looking at her, he went to an antique, jeweled chest beside the bookshelf. He twisted a key in the lock and opened it. Reaching inside, he pulled something out and returned to where she sat, clothed and numb on the bed.

He held out her emerald necklace, dangling it from his hand. She stared at the green facets of the stone, without moving.

He took her hand and placed the emerald in her palm, folding her fingers over the gold chain.

She heard the ragged gasp of his breath. Then his posture became hard as granite. He placed his hand over hers. When he spoke, his voice was deep and cold, echoing in the cavernous royal bedchamber.

"Jasmine, I divorce you."

CHAPTER NINE

THE next morning, Jasmine stepped out of the helicopter, craning her neck to stare up at the modern, gleaming racetrack that split the desert flatlands from the wide loneliness of the blue sky.

Qais. The desert she loved. But now the freedom had a sting. Horizons stretched out around her, mocking her as she stood dressed from head-to-toe in clothes chosen for her by someone else.

Her clothes had finally arrived from Paris, and she was now dressed to please her future husband, in a belted red silk dress from Christian Dior, Christian Louboutin black heels, a black vintage Kelly bag and a wide-brimmed black-and-white hat. Her beautiful designer clothes felt like a costume from the 1950s, stylish and severe.

She no longer had freedom here. Not even in the clothes she wore.

Jasmine looked up at the glass stadium that Kareef and Umar had built together. It wasn't the only thing the two men would soon share. When the Qais Cup was over, her wedding would begin.

Kareef followed her with the rest of his bodyguards

and assistants. She saw him hesitate, then grimly push forward. What more was there to say?

He'd already given the bride away.

Jasmine stared at his tense, muscular back as he walked ahead of her. She memorized the turn of his head, the line of his jaw. The shape of his supremely masculine body as he walked in his white robes.

Unwillingly, she remembered the feel of his naked body against her own. The sweet satisfied ache of pain as he possessed her, the way her lips felt bruised from his kiss, her inner thighs scratched from the sandpaper-roughness of his jaw. The memory made her body tighten with a rush of heat, even as her soul shook with the anguish of loss.

With a deep breath, she forced herself to look up.

Rising from the desert, the glass stadium competed with the blinding sun for brilliance. But even the desert sun couldn't burn away the taste of Kareef, the exotic scent of his skin. It couldn't burn away the memory of his hard body covering hers. Or the look in his blue eyes last night when he'd spoken the words to divorce her.

"My dear." Umar stepped forward from a private side door of the stadium and leaned forward to kiss her cheek gently. "I am so glad to see you at last."

In spite of his words, he looked pale. As he pulled away from her, she made no move to kiss him back, no attempt to even smile. "Where have you been, Umar?"

Umar's pale cheeks turned pink. "France," he muttered. "There was a family emergency. With Léa."

"With your nanny?" Jasmine said. "Is everything all right?"

"Fine. Fine," he said with an uneven smile. He

seemed strangely nervous and jittery compared to the urbane, sophisticated man she knew.

Turning away, he started walking, practically running toward the door, though propriety demanded that the king should have gone first. They had to hurry to keep up with him, or else be left behind.

"And that's all you have to say to me?" she demanded.

"The race is about to start." Umar glanced back at her, his nose wrinkling like a rabbit's before he sighed. "When it's over, we'll talk."

Jasmine stared at him. Had he heard the rumors about her and Kareef being lovers? Did he no longer wish to marry her?

Was he going to abandon her at the altar, to her family's eternal shame?

"Wait," she choked out. "Whatever you've heard, I can explain—"

"Later." Umar hurried toward the door. "Your family is already here. I had them seated in a place not too far from the royal box, in a place of honor." He paused. "I'll be sitting with my children in the box next to yours. You're in the royal box with the king."

So he'd heard!

"Wait!" she cried. "You don't understand!"

Kareef came up behind her. "Afraid to be alone with me?" he said in a low voice.

She glanced back at him, and trembled at the darkness in his blue eyes. She swallowed, fighting back tears. This was hard. So much harder than she'd thought it would be!

"Is my arrangement acceptable, my king?" Umar asked Kareef with a bow of his head.

Kareef answered with a single hard nod, then looked back at Jasmine with glittering eyes.

Divorced. They were divorced. But that hadn't changed her feelings. It didn't keep her body from crying out for his touch. The divorce changed nothing.

"Thank you, sire." Umar ducked inside the grandstand.

She felt Kareef's fierce blue gaze upon her like the merciless desert sun, charring her soul, turning it to dust. He glowered, then walked past her.

Lifting her chin, she put one hand on her head, balancing her wide-brimmed hat as she followed him through the private door and up the stairs. They passed through an enclosed, air-conditioned private room with a one-way mirror overlooking the track, and finally came out into the open-air royal box.

Kareef went outside first.

When he was visible to the crowds in the stadium, forty thousand people rose to their feet, screaming his name.

He raised his hand to them.

The screaming intensified.

Coming out into the royal box behind him, Jasmine pressed her hand against her belly, holding her black handbag against her body like a shield against the roar of the crowd.

She looked at his beautiful, savage face. Saw the lines of strength and wisdom at his eyes, saw the powerful jut of his jawline. Honor was the heart of who he was.

She'd done the right thing, no matter how it killed her.

She'd set him free to be the king he was born to be.

Kareef finally sat down and she sank into the chair beside him. She was aware of him at every moment but didn't look in his direction. Instead, she pressed her fingers against her wide-brimmed hat, blocking the sun from her eyes as she stared out at the racetrack.

Thousands of people stared back at her. Sitting beside the handsome, powerful young king, Jasmine knew she must appear to be very fortunate. Even though some of the older women whispered maliciously behind their hands, she could see their modern daughters looking at her belted, form-fitting red silk dress and handbag with envy. Looking at her expensive, pretty clothes and the handsome, powerful man beside her, they were no doubt thinking a lost reputation would be a small price to pay for such a glamorous life.

If only they knew what Jasmine really felt like on the inside. The truth was that she wished she had a spoon, so she could cut her heart out with it.

Beautiful clothes, wealth, attention and power—none of that mattered. Not when she couldn't have the man she loved.

"Did you sleep well?" Kareef said in a low voice beside her.

"Yes," she lied over the lump in her throat, turning away as she fought back tears. "Very well."

The gunshot sounded the start of the race, and the horses bolted from the gates.

She felt the hot burn of Kareef's gaze on her. Felt it by the way her neck prickled. By the way her nipples tightened and her breasts became heavy. She fanned herself with a program, sweating from a blast of heat that had nothing to do with the white desert sun above the grandstand.

In the next box over, she could see Umar sitting with his four young sons. The two-year-old baby was snuggled contentedly in the lap of the French nanny, Léa, who while not strictly pretty, had a sweet look to her plump face. She was only a few years older than Jasmine. Umar sat back in his chair until the horses pounded by their seats in a loud torrent of thundering hooves, and he rose to his feet, shouting at his horse in a mixture of cursing and praise.

The four boys were all adorable, Jasmine thought. She would soon be their stepmother. But even that thought didn't cheer her as it used to. None of the children wanted her. They already seemed to have a mother—Léa.

As the horses neared the finish line, Umar gripped the railing, pumping his fist in the air as he watched. "Go! Go, damn you!"

Jasmine saw her mother and father sitting in a different section with her sisters, along with her sisters' husbands and children. She hesitantly lifted her hand in greeting at her father.

Her father scowled at her in the royal box. He coldly turned his head away.

Jasmine set her shoulders. It didn't matter, she told herself over the lump in her throat. Once she was married—if Umar still married her—her father would finally be proud of her. She would do the right thing. Even if it killed her.

She heard Umar shout with delight, heard him clap his hands. His horse had won. Ruffling the hair of one of his older sons, he rushed off to accept his prize, his children following behind with the nanny. Watching them, Jasmine felt more like an outsider than ever.

She rose to her feet and went to the front of the royal box. She watched Umar walking out onto the race-track, waving to the crowd as he crossed the grass.

"It means nothing to you, does it," Kareef said behind her in a low voice, "that you'll give your body to him tonight, when you were in my bed only yesterday?"

She pretended to smile down at Umar on the race-track as he exuberantly accepted flowers, patting his horse's nose and shaking his jockey's hand. "We are divorced," she said, fighting to keep her voice even. "You mean nothing to me."

"Don't marry him, Jasmine." His voice was hoarse and deep. She heard him rise from his chair. "Don't."

She saw her fiancé waving and smiling. He lifted his two-year-old son on his shoulder, and the crowd roared their approval.

She felt Kareef come up behind her, close enough to touch. She didn't turn around. She couldn't. The cheers of the crowd became deafening white noise, like static. Until all Jasmine could hear was the pounding of her own heart and the rush of blood in her ears.

She felt Kareef slowly pull off her wide-brimmed hat. The back of her neck was washed in the warmth of his breath. Her body tightened from her scalp to her breasts, and a sweet agonizing tension coiled low and deep inside her.

"Stay with me," Kareef said in a low voice. "Not because you're bound to me, but because it's your free choice. Be my mistress."

The king's mistress.

For that kind of joy, Jasmine would have willingly sacrificed anything. Except one thing. Her gaze fell upon her family.

She squeezed her eyes closed. She'd thought she'd known pain before, but this was more than she could bear. With an intake of breath, she whirled around in his arms. Ripping the hat out of his grasp, she held it against her handbag as she backed away. "I can't."

"Jasmine—"

"Go back to the palace, Kareef," she choked out. "Don't stay for my wedding. It kills me to have you so close—don't you see you're killing me?"

She turned and rushed up the steps toward the air-conditioned private room, disappearing behind the door.

Kareef caught up with her almost instantly on the other side of the mirrored window. Grabbing her, he pushed her roughly against the wall. Both hat and handbag dropped hard on the floor. She struggled, but his hands wrapped around her wrists, holding her fast. She couldn't run. She couldn't escape. She couldn't resist.

She braced for a savage plundering of her lips. She waited for him to crush her. Instead, he did something far worse. He lowered his mouth to hers in a kiss far more brutal than any mere force could ever be.

He kissed her…as if he loved her.

Kareef moved his hands over Jasmine's red silk dress, savoring the feel of her curvaceous body in his arms. Relief filled him that she was back where she belonged. Desire sizzled through his veins like a drug as he tasted the exquisite sweetness of her lips.

He'd thought he'd almost lost her. He'd divorced her, as he'd given his word of honor to do. But he still wanted her. He wanted her to choose to be with him, of her own free will. To choose him over all other men, no matter how inconvenient or difficult their love might be.

Didn't she realize that they'd already lost too many years of their lives apart?

She belonged to him. As he belonged to her.

He cupped her breasts through her dress, stroking her shoulders, her swanlike neck. He kissed her skin, biting almost hard enough to bruise. He wanted to mark his possession, to remove any memory of another man's claim on her. *To rip that damned diamond off her left hand.*

"You belong to me," he growled. "Say it."

Her beautiful chocolate-brown eyes gleamed and shimmered, sliding over him with the sensuality of a hot desert night. His body's memory of making love to her so many times, so urgently, roared through him like a blaze. His hands tightened.

"I belong to you," she whispered with an intake of breath. "But Kareef, you must know that we—"

He stopped her with a hard kiss. He felt her tremble beneath him as he stroked her body through the red silk. He wrapped his hands in her lustrous dark hair, amid chestnut streaks like woven gold in the daylight.

They belonged together. Now, he would let the whole world know it. He would no longer hide his love for Jasmine in the shadows.

His love.

Oh my God. He loved her.

He didn't just desire Jasmine. He didn't just wish to spend his every moment with her.

He loved her. He'd never stopped loving her. It was why he'd never once felt tempted by the endless succession of women who'd tried to throw themselves into his bed. His body, his heart, were for one woman only.

Jasmine.

Even if it cost him his crown. Even if it cost him his life. He would have them together. In the open. *In the sun.*

Cupping her face, he kissed her tenderly, kissing her closed eyelids, her cheeks, her mouth. A sigh escaped her lips as she swayed in his arms, turning her face toward his.

He wrapped her left hand in his own, pressing it up against his heart as he looked down at her. "I'll tell Hajjar the wedding is off."

Smiling, he grasped the enormous diamond ring and started to draw it off her finger.

But she closed her hand into a fist. He stared at her in exasperation.

"Jasmine," he demanded.

Her face was blank of expression as she shook her head.

"You will be my honored mistress," he said, his brow furrowed. "My queen in all but name. There will be no more sneaking in the shadows, no shame for your family. I will treat you as the highest lady in the land, and the whole country will follow my lead."

"And Umar?"

"He will forgive us."

"And you?" She slowly looked up at him. "When you take your bride, Qusay's queen? What will become of me then?"

He set his jaw. The thought made him sick.

"Perhaps I will die a bachelor," he growled.

"But you need an heir," she whispered.

He shrugged, a casual gesture that belied the repressed emotion in his eyes. "My brothers' children can inherit," he said lightly. "Or their grandchildren. I intend to live a very long life."

"But your brothers are not even married. What makes you think they ever will be?"

He felt brief uncertainty, which swiftly changed to anger and impatience. "They will."

"They don't even care enough about Qusay to live here. Do you think Rafiq would give up his billion-dollar business empire to come back from Australia and rule? And from what I've heard, Tahir is squandering his life away on the international party circuit—"

"People can change—"

"Are you willing to risk the throne of Qusay on that? To place that kind of burden on your younger brothers?" She shook her head desperately. "Even if they do someday have children or grandchildren… those grandchildren will know nothing of Qusay. You think our people would tolerate being ruled by someone ignorant of our languages, our customs?"

His jaw clenched as he looked away. When he looked back at her, his voice was full of agony he no longer tried to hide.

"Is there no chance you could get pregnant, Jasmine?" he said hoarsely. "Not even a small chance? We could see the best fertility specialist in the world, spare no expense, do whatever it took for you to bear my child—"

"No," she said brutally. "I've visited some of the top obstetricians in Manhattan. I got second and third opinions. I can never get pregnant." A sob rose to her lips. "I won't destroy my family by becoming your mistress." She wiped her eyes, lifting her chin. "I deserve more than that. And so do you," she whispered.

He grabbed her shoulders savagely.

"I've waited for you for thirteen years. I'm not going to lose you again." His hands tightened on her painfully. "Even if the whole world goes down in flames for it. I'm not going to let you go."

She looked up at him, so impossibly beautiful. Unreachable.

Behind her, the bright flowers and garish red-and-gilt of the private room seemed flat, as if covered by dark mist. Outside the mirrored window, the green grass and brown horses and colorful shirts of the jockeys seemed to fade to black as Jasmine pushed away from him coldly, kneeling to pick up her hat and purse from the carpet.

"Marry another," she said in a low voice, not looking at him. "Be the king you were born to be."

He stared at her. "Is it so easy for you to thrust me into the arms of another?"

She sucked in her breath. Her eyes were stricken.

"No," she choked out. "I hate the woman you'll marry. Whoever she might be."

"And I'll hate any man who has you in his bed. Even the friend who saved my life." He looked down at her, his jaw hard. "You won't be my mistress. So there is only one answer. You will marry me."

Her jaw dropped. "What?"

"Marry me. *You* must be my queen, Jasmine. Only you."

Her eyes were huge. Then she seemed to shudder, blinking her eyes as if closing a door in her heart.

"It cannot be. You need an heir. If you married me—whatever you might think—you would be forced to abdicate."

"I have the right to choose my own bride—"

"No," she cut him off harshly. "You don't."

"But Jasmine…" he started, then stopped. He'd offered her everything. His kingdom. His name. He'd offered her everything he had, and she'd refused.

But he hadn't offered her everything. There was one risk he hadn't taken.

"But you have to marry me, Jasmine," he said. "You have to be my wife, because I…" He took a deep breath and looked straight into her eyes. "I love you."

Her eyes widened. He saw her tremble. Then slowly, ruthlessly, she squared her shoulders.

"Then you're a fool," she said evenly. "I pity you with all my heart."

With a growl, he started toward her. "But you love me," he said. "Tell the truth. You love me, as I love you!"

She held up her hand.

"The truth is that I want what you cannot give me." Her voice was cold as ice, like a sharp icicle through his heart. "Marrying Umar might be my only chance to ever have children." Her eyes narrowed as she delivered the killing blow. "You took away my chance to be a mother, Kareef," she whispered. "You took away my chance to ever have a child."

It was his greatest grief. His greatest fear. The guilty thought he'd whispered silently around the desert fire by night. Only this was a thousand times worse, since the accusation fell from the lips of the woman he loved.

His agonized blue eyes were focused on her. He took a single stumbling step backward, bumping a nearby silver champagne bucket on a table. It crashed to the floor in an explosion of ice. The bottle rolled against the wall, scattering ice and champagne across the carpet.

But he didn't notice. Pain racked his body, ripping him into little pieces more completely and ruthlessly than any sandstorm.

You took away my chance to ever have a child.

Pain and grief poured through him, burning like lava.

She'd told him it had been an accident. She'd told him he was forgiven.

Lies—all lies!

Suddenly, he could not contain the rage and grief inside his own body. Savagely, he turned and smashed a hole in a nearby wall. She flinched back, gasping.

"Teach me how to feel nothing, like you," he said in a low voice. "I'm tired of having a heart. From the moment I loved you, it has never stopped breaking."

Walking away from her, he paused in the doorway without looking back. He didn't want her to see his face. When he spoke, his voice was choked with grief.

"Goodbye, Jasmine," he said, leaning his head against the door as he closed his eyes. "I wish you a life filled with every happiness."

And he left her.

CHAPTER TEN

An hour later, Jasmine looked blankly at her own image in the large gilded mirror of the late Mrs. Hajjar's pink bedroom.

"Oh, my daughter," her father said tenderly as he pulled the veil over her head. "You're the most beautiful bride I've ever seen."

"So beautiful," her plump, gray-haired mother agreed, beaming at her. "I'll go tell them you're ready."

Jasmine stared at herself in the mirror. The round window behind her lit up her white veil with afternoon sunlight, leaving her face in shadow. She was having trouble breathing and could barely move, laced into a tight corset, locked into a wide hoop skirt beneath the layers of tulle.

Umar had ordered every component of this gown for her, even her underwear, from a Paris couture house six months before she'd agreed to be his bride. She looked at the mirror. The perfect gilded princess for this garish palace.

She could see the desert through the window behind her. She could almost imagine, in a far distance, a low-slung ranch house of brown wood, with trees and simply tended flowers beside a swimming pool of endless blue, and a loggia where she'd once held the man she loved, naked against her body.

Here in the desert, the harsh sun burned away all the lies.

Except for one.

The lie Jasmine had told to drive Kareef away.

Staring at the perfect bride in the mirror, she felt dizzy from the frantic beat of her heart.

Kareef had told her he'd loved her.

And she'd tossed his love back in his face!

I had no choice, she told herself as her knees shook beneath her. *I had no choice! He asked to marry me. He would have been forced to abdicate the throne for me!*

To push him away, she'd conjured the most cruel spell, the most vicious accusation she could imagine to drive him away from her. She'd used his own grief and guilt against him.

It made her sick inside. No matter how pure her motives, she knew she'd committed the deepest betrayal of the heart. And if she married Umar today, she would be committing suicide of the soul.

And suddenly, she knew she couldn't do it.

She could not marry a man she did not love.

For any reason.

"Where is Umar?" she whispered, pressing her hands against her tightly corseted waist, struggling for breath. "He said we would talk before the wedding. Please find him."

"I don't think that's such a good idea—" her father began ponderously.

"We'll find him," her mother said, giving her husband a sharp look. She smiled at Jasmine. "Don't worry."

"Wait." She grabbed her mother's wrist. A lump rose in her throat at the sudden fear that Jasmine would never see her again.

"Why Jasmine," her mother said softly, stroking her hair though the veil as if she were still a little girl. "What's wrong?"

Would they forgive her for calling off the wedding? Would they ever forgive her?

She would pray they would. She'd do everything she could to help her sister. She'd do everything she could to show her family she loved them.

But not sacrifice her soul.

"Mother," Jasmine said, fighting back tears, "I know I haven't always made you proud but…" Sniffling beneath her elegant veil, she looked from her mother to her father, then shook her head. "I love you both so much."

"And we've always loved you, Jasmine," her mother said, squeezing Jasmine's hand. "We always will."

"Come," her father said gruffly, pulling his wife away. "Let us leave Jasmine in peace."

Her mother's hand slipped away. The door shut softly.

With a deep breath, Jasmine opened her eyes in the flowery pink bedroom designed by Umar's dead wife. Jasmine saw moving rainbows against the wallpaper. She looked down to see the enormous diamond on her hand with its endless reflecting facets. She pulled the ring off her finger.

The stone was so cold, she thought, looking down at it in her palm. So hard. So dead.

Teach me how to feel nothing, like you. I'm tired of having a heart. From the moment I loved you, it has never stopped breaking.

Kareef had already left Qais, she'd heard, returning to the city on his helicopter. Tomorrow morning, he would be crowned king—alone.

Jasmine had finally gotten what she wanted. She'd finally pushed him away.

The ring fell from her lifeless hands. Jasmine sank to the floor, enshrouded by layers of white tulle as she fell forward into the voluminous white skirts. Her head hung down as her whole body was racked with sobs of grief.

"Oh my God," she heard Umar say in the doorway. "Someone told you."

"I'm sorry," she whispered, covering her veiled face with her hands. "I'm so sorry…."

She felt Umar's arms around her. "I'm the one who's sorry," he said. "I should have told you days ago."

Staring up at him, she said, "Told me what?"

"I've been courting you for so long, but you pushed me away…and she was right there, warm and loving. She was never the type of woman I thought I would take for a bride. She has no money, no connections, no particular beauty." Shaking his head, he stared at the floor. "In the middle of our engagement party, she called me. She said she thought she might be pregnant."

"Pregnant," Jasmine breathed. "Who? Who are you talking about?"

"Léa," he whispered. He shook his head. "I never should have allowed my courtship of you to continue while I was sleeping with another woman. I told myself Léa didn't count. She was a servant. But my children love her, and she's pregnant with my child. I must marry her." He pressed his hands over hers, his voice pleading for understanding. "I *want* to marry her. Though she is nothing like the bride I imagined…I think I could love her." He pressed her hands to his forehead as he bowed his head. "Forgive me," he said humbly.

"There's nothing to forgive," she said. A half-hysterical laugh burbled to her lips. "Because I myself…"

He gave her a sideways glance. "You and the king?" He smiled. "Gossip that rich travels swiftly, even to Brittany, where I was getting permission from Léa's father to marry her."

Umar had four children already, and would soon have a new baby. Shaking her head, Jasmine stared at the carpet. In the shifting patterns of colored light from the round window, she could imagine a meadow of flowers, hear a child's laughter. She looked up into his face. "I wish you every happiness," she said softly. "You and your precious little ones."

He kissed her hand in gratitude. "You are too good," he whispered.

She stared at the patterns of sunlight on the floor. Good? She was far from good. Picking up the ring, she handed it to him.

"What will you do?" he asked.

She took a deep breath. "Go back to New York. Run my business. Help my sister however she needs me."

"And the king?"

She shook her head. "His duty lies elsewhere."

"Are you sure?"

Trembling, she rose to her feet. "He must marry a woman who can give him children."

"Sometimes, Jasmine," Umar said, looking at her quietly, "you must put aside the person everyone wants you to be—to become the person you were born to be."

She stared at him.

For years, Jasmine had lived alone in New York, working to build her investment portfolio. She'd focused on the past and the future, but never the present.

Now the past was done. The future was unknowable. But she was only twenty-nine years old. There could be a life for her back in New York, if she chose to create one. She could make her sterile Park Avenue apartment a comfortable home. She could start with a fresh clean slate.

"Is there anything I can do for you, Jasmine?" he asked. "Perhaps explain to your father?"

She gave a deep, shaky laugh. "That's an idea," she said wryly, then shook her head. "There is one thing. You have that private plane…."

"Done."

She pulled the white veil off her head, dropping it to the floor in a shimmering cascade of translucent light.

"I cannot allow Kareef to sacrifice himself for me. But there is one thing I can do." She glanced out the round window, thinking of the ranch house, far across the unseen desert. She straightened. "I can watch him become a king. And before I leave Qusay, I can take back a lie. I can tell him…" She took a deep breath. "I can tell him the truth."

Kareef looked around the royal bedchamber in the bright sunlight.

His coronation day.

His enormous bedroom was richly appointed, lavishly decorated and big enough for the ten servants that usually insisted on waiting on him. This morning, he'd thrown them all out. He would dress for his coronation—alone.

Slowly, he picked up the ceremonial sword with emeralds on the scabbard and wrapped the belt around his white robes. So much had changed in the last week. And yet nothing had changed.

He was king.

He was alone.

And he felt nothing.

He had dim memories of flying back from the desert last night after the Qais Cup. He was fairly sure he'd spent the evening making small talk with foreign dignitaries. But he could not recall any conversation or whom he'd spoken with. When he tried to think of last night all he could recall was the image of Jasmine's pale expression, the way she'd flinched when he'd punched the hole in the wall.

You took away my chance to ever have a child.

Punching the wall, he'd been trying to rid himself of the pain. In a way, it had worked. His hand still felt numb. Just like the rest of him.

He'd offered Jasmine everything. His name. His throne. His love. And she'd still refused him.

You're a fool. I pity you with all my heart.

The servants waiting outside his bedchamber door followed him in a line as he went down to the breakfast room for his final meal before the formal coronation.

Final meal, he thought dully. *The condemned man ate a hearty breakfast.*

He'd loved her. He loved her still. But he could not have her.

"Ah, sire!" the vizier said brightly as he entered the room. "Good morning! A fine joyful day, sunny and perfect for the first official day of your reign. Now that you are free of…er…entanglements, perhaps after the coronation, I might have your permission to begin the process of seeking a royal bride?"

Kareef looked up at him wearily at the word *entanglements*. Akmal Al'Sayr gave a single discreet grimace. The man had somehow discovered already that Jasmine had thrown him over, and he was so damn happy about it. It made Kareef grind his teeth.

"Fine," he bit out. If Jasmine could move on, then so could he. He'd lived without love before. He could do it again.

Duty was all he had left. Cold, endless duty.

"Perfect, sire! I have several lovely princesses to choose from."

"Choose whomever you like," Kareef said heavily.

"I know the perfect bride. She's already here to attend the coronation. I will speak with her family immediately, and if they agree, we will begin negotiations later this afternoon." He paused. "Unless you'd care to meet the girl first?"

"I don't need to meet her," he said flatly. "Just make sure she understands this is a political marriage, nothing more."

"Of course, sire. I will tell her." Akmal paused delicately. "Although of course there must be children.…"

Kareef looked down at his plate and saw that it was empty. Somehow, without tasting any of his food, he'd gotten it all down. The thought made him grimly glad. He would survive. At least his body would, and that was all that was required, wasn't it?

"Ready?" His brother Rafiq entered the breakfast room.

"Is Tahir here?"

"No sign of him."

"Right." Why was he not surprised? Of course his youngest brother had changed his mind about coming home, promise or no promise. Kareef thought of his own optimism and joy a few days ago and felt like the exact same fool Jasmine claimed him to be.

Rising slowly to his feet, Kareef followed his brother down the long hall. But as he went outside the door and into the courtyard overlooking the cliffs above the Mediterranean, he heard someone scream his name. One sweet voice above the rest. A ghost from a long-forgotten dream.

But he kept walking. He didn't even turn his head.

Then Kareef heard it again. He stopped.

"Did you hear that?"

"I heard nothing," the vizier said nervously, then tried to sweep them forward. "This way, if you please, sire. You don't wish to be late.…"

Kareef took another few steps. Above the roar of the common crowd that had gathered to watch the coronation from outside the palace gates, he heard her voice again. Screaming his name desperately. He took a long, haggard breath.

"I must be losing my mind.…" Kareef whispered. "I keep imagining I hear her."

"Who? Jasmine?" Rafiq said. "She's right there."

Kareef whirled sharply. And there, on the other side of the palace gate, surrounded by shoving, cheering crowds, he saw her.

He whirled back to the vizier. "Get her in here!" he thundered.

"Sire," Akmal Al'Sayr begged, "please. She's been trying to get in all night but I've done my best to keep her out. For the good of the country you must consider…"

With a gasp, Kareef grabbed the older man by the neck. Then, with a shuddering breath, he regained control.

"Bring her to me," he ordered between his teeth. Terrified, his vizier gave the frantic order to the guards. A moment later, Jasmine was inside the gate.

She ran straight to his arms. She was dressed in a simple red cotton smock and sandals, her dark hair loose and flying behind her.

"Jasmine," he breathed, holding her against his chest. Half the world's leaders were waiting to see him crowned king, and yet he could not let her go. He pulled her back inside the royal garden, to a private spot behind stone walls.

"It was a lie," she gasped out with a sob. "I said those horrible things because I thought I had to push you away. I don't blame you for the accident. Forgive me," she whispered. "I thought I had no choice."

His eyes fell upon the emerald hanging on a gold chain around her neck. Then he saw her left hand…was bare!

"Did you marry him, Jasmine?" he asked, his heart in his throat.

She shook her head. "No. I couldn't do it. I know we can never be together, Kareef, but I couldn't leave Qusay without telling you the truth. I love you. I always have, and I always will."

With a shuddering intake of breath, Kareef held her against his chest, holding her tight as he closed his eyes, turning his face to the sun. A warm breeze swirled against his white robes, against his skin.

And for the first time since yesterday, he felt himself live again. Felt his blood rushing back through his veins. Felt air fill his lungs with every breath. *Jasmine loved him.*

"You had to know," she whispered. "I had to tell you. I couldn't leave with that lie."

"Leave?" His eyebrows furrowed. "Where are you going?"

"To New York." She gave a small laugh. "To start a new life. My new old life. And it's where," she said softly, "the king of Qusay will always have someone who loves him from afar. I will never forget you. Never stop loving you. Even after you take a wife—"

He stopped her with a kiss. And when he felt her lips against his—her soul against his own, so sweet and strong—he knew what he had to do.

Kareef would honor the vow he'd made long ago. He would hold true to his deepest obligation.

Taking her hand in his own, he led her out of the royal garden. His brother Rafiq was waiting patiently on the other side of the courtyard. Kareef felt a pang, then hardened his heart. It was the right choice. The only choice. Ancient honor demanded it of him, honor deeper than bloodlines. This promise superseded any other.

But still…

Forgive me, he thought, closing his eyes. Then he turned to Jasmine. "Come," he said quietly. "Before you leave this city forever, you will watch me speak the words that bind me."

CHAPTER ELEVEN

As Kareef led her across the courtyard toward the old Byzantine ruin on the edge of the cliff, Jasmine knew it would be painful to watch him speak the words that would make him forever Qusay's king. But she took a deep breath and followed him anyway. She loved him, and knew this would be the last time she would ever see him. She wanted their last memory together to be of her face shining with love—not those horrible words she'd said to him last night.

He abruptly let go of her hand, leaving her behind the three hundred guests seated in chairs placed tightly amid the old stone columns. Kareef and his brother Prince Rafiq continued walking, straight up the aisle of the ancient, roofless ruin.

She felt some people turn to look at her, a few with scorn, others with envy. Then they turned back around as Kareef faced them. He shook hands with his brother before Rafiq bowed and left to sit in the audience beside her old friend Sera. Those two seemed rather cozy, Jasmine thought. Was there something going on between Prince Rafiq and the Sheikha's widowed companion? Then the music swelled, and suddenly no one was looking at Jasmine at all.

Kareef stood at the front in his white ceremonial robes with the jeweled sword at his hip, set in emeralds, and no one could look anywhere else. Tears rose to Jasmine's eyes. He was strength. He was power.

He was her love.

As the vizier started to speak in the old dialect of Qusay, her heart lifted as she stared at Kareef, so regal before the crowd. Even now, after it had ended in heart-break, Jasmine couldn't regret their affair.

She wouldn't regret loving him—ever.

The music suddenly stopped. She heard the wind, the sound of the waves crashing beneath the cliffs. The ruins of the thousand-year-old citadel seemed to vibrate beneath their feet.

The vizier paused, and as the ceremony demanded, Kareef turned to the crowds. He was darkly beautiful. The perfect king.

His eyes met hers across the audience. And he spoke.

Not in the old dialect, as the ritual decreed, but in words everyone could understand, in a clear, low voice that rang across sand and sea.

"I renounce the throne."

There was a gasp like thunder, echoing across the crowd. She heard the vizier cry out in distress. Someone else gave a low shocked hiss—was it his brother?

Kareef remained steadfast and calm, the eye of the storm.

"Thirteen years ago, I asked a woman to marry me. A young virgin, pure and true." Everyone fell silent, struggling to listen as he said with a harsh lift of his chin and glittering eyes, "That woman was Jasmine Kouri."

A gasp arose from half the crowd as they turned to look at her. "The Kouri girl." The whispers were repeated, even as the foreign dignitaries frowned in bewildered confusion. "The old scandal."

Kareef's face hardened. "Jasmine bore the scandal—alone. But there was no shame. She lost our child in an accident. But before that, she was my bride." He stretched out his arms and proclaimed, "I owe her a debt that supersedes any other duty or obligation."

She was in shock, her heart in her throat as people got whiplash looking between them.

He took a single step down from the dais, his blue eyes locked on hers.

"Jasmine Kouri, you will marry me."

"No," she gasped.

He stepped down to the aisle.

"Jasmine Kouri, you will marry me," he commanded.

She stared at him, unable to answer against the pounding desire of her own heart.

He continued to come down the aisle, his eyes never looking away from hers. Suddenly, he was right in front of her. He towered over her, his body inches from hers. All eyes were upon them.

"Jasmine Kouri," he said softly, "you will marry me."

There was a breathless hush across the ruin.

She looked up at him with tears in her eyes.

"Yes," she choked out, her heart full of joy. "Yes. Yes!"

The smile of happiness across his handsome face

was like nothing she'd ever seen. He took her in his arms and kissed her.

"Now," he whispered urgently when he finally pulled away. "Right now."

"I love you," she whispered in reply.

The vizier rose behind him like a furious serpent. The old man's beard waggled in rage and frustration before he turned away sourly.

"Kareef Al'Ramiz has renounced the throne," the vizier pronounced in a hollow voice that echoed beyond the ancient ruin, across the sea. "There must always be a king of Qusay. Long live…King Rafiq!"

With a gasp, everyone turned to stare at Kareef's brother, the tycoon from Australia. The most shocked of them all appeared to be Rafiq himself. His blue eyes went wide as he looked down at the woman beside him. Jasmine saw Sera's lovely face constrict in shock and pain.

But as all chaos broke around them, her view of Sera and Rafiq was blocked by Kareef's strong, powerful body.

"Say it," he ordered, looking down at her.

"I marry you," she whispered in a voice almost too quiet to hear.

"Louder."

"I marry you."

He looked down at her, his eyes shining with love. "One more time."

And this time, when she spoke, her shout was loud and pure and true. "I marry you!"

He pulled the emerald necklace from her neck and placed it around his throat. Cupping her face in his hands in front of half the world's princes and ambassadors, he gently kissed away the tears now streaking her face.

"And I marry you," he said, completing the ancient Qusani ritual of marriage. As some of the audience burst into applause, and the rest muttered their shock, Kareef took her hand. As she looked up into her husband's handsome, brutal, beloved face, all the storm disappeared around them, blowing away like sand.

"Come, my love," he whispered tenderly. "Let's go home."

Six months later, Jasmine brought her baby out of the house to sit in the morning sun. Cuddling Aziza in her lap in a comfortable, shaded chair, she took a drink of ice water from her own cool glass as she watched her husband train a new yearling in a nearby paddock outside the desert ranch house.

The sun was hot and bright in the blue sky, and around their snug, comfortable home, the horizon stretched out with endless freedom.

But the desert was more than just a horizon. It was more than just sand. If a person looked closer, they'd see so much more, Jasmine thought. Tiny pink flowers. Cactus trees. Hawks soaring through the sky and tiny rabbits darting beneath the rocks. What appeared to be barren was truly full of life and color and joy.

"Jasmine!" When Kareef saw them, he left the other trainers and came over to them. Climbing through the fence, he bent to kiss her, then took the happily gurgling baby in his arms. "Come to teach our daughter how to ride?"

Jasmine choked back a laugh. "She's a bit young yet."

The baby cooed, watching the unbroken horses run in a nearby field. She waved her pudgy arms excitedly. Kareef glanced from his daughter to his wife with a lifted eyebrow.

"All right, it'll happen soon enough," Jasmine said, smiling. "She has your recklessness."

Kneeling before her, he wrapped his arms around them both and looked intently into Jasmine's eyes. "She has your courage."

As he held them both in the strong, protective circle of his arms, the sun was warm on Jasmine's back. She leaned against him as they watched the wild horses running across the field. And Aziza laughed. It was a precious sound, one she never tired of hearing, like the ringing of joyful bells across the desert.

What a precious gift. What a precious life.

Jasmine had set out to give her youngest sister the chance for a fresh start, but Nima had done it for her instead. She'd never wavered on wanting to give her child up for adoption, insisting she was too young and immature to be a decent parent. The day after Jasmine's marriage to Kareef, Nima had called her with a tearful, solemn request. "Take my baby, Jasmine. No one on earth would be a better mother."

It had taken months before Jasmine had finally accepted that Nima wouldn't change her mind. She hadn't really believed it until the day she and Kareef had brought their newborn baby back home.

Nima now lived in New York City, where she attended prep school and next year would start university, with dreams of studying chemistry and biology. She'd visited Qusay several times since the adoption, but she'd made her position clear. "I'm her aunt," Nima had said firmly, then glanced between Jasmine and Kareef with warmth and gratitude shining from her face. "Aziza knows who her real parents are."

Jasmine's parents and sisters already doted on the newest member of the Kouri family, and had visited their home in Qais multiple times. Even her father could not complain—how could he be anything but proud of the daughter who'd snagged a king, pulling him from his throne into a respectable marriage?

Or at least that was her father's gruff excuse, but the truth was that even his iron pride hadn't been able to resist their baby. No one could resist Aziza. Least of all Jasmine.

The happiness of getting everything she'd ever wanted—just when she'd thought all chance was lost—caused her heart to expand so wide in her chest she thought it might break with joy.

Kareef kissed their gurgling baby's chubby cheeks, then moved to kiss his wife's forehead. With a new spark in his eyes, he gave Jasmine a hungry look and lowered his mouth to hers. His kiss was tender and full of passion and promise for the night. When he pulled away, she sighed with happiness.

Each day, he kissed her as if for the first time.

Against all expectation, her life, like the desert, had bloomed. And she knew the heat of the sun, the vast blue sky, and the warmth of their love would last forever.

Forbidden: The Sheikh's Virgin

TRISH MOREY

Trish Morey is an Australian who's also spent time living and working in New Zealand and England. Now she's settled with her husband and four young daughters in a special part of South Australia, surrounded by orchards and bushland and visited by the occasional koala and kangaroo. With a life-long love of reading, she penned her first book at the age of eleven, after which life, career and a growing family kept her busy until once again she could indulge her desire to create characters and stories—this time in romance. Having her work published is a dream come true. Visit Trish at her website, www.trishmorey.com.

To Romance Writers of Australia, an organisation that has taken this one raw writer with a dream, held my hand through the long lean years of rejection, inspired me, educated me and celebrated with me every success along the way. Most of all, thank you for giving me the best friends a girl could have.

I owe you so much!

PROLOGUE

IT SHOULD have been something to celebrate. Business was booming, the Aussie dollar soaring, and people were buying imports like never before. Combined with a sharp recovery in property prices, Rafiq Al'Ramiz's import business and property investments were doing better than ever.

It *should* have been something to celebrate…

With a growl, he turned his back on the reports and swivelled his leather high-backed chair through one hundred and eighty degrees, preferring the floor-to-ceiling views of Sydney Harbour afforded by his prime fortieth-floor office suite to the spreadsheets full of black numbers on his desk.

He didn't feel like celebrating.

What would be the point?

Because it was no fun when it was too easy.

He sighed and knotted his hands behind his head. Challenge had been the thing that had driven him over the last ten-plus years, adversity the force that had shaped him, and for a man who had built himself up from nothing into a business phenomenon, conflict had always been a driving force. Making money when everyone else was, even if he made ten times more than they did, was no achievement. Succeeding when times were tough was his challenge and his success.

Beyond the glass windows of his office the waters of Sydney Harbour sparkled like jewels, passenger ferries jostling with pleasure craft for the perfect view of the Harbour Bridge and the Opera House. For the first time he could remember he felt the insane urge to abandon the office during business hours and take his yacht out and join the pleasure craft taking advantage of the spectacular harbour while the weather was so perfect.

And why not? Business couldn't be better. Why shouldn't he cut himself some slack? He tugged at the knot in his tie, already warming to the notion. He could have Elaine call up that society princess he'd met at last week's charity do. He couldn't remember the cause, or her name for that matter—he was invited to so many of those things and he met so many women—but he could remember the way the blonde had sashayed up to him, so hot in her liquid red dress that she'd all but melted the ice in his glass. His PA would know who she was. That was Elaine's job. And maybe by the time he'd finished with the blonde the economy would have taken a tumble and life might be more interesting again.

He could only hope.

He'd already swivelled his chair back, ready to pick up the receiver and hit the button that would connect him to his PA, when his phone buzzed.

He raised one eyebrow. Elaine had a sixth sense for his requirements, almost uncanny at times, but if she already had the blonde bombshell on line one, her bonus this year would be an all-expenses-paid holiday to the Bahamas.

He picked up the receiver and listened. It wasn't the blonde, and there would be no all-expenses-paid holiday to the Bahamas for his PA, but life was already one hell of a lot more interesting.

CHAPTER ONE

THE sun belted down on the tarmac of Qusay International Airport, the combination turning the air oppressive as Rafiq stepped from the Gulfstream V. He took a moment to let his eyes adjust to the dazzling light, and even over the smell of avgas he breathed it in: the unmistakable scent of his homeland, the salt-tinged air fragrant with a thousand heady spices and dusted with the desert sands that swept so much of the island kingdom.

'Rafiq!'

He smiled as his brother emerged, his robes stark white and cool-looking, from the first of two limousines waiting near the foot of the stairs. At their front, flags bearing the royal insignia fluttered, and four uniformed motorcyclists sat ready nearby, bringing home to him the reality of the bombshell his brother had dropped during his phone call. King Xavian had abdicated after learning that he was really the missing Prince Zafir of Calistan, which meant that his brother, Kareef, would soon be crowned King of Qusay.

Which made him, Rafiq, a prince.

A fleeting hint of bitterness infused his thoughts and senses—*if he'd been a prince back then*—but just as quickly he fought it down. That was history.

Ancient history.

There were far better things to celebrate now, even if the bad taste in his mouth would not disappear completely. He jogged down the stairs, ignoring the heat that seemed to suck the very oxygen from the air, and took his brother by the arm, pulling him close and slapping him on the back. 'It is good to see you, big brother. Or should I call you Sire?'

Kareef waved his jest aside as he ushered his brother into the cool interior of the waiting limousine, the chauffer snicking the door softly closed behind them before sliding into the driver's seat. 'It's good you could come at such short notice,' Kareef acknowledged as the cavalcade pulled away.

'You think I would miss your coronation?'

'You almost missed Xavian's wedding. How long were you here? Three hours? Four at most.'

'It is true,' Rafiq acceded, unable to deny it. Business had been more pressing a few weeks ago—new emporiums opening almost simultaneously in Auckland and Perth, his presence required everywhere at once—but he had managed to get here, only to have his snatched visit cut even shorter with news of a warehouse fire that had threatened some of his employees' lives. 'Although as it turns out he wasn't Xavian our cousin after all. But there was no way I was not coming for your coronation. And if there is one thing I am sure of, Kareef, it's that you are indeed my brother.'

Nobody could have doubted it. The brothers shared the same height and breadth of shoulder, and the same arresting dark good-looks. Those things would have been more than enough to guarantee the family connection, but it was their uncannily blue eyes, eyes that could be as warm as the clearest summer sky or as cold as glacial frost, that cemented the family connection and took it beyond doubt.

'Speaking of brothers,' he continued, 'where is Tahir? Is our wayward brother to grace us with his presence this time?'

A frown marred Kareef's noble brow. 'I spoke with him…' He paused, and seemed to take a moment to gather his thoughts before looking up and smiling broadly. 'I spoke with him yesterday.'

'I don't believe it!'

'It's true. Though it wasn't easy to track him down in Monte Carlo, he's coming to the coronation.'

Rafiq raised a brow as he pushed himself further back into the supple leather upholstery. 'All three of us, back here at the same time?'

'It's been too long,' Kareef agreed.

The journey from the airport through the bustling city of Shafar, with its blend of the traditional low mud-brick buildings amongst modern glass skyscrapers, passed quickly as the brothers caught up on events since they had last seen each other, and soon the limousine was making its way through the massive iron gates that opened to the cobbled driveway leading to the palace. It never failed to impress. In the noonday sun, the palace glowed like the inside of a pearl shell—so massive, so bright, standing atop its headland, that travellers at sea must be able to see it from miles around, whether in the dazzling light of day or glowing brightly in the pearly light of the moon.

And as the car pulled to a halt under a shadowed portico, and a uniformed doorman swept close and saluted as he opened the door, the reality of recent events hit home once more. Now Rafiq wasn't just entering the royal palace as a member of the extended family. Now he *was* royalty. A prince, no less.

How ironic, when he had built himself up to be king of the business he had created for himself—ruler over his own empire. For now he was one step away from being ruler of the country that had given him birth, the country he had turned his back on so many years ago.

How life could change so quickly.

And once again an unwelcome trace of bitterness sent him poisoned thoughts.

If he'd been brother to the King back then, would she have waited for him? If he'd been a prince, how might things have been different?

He shook his head to clear the unwanted thoughts. The savage heat was definitely getting to him if he was dwelling on things that could not be changed. He hadn't been a prince back then and she had made her choice. End of story.

His brother left him then, putting a hand to Rafiq's shoulder. 'As I mentioned, there are matters I must attend to. Meanwhile Akmal will show you to your suite.'

His suite proved to be a collection of high-ceilinged, richly decorated rooms of immense proportions, the walls hung with gilt-framed mirrors and colourful tapestries of exploits otherwise long forgotten, the furnishings rich and opulent, the floor coverings silken and whisper-soft.

'I trust you will be comfortable here, Your Highness,' Akmal said, bowing as he retreated backwards out the door.

'I'm sure I will,' he said, knowing there was no way he couldn't be, despite the obvious difference between the palace furnishings and the stark and streamlined way his own house in Sydney was decorated. His five-level beachside house was a testament to modern architecture and structural steel, the house clinging to the cliff overlooking Secret Cove, Sydney's most exclusive seaside suburb.

And inside it was no less lean and Spartan, all polished timber floors and stainless steel, glass and granite.

Strange, he mused, how he'd become rich on people wanting to emulate the best the Middle East had to offer, when he'd chosen the complete opposite to decorate his own home.

'And Akmal?' he called, severing that line of thought before he could analyse it too deeply. 'Before you go…'

The older man bowed again, simultaneously subservient and long-suffering in the one movement. 'Yes, Your Highness?'

'Can we drop the formalities? My name is Rafiq.'

The old adviser stiffened on an inhale, as if someone had suddenly shoved a rod up his spine. 'But here in Qusay you are *Your Highness*, Your Highness.'

Rafiq nodded on a sigh. As nephews to the King, he and his brothers had grown up on the periphery of the crown, in line, and yet an entire family away, and while the possibility had always existed that something might happen to the heir they'd known as Xavian before he took the crown, nobody had really believed it. Their childhood had consequently been a world away from the strained atmosphere Xavian had grown up in, even with their own domineering father. They'd had duty drilled into them, but they'd had freedom too—a freedom that had allowed Rafiq to walk away from Qusay as a nineteen-year-old when there'd been nothing left for him here.

He'd made his own way in the world since then, by clawing his way up from being a nothing and nobody in a city the other side of the world. He hadn't needed a title then. He didn't need a title now, even if he was, by virtue of Xavian's abdication, a prince. But what was the point of arguing?

After all, he'd leave for Sydney and anonymity right after the coronation. He could put up with a little deference that long. 'Of course, Akmal,' he conceded, letting the older man withdraw, his sense of propriety intact. 'I understand. Oh, and Akmal?'

The vizier turned. 'Yes, *Your Highness*?'

Rafiq allowed himself a smile at the emphasis. 'Please let my mother know I'll visit her this afternoon.'

He bowed again as he withdrew from the room. 'As you wish.'

Rafiq took the next hour to reacquaint himself with the

Olympic-length swimming pool tucked away with the men's gym in one of the palace's many wings, the arched windows open to catch the slightest breeze, while the roof protected bathers from the fiery sun. There weren't any other bathers today; the palace was quiet in the midday heat as many took the opportunity for the traditional siesta.

And of course there were no women. Hidden away in the women's wing, there was a similar pool, where women could disrobe without fear of being seen by men. So different, he thought, from the beach that fronted his seaside property and the scantily clad women who adorned it and every other piece of sand along the coast. He would be a liar if he said they offended him, those women who seemed oblivious to the glances and turned heads as their swimming attire left little to the imagination, but here in Qusay, where the old ways still had meaning, this way too made sense.

The water slipped past his body as he dived in, cool but not cold, refreshing without being a shock to the system, and he pushed himself stroke after stroke, lap after lap, punishing muscles weary from travel until they burned instead with effort. He had no time for jetlag and the inconveniences of adapting to a new body clock, and physical exercise was the one way of ensuring he avoided it. When finally his head touched the pillow tonight, his body, too, would be ready to rest.

Only when he was sure his mother would have risen from her siesta did he allow his strokes to slow, his rhythm to ease. His mind felt more awake now, and the weariness in his body was borne of effort rather than the forced inactivity of international travel. Back in his suite, he showered and pulled open the wardrobe.

His suits and shirts were all there, freshly pressed and hung in his absence, and there were more clothes too. White-as-snow robes lay folded in one pile, The *sirwal*, worn as trousers underneath, in another. He fingered a *bisht*, the headdress favoured by Qusani men, his hand lingering over the double black cord that would secure it.

His mother's handiwork, no doubt, to ensure he had the 'proper' clothes to wear now he was back in Qusay.

Two years it had been since he had last worn the robes of his countrymen, and then it had only been out of respect at his father's funeral. Before that it would have been a decade or more since he'd worn them—a decade since his youthful dreams had been shattered and he'd turned his back on Qusay and left to make his own way in the world.

And his own style. It was Armani now that he favoured next to his skin, Armani that showcased who he was and just how far he'd come since turning his back on the country that had let him down. With a sigh, he dropped the black *igal* back on the shelf and pulled a fresh shirt and clean suit from the wardrobe.

He might be back in Qusay, and he might be a prince, but he wasn't ready to embrace the old ways yet.

The palace was coming to life when he emerged to make the long walk to his mother's apartments. Servants were busy cleaning crystal chandeliers or beating carpets, while gardeners lovingly tended the orange and lemon trees that formed an orchard one side of the cloistered pathway, the tang of citrus infusing the air. All around was an air of anticipation, of excitement, as the palace prepared for the upcoming coronation.

He was on the long covered balcony that led to his mother's suite when he saw a woman leaving her rooms, pulling closed the door behind her and turning towards him, her sandals slapping almost noiselessly over the marble floor. A black shapeless gown covered everything but the stoop of her shoulders; a black scarf over her head hid all but her downcast eyes. One of his mother's ladies-in-waiting, he assumed, going off to fetch coffee or sweets for their meeting.

And then he drew closer, and a tiny spark of familiarity, some shred of recognition at the way she seemed to glide effortlessly along the passageway, sent the skin at the back of his neck to prickly awareness.

But it couldn't be.

She was married and living the high life in Paris or Rome, or another of the world's party capitals. And this woman was too stooped. Too sad.

He'd almost discounted the notion entirely, thinking maybe he hadn't completely swum off his jetlagged brain after all, when the woman sensed his approach, her sorrowful eyes lifting momentarily from their study of the floor.

A moment was all it took. Air was punched from his lungs, adrenaline filled his veins, and anger swirled and spun and congealed in his gut like a lead weight.

Sera!

CHAPTER TWO

HER kohl-rimmed eyes opened wide, and in their familiar dark depths he saw shock and disbelief and a crashing wave of panic.

And then the shutters came down, and she turned her gaze away, concentrating once more on the marble flagstones as her steps, faster now, edged her sideways, as far away from him as she could get, even as they passed. Her robe fluttered in the breeze of her own making, and the scent of incense and jasmine left in her wake was a scent that took him back to a different time and a different world—a scent that tugged at him like a silken thread.

He stopped and turned, resenting himself for doing so but at the same time unable to prevent himself from watching her flight, bristling that she could so easily brush past him, angry that once again she could so easily dismiss him. So many years, and she'd found not one word to say to him. Didn't she owe him at least that? Damn it to hell if she didn't owe him one hell of a lot more!

'Sera!' The name reverberated as hard as the stone of the cloister, no request but a demand, yet still she didn't stop, didn't turn. He didn't know what he'd say if she did. He didn't even know why he'd felt compelled to put voice to a name he'd refused to say even to himself these last ten years or more. He had no doubt she'd heard him, though. Her quickening footsteps were even faster now, her hands gathering her voluminous gown above her feet to prevent her from tripping on its length as she fled.

'Sera!' he called again, louder this time, his voice booming in the stone passageway, although she was already disappearing around a corner, her robes fluttering in her wake.

Damn her!

So maybe he was no more interested in small talk than she was, but there was a time once when his voice would have stopped her in her tracks—a time when she could no more have walked away from him than stopped breathing.

Fool!

He spun around on his heel and strode swiftly and decisively to his mother's apartments. Those days were long gone, just as the girl he'd known as Sera had gone. Had she ever existed, or had she been fantasy all along, a fantasy he'd chosen to believe because it had been the only bright spot in a world otherwise dominated by his father's tyranny? A fantasy that had come unstuck in the most spectacular fashion!

He was still breathing heavily, adrenaline coursing through his veins, when he entered his mother's suite. He was led to one of the inner rooms, the walls hung in silks of gold and ruby around vibrant tapestries, the floor covered with the work of one artisan's lifetime in one rich silk carpet, where his mother sat straight and tall amidst a circle of cushions, a tray laden with a coffee pot and tiny cups and small dishes of dates and figs to one side.

She sat wreathed in robes of turquoise silk, beaming the smile of mothers worldwide when she saw him enter, and for a moment, as she rose effortlessly to her feet, he almost forgot—*almost*—what had made him so angry.

'Rafiq,' she said, as he took her outstretched hand and pressed it to his lips before drawing her into the circle of his arms. 'It's been too long.'

'I was here just a few weeks ago,' he countered, as they both settled onto the cushioned floor, 'for Cousin Xavian's wedding.' He didn't bother to correct himself. Maybe Xavian wasn't his blood cousin, and his real name wasn't Xavian but Zafir, but as children they'd grown up together and he was as much family as any of them.

'But you didn't stay long enough,' his mother protested.

He hadn't stayed long, but it had been the warehouse fire in Sydney that had cut his visit even shorter than he'd intended. He'd made it to the ceremony, but only just, and then had had to fly out again before the festivities were over.

Only now could he appreciate how disappointed his mother must have been. The two years since her husband's funeral had not been hard on her, her skin was still relatively smooth, but there were still the inevitable signs of aging. Her hair was greyer than he remembered, and there were telltale lines at the corners of her blue-grey eyes that he couldn't remember. Sad eyes, he realised for the very first time, almost as if her life hadn't been everything it should have been. Sad eyes that suddenly reminded him of another's...

He thrust the rogue thought away. He was with his mother; he would not think of the likes of *her*. Instead, he took his mother's hands, squeezing them between his own. 'This time I will stay longer.'

His mother nodded, and he was relieved to see the smile she gave chase the shadows in her eyes away. 'I am glad. Now, you will have coffee?' With a grace of movement that was as much a part of his mother as her blue-grey eyes, she poured them coffee from the elegant tall pot, and together they sipped on the sweet cardamom-flavoured beverage and grazed on dates and dried figs, while his mother plied him with questions. How was business? How long was he staying? What items were popular in Australia? What colours? Had he come alone? What style of lamp sold best? Did he have someone special waiting for him at home?

Rafiq applied himself to the questions, carefully sidestepping those he didn't want to answer, knowing that to answer some would lead to still more questions. Three sons, all around thirty years old, and none of them married. Of course their mother would be anxious for any hint of romance. But, while he couldn't speak for his brothers, there was no point in his mother waiting for *him* to find a woman and settle down.

Not now.

Not ever.

Once upon a time, in what now felt like a different life, he'd imagined himself in love. He'd dreamed all kinds of naive dreams and made all kinds of plans. But he'd been younger and more foolish then—too foolish to realise that dreams were like the desert sands, seemingly substantial underfoot and yet always shifting, able to be picked up by the slightest wind and flung stinging into your face.

It wasn't all bad. If there was one thing that had guaranteed the success of his business, it was his ability to learn from his mistakes. It might have been a painful lesson at the time, but he'd learned from it.

There was no way he'd make the same mistake again.

His mother would have to look to his brothers for grandchildren, and, while he had difficulty imagining their reckless younger brother ever settling down, now that Kareef was to be crowned he would have to find a wife to supply the kingdom with the necessary heirs. It was perfect.

'Give it up, Mother,' he said openly, when finally he tired of the endless questions. 'You know my feelings on the subject. Marriage isn't going to happen. Kareef will soon give you the grandchildren you crave.'

His mother smiled graciously, but wasn't about to let him

off the hook. Her questions wore on between endless refills of hot coffee and plates of tiny sweet pastries filled with chopped dates and nuts. He did his best to concentrate on the business questions, questions he could normally answer without thinking, but his heart wasn't in it. Neither was his head. Not when the back of his mind was a smouldering mess of his own questions about a raven-haired woman from his youth, his gut a festering cauldron poisoned with the bitterness of the past.

Because *she* was here, in Shafar.

The woman who'd betrayed him to marry another.

Sera was here.

'Rafiq?' His mother's voice clawed into his thoughts, dragging him back. 'You're not listening. Is something troubling you?'

He shook his head, his jaw clenched, while he tried to damp down the surge of emotions inside him. But there was no quelling them, no respite from the heaving flood of bitterness that threatened to swamp his every cell—and there could not be, not until he knew the answer to the question that had been plaguing him ever since he'd recognised her.

'What is *she* doing here?' His voice sounded as if it had been dragged from him, his lungs squeezed empty in the process.

His mother blinked, her grey-blue eyes impassive as once again she reached for the coffeepot, the eternal antidote to trouble.

He stayed her hand with his, a gentle touch, but enough to tell his mother he was serious. 'I saw her. Sera. In the passageway. What is she doing here?'

His mother sighed and put the pot down, leaning back and folding her long-fingered hands in her lap. 'Sera lives here now, as my companion.'

'*What?*'

The woman who had betrayed him was now his mother's companion? It was too much to take in, too much to digest, and his muscles, his bones and every part of him railed against the words his mother had so casually spoken. He leapt to his feet and wheeled around, but even that was not movement enough too satisfy the savagery inside him. His footsteps devoured the distance to the balcony and, with fingers spearing through his hair and his nails raking his scalp, he paced from one end to the other and back again, like a lion caged at the zoo. And then, as abruptly as he'd had to move, he stopped, standing stock still, dragging air into his lungs in great greedy gasps, not seeing anything of the gardens below him for the blur of loathing that consumed his vision.

And then his mother was by his side, her hand on his arm, her fingers cool against his overheated skin. 'You are not over it, then?'

'Of course I am over it!' he exploded. 'I am over it. I am over her. She means nothing to me—less than nothing!'

'Of course. I understand.'

He looked down into his mother's age-softened face, searching her eyes, her features, for any hint of understanding. Surely his mother, of all people, should understand? 'Do you? Then you must also see the hatred I bear for her. And yet I find her here—not only in the palace, but with my own mother. Why? Why is she here and not swanning around the world with her husband? Or has he finally realised what a devious and power-hungry woman she really is? It took him long enough.'

Silence followed his outburst, a pause that hung heavy on the perfumed air. 'Did you not hear?' His mother said softly. 'Hussein died, a little over eighteen months ago.'

Something tripped in his gut. Hussein was dead?

Rafiq was stilled with shock, absorbing the news with a kind of mute disbelief and a suspension of feeling. Was that why Sera had looked so sad? Was that why she seemed so downcast? Because she was still in mourning for her beloved husband?

Damn the woman! Why should he care that she was sad—
especially if it was over *him*? She'd long ago forfeited any and
all rights to his sympathy. 'That still doesn't explain why she
is here. She made her choice. Surely she belongs with Hussein's
family now?'

The Sheikha shook her head on a sigh. 'Hussein's mother
turned her away before he was even buried.'

'So her husband's mother was clearly a better judge of character than her son.'

'Rafiq,' his mother said, frowning as her lips pursed, as if
searching for the right words. 'Do not be too hard on Sera. She
is not the girl you once knew.'

'No, I imagine not. Not after all those glamorous years
swanning around the world as wife to Qusay's ambassador.'

The Sheikha shook her head again. 'Life has not been as
easy for her as you might think. Her own parents died not long
before Hussein. There was nowhere for her to go.'

'So what? Anyone would think you expect me to feel sorry
for her? I'm sorry, Mother, but I can feel nothing for Sera but
hatred. I will never forgive her for what she did. Never!'

There was a sound behind them, a muffled gasp, and he
turned to find her standing there, her eyes studying the floor,
in her hands a bolt of silken fabric that glittered in swirls of tiny
lights like fireflies on a dark cave roof.

'Sheikha Rihana,' she said, so softly that Rafiq had to strain
to catch her words—and yet the familiar lilt in her voice
snagged and tugged on his memories. He'd once loved her
softly spoken voice, the musical quality it conveyed, gentle and
well bred as she was. *As he'd once imagined she was.* Now,
hearing that voice brought nothing but bitterness. 'I have
brought the fabric you requested.'

'Thank you, Sera. Come,' she urged, deliberately disregard-
ing the fact that Sera had just overheard Rafiq's impassioned

declaration of hatred as if it meant nothing. He wanted to growl. What did his mother think she was doing? 'Bring it closer, my child,' his mother continued, 'so that my son might better see.' And then to her son, 'Rafiq, you remember Sera, of course.' Her grey-blue eyes held steady on his, the unsaid warning contained therein coming loud and clear.

'You know I do.' And so did Sera remember him, if the way she was working so hard at avoiding his gaze was any indication. She'd heard him say how much he hated her, so it was little wonder she couldn't face him, and yet still he wanted her to look at him, challenging her to meet his eyes as he followed her every movement.

'Sera,' he said, his voice schooled to flat. 'It has been a long time.'

'Prince Rafiq,' she whispered softly, and she nodded, if you could call it that, a bare dip of her already downcast head as still she refused to lift her gaze, her eyes skittering everywhere—at his mother, at the bolt of fabric she held in her hands, at the unendingly fascinating floor that her eyes escaped to when staring at one of the other options could no longer be justified—everywhere but at him.

And the longer she avoided his gaze, the angrier he became. Damn her, but she *would* look at him! His mother might expect him to be civil, but he wanted Sera to see how much he hated her. He wanted her to see the depth of his loathing. He wanted her to know that she alone had put it there.

Through the waves of resentment rolling off him, Sera edged warily forward, her throat desert-dry, her thumping heart pumping heated blood through her veins.

She knew he hated her. She had known it since the day he had returned unexpectedly from the desert and found her marrying Hussein. She'd seen the hurt in his eyes, the anguish that had squeezed tight her already crumpled heart, the anguish that had turned ice-cold with loathing when he'd begged her to stop the wedding and she'd replied by telling him that she would never have married him because she didn't love him. Had never loved him.

He hadn't quite believed her then, she knew. But he'd believed it later on, when she'd put the matter beyond doubt…

She squeezed her eyes shut at the pain the memories brought back. That day had seen something die inside her, just as her lies and her actions had so completely killed his love for her.

Yet walking in just now and hearing him say it—that he felt nothing for her but hatred, and that he could never forgive her—was like twisting a dagger deep in her heart all over again.

And she had no one to blame but herself.

Her hands trembling, she held out the bolt of fabric, willing him to take it so once again she could withdraw to somewhere safe, somewhere she could not feel the intensity of his hatred. She could feel his eyes on her face, could feel the burn as his gaze seared her skin, could feel the heat as blood flooded her face.

'What do you think?' she heard the Sheikha say. 'Have you ever seen a more beautiful fabric? Do you think it would sell well in Australia?'

At last he relieved Sera of the burden in her arms. At last, with him distracted, she might escape. She took a step back, but she couldn't resist the temptation that had been assailing her since she'd first seen Rafiq again, couldn't resist the compulsion that welled up within herself to look upon his face. Just one glance, she thought. Just one look at the face of the man she had once loved so much.

Surely that was not too much to ask?

Tentatively she raised her lashes—only to have the air punched from her lungs.

Because he wasn't looking at the fabric!

Blue eyes lanced hers, ice-blue, and as frozen as the glaciers that adorned mountaintops in the Alps. So cold and rapier-sharp that just one look sliced deep into her psyche.

And she recognised that this was not the man she had loved. This was not the Rafiq that she had known, the man-boy with the warm smile and the liquid blue eyes, eyes that had danced with life and love—love for her. Oh, his features might otherwise look the same, the strong line of his nose, the cleft jaw and passionate slash of mouth, and the thick dark hair that looked like an invitation in which to entangle one's fingers, but his eyes were ice-blue pits, devoid of everything but hatred.

This man was a stranger.

'What do you think, Rafiq?' she heard his mother say, and a moment later his eyes released their icepick hold, leaving her sagging and breathless and weak in its wake. 'Come, sit here, Sera,' Sheikha Rihana continued, pouring another cup of coffee as she patted the cushions alongside her.

And, while escape would be the preferred option, with Sera's knees threatening to buckle underneath her it was all she could do to collapse onto the cushions and pretend that she was unshaken by the assault his eyes had just perpetrated against her. Maybe now Rafiq would ignore her, for there was no reason for him to so much as look at her again. Hadn't he already made his hatred plain?

Rafiq tried to concentrate on the fabric. He wasn't formally trained in such things, but once upon a time he'd single-handedly selected every item that would be shipped to Australia for sale in his emporiums. Times had changed since those heady early days, and now he had a handful of trusted buyers who circled the Arab world looking for treasures to appeal to his customers, but still he knew something special when he saw it. Even now, while his blood pumped hot and heavy through his veins, he felt that familiar spike of interest, that instant of knowing that what he held in his hands was extraordinary.

'Hand-stitched,' announced his mother, as proudly as if she'd made it herself, 'every one of those tiny gems stitched by hand into place.'

He didn't have to pretend to be interested to indulge his mother; he was genuinely fascinated as he ran the gossamer-thin fabric through his hands, studying the beads, searching for their secret.

'Emeralds,' he realised with surprise. The tiny chips were sculpted and shaped to show off their magnificent colour as if they were the most spectacular gems. The workmanship in cutting the beads would be horrendous in itself, the craft of stitching them to a fabric so light a labour of love.

'Is it not magnificent?' his mother said. 'The beads are fashioned from the off-cuts after the best stones from the emerald mines are cut. This fabric is light, and suited to gowns and robes, but there are heavier fabrics too, suitable for drapes and cushions, of all colours and weights. Could not something this beautiful sell well in your stores?'

'Possibly,' he said, making a mental note to inform his buyers to check it out, and then put the fabric aside, his curiosity once more drawn to the black-clad figure kneeling next to his mother. She was studying the floor again, her long-lashed eyes cast downwards, looking the very essence of meek and submissive. Surely his mother wasn't taken in by such a performance? This was a woman who had married for wealth and privilege and status. She might look innocent and meek, but he knew differently. She was as scheming as she was beautiful.

The thought stopped him in his tracks. Beautiful? But of course she always had been, and even now, with the air of sadness she carried with her, there was a haunting beauty in her slumberous eyes and the curve of her lashes that could not be denied. Beauty and cunning. She had both, like a viper poised ready to strike.

He turned to his mother, only to find her watching him, her eyes narrowed. For a moment he got the impression she was going to say something—could she read his thoughts in his eyes? Was she about to defend the woman again? —but then she shook her head and sniffed, and gestured towards the roll of material instead.

'How can you say possibly? Fabric of this quality, and yet you think it could only *possibly* be good enough to sell?'

'I'll have one of my buyers come over and check it out.'

'Ah, then you may be too late.' She collected the bolt of fabric in her hands, winding the shimmering loose material around it and passing it to Sera. 'I am sorry to have troubled you. Sera, you might as well take this back.'

Sera was rocking forward on her knees, preparing to rise to her feet, when Rafiq reached out and grasped one end of the bolt. 'Stay,' he ordered Sera, before turning to his mother. 'What are you talking about, too late? Why should it be too late?'

Sera looked to the Sheikha, who smiled and put her henna-stained hand over the younger woman's. 'One moment, my child.' And then his mother turned to Rafiq and sighed wistfully. 'There is another party interested and ready to sign for exclusive rights to the collection. If you delay, and wait for your buyer to arrive…' she shrugged for effect '…it will no doubt already be too late.'

'Who is this other party?' But he already suspected the answer, even before his mother confirmed it by giving the name of the biggest importer of Arab goods in the world. Strictly speaking they weren't competitors. He was content to dominate the southern hemisphere while they took the north, each keeping out of the other's way. But to demand exclusivity on a range of goods made right here, in the country of his birth? That had never been part of their unspoken agreement.

He caught his mother's cool-eyed gaze assessing him again,

and allowed himself a smile. It had never occurred to him before, but maybe he owed at least some of his business acumen to his mother. What else could have prompted him to look up a business opportunity while he was here for his brother's coronation but the thrill of the chase?

'I suppose,' he conceded, 'I could go and look at the collection while I am here. Is the workshop here, in Shafar?'

She shook her head. 'No, it is in the town of Marrash, in the mountain country to the north.'

He summoned up a mental map of Qusay, trying and unable to place the town, but knowing that if it was in the rugged red mountains of the north transport would be difficult and by necessity slow. He shook his head. 'Travelling there would take at least a day. It is not practical, given it is so close to the coronation. Is there nowhere in Shafar to view this so-called collection?'

'There is only this one sample here in the palace, but there is plenty of time before the coronation—it is no more than an overnight trip. And you would have to travel to Marrash if you wished to deal with the tribespeople. They would not do business otherwise.'

'But what of Kareef? I have only just arrived in Qusay. What kind of support would I be to my brother if I were to up and leave him a few short days before his coronation?'

'He would think you are a businessman with an eye to business. He would be more surprised if you did *not* pursue an opportunity such as this. Besides, I suspect he will be busy enough with arrangements as it is.'

He supposed she was right. And it was one way of making the most of his time in Qusay. Why not combine business with pleasure? It had been a long time since he had ventured across the desert to the mountains of red stone. A very long time…

'I'll go,' he said, nodding, 'I'll explain to Kareef and get Akmal to organise a driver.'

'You'll need a guide too, to smooth the negotiations.' He was about to protest when she held up one hand softly. 'You might now be a prince, my son, but you are still a man. You will need someone who knows the women and understands their needs, someone who can talk to them as an equal. I would go myself, but of course...' she shrugged '...with so many guests in the palace, and while we wait on news of Tahir, there is no way I can excuse myself. I can send one of my companions. They have all travelled extensively throughout Qusay with me, talking to the women, listening to their needs so that we might better look after our people.'

He noticed the sudden panicked look in Sera's eyes as she sought out his mother's, and wondered absently what her problem was. There was no way his mother would send *her* to accompany him; she knew only too well what his feelings would be at the suggestion. And there was no way he would take her if she did. In fact, instead of looking panicked she should look relieved. With him out in the desert for a couple of days and no chance of running into each other, without the constant resurfacing of memories best left forgotten, she should be relieved. He knew he was.

'Who did you have in mind?'

His mother gestured to a woman sitting patiently in one corner amongst the drapes that lined the walls. 'Amira can accompany you.'

She was older than his mother, with deep lines marking the passage of time in her cheeks, and her spine curved when she stood, but it was the expression of another woman that snared his attention. Sera looked as if she'd just escaped a fate worse than death.

It rankled. He had no wish to spend time with her, but did her relief have to be so palpable? Anyone would think she regarded the prospect of two days in his company with even more revulsion than he did. How could that be possible? It wasn't as if he was the one who had betrayed her. What was she so afraid of—unless she feared that he might somehow try to exact his revenge?

Revenge?

His mother was talking, saying something to Amira, but he wasn't listening. He was too busy thinking. Too busy making his own plans. He looked across at the figure in black, hunched and cowed, her eyes looking everywhere but at him, no doubt wanting nothing more but that he might disappear into the desert with Amira to accompany him.

Did she really find the idea of being with him more appalling than he found the prospect of being with her? The gears of his mind crunched in unfamiliar ways, dredging up memories in their cogs, reassembling them into a different pattern, different possibilities.

Maybe there was something here he could turn to his advantage after all.

She'd never paid for what she'd done. She'd never so much as been called to account. She'd simply turned her back on him and walked away.

Why shouldn't he take advantage of this opportunity to even things up?

'I thank Amira,' he said, turning back to his mother and smiling at the older woman. 'But it is an arduous journey into the mountains that will by necessity be rushed and uncomfortable. I would hate to subject Amira to that. Perhaps I might suggest another idea—someone younger perhaps?'

It was the turn of the older woman to look relieved, while the hunched form alongside his mother tensed, the colour draining from her features. He allowed himself a smile. This might be even more satisfying than he'd imagined.

'Sera can accompany me.'

His mother's eyes turned to him in surprise, but it was nothing compared to the look he saw on Sera's upturned face. Disbelief combined with sheer horror, her black eyes brimming with fear.

An expression he would treasure for ever.

CHAPTER THREE

HE COULD not be serious! 'Please, no,' she pleaded of the Sheikha, who must see the moisture clinging to her lashes, who must know how impossible was the thing he was asking. 'Sheikha, please…'

But, while the Sheikha looked troubled, and squeezed her hand, it was to Rafiq she turned—Rafiq, who looked as if he was about to declare war. 'You are my son,' she said, 'and a Qusani prince. You know I can deny you nothing. But are you sure about this?'

'I have never been more sure in my life.'

'But, Sheikha, please…'

'Sera,' she said with a sigh, patting the younger woman's hands where they lay twisted and knotted in her lap, 'it will be fine. My son is nothing if not a gentleman. You have nothing to be concerned about. Has she, Rafiq?'

And through the screen of her lashes she saw Rafiq smile, the slow, lazy smile of a jungle cat sizing up its next meal. It was a miracle, she thought, that he managed not to lick his lips. She shivered as a chill descended her spine.

'Of course, not. Nothing to worry about at all,' he said, in a steady, measured voice that terrified her all the more for its calm, yet deadly intent.

Nothing to worry about? Then why had she never been more afraid in her life?

* * *

The two four-wheel drives were packed, loaded with water and supplies in case of breakdowns while crossing the vast desert sands on their way to the mountains, and their drivers were waiting. Already a truck had been sent out to make camp where the desert met the sea, where Akmal had recommended they stop for the night before attempting the steep ascent up into the mountains.

Rafiq just shook his head. It almost seemed like overkill, to pack so much for no more than a two-day trip, but he knew from experience that the desert was an unpredictable mistress, fickle and capricious, and as lethal as she was beautiful. Still, he had no plans to prolong this trip, and with any luck the camp would not be necessary. He intended to get there and back as quickly as possible.

Sera hung back, clinging close to where his mother stood in the shade of the porticoed entrance, her eyes, when he did managed to catch sight of them, troubled and pained.

Finally Akmal was satisfied that the last of the provisions had been properly stowed, the engines idling to power the air-conditioning units that would cool the interiors and make the arduous journey through the desert bearable. He bowed his head in Rafiq's direction. 'All is in readiness, Your Highness. Whenever you are ready?'

'Thank you, Akmal.'

'Safe journey, my son,' said his mother, meeting him halfway as he leaned down to kiss her age-softened cheek. 'Take care of Sera.'

'Of course,' he promised. 'I intend to do just that.'

And then he smiled and accepted her blessing, before making for the first car to talk to the driver.

He pulled open the passenger door and saw in the rear-vision mirror his mother holding Sera's hands, their heads close together as his mother uttered a few last words to her. Was she once again guaranteeing her son's good behaviour? Promising Sera that her virtue was safe with him? She needn't bother. Knowing she was uncomfortable in his presence was all the sport he desired. He had no wish to touch her.

He would not give her the satisfaction.

There was a flash of black robes as he saw Sera dash for what she must have assumed was the relative safety of the second car. He allowed himself a smile as he finished what he wanted to say to the driver, before closing the door and raising his hand to his mother one last time before striding towards it himself.

Shock turned her black-as-night eyes wide as he slid into the seat alongside her. A moment later she turned both her face and body away, shrinking against the door as if she might will herself right through it, and his feeling of satisfaction deepened.

She was terrified of him.

Strange how that knowledge had altered his long-held vow. Ten years ago he'd never wanted to see her again. And ever since then he'd always believed that what she'd killed that day was better left buried, his memories of his time with her buried along with it. Being forced to share the same space with her for two days should have been the very last thing on his agenda. And yet seeing her squirm and cower in his presence…oh, yes, this way was infinitely more satisfying than he could have ever imagined.

He took advantage of the space she left, angling himself to stretch out his legs in the space between them, and even though she didn't look, didn't turn, he knew she was aware of every move he made, knew it in the way she shrank herself into an even smaller space.

Oh, yes, infinitely more satisfying.

Why did he have to travel in this car if he needed so much legroom? Sera battled to control her breathing, willing away the tears that pricked at her eyes even as she wedged herself harder against the very edge of the wide seat, squeezed tight against the door, too hot and much too bothered by this man who seemed to think he owned the entire world, if not the entire vehicle. Maybe he did—he was part of Qusay's royal family now—but that didn't change the fact he was going out of his way to make her feel uncomfortable.

But why?

He hated her. He'd said as much to his mother, practically shouted it. He might as well have announced it to the world.

And he knew she'd heard him.

Didn't he think it was enough, just knowing it? Did he think he had to prove it by insisting she come with him, just so he could keep showing her how little he thought of her? Did he have to make her feel any worse than she already did?

Did he hate her that much?

Agony welled up inside her like a mushroom cloud, a familiar pain that tore at her heart and threatened to shred her sanity. But why shouldn't he hate her? Why should Rafiq be any different?

How many times had she been told that she was the one at fault? How many times had she been told that she was worth nothing? That she deserved nothing?

And now Hussein was gone, and still she was hated.

But how could she expect anything else?

And, in Rafiq's case, it was surely no more than she deserved.

'Maybe it's a chance to put the past behind you,' his mother had said when Sera had pleaded one last time to be allowed to stay behind. *'A chance to heal.'* She loved the Sheikha, who had taken her in when she'd had nowhere else to go. She loved her warmth and her wisdom, and the stories she'd shared of her own imperfect marriage. The Sheikha understood, even though what was left of her own family had believed the lies whispered by

her mother-in-law and abandoned her to her fate. Sera trusted her. And yet the past was behind her—long gone. What was the point of dredging it all up? What was the point of reliving the pain? Rafiq hated her. He would always hate her. And who could blame him?

She sucked in a breath, wishing she could concentrate on the passing streetscape as the small convoy left the palace precincts and headed past flat-topped buildings and narrow market streets towards the outskirts of the city, willing her eyes to find something to snag her attention—but it was the reflection in the window that held her captive, the long legs encased in cool-looking linen trousers, the torso wrapped in a snowy white T-shirt that hugged his body where the sides of his jacket fell apart…

She watched him in the window, his long legs sprawled out, his lean body so apparently at ease, and she grew even hotter and tenser as she huddled under her robes.

Curse the man that he hadn't grown old and fat in the intervening years!

She leaned her head against the window and squeezed her eyes closed, trying to concentrate on the warmth of the glass against her cheek and shut out the image of the long, lean body beside her, trying to think of anything but—and still she could see him clearly in her mind's eye. But when would she ever *not* be able to picture him clearly?

Eleven years ago he'd been the best-looking man in Qusay, with his dark-as-night hair and startling blue eyes. Strong-jawed and golden-skinned, he'd won her adolescent heart the moment she'd first set eyes on him. If she could have imagined her perfect man, it would have been Rafiq. Long, muscled legs, broad shoulders, and a chest that had been like a magnet for her innocent hands.

She would glide them around him, and he'd wrap her in his

arms and tell her that she was the most beautiful woman in the world and that he would love her for ever…

Pain sliced through her, deep and savage, old wounds ripping open so jaggedly that she had to bury her face in her hands and cover her mouth to stop herself from crying out. What was the point of bringing it all back? It was so long ago, and times had changed.

Except Rafiq hadn't. He was magnificent. A man in his prime. *A man who hated her.*

'Is something wrong?'

His voice tangled with her thoughts, and she opened her eyes to see that they had left the city behind. Only the occasional home or business lined the bitumen highway out of the city, the landscape giving way to desert as they headed inland.

Two days she must spend in his company, and he had to ask if something was wrong? What did he think? 'I'm fine,' she answered softly. There was no point saying what she really thought or what she really felt. She'd learned that lesson the hard way.

'You don't look fine.'

She bit her lip, refusing to face him, gathering her robes a little tighter around herself, resenting the fact he wouldn't just let her be. It was true she would feel better if he wasn't right there next to her, brooding and magnificent at the same time. And she would feel much better if the air didn't carry the faint hint of his cologne, seductive and evocative. But right now she was stuck with both, and there wasn't one thing she could do about it but survive. And if there was one thing Hussein had taught her to be good at, it was survival.

'I am sorry to offend.' She folded her hands in her lap and sat up straighter against the leather upholstery, watching the desert speed by.

What had happened to her? This was not the Sera he knew.

Or had she always been destined to turn into this bland, cowering shadow of a woman? Had her character been flawed from the very beginning and he'd been lucky to escape from her clutches when he had? Would he now be regretting it if she hadn't found a higher-ranking, more wealthy target to get her claws into? Wouldn't that be ironic? He was a prince now. What would that have meant to a woman who had married for wealth and prestige? Maybe there was another reason for her to look so sullen—mourning the big fish she had inadvertently thrown back and that had got away.

He sat back in his seat, the Arabic music the driver had found on the radio weaving patterns through his mind, giving birth to yet another unsatisfactory line of thought.

For, whatever troubled her, and however her mind worked, she was closing him out again, fleeing from him in mind and spirit as surely as she had fled from him in the stone passageway. Was this her tactic, then, to stay silent in the hopes he would leave her alone?

Not a chance.

He hadn't dragged her out here simply so she could cower in a corner and pretend he wasn't here.

'How long have you been with my mother?'

He caught her sigh, felt her resignation and more than a hint of resentment that she would not be able to avoid answering his questions, and was simultaneously delighted that his tactic was working and annoyed at her reaction. Was it such a chore for her to be with him? Such an imposition? Once upon a time she would have turned and smiled with delight at the sound of his voice. She would have slid her slender hands up his chest and hooked them around his neck and laughed as he spun her slim body around, laughed until he silenced her laughter with his kisses.

Once upon a time?

Since when did nightmares start with 'once upon a time'?

'How long?' he demanded, when she took too long to answer.

Tentatively she turned her head towards him, her gaze still hovering somewhere around his knees. 'A year. Maybe a little longer.'

'I didn't see you at Xavian's—*Zafir's*—wedding. But you must have been in the palace then.'

'I chose not to go.'

'Because I was there?'

Her eyes flicked up to his. Skittered away again just as quickly.

'Partly. But my h… Hussein's family were also in attendance. And some of his associates. It was wiser for me to keep my distance.'

He wondered why she had hesitated over calling him her husband. But if he was honest he was more annoyed that it wasn't his presence that had kept her away. 'You don't get on with them?'

She seemed to consider his question for a while, sadness welling in her eyes. 'It is easier for all concerned if I remain in the background.'

He took it as confirmation. 'And so my mother took you in.'

She nodded, the long dark curve of her lashes fluttering down. She was all about long lines, he realised. Always had been. Still was. The long sweep of her lashes, the smooth line of her high cheekbones and the sweeping curve to her jaw, the generous symmetry of her lips.

And maybe for now the rest of her was hidden under her voluminous robe, but he remembered how she looked. How she felt under his hands and the way she moved. Though the robe covered her completely, he knew she was little changed from those days.

His head rocked back, his hands raking through his hair as he was overcome by the sheer power of the memories of the past.

She could have been his. She *should* have been. She had

already been part of him, as much a part of him as breathing, and he could have had her—all of her. Oh, God, and he'd been tempted…so tempted. And in the end only the vow he'd made had held him back.

Because she'd been so perfect. And he'd wanted everything to be right for her. He'd wanted everything to be as perfect as she was. And for that reason he had not touched her that way. Not until their wedding night, when they could be united for ever. Legally and morally.

Body and soul.

A wedding night he had wanted and planned and longed for with all his heart. A wedding night they had never had.

Because she'd given herself to someone else first.

God, what kind of madness had made him think he was ready to face again the woman who'd done that to him?

He brought his head back down on an exhale, opened his eyes and saw her watching him, her dark eyes so filled with concern that his fingers stalled in his hair. *Damn it, he didn't want her sympathy!* He let his hands drop into his lap.

Her eyes followed the movement, a frown marring her perfect brow. 'Are you all right?'

And it took him a breath or two until he was sure he was back in control, until he'd clamped down on the memories of heated kisses and shared laughter, of silken skin and promises of for ever that had come surging back in such a tidal force of emotion, the feelings that had lain buried for so long under a concrete-thick layer of hatred.

'Jetlag,' he lied, his voice coarse and thick, and designed to close off all conversation as he turned away to stare unseeingly out of his window.

CHAPTER FOUR

Two hours out of Shafar the cars turned off the highway, heading along a sandy track through the desert. They would meet up with the narrow coast road much further on, where the track met the coastline, and where their camp should be ready for them if they needed to stop.

The going was tougher here, and the cars ground their way over the uneven and sometimes deeply rutted track, their passengers bouncing upon the upholstery as the car jolted them around. Far ahead they could just make out the smudge on the horizon that marked the beginning of the red mountains, where they were headed—a smudge that slowly grew until their jagged peaks rose high in the windscreen as they made progress over the bumpy and desolate terrain.

They stopped further on for a break at a welcome oasis, the cars pulling under the shade of a stand of date palms, the passengers more than ready to rest their jolted bones. A short break now and they would still make Marrash tonight, leaving enough time tomorrow for the necessary inspections and at least the preliminary negotiations. If all went well they would be back in Shafar no later than tomorrow evening.

Sera climbed from the car, happy to stretch her legs, but even happier to escape the hothouse atmosphere in the back seat for a few minutes. Her temples and neck promised the onset of a tension headache. Even the fiery ball of the sun and the super-heated air was some kind of relief. She knew it would only be a matter of time before he'd find another angle of attack, another means to criticise her and find fault, but for now she'd had enough of the brooding silence and the constant anticipation of yet another volley.

The drivers were busy pulling things from the backs of the vehicles, organising refreshments and checking the vehicles, their conversation like music on the air. Rafiq was there too, she noticed, wanting to help even over their protests that they should be serving him.

She walked towards the inviting pool, breathing a sigh of relief, certain he wouldn't listen—not if it meant the alternative was spending more time with her. Which meant that at least for a few blessed minutes she had some space to herself.

The oasis was small, no more than a scattering of assorted palms clustered around a bubbling spring that spilled into a wide pool, with an ancient stone shelter to protect travellers caught in the sandstorms that rolled from time to time over the desert that surrounded them on all sides. A tiny slice of life in the midst of nothingness. And there *was* life. Tiny birds darted from bush to bush, and brightly coloured butterflies looked like flowers against the dark green foliage. Immediately Sera felt more relaxed, felt the peace of the oasis infuse her veins.

Rafiq had sat like a thundercloud beside her, silent and threatening, ever since that moment in the car. Sera had recognised the change—as if something unseen had shifted in the space between them, as if he too was remembering a time that both of them would rather forget. Whatever it was, Rafiq hadn't welcomed it. She'd witnessed the turmoil that had turned his cool eyes to the troubled blue of a stormy sky; she'd felt the torment she'd seen there as if it were her own. She'd recognised it.

The water in the pool beckoned, crystal-clear and inviting. She knelt down in the long reedy grass at the water's edge, trailing her fingers through the refreshingly clear water, pouring some over her wrists to cool herself down, patting some to her throbbing temples. She sighed with relief.

It was too much to expect that it would last—they couldn't stop long—but right now, it was bliss.

A plume of sand rising from the desert drew Rafiq's attention. He shaded his eyes from the sun and peered into the distance, where the mountains now loomed in jagged red peaks. The billowing sand drew closer. It was too early to hear the car, but no doubt they would soon have company.

He swung his eyes around, to the place he'd been studiously avoiding up till now, to the place where Sera sat serenely at the water's edge, eyes closed, her face turned up towards the sky in profile, her features for once at peace. Without thinking his feet took him a step closer. She'd loosened the scarf around her head and her glossy black hair flowed down her back, shining blue in the same dappled light that moved shadows across her satin skin and showed off the silken curve of her throat.

And something shifted deep inside him. She was still so beautiful. Dark lashes kissed her cheeks, and the curtain of black hair hung in a silken stream over her shoulders and beyond, and her generous mouth held the promise of a kiss. In the dry heat, his blood started fizzing. Eleven years after she'd married someone else, he still thought her the most beautiful woman he'd ever seen.

And under the robe? Would she still be as perfect as he remembered? Would she still feel as satin-skinned in his hands? Would she still melt into his touch as if she was part of him?

He took another step closer before he heard the car, before the sound filtered into his brain and he realised what he was doing. He looked back at the source of his confusion. What the hell was wrong with him? The sun must be getting to him.

But Sera had heard the sound too, her head swinging around, but her dark eyes' mission forgotten when they found him watching her. She swallowed. He followed the upward movement of her chin, followed the movement in her throat, knew the instant she'd taken her next breath.

Even across the space between them he was aware of every tiny movement, every minute change in her eyes, in the flare of her nostrils. And as he watched her, and as she watched him, the dry air crackled between them like fireworks.

Until above it all he heard voices and the sounds of an engine, brakes squealing in protest, and he spun away, his mind and his senses in disarray.

It was a relief to see that some things still made sense. A four-wheel drive had pulled up at the oasis in a cloud of sand. A distraction. Thank God.

The driver emerged, cursing and gesticulating wildly, while a woman climbed wearily out of the other side, reaching into the passenger seat behind and removing first two dark-haired toddlers and then a tiny baby from their seats in the back. She herded the small children before her towards the pond, her voice a slice of calm over motherly panic as she clutched the baby, even as the man opened the hood and let loose with a new string of invective.

Steam poured up from the engine. The man flapped his hands uselessly, then clutched at the side of his white robe with one hand and simultaneously reached for the radiator cap.

It was Rafiq who stopped him, Sera saw. Rafiq who was there first, stopping his hand, urging him to wait. Their drivers followed, reiterating his advice, and she looked back as the woman neared, her toddlers stumbling before her, the crying baby clutched tight in her arms.

'Be careful!' the mother called out, following as fast as she could. 'Stop before you reach the water.'

Sera was only too happy to assist, stretching out her arms to form a barrier that the twin girls collapsed into at the last moment, laughing and shrieking, thinking it was a game. The mother breathed a sigh and thanked her, before settling with her brood at the water's edge, taking the time to make the traditional greetings even as she settled her baby to feed now that she knew her other children were safe.

Sera smiled, her spirits lifting at meeting Aamina and her children. A visitor was a welcome distraction—especially a young mother with such a young and energetic family. The woman had a beautiful round face, and a generous smile that persisted patiently, even when the children got too excited and jostled the feeding infant impatiently in her arms. Only the shadows under her eyes betrayed how much she yearned for sleep. Sera was plagued with shadows under her eyes too, she knew, but she could only wish they were for the same reason. But this woman was so young, and yet already with three children...

That could have been her, she thought, in a sudden and selfish moment of madness that had no place or no relevance in her real world, and yet which still refused to give way to sanity.

That could have been her if she'd followed her heart and not her head.

If she'd ignored her family's demands and the threats made against them.

That could have been her if she'd married Rafiq.

Sera clamped down on the unwelcome thoughts. Because that was all in the past, and marrying Rafiq had never been an option, not really, no matter how much she had wanted it, and she couldn't blame her family alone.

It was pointless even thinking about it, no matter how much Rafiq's return to Qusay had made her wonder how things might have been if she'd made a different decision all those years ago.

Instead she tried to focus on the young woman's story, and

why she was here now, travelling across the desert with such a tiny infant. It was not ideal, the woman acknowledged, but necessary, as her husband's mother was seriously ill in hospital in Shafar, and they had promised to take their new baby, named Maisha in her honour, to meet her. But her husband was impatient, and had been pushing their aging vehicle too hard. It was lucky they had made it as far as the oasis before the radiator had blown completely.

The toddlers, no more than eighteen months old, had been content to wait at their mother's side while she fed the baby, but now demanded more of their mother's attention. They wanted to paddle in the shallows, and they wanted their mother to take them. Both of them.

Their mother looked lost, though the babe at her breast had thankfully finished feeding and was now sleeping, and Sera could see the woman was trying to work out how to juggle them all.

'Mama, plee-ease,' the toddlers insisted, and their mother looked more conflicted than ever.

'I could hold the baby,' Sera suggested, 'if it might help?'

And the mother looked at her briefly, taking less than a second to decide whether to entrust this stranger with her tiny baby before making up her mind. She smiled, propping the baby up on her shoulder and patting its back. 'Bless you,' she said.

The baby joined in with a loud burp that set the girls off with a fresh round of giggles. The girls' laughter was infectious, and Sera found herself joining in the glee before the mother passed the baby over to her waiting arms. The infant squirmed as it settled into the crook of her arm, nestled into her lap, while the mother swooped her robe over one arm and kicked off her sandals, her own smile broadening. She held a twin's hand securely in each of her own, and the trio ventured gingerly into the water, the girls shrieking with delight as they splashed in the shallows.

In her arms the baby stirred and sighed a sigh, blowing milky bubbles before settling down into sleep, one little arm raised, the hand curled into a tiny fist. So tiny. So perfect. Sera touched the pad of one finger to its downy cheek. So soft.

She smiled in spite of the sadness that shrouded her own heart—sadness for the missed opportunities, the children she'd never borne and maybe now never would, and ran her fingers over the baby's already thick black hair, drinking in the child's perfect features, the sooty lashes resting on her cheeks, the tiny nose, the delicate cupid's bow mouth squeezed amidst the plump cheeks.

So utterly defenceless. So innocent. And then her mind made sense of it all. Maybe it was better that she'd never had children. After all, she'd proved incapable of even taking care of her own tiny kittens.

The children laughed and splashed and squealed in the shallows, and the baby slept on, safe in Sera's arms.

When one of the drivers laid out a blanket with refreshments for them, and the children whooped and fell on the picnic, their hunger now paramount, Sera told the mother to look after the girls first. Once again the mother smiled her thanks as she helped her hungry toddlers feast.

Not long after, with the radiator cooled and refilled, their car was pronounced fit to go and the mother thanked Sera as she scooped her sleeping infant back into her arms. 'But you haven't had anything to eat yourself yet,' she protested, as the remains of their quick repast were already being cleared away.

'It doesn't matter,' Sera replied honestly, for the woman had given her a greater gift—the feel of a newborn in her arms and the sweet scent of baby breath.

Although that gift had come with a cost, she realised, as she waved the mother and her children goodbye, smiling as she wished them well in spite of the tears in her eyes. She'd almost forgotten in the past few years how much she'd wanted children. She'd almost come to terms with the fact she might never have them.

And right now that reawakened pain was almost more than she could bear.

She turned and walked slowly towards the pool again, the sadness squeezing her heart until she was sure it would bleed tears.

She sniffed down on her disappointment, willing it back into the box where she'd kept it locked away until now. They would be resuming their journey shortly; the drivers were already making their final checks of the vehicles and re-stowing their gear. Rafiq had thankfully kept his distance while the woman and her children were here, but soon she would have to put up with his thundercloud-dark presence again. She needed to get herself under control before then.

Rafiq looked at the map one more time, trying to focus, trying to assimilate what the father of the small family, a local, had informed them—that the mountain track up to Marrash had suffered in recent landslips and that progress could be slower than they expected.

It was news Rafiq hadn't wanted to hear, for it meant that there was a chance they mightn't make Marrash tonight. The local man had advised that it would be madness to try to negotiate the treacherous mountain road in the dark. Both drivers had agreed, suggesting that perhaps they should make use of the camp at the coast. The truck that had set out earlier would have prepared for their arrival, and the camp was even now being readied for them.

But he didn't want this trip taking any longer than one night, and if they stopped tonight and negotiations in Marrash took too much time they might well have to spend a second night at the camp, so he'd argued that if they cut their break short and pressed on now they could still be in Marrash by nightfall.

He didn't want to run the risk of having to spend two nights away from the palace.

And it wasn't only because he had to get back for the state banquet being held in Kareef's honour.

He gave up pretending to study the map and looked over to the pool, where the real source of his irritation sat at the edge, gazing fixedly at…

He tried to follow her line of sight, but there was nothing but sand beyond the fringe of trees and nothing to see.

He'd thought this trip would be so easy, that he would be the one irritating her, but her presence was akin to the rub of sandpaper against flesh, the continual abrasion stinging and ferocious on flesh raw and weeping, and he wondered about the sanity of making this journey at all. Would not his business survive without his hunting down a fabric made by some village high up in the mountains? And it could still be a wild goose chase. He didn't even know at this stage if he was all that interested.

It was bad enough that he would be forced to spend the next twenty-four hours with her. The last thing he needed was to spend more because of the parlous state of the roads. He would speak to Kareef about those. For all Qusay's wealth from its emerald mines, and the wide highways leading out of the city, there remained plenty of places where money could be used. The roads in this part of the desert were definitely one of them.

He growled his irritation and looked back at the map. Just as quickly he looked back again, frowning this time. For she looked sad again, her expression hauntingly beautiful, but sad all the same.

He'd seen her smile when she'd been holding the child, and he'd even heard her laughing—or had he just imagined that? But she'd definitely smiled. He had seen her face light up, filled with love as she had rocked the sleeping baby in her arms.

It had been hard to look away then, because for a moment,

just a moment, he had seen the face of the girl he had fallen
in love with.

'She is not the girl you once knew.'

Like a blow to the body, his mother's words came back to
him in a rush.

No, she was not the girl he'd known before. She was a
widow now.

Hussein's widow.

Impatiently he tossed the map aside. Regardless of the
advice from their visitor, they would have to get going. He was
determined to make Marrash this evening.

She started as he drew close, her eyes widening in surprise
as he approached, before her head dipped, her gaze once again
going to the ground. 'Is it time?'

Her voice was serenity itself, and he knew the shutters were
back, slammed ever so meekly and serenely, but nevertheless
slammed effectively in his face. What would it take to shake
her up? What would it take to shake her out of that comfort zone
she retreated to every time he so much as looked at her?

'I always thought you wanted a big family—six children at
least.'

There was a rapid intake of breath, a pause, and he wondered
if she was remembering that very same day, when they'd raced
their horses along the beach, hot rushing air accompanied by
the splash of foam and the flick of sand, their mounts neck and
neck along the long sweep of coast. And finally, with both
horses and riders panting, they'd collapsed from their mounts'
backs onto the warm sand and shared their dreams for their
future together. *'A big family,'* she'd said, laughing, her black
hair rippling against the arm her head had nestled against. *'Two
boys and two girls, and then maybe one or two more, because
four will surely not be enough to love.'*

And he'd pretended to be horrified. *'So many children to*

provide for! So many children to love. Who will have time to love me?'

And she'd leaned over him and brushed a lock of hair from his brow, her hand resting on his cheek. *'I will always love you.'*

He still remembered the kiss that had followed, the feel of his heart swelling in his chest with so much joy that there had been no room left in his lungs for air. But he hadn't needed air then—not with her love to sustain him.

More fool him.

'Maybe,' the woman before him finally admitted, dragging him back to the present. 'Maybe once.'

'And yet you never had children of your own.'

Her hands wrung together, her bowed head moving from side to side, agitated, as if his line of questioning was too uncomfortable, as if looking for a means of escape. He wasn't about to provide it, not when he needed so many answers himself.

'Why not?'

Now the movement of her head turned into a shake. One hand lifted to her forehead to quell it, and her voice, when it came, was nowhere near as steady as she would no doubt wish. 'It… It didn't happen.'

'Didn't Hussein want children?'

Her agitation increased; her eyes were raised now, and appealing for him to desist. 'Why does it matter to you? Why can't you accept it? It just didn't happen!'

'What a waste,' he said, not prepared to give up yet—not when there were so many unanswered questions and when she looked so uncomfortable. 'Because I saw you with that baby.' She looked up at him, her eyes wide, suddenly vulnerable, as if wondering at this change of tone. 'You looked good with it. I always thought you would make the perfect mother.'

Her mouth opened on a cry, and she snapped it shut, turning

her head away, but not quickly enough that he could miss the moisture springing onto her lashes.

'Did you love him?' Anger surged in his veins like a flood tide. Was that why she was crying? Because she'd wanted her husband's children so desperately and she would forever mourn not having them? It pained him to ask, but he was here with her now, and somehow it was more important than ever that he know the truth. 'Did you love Hussein?'

She squeezed her eyes together, and then near exploded with her answer. 'He was my *husband*!'

Her words sparked a short-circuit in his brain. 'Tell me something I don't know!' he said, snapping back with equal ferocity, his voice as raw as his emotions. 'I was there—remember? One year in the desert I had to endure, to learn the skills to be a man, but one month in and all I learned was that I couldn't survive without you, that I needed to be with you. But you couldn't wait one year. In fact, you couldn't even wait four short weeks!'

She dropped her face into her hands. 'Rafiq, please—'

'And I found my would-be bride, all dressed up in her wedding finery, the most beautiful bride I could ever imagine, and for a moment—just one short, pathetic moment—I thought that you had somehow known I was returning. And that this was to be the day we would be bound together as man and wife for ever.' He looked down at her, his fury rising, seeing only the vision of her back at the palace, a gown of spun gold clinging to her slim form, row after row of gold chains around her neck, her dark kohl-rimmed eyes wide with shock as he appeared in the doorway, the cry rent from his lungs, the cry of a beast in agony. 'But it was not to be our day, was it? Not when you were standing at the altar ready to marry another man!'

'Rafiq,' she said softly, and he recognised her trying to

reason with him when he knew there was no reason. 'It wasn't supposed to happen that way. But… But I had no choice.'

'You had a choice! You chose Hussein. You chose life as a wealthy ambassador's wife over life with me.'

'Please, that's not true. You knew my father had promised me to him. You knew it could happen.'

'While I was away? Yes, there was talk of an arrangement. But you saw me leave for the desert for a year. You let me go. You kissed me goodbye, promised that you would be waiting for me on my return and that we would overcome our families' objections. I thought you would be strong enough to wait that long. But you were too much of a coward. I had no sooner disappeared from sight before you formalised the arrangements to marry Hussein behind my back.'

'It wasn't like that!'

'No? Then what *was* it like?'

She raised her face to the sky and shook her head from side to side. 'What did you expect me to do? I had seen what happened after my best friend Jasmine returned from the desert, close to death, because she and your brother had chosen to defy their parents' wishes for their future.'

She paused, remembering Rafiq's father and how he had laughed at her when she had protested at marrying Hussein, pleading that she had promised to marry Rafiq. *'I will choose my sons' brides,'* he had decreed. *'Look at the mess Kareef has made of his life. That will not be allowed to happen to Rafiq.'* She swallowed back on the memories. How could Rafiq pretend not to understand?

'How could I do the same to my family—*to yours!*—after that? How could I shame them that way when I had seen what it had cost everyone?'

He brushed her words aside. 'You told me you loved me!'

'I know, but—'

'Which is why you married Hussein when I had been gone less than a month. *Because you loved me!* What a total fool you made of me.'

'Rafiq, please, you must listen…'

'Do you know how I felt standing there? Do you have any idea what it was like to have everyone's eyes upon me, to have your father and Hussein openly sneering in victory, others filled with pity, feeling sorry for me, poor Rafiq, the last one to know what everyone else had known all along. That you never had any intention of marrying me.'

She shook her head. 'I didn't mean—'

'But even that wasn't enough for you, was it? Because, not content with simply humiliating me in front of the entire palace, you then had to grind my love into the dirt!'

She shook her head again, one hand at her brow, the other over her mouth, and he wanted to growl and shake her. If there was a prize for affectation, a prize for acting melodramatic, *pretending that she cared*, she would win it hands-down. 'I didn't want to hurt you.'

He snorted his disbelief. 'Like hell! You delighted in it. Because when I pleaded with you, when I begged you to halt the wedding, to tell me—to tell everyone—that it was me you loved and not Hussein, you looked me in the eye and told me and everyone else there that you had *never* loved me.' His chest heaved, his breath ragged and rasping, as if the muscle that was his heart was remembering that day and the pain that had torn through it, leaving it in tattered shreds. 'Tell me, then, that you didn't love Hussein.'

Silence met his demands, with only the sound of their laboured breathing filling the space between them, the low rumble of the idling engines coming from the vehicles nearby. Under the shade of the palms the drivers squatted, waiting, sipping coffee and keeping their distance, knowing their business was not to interfere, even though they could certainly hear their raised voices, and even though Rafiq himself had pressed upon them the urgency of moving on.

'Oh, Rafiq,' she whispered, reaching out a tentative hand to him, a hand that wavered in the air before it dared land on his skin.

He scowled at it as he might regard some annoying insect, ready to slap it away.

'Rafiq. I...I'm so sorry.'

She was sorry? She had done all that she had done and all she could find to say to him was that she was sorry? She had humiliated him, stomped all over his teenaged hopes and dreams, thrown his life into total disarray, and she was *sorry*?

Blood pounded in his veins, crashed loud in his ears, and when he closed his eyes it was blood-red that he saw behind his lids. 'You're sorry? What exactly are you sorry for? That you lost your rich husband, your entrée to the party capitals of the world? Or that you married him and missed out on landing an even bigger fish? You could have been sister-in-law to the King if you'd waited like you'd promised and married me. How would that have been? All that prestige. All that pomp and ceremony to lap up.

'Except back then you didn't know my brother was going to be King, did you? So you chose someone older, someone rich. You chose Hussein and a guaranteed good life. The high life. Well, I hope you're enjoying life, Sera, because I sure am. The last thing I needed was someone like you, no better than a gold-digger in search of a dynastic marriage. If Hussein were still alive I'd shake his hand right now. He saved me from a fate worse than death. Marriage to you.'

'No! Rafiq, don't say that!' Her face was crumpled now, liquid flowing freely from her eyes, coursing down her cheeks, her hands useless at stemming the tide. 'It wasn't like that. I...I loved you.'

His fist smashed through the air, collided with his open palm with a crash. 'It was *exactly* like that! You wanted a rich husband. You got one. It was just bad luck for you that you picked the wrong one. And as for your so-called love, it proved to be as worthless as you.'

She heard a sound, a garbled cry, misery mixed with anguish, grief rent with despair, before realising it had emerged unbidden from the depths of her own agonising hopelessness.

He hated her. She knew he did. And she knew she deserved it. But she had not realised how deeply his hatred went, nor how much pain she had caused him.

In letting him go, in thinking she was setting him free by doing what she had, she might just as well have chained him to her betrayal.

But why could he not see that she was hurting as well? How could he have believed for a moment, let alone all these years, that she had never loved him? So she'd tried to be convincing in her rejection of him—she'd had to be—but didn't he know her better than that? Couldn't he see the lie she'd lived all these years?

Tears stung her eyes. She heard her name called behind her, but her feet kept pounding across the hot sands. She could not stay. Not like this. Not with him. Only apart could their wounds ever heal. Only apart was there a chance she might forget.

She was behind the wheel of one of the cars before anyone could stop her. The doors locked as she clutched hold of the steering wheel, feeling sick to her stomach as she looked down at the dashboard and its assortment of dials and gauges. Escape was suddenly more complicated, and she cursed Hussein for not letting her learn to drive. She'd had only two lessons before he'd discovered her secret. She squeezed her eyes shut, wishing as she'd wished a thousand times before that he'd had her beaten, instead of an innocent man, wishing that he'd hurt her rather than an innocent kitten. But hurting her had never been Hussein's way. Not physically, anyway.

Rafiq was shouting something, and she looked around through the haze of her tears to see him close, perilously close, the two drivers running behind, their arms flapping as uselessly as their white robes. Two driving lessons would have to be enough. She'd learned the basics in those. Start. Go. Stop. How difficult could it be?

She threw the car into 'drive' and pressed her foot hard down on the accelerator. It moved like a slug, and she slammed her fist against the steering wheel. 'Come on,' she urged, and floored her foot again, this time remembering the handbrake at the last moment. She jerked it up, releasing it, and the car lurched forward. She spun the wheel, spraying sand behind her in an arc, and took off in the direction the family had disappeared. She would catch up with them, plead with them to let her return to Shafar with them. It was not as if she was going to keep the car. The family had only just gone. They couldn't be too far ahead.

The vehicle snaked down the rutted track, difficult to follow and worse so through the blur of tears. He thought she'd married Hussein because she'd wanted a trophy husband? How could he think that, even if she *had* betrayed him? He should never have been there. Eleven months longer in the desert and he would probably have been over her. He wouldn't have cared so much that she'd gone. A year in the desert and he'd probably have grown out of her, been relieved she was no longer an issue for him on his return.

A fresh flood of tears followed that thought, refusing to be staunched. He should never have come back early from the desert! He should have stayed away. Then he wouldn't have seen her. And then she wouldn't have been forced to lie to him. Forced to try and prove it…

She sniffed. She'd played her hand too well and convinced him with her words and her actions that she'd never loved him. And somehow that had been the cruellest blow of all. For hadn't he seen her family gather around her, as if she was more a prisoner than a bride? Hadn't he witnessed his own father in the audience, smirking as his plans to rid himself of another woman unworthy of being his daughter-in-law had gone even better than he had expected?

A wail erupted from her throat, chopped up into sobs as the car bounced over the rutted track.

And hadn't he seen the sickness on her face at the reception, when Hussein had made her touch him—there—while Rafiq was watching?

How could he not have seen that? And he'd believed her lies, believed what his eyes had told him, and now he hated her. Damn him!

The car bounced and bucked its way along the desert track, past a sign that was behind her before she could read it, the wheel jerking out of her hands at times, the tyres finding it hard to get traction on the sandy hill. She couldn't remember a hill, but surely they had passed this way earlier, hadn't they?

All she could see through the mists of her vision was sand and more sand, red and endless, and if there were tyre-tracks anywhere the wind had long since blown them away.

Where was the track? Surely it was here somewhere. She blinked the tears from her eyes. Surely she hadn't lost it? Fear gripped her, and she pushed her foot harder down on the accelerator, desperate to get to the top of the dune so that she might get her bearings. But there was no stopping at the top of the rise. The tyres suddenly found purchase and the car roared up the slope, launching itself into space before crashing down on the other side in a crunch of springs and a grinding of metal. Pain blinded her as her head smashed against the door pillar, stunning her momentarily. The car was steering itself down the other side of the dune, half sliding, half careening, until the terrain thankfully flattened out, the car slowing as her foot slid from the accelerator.

Sera took a breath, blinked away her shock as she reclaimed control of the steering wheel. The side of her head throbbed where it had collided with the pillar, and she knew she'd have a headache later, but at least the shock had stopped the flow of tears and she could see where she was going. The dunes were lower here, with a wide, flat depression between. At last something was going right for her. This would definitely make for easier going until she regained the track.

She pressed down on the accelerator and the car surged over a last small dune. She was starting to relax, her racing heartbeat finally settling, when the car lurched, nose-first, its front wheels digging into the desert sands. She tried to power her way through, but the wheels spun uselessly, only digging themselves deeper. She battled with the gearstick, trying to coerce it into reverse gear, by chance happening on the button that allowed her to move it.

The tyres spun wildly in the other direction. Sera willed them to pull free of the clinging sands, and yet still the car refused to budge. If anything, it felt as if the car was burying itself still deeper.

Great. Her head sagged against her arms on the useless steering wheel and she felt despair welling up inside her once again. So much for escape. She was bogged down, stuck fast, up to her axles in sand in the middle of a desert, and she wasn't going anywhere until she dug herself out. *If* she could dig herself out. What a mess!

She pushed open her door to climb out and the car groaned and tilted, as if the weight of the open door had somehow pulled it over. It seemed to rock unsteadily for a moment then, for a moment in which she wondered if she'd imagined the movement, and whether the knock on the head was affecting her balance, and then she saw it—the almost imperceptible movement in the sand below her, the slip and suck as it embraced the car's tyres and drew the car even deeper, the slow vortex that made clear its deadly mission.

And a new and chilling horror unfurled in her gut.

CHAPTER FIVE

HE WAS as angry as hell, and it wasn't all directed at the woman behind the wheel in the car ahead. Sand showered his windscreen, making it even harder to work out which way she was going. Who the hell had taught her to drive? She was all over the place, making no allowances for the rough terrain, least of all with the accelerator. Anyone would think the hounds of hell were after her.

He'd like to have a few words with the person who'd taught her to drive. Most of all, though, he was looking forward to having a few choice words with her. What the hell was she thinking, taking a car and driving off into the desert like that? What did she think it would solve?

Nothing.

All he'd done was deliver a few home truths and, like the spoilt society princess she was, she'd bolted. So maybe the truth hurt. Well, he had news for her: he had a few more home truths to get off his chest before their time together was over. And if she'd thought him angry before, she hadn't seen *anything* yet. Once he got her to stop he'd show her just how bad his temper could get.

She had that car all over the place, the vehicle bouncing and sliding from side to side, but it was when she suddenly veered off the rutted path and took off across the desert sands that fury turned to fear. He jerked the wheel around to follow, the heel of his hand hard against the horn, trying to get her attention, trying to warn her. But there was no stopping her, just as there had been no reasoning with her. She kept right on going.

What the hell was she thinking? She'd roared past a warning sign as if it had been nothing. But he'd seen the map. He'd seen the warning not to leave the road, and he'd seen the hatched areas that signalled the danger zone.

Sinking sands.

The desert around here was full of them, their appearance indistinguishable from the surrounding desert, traps for unwary travellers or wayward beasts.

He'd learned that lesson the hard way. He'd seen one swallow an entire camel during his month in the desert—the doomed animal's neck and head flailing hopelessly, its limbs already stuck deep within the remorseless sucking sand, its eyes wide and desperate, its panicked bleats sounding more like screams. The unnatural sound was what had drawn him to the pit's edge, and the noise had continued while he fought to save the doomed animal. But there had been no saving it, and soon, despite his efforts, both the camel and the sound had been swallowed up, and the desert had fallen silent but for the howl of the empty wind.

Oh, God, he'd seen first-hand what those sands could do.

The car in front screamed up a dune, launching itself into the hot, thin air, disappearing at a crazy angle over the other side and sending his gut lurching. He wanted her to stop—but not because she'd rolled the car!

It seemed to take an eternity to get there, until he topped the dune and could breathe a sigh of relief. He was in luck. She'd stopped at last. Maybe she'd come to her senses. Or maybe…

His blood chilled as he drew closer and skidded to a halt,

sending a cloud of red sand into the air. There was a reason she'd stopped. Her tyres were buried deep in sand, the car stuck fast.

And then he saw her door swing open and the car tilt ever so slightly with it, shifting ever deeper to one side, and something curdled in his gut.

'Sera, no!' he yelled. 'Don't get out!'

She turned her head, her eyes wide, but it was surprise he read in them first and foremost, as if she thought it odd that he should be here. What did she think? That he would let a lone woman drive off into the desert by herself? She didn't know him at all if she thought that.

'Stay there. Close the door.'

She looked at him as if he was mad, and he could understand why. She no doubt wanted to get out of the car, not lock herself inside while the car worked its way into a sandy grave. There was no point trying to explain to a society princess and no time, but the last thing he wanted was for the car to slip sideways and make it even harder for her to climb out.

Besides, it was a car and not a flailing-limbed camel, too panicked and too stupid to know that fighting the wet sand was the worst thing it could do and would only hasten its demise. The car would sink slower if it didn't go down nose first, but not with the doors open.

Maybe Sera was just too afraid to argue, because she reached out, trying to pull the heavy door back. 'It won't budge,' she cried, and he cursed when he saw why.

Already the bottom corner of the door was dragging at the sucking sands. Soon the soft sand would pour through the open door, claiming the car for its own. 'Leave it,' he ordered, 'and get into the back.'

The car tilted further as she scrambled over the front seats. Meanwhile he moved cautiously closer, testing each step before giving it his full weight. 'Watch out!' he heard her call, as if he were the one stuck in the middle of a pit of sinking sand.

His foot found the edge of the pit, sinking into the soft, damp sand just a couple of feet short of the car's tailgate, but at least she hadn't landed the car any further in. He might have to congratulate her for that once they were out. Still, it would be a stretch, but he should be able to reach the tailgate. He made sure both his feet were on solid sand and then leaned over, letting himself fall the last few inches to the doors, wrenching the handle, fighting the angle of the sinking car to pull the back doors open.

'I'm sorry,' she cried, from where she sat huddled in the back seat. 'But I couldn't stay back there. I had to get away.'

The car slipped deeper then, tilting further, the metal groaning an unearthly groan, metal and rubber against the sucking forces of sand, and she winced, her fingers clutching the back seat like claws. The acid reply that he'd been so ready to let fly from his lips died a rapid death. 'Forget it,' he simply said, pulling stuff out of the back of the car and tossing it behind him, hoping it reached solid ground but more intent on making space right now for her to climb through. 'Just be ready to jump over when I tell you.' He found a folded tarpaulin and flapped it open with one hand, spreading it out on the soft ground below him as best he could. It wasn't much, but at least it would be some protection if anything they needed fell in his rush to clear space.

'I'm sorry about the car,' she babbled. 'I didn't know.'

'I said forget it!' He did a rapid assessment and decided he'd made enough space for her to climb through. 'Now, let's get you out of there. Are you ready?'

She nodded uncertainly and he leaned out of the way to give her more room. She hauled up her robe to clamber inelegantly over the tilted seat, revealing a long sweep of golden skin followed by another just as perfect, just as lean and smooth and long, distracting him when he least needed a distraction.

The car dipped sideways into the sand and his hold slipped with it. 'Rafiq!' Sera screamed, reaching for him as he fell, but he had landed on the tarpaulin, his weight spread, and was able to roll away and be on firm sand again before he could sink.

'Now, get ready,' he told her, relieved to see she had tucked the offending legs back under her robe, where they could not distract him again. 'Reach for my hand, and when I give the word, you jump. Got that?'

She nodded and dragged in a breath, as if steeling herself, her eyes a mixture of fear and apprehension.

He leaned out towards her and she balanced as best she could in the sloping doorway, reaching out her own hand to him. His fingers curled hungrily around her small hand even as the car pitched nose-down, with sand pouring into the front seat. Sera gasped, lifted higher with the back of the car, her fingers slipping from his as her arm stretched. But his grip only tightened. There was no way he was letting her go.

'Now!'

She sprang at his command, the same instant as he pulled on her hand, launching her across the distance with so much force that she collided against his chest. His arms immediately wrapped around her as he spun her away from the edge of the pit and to safety.

'What the hell were you thinking?' he yelled. 'What the hell were you playing at?'

And her response came not with words but as tremors. They started out as a shiver that set her body quaking in his arms. He looked down at her flustered face, at the black-as-night eyes that looked up at him, eyes wounded by the verbal attack that had come so close on the heels of her rescue, and he looked at the open mouth as she dragged in air, at those lips, so close to him now that their proximity must surely equate with possession.

Possession he had no choice but to take.

His mouth crashed down upon hers in a brutal kiss, a kiss that he tore from her, a kiss that spoke of dread and fear and loss, of agony and relief as his mouth plundered hers, his hands sliding up her slim back to bury themselves in that silken curtain of black hair and anchor her close to him. Remorseless and ruthless. Avenging himself for the wrongs of the past. Like a man dying of thirst, he drank deeply of that first heady stream. Unable to stop even when good sense dictated he should, even when he knew his life depended on restraint.

There was no restraint here.

Instead, all the things he felt, all the things he'd wanted to say to her in the past years, all the strain of the last few short hours—everything spilled out into that kiss as his mouth savaged hers while they stood amidst the sandy dunes under a scorching desert sun.

Until she flinched, and his hand in her hair came away sticky and damp.

Breathless and conflicted, searching for answers to questions he didn't understand and finding none, he pushed her away from him as abruptly as he'd pulled her into his kiss, his chest labouring, his senses shot as he tried to make sense of the discovery.

He looked down at his fingertips, felt something twisting and curling inside him. 'You're bleeding.'

Somehow Sera managed to keep upright, although her legs felt boneless, her senses in a shambles. He'd been angry with her, hadn't he? So angry after he'd pulled her out of the car. But then he'd kissed her—a kiss that had knocked her remaining breath clean out of her lungs and left her more confused than ever.

And all he could worry about was a bang on the head she'd forgotten completely in the thunderclap of a kiss that had blanked her mind, wiping clear the terror of her escape, the relief at being safe, the fact that he hated her.

He hated her. He'd told her so. He'd shown her in his words and his actions.

So why had he just kissed her?

'Your Highness!' The breathless cry came from the dunes behind and she turned her head to see one of the drivers, half jogging, half stumbling through the sand, his face red and sweat streaked from his exertions, his white robe sticking to him and stained with sand. The other followed a few paces behind, looking no less stressed, and guilt sliced into her as cleanly as a surgeon's scalpel.

She was the cause of their distress. And their concern for their prince meant they must follow even as he chased the crazy woman in the car. Rafiq would not have thought of such things—he had been so many years in Australia that he would not understand the depth of their responsibility to a member of their royal family. But she knew how the palace worked. And she should have realised Rafiq would follow. He probably hadn't finished telling her how little he thought of her—for that reason alone he would have been driven to pursue her.

But out here, deep in the desert, when she hadn't cared what might happen to her, she should at least have realised how dangerous her actions were for everyone else.

When had she become so selfish? She had not thought through her actions. She had not thought of anyone else at all.

But of course the men did not take issue with her—it was not their place to judge. Instead, both men stared at the doomed car, now sinking its way deeper into the desert itself, offering prayers of thanks for their prince's safekeeping as they neared.

'Your Highness,' one of them panted, his hand over his chest as he dipped his head with respect. 'We feared for your safety.' His eyes were once more drawn to the bizarre sight of the doomed vehicle, and he caught his breath before he could continue. 'Are you all right?'

'I'm fine,' Rafiq said, handing water to the men. 'Drink. Then one of you see to Sera. She has a wound on her head. The other one, help me. The car is beyond winching now, but there's still time to save a few more things.'

In a daze, Sera allowed herself to be guided to the blissfully cool air-conditioned car, where the first aid kit was accessed. 'I'm sorry to cause so much trouble,' she said to the man as he tended her wound, but he merely shrugged philosophically, as if there was nothing unusual in a woman going crazy and causing mayhem in the desert.

Her actions had lost them a vehicle.

She'd lost them hours of daylight.

And somewhere along the line she seemed to have lost a grip on herself.

It must be a kind of crazy, she thought, wincing as his fingers prodded at her head. A few short hours ago she'd been perfectly content with her life, or at least as content as someone with her past could hope to be. She had a role at the palace with a woman who understood, and she performed her duties well. She was quiet. Thoughtful. Responsible.

Until Rafiq had returned and her world had been turned upside down. Who was she that she could forget who she was so easily? That she could be swept away on this unfamiliar tidal rush of memories and emotion?

She squinted past her carer to where Rafiq was bundling the goods he'd salvaged from the car before she'd jumped. His pale shirt and trousers were smudged with sand, tendrils of his dark hair clung damp against his brow and his features were set. Even under the hot sun, his eyes had returned to their glacial blue.

They hadn't looked cold before.

He'd held her in his arms and looked down at her and her

heart had skipped a beat. For his blue eyes had simmered with heat, a boiling spring steaming with desire, a summer storm that promised lightning set to rent the sky in two. And then his desperate eyes had found her mouth and her trembling had changed direction. She had trembled not from the shock of the near disaster; she had trembled from the shock of knowing he wanted her.

And from the shock of wanting him.

Her hands twisted into knots in her lap. *She must be crazy to even think it*.

And yet there had been no mistaking Rafiq's desire. She had witnessed the need in his storm-tossed eyes. And while it had shocked her, and sent her trembling anew, she could not deny that the knowledge had secretly thrilled her, even while it had terrified her.

Rafiq still wanting her?

It was beyond comprehension. Beyond belief.

Even his kiss made no sense. For his kiss, when it had come, as his turbulent eyes had promised it must, had been nothing like the tender kisses they'd exchanged in their youth. This kiss had been ruthless and hard, savage in its intent, almost as if he'd wanted to punish her, and yet still it had brought with it an awakening of her senses, an unfurling of emotions and passions that she'd been long since denied.

Had long since denied herself.

A kiss so momentous it had reawakened both her heart and her soul.

But at what cost?

Her hands twisted and retwisted while she sat patiently, an expression of the turmoil going on inside herself, until the driver pronounced his work done. A graze and a bruise was the only visible external damage, but he gave her a warning to let him know if her pain worsened.

Could her pain worsen? Surely it wasn't possible. For this pain she felt now, the pain uppermost and foremost in her mind, was not just the mere throb of a temple; this pain was akin to the intense sting of a numbed limb whose blood supply had been cut off and then suddenly resumed, whose numb flesh had reawakened to the stabbing pins and needles of sensation as the flow returned.

Except that pain did not normally last longer than a minute or two, and this was not some arm or leg that felt the pain of sensation returning.

This was her heart.

Their party made camp where the desert track met the sea. The sun was already low on its downward track towards the water, a fireball already sinking, almost extinguished, and the mountains that were their goal loomed dark and threatening before them.

Rafiq had not been happy, but there was nothing else for it. In the light of the advice from the travellers at the oasis, and supported by his drivers, Rafiq had agreed that they had lost too much time today, and that the path up to Marrash would be too treacherous in the dark. They would camp by the coast.

And while he didn't say it outright, while the drivers remained silent on the subject, Sera knew he held her responsible. Knew that he was angry.

For, when once his eyes had all but demanded her attention, he'd been avoiding her ever since the accident, ensuring he sat in the front with one driver while she sat in the back seat with the other, guaranteeing they wouldn't have to share the same seat or inadvertently make eye contact. Guaranteeing he wouldn't have to so much as look at her.

Even now, while the camp buzzed with activity around them, while a meal was prepared and the final touches put to the tents that would house them tonight, he kept his distance, leaving her to her own devices.

How could he make any plainer the fact that he regretted their kiss? And how could he have better shown his contempt for her but to bend her to his will and then drop her cold?

Which didn't make forgetting it any easier for her.

For his taste lingered on her lips.

And the memory of the touch of his fingers raking through her hair while his mouth had plundered hers still set her scalp to tingling. How was she expected to just forget those sensations? That kiss had awakened something inside her. A yearning. Long-forgotten feelings.

She swallowed, squeezed her eyes shut, and wished she could so easily shut out the tangle of unwanted emotions. Because she didn't want to feel. She had taught herself long ago not to feel. It was the only way she'd been able to close out the revulsion. The disgust.

And yet his kiss had brought feeling back, sharp and prickling and uncomfortable.

Later, after a meal heavy with silence, she wandered alone along the long sweep of sandy beach, the caw of gulls and the foaming crash of the waves and the sea-softened wind that toyed with her hair her only companions.

Her feet left imprints in the damp sand, footprints the next incoming swoosh of wave wiped away, as if she'd never walked that way.

On and on she walked, until the lure of the beckoning sea became too much, and she stopped and decided she was far enough away from the camp. She walked higher up the shore, to where the foaming waves would not reach, and stood there, contemplating the endless sea, shimmering silver under the moon's pearlescent glow.

The tug of the water and the promise of the ocean's soothing caress became too much, and she picked up her hem and scooped her bulky *abaya* over her head, shaking her long hair free as she dropped the garment to the sand.

She strode into the welcoming water, felt the refreshing rush as a wave came to greet her, then the suck as it receded, coaxing her deeper. She waded in until she was waist-deep and then dived under an incoming wave, setting her nerve-endings alight with the sensual slip of water against skin.

He hadn't really believed she'd been running away. He didn't really believe she'd try anything like that again. But that didn't mean he didn't think she was an accident waiting to happen. Just a short walk, she'd said after their meal, to clear her head—and yet already she'd walked the length of the beach and then some before she'd finally stopped. He'd wondered if he should turn, or just wait for her there in the dark. She was bound to be unimpressed if she learned he'd followed her.

And then she'd done the unexpected and pulled her dress up and over her head, and the air had been punched from his lungs.

In the light of the moon her skin glowed gold, her hair shining black, tumbling down to her slim waist as she shook it free from her dress. Long-limbed, and with curves where they should be, she stood under the moonlight like a golden goddess, before she moved to meet the water, her hips swaying, her long hair rippling down her back, as graceful and elegant as a water bird.

Sera.

His Sera.

CHAPTER SIX

NEED punched into him like a curled fist. It had hit him hard the first time, when he had kissed her in the desert after pulling her to her escape. Hit him unexpectedly, with its force and sheer ferocity. Because he'd realised finally that his kiss hadn't just been about vengeance. It had been need that had driven him to taste her lips. Need that had made him crush her to him as if he'd never let her go again.

A need that had rocked him to the core when he had put her away from him, determined to keep her at arm's length, where the siren could no more mess with his head.

But now, seeing her like this, golden-skinned and lithe, and with the water slipping its cool magic up her silken thighs, it was as if his need had taken root and become a living thing.

How could one be jealous of the water in the sea? But right now he was. He wanted to be there in place of it, caressing the secret places he never had, sliding past that silken skin, holding her flesh in his thrall.

Why shouldn't he have her?

She was nothing to him now but a dark memory. Nothing but an itch that had never been scratched. Once upon a time he'd respected her innocence, had been prepared to wait until the right moment, until the ceremony that would see them tied

together for ever. But why should he wait now? There was
nothing left to wait for. There would be no ceremony, no
forever, and she was a widow, no longer the innocent.

Why shouldn't he have her?

She hadn't fought against his kiss. Even if she had not
wanted it, as he himself had not, she had not protested or struggled to be free. Instead her body had swayed into his, melted
against his, her mouth opening at his invitation just as surely
as he knew her body would open for him. After all, she was a
woman now practised in such moves.

What was one more man to her now?

He wandered closer to where she'd left her *abaya*, crumpled
on the sand, and dropped the sandals he'd been carrying in his
hands. Out in the sea she was diving through the waves like a
dolphin, her body sleek, her back curved, the moonlight turning
her body to a swish of silk through the water. He envied the
black hair that hugged her skin and curved around her breasts
just as he envied the sea that embraced her.

She was beautiful. A goddess. And he wanted her.

She should have been his a long time ago.

She could be his now.

And he would have her.

Sera wanted to stay there for ever, but she knew that she had
already been away too long, that her presence would be missed
and that Rafiq had probably sent out a search party.

Besides, the water had not numbed her heated skin as she
needed. Instead the waves had been a sensual massage against
her skin, its motion past her skin feeding the tension that had
beset her body ever since Rafiq had appeared outside his
mother's apartment, the remorseless tension that had cranked
up one-hundredfold when he'd folded her so tightly in his arms
and kissed her senseless.

She shivered in the water, suddenly feeling cold, and turned for shore, catching a wave and riding it into the shore, where she stood in the shallows, put her arms behind her head to squeeze the water from her hair, and looked up the beach for the place where she had left her gown.

The tremor squeezed every muscle tight when she found it, and she dropped her arms and crossed them defensively across her belly when she saw who was sitting beside it.

Rafiq.

How long had he been sitting there, lounging back against the sand like a modern-day pirate, his white shirt bright in the moonlight, his pants rolled up at the ankles? How long had he been watching her?

What defences the sea had managed to wash away were hastily re-erected. The relaxing benefits of the motion of the waves were suddenly for naught. With her water-cooled flesh exposed to both the balmy breeze and to his gaze, her flesh was turning to goosebumps.

Couldn't he at least look away?

She forced herself forward, crossing the sand on uncertain legs, refusing to meet his gaze, wishing she'd thought to pack a swimsuit in her hastily packed bag. She made a swipe for her *abaya*, but he got there first, picking it up in his hands, resting his elbows on his knees as he held the garment. But at least he wasn't looking at her any more. His gaze was turned out to sea, no doubt so that he could pretend he hadn't noticed she had just been reaching for it.

'Have a nice swim?' he asked, the sides of his mouth turned up.

He dared to smile? As if this was some kind of game? 'What are you doing here?'

'Don't you know it's dangerous to swim alone at night?'

'Don't you know it's rude to spy on people?' The words were

out before she could stop them, her boldness shocking her so much that she took an involuntary step back across the sand in defence. She wasn't used to thinking such thoughts any more, let alone speaking them aloud—not when she knew what the consequences could be.

But Rafiq's smile merely widened, as if he hadn't noticed her transgression. He kept his gaze seawards. 'I was worried about you.'

'You thought I'd run away?'

'Not really. But you do have this thing with sand. I didn't want to take any chances.'

Was that supposed to be funny? Or her cue to fall down and thank him for rescuing her today, even when he'd frozen her out and treated her as if she didn't exist ever since he'd rescued her? When he'd snatched up her clothes so she couldn't get dressed? Not a chance.

'As you can see, I'm fine.'

Now he did look at her, his eyes searing a path all the way from her knees to her face, the slow way, until her skin burned and she cursed herself for inviting him to look.

'Would you mind handing me my dress?'

His white teeth flashed in the moonlight. 'What if I said I liked the view just the way it is?'

It wasn't what she wanted to hear, but even while her flesh tingled a tiny part of her wanted to rejoice in his words, because it had been Rafiq himself who had uttered them. But it was still wrong—for so many, many reasons. He shouldn't look at her that way. Couldn't he see her shame? Couldn't he tell?

She remembered the men who had admired her body and her looks, the men who had run their pudgy fingers through her hair, their alcohol-heavy breath perilously close to her own as they had whispered secret wishes in her ear that had turned her stomach.

And she remembered too the men who had recoiled from

her, their faces shocked and appalled, as if she were no more than a piece of dirt.

She was worthless. Could he not tell?

She spun around on the soft sand, banishing the poisonous memories as she turned her back on Rafiq for evoking the twisted memories of days thankfully gone, for the long-forgotten desires of her own wayward body combining inside her into a potent mix. 'I just wanted to have a swim in private. Is that too much to ask?'

And something in her tone must have worked its way into his arrogant brain, for suddenly he was next to her, holding out her *abaya*. She snatched it from his hands, bundling it over her head and punching through her arms, struggling to get it down over her still-damp body, not waiting to get it right down over her legs before she set off down the beach, away from him, desperate now to return to the camp where there were others, where there could not be this talk of 'liking the view' of her, undressed or otherwise. Where the conversation would be on safer territory and not in this permanent quicksand that seemed to surround their every exchange.

She sighed. She'd hoped earlier that she'd had her last encounter with the sinking sands, and yet they were all around her, in his words and in his heated looks, ready to trap her and suck her down.

'I don't need you to follow me,' she protested, enjoying her newfound freedom to speak her mind as he drew level alongside her. 'I don't want you here now.'

'You are a woman walking in the dark alone. Your safety is my responsibility.'

'This is Qusay. It is safe for women here.'

'There are still strangers. Tourists.'

Ridiculous! There was no one else here in this remote corner of their country. The roads were too basic, the infrastructure negligible, and the closest this part of the coast had to a tourist resort were the tiny villages that scraped an existence from the sea and he knew it. But there was a better way of showing how flawed his argument was. 'Are not you a tourist yourself? Should I then be fearful of you?'

His intake of air was audible, and his already gravel-rich voice deepened. 'I am Qusani, born and bred.'

'But you don't live here. You're only here until Kareef is crowned, and then you'll return to your home halfway around the world. That makes you little more than a tourist. And, based on your own assertion, that makes you someone I should be wary of. Given the way you snatched up my *abaya* so I could not cover my body, I'd say you were right.'

He grabbed her arm, his fingers like a manacle around her, wheeling her around. Her eyes widened with something that looked more like fear than the surprise he'd anticipated. Only there was no time to try to work out why—not when he had a point to make. 'I am not a tourist! What the hell is wrong with you? I am Prince of Qusay.'

She blinked, and when she reopened her eyes the fear had gone, but there was a brightness there that he hadn't noticed before. A life force that had been missing. 'So they say,' she whispered, soft as the silken sands on which they stood. 'But are you really? Why is it that you cannot even look like a prince of Qusay?' She waved her free hand towards him. 'Look at what you wear. Armani suits. Cotton shirts with collars. This is not the Qusani way. Why do you insist on turning your back on your heritage if you are so proud to be Qusani?'

'Because this is not my home!'

And she smiled, and thanked the force that had released her from having to hold her tongue every second of every day, even if that force had a little too much to do with Rafiq's unwanted kiss.

'Exactly my point. A tourist. In which case, I'd better get back to camp before I put myself in any more danger.'

Breathless and heady, she jerked her arm out of his hand and strode off down the beach, expecting any moment for him to run after her and grab her again, to show her how wrong she was. But there was no thud of footsteps across the sand behind her and no iron-fingered clasp to stop her.

Rafiq watched her walk away, wanting to growl, wanting to argue, wanting to protest. A tourist she'd likened him to. A mere holidaymaker who had no right to be here in Qusay.

Yet those protests died, his words stymied, as he remembered. She'd smiled. Maybe at him rather than with him, but she'd actually smiled. And didn't that turn his growl of irritation into a growl of something infinitely more satisfying?

He turned to watch her go, hypnotised by the sway of her hips under the *abaya* that now clung to her sea-moistened curves. Curves that he had seen in close proximity. Curves that he had ached to reach his hands out to—curves he could have reached out for if only they hadn't been filled with the fabric of her dress.

A siren he'd thought her before. A sea witch who lured men to their deaths.

Maybe so—but not before he'd had her first.

She was lucky to have escaped him this time. Even now he should be tumbling her down on the soft sand, rolling her under him, instead of watching her march alone up the beach like a victor.

But then she'd changed. He snatched up the sandals he'd left where he'd sat waiting for her, meaning to turn and follow Sera, but stopped, dropping down onto the sand instead, wondering at this new revelation.

She *had* changed. The woman he'd seen outside his mother's apartments—the woman who'd refused to look at him let alone speak to him, the woman whose eyes were bleak and filled with despair, the woman he'd barely recognised as the Sera he'd known—was gone.

A new Sera seemed to have taken her place. Not his old Sera, for the Sera he remembered had been sweet and filled with light and laughter. The Sera who was emerging from that bleak shell was different. Tougher underneath. And yet with such an air of fragility, as if at any moment she might shatter into a thousand pieces. But at last she'd smiled.

A tourist, she'd called him, challenging him to deny it, refusing to accept his arguments when he had offered them.

Was that how he was seen? Rafiq the tourist prince?

The idea grated, even as he could see some kind of case for it. For what thought had he really given to Qusay? No more than he'd ever given it before—it was the island of his birth, and the place that had let him down. The place he'd ultimately turned his back on. He hadn't considered what it would mean to be its prince, even while his own brother was about to be crowned.

Instead he'd put his homeland behind him a very long time ago. Self-defence, he knew, because the best times in his life had not been with his brothers or with their domineering father, but with a black-haired girl who had seemed like an extension of himself, who had been the light of his life.

No, he knew that if he had thought of Qusay at all it would only have brought back memories of Sera, and he'd had no intention of inflicting that upon himself.

So much for being a prince of Qusay. What did he really know of this land, when he had abandoned his existing responsibilities and his links so readily?

The moon provided no answers, and the dark sea refused to come to his rescue.

Could Sera be right? he wondered, as he set off back towards camp long after she had departed. He *was* little more than a tourist here. An accident of birth might have made him their prince, he might be ruler of a business empire of his own making, but there was precious little else to commend him.

It was just lucky he was not the eldest. Kareef would make a good king. A just king. Kareef would be the king Qusay needed.

Sleep eluded Rafiq in his tent that night, no matter his recent long journey, the comfy wide bed with plush pillows and comforter, and the otherwise relaxing sound of the waves crashing in, wave after endless wave, rolling in along the shore. But Rafiq did not mind the sleepless hours. Because when he did sleep it was his own private agony, and his dreams were filled with the song of sirens, of a beauty once forbidden to him, of a beauty that still called to him.

It was hard enough not to think of her when he was awake—impossible not to remember her long-limbed perfection as she'd risen from the sea, the water streaming from her golden body. And when he slept his dreams were owned by her, closeted away under the curtain of her thick black hair—the hair he'd once buried his whispers in, the hair he'd worn heavy across his chest as she'd laid her head upon his shoulder.

He jerked awake suddenly, certain he could smell the herb-rinsed scent of her hair on his pillow. But he flopped back down alone, strangely disappointed, his breathing ragged as the spindly fingers of dawn squeezed their way through the tiny gaps in his tent.

What the hell was wrong with him?

The mountain road was in no better state than reported—no more than single lane in many places, with mountain slippages making it even more risky in others. Below them as they rose up the twisted road, the endless desert rolled on. Somewhere out there was Shafar, Sera reflected, and the palace. Soon

Kareef would be crowned, and Rafiq would return to his other world, and things would return to some kind of normality.

She could hardly wait.

And then she glanced across at Rafiq, sitting alongside the driver in the front seat, and thought, *liar*.

For, while she wished he'd never bothered to turn up for his brother's coronation, and as much as she wished to get her emotions back under control, seeing him go, watching him leave again after he'd reawakened feelings that should have been left dormant, would be devastating.

He looked over his shoulder then, snaring her gaze. Questions swirled in his own blue depths before she could turn her head away, her skin tingling under her *abaya*, her breasts suddenly sensitive and full. It hurt, this sudden reawakening of her senses. It stung physically and mentally.

She closed her eyes, feigning sleep, trying to block out both him and the uncomfortable sensations, trying to cut the invisible tie that seemed to bind them even now, after so many empty years.

But when she gave up on the pretence and opened them again he was still studying her, his eyes steel-blue with intent, and her body shuddered anew. Spot fires were starting under her skin, their flames licking secret places, building secret needs that made her more ashamed of her body than ever. Evidence, if she'd needed anything more, that her body welcomed his attentions and would miss him when he was gone.

Evidence that the sooner he left, the better.

The vehicle rattled and bumped up the steep escarpment. Their ascent up the mountainous path was seeming to take for ever, although it was at most a couple of hours. Finally the narrow track opened out, widening where the land levelled between two craggy mountain peaks, and stunted trees and bushes clung to the roadside. Buildings appeared, low and squat—mud brick buildings made from the same red cliffs of the mountains.

They had reached Marrash. Goats brayed where they were tethered at the sides of the road, and children gathered in groups under the shade of spindly trees, jumping up and shouting as they approached, as if the arrival of visitors was a rare treat. Given the state of the one road leading into it, it probably was.

Rafiq surveyed the town suspiciously. *This* was the place where a fabric of such beauty had been created? In this dry and dusty mountain village? It hardly seemed possible.

Had his mother sent him on a wild goose chase? And, if so, for what purpose? And then a movement behind him caught his eye, a flash of black as Sera lifted her hand to shade her eyes as she looked out of her window.

And he remembered her moonlit skin as she'd emerged from the water, a goddess from the sea, and he didn't care if it was a wild goose chase, because it had given him the chance to even the score with Sera. If he was going to lose sleep, he might as well be better occupied than spending the hours in tortured and fractured rest.

Last night she'd thrown him with her accusations of being a tourist prince. Last night he'd let her go.

He wouldn't let her go again.

He *was* a prince, whether she liked it or not. And, just as he'd set himself the task of making a business success of himself, so too would he be a success in his role as prince.

And when it came to dealing with Sera he was the one who would set down the ground rules.

The car came to a stop in a largish square in the centre of the village, with the dusty squeak of brakes and the sound of the children laughing and calling as they swarmed around the car.

Soon the square was filled, as people emerged from their houses, squinting against the bright daylight, smiles lighting up their faces. A white-haired man came forward, his spine bent, his skin tanned like leather, the lines on his face deep like the crevasses of the very mountains themselves.

'Your Highness,' he said, bowing low as Rafiq emerged from the car. 'It is indeed a pleasure to have you visit our humble village. I am Suleman, the most senior of our village elders. You have come to see our treasures, I believe? Come, take refreshment, and then it will be our pleasure to show you those things of which Marrash is justifiably proud.'

So there were treasures to be seen after all? Rafiq followed the elder, and the small party made its way through the crowded square. Wide-eyed children reached out to touch him, and women holding babies asked for his blessing as he passed, or sent their blessings to Kareef for his upcoming coronation.

How many hands he held, how many babies' cheeks he touched and murmured soft words to he quickly lost count— but he could not forget Sera's accusation of last night.

Tourist prince.

She would pay for that.

CHAPTER SEVEN

RAFIQ was impatient. He had two priorities now. Seal the deal with the Marrashis, if there was to be one, and bed Sera. But the second could not happen until the first was completed, and so far he hadn't seen any treasures. Instead the rounds of coffee seemed endless, the plates of tiny treats never-ending—as if they had all the time in the world to engage in polite conversation with the dozen elders of the village, about everything but the reason they'd come.

After ten years building his empire in Australia, he was frustrated. This was not the way he did business. But he was in Qusay, and things were done differently here. Time seemed to pass more slowly, formalities had to be observed, niceties endured.

And so he observed and endured and smiled through gritted teeth, and made a note to thank his buyers, who did this all the time in order to source the goods for his emporiums. They must have patience in abundance.

Sera, he noticed with mounting irritation, looked like patience personified. She sat elegantly, her feet tucked out of sight underneath her, her back straight and her attention one hundred percent on whoever was speaking.

Or maybe not quite one hundred per cent.

For the second time he caught the slide of her eyes towards

him, the panicked flight when she saw she'd been caught, the colour that tinted her smooth-skinned cheeks.

It was all he could do to drag his attention back to the ceremony.

Finally, with the last question as to the health of his brother and his mother answered, the coffee pot withdrawn, Suleman appeared satisfied. 'Now,' he said, his eyes lighting up like one about to bestow a special gift on a child, 'shall I show you our treasures?'

Rafiq smiled and nodded. *At last.* If there was little to see they could be out of here and back in Shafar in plenty of time for tonight's state banquet. He stepped back to allow Sera to precede him as Suleman led the way, and breathed in the scent of her hair, remembering a golden goddess emerging from the sea.

Although there was something to be said for staying one more night in the camp by the sea.

The palace would be crowded with visitors arriving for the coronation, noisy and demanding, and it would be near impossible to lever Sera from his mother's apartments even if there were somewhere private to take her.

Whereas at the camp by the sea they would be practically alone.

A deep breath saw oxygen-rich blood jump to the ready, like an army eager to do battle.

There was no rush to leave.

It was perfect.

Suleman led them out into the street again, and onto a narrow path that ran along a thin stream. Fed by a spring, Suleman told them, a gift from the gods. Instantly it felt cooler, the path lined with grasses and shaded by trees. There was a grove of orange trees too, the tang of citrus on the air.

The path led them past a tiny shop, selling everything from rugs to lace to knick-knacks, where an old woman sat in a chair in front, fanning her face. She broke into a big gappy smile when she saw Rafiq, swinging herself up onto her bowed legs.

'Prince Rafiq,' she cried, her voice frail and thin—and how she even saw him, let alone recognised him with the cataracts clouding her eyes and turning her lenses almost white, was a miracle. He went to greet her, and she pressed his hand between her bony, surprisingly strong hands. 'Please, have something from my shop.'

Suleman stood behind them patiently, his fingers laced in front of him, while Sera could not resist looking closer at the table laden with trinkets set amongst tiny lamps and coffee pots. She picked up one of the lamps, the chips of green stuck to the brass twinkling in the dappled light.

'This is beautiful,' she told the woman. And then to Rafiq, 'Your mother would love this.'

'How much is it?' he asked, reaching into his pockets.

'Take it for the Sheikha!' the old woman insisted, picking up another, larger and more resplendent in its decoration. 'And one for Prince Kareef, to celebrate the upcoming celebrations— a gift from Abizah of Marrash.'

He wanted to argue the point—clearly the woman was scraping out an existence without giving away her stock—but she was already reaching for paper to wrap the gifts, pressing them into his hands when she was finished.

'And now something for your beautiful wife...' Her hand hovered over the table of wares.

Rafiq coughed. Sera at his side bowed her head, her face suddenly colouring. 'Sera is the Sheikha's companion,' he corrected, as gently as he could.

'Yes, yes,' the old woman said, waving one hand and taking no notice. 'For now, perhaps, yes. Aha!' Her hand scooped up the prize—a choker Sera hadn't noticed behind all the other trinkets, made up of clusters of the same green chips that had adorned the fabric she'd fetched for the Sheikha, the same green chips that shone on the tiny lamp, but these chips were threaded on gold thread, with trails of the tiny gems hanging from it in a wide V-shape. Sera gasped. It was divine. A work of art.

'It is too much!' Sera protested. 'I cannot accept such a gift from you.'

The old woman brushed her concerns aside with a sweep of one hand. 'Nonsense.' She passed the necklace to Rafiq. 'Put this on your wife. My eyes and fingers are not as good as once they were.'

He held the ends of the sparkling necklace in each hand, not even bothering to correct her this time, still rattled by her earlier words and not sure she would listen anyway. 'Turn around,' he told her, and saw Sera's slight shake of her head, her dark eyes helpless, deep velvet pools. But dutifully she turned. He put his arms over her head, dropping the necklace onto the skin of her throat. There was a pulse beating there, urgent, bewitching, and he had the insane desire to press his mouth to it and feel her very life force beneath his lips.

As if she read his thoughts, he felt her breath hitch, her chest rising with it.

He drew back, enclosed the golden chain around her hair, fastened the closure.

He could have left it at that. Stepped away and let her free her hair from the circle of the chain. But he could not.

Instead he slid his hands under her heavy black hair, like silk in his hands as he lifted its weight, feeling the tremors slide through her as the backs of his fingers skimmed her neck.

And again he could have left it at that.

But still he could not walk away. Not until he had smoothed her hair down—hair that was a magnet for his fingers, hair that he wanted to bury his face in so he might drink in more of the scent of herbs and flowers.

The old woman handed him a mirror, and reluctantly he had no choice but to take it. 'Take a look,' he invited, his hand on

Sera's shoulder as she slowly turned. Against her golden skin the emerald chips winked and sparkled, the perfect foil for her dark eyes and black hair.

Colour, he realised. That was what she needed. Colour to accentuate her dark beauty, not bury it under so much black. 'You look beautiful,' he said, not sure whether he should have said *it* looks beautiful, suddenly not certain which he meant.

Sera gasped when she looked in the mirror. 'It is exquisite. But, please, you must let me pay for it.'

The old woman nodded and smiled. 'You may pay me with your smile—it is all that I ask. For one so beautiful should not be sad. Listen to Abizah, for she knows these things. Soon you will find your happiness.' And in the next instant she was waving them away, as if they were keeping her from other customers, of which there were none. 'Now, you who could be King, be away on your business, and thank you,' she said, bowing, as if he'd just done her the favour of her life. 'Thank you for stopping at my shop.'

'She is a generous woman,' Rafiq said to Suleman, and he smiled indulgently as they continued along the path.

'Abizah is Marrash's wise woman. Her eyes are not so good, as she says, yet still she sees things.'

'What kind of things?' asked Sera.

'The future, some say.' And then he shrugged. 'But others believe she speaks nothing but nonsense. Sometimes it can be one and the same. Come this way; the factory is waiting for us.'

The future? Rafiq wondered. Or nonsense?

Why had she addressed him as 'you who *could* be King'? Did she mean if not for Kareef? It seemed a strange way to refer to him.

But not half as strange as it had felt when she had called Sera his wife. Even after his correction still she'd persisted, half the time speaking in riddles. No wonder some said she spoke nonsense!

* * *

Sera put a hand to her throat, where the tiny stones of the choker lay cool and smooth against her flesh. She was still trembling, although whether from the words of the old woman or as a result of Rafiq's sensual touch and the fan of his warm breath against her throat, she wasn't sure.

Why should she feel so much now, when she had felt nothing for so long? Why had feelings come back to life, turning everything into colour instead of black and white?

And why had the old woman assumed she was Rafiq's wife? They were travelling together, it was true, and Rafiq might not be as well known to the Qusanis as his brother Kareef. But she had persisted even after Rafiq's gentle attempt to correct her. And what had she meant about Sera being the Sheikha's companion *'for now'*?

Despite the warmth of the day, Sera shivered as she followed their guide, haunted by Abizah's words, trying to make sense of them. How did the old woman know she'd not been happy for a long time? Had she found it written on her face, or guessed it from the black robes she favoured? But how could she have known when she was nearly blind?

Whatever, the encounter with the old woman had shaken her, and the magnitude of the gift she'd bestowed upon her was unsettling. Even though of polished emerald chips rather than cut stones, the necklace was such a beautiful thing, the craftsmanship superb. How could she ever repay her?

In a momentary pause in their guide's monologue, she touched a hand to Rafiq's arm. 'There must be something we can do to repay her. There must be.' And Rafiq's eyes turned from what had looked like shock at her touch to understanding, and without his saying a word she somehow knew he understood.

The path had widened to a courtyard, and a squat, long

building that seemed to disappear into the very mountain peak behind, its timber door knotted and pitted with age. Suleman stood before it, his hand on the latch.

'Welcome,' he said, smiling broadly, 'to our Aladdin's Cave.' And then he bowed theatrically and pushed open the door.

Sera gasped as she entered the long, surprisingly cool room, as an explosion of colour greeted her: jewel colours in bolts stacked high on shelves, more bolts lined up to attention on the floor like soldiers, all adorned with glittering gems in patterns reminiscent of starbursts or flowers or patterned swirls, sparkling where the light caught them. It was an endless array of colour—wherever she looked an endless source of delight.

Tucked into one corner of the vast room, a small display had been set up. Inadequate. really, given the extent of the range, but there was a bed, with covers and drapes and cushions, all aimed to show how the fabrics could be used. And alongside was set a trio of dummies, wearing gowns fashioned from the lightest fabric. The colours were intense, in ruby-red and sunset-gold and peacock-blue, the fabrics diaphanous, gossamer-thin, the emerald chips blazing upon them as if they were alive.

They were superb.

Rafiq was no less impressed. In truth, he'd expected a few bolts of fabric, some of it failing to live up to the sample his mother had shown him, because surely they would have sent their best to the Sheikha. But, looking at the vast selection around him, Rafiq wondered how anyone could have chosen the best.

He walked around the room, testing a sample of fabric here and there, admiring the handiwork, feeling the difference in the weights. He knew little of fabric, preferring to leave the finer details to his buyers' expertise, but he did know from the sales reports that anything of this quality would be snapped up in a heartbeat. Curtains, cushions, soft furnishings—even without the benefit of the mocked-up display, he could see the applications would be vast.

'Why is there so much here?' he wondered out loud, while Suleman stood rocking back on his heels, clearly delighted with his visitors' reactions.

'Abizah told us it was not the time to sell before now, and so we waited. The materials have been stockpiled here.'

Rafiq looked up. 'Abizah? The old woman we met?'

The elder nodded. 'Some said that she knew nothing of what she spoke, but others, mostly the women, overruled them.'

'Then how is it that I saw a bolt of this fabric at the palace just yesterday?'

'Ah.' Their guide nodded. 'There was one bolt, sent to the palace as a gift in the hope that it would be found suitable for a role in the coronation. Alas, we sent the fabric too late. The ceremonial robes had already been decided upon.'

Rafiq considered his words, accepted the sense they made. 'And your Abizah believes now is the right time to sell?'

'The moon is past full this month, and so, yes, she has given her approval. The time is upon us, she said.'

'My mother mentioned you already have somebody interested in the collection. How did they find out about what you have here?'

Suleman shrugged, holding his hands up, tilting his head, his brown face collapsing into craggy ravines as he smiled. 'Chance. Destiny. Who can say? A tourist couple, a businessman and his wife, they chanced across Marrash and stopped for refreshment. The women invited the wife in to view their treasures. As fate would have it, her husband was an executive for a large import company. He sent out a representative as soon as he returned home.'

Rafiq nodded. The man would have to have been certifiable not to. 'And an offer has been made?'

Suleman's chest puffed up with pride. 'A very good offer. Some said we should accept it straight away, that good fortune had shone down on Marrash the day the travellers happened by.'

'And others?'

Again that shrug, less pronounced this time. 'Others said that we should wait, that we had already waited this long and that we need not rush at the first sheep through the pen.'

The old Qusani proverb brought a smile to Rafiq's lips. It was a long time since he'd heard it, but the saying was uncannily pertinent. Why get excited chasing the fastest beast when it could be leaner and less tasty, when the slower animal might have more meat, more fat, and be more succulent and tender?

Rafiq's business sense kicked in, his pulse quickening at the thrill of the chase. He'd been given this opportunity, this chance to find something truly unique, and, while running his business and overseeing the big picture had consumed his time in the last few years, there was something to be said for the nitty-gritty of finding the actual items that would sell.

His gut had made him rich when he had first started out, many years ago, before he'd had buyers scouring the Arab world for the best. His gut had told him what items would work in the Australian market. His gut was telling him now that this was a rare find.

He owed his mother thanks. If she had not thought to show him the bolt of fabric he could have been too late, the deal already done.

'Are you able to tell me what this representative offered?'

Suleman gave an average figure per bolt—hopelessly inadequate, Rafiq recognised right away, even if Suleman had, as he expected he would have, inflated that figure with a decent margin to ensure any counter-offer would be better. But even if inflated, the quality of the fabrics at stake, let alone the rights to exclusivity, demanded at least that much again. Clearly the people of Marrash were being taken advantage of.

'It is not nearly enough,' he announced. 'You should be demanding at least double that.'

Beside him Sera gasped, as if she'd mentally calculated the worth of the room at the mention of the first offer, only to find Rafiq willing to offer double that price. But it was Suleman who looked the most taken aback, his face pale with shock. 'Are you making an offer, Your Highness?'

'Would it be accepted, Suleman?'

He bowed, his features quickly schooled, though his eyes shone with an excitement that refused to be masked. 'I would have to refer your offer to the council.'

'Of elders?' If so, with Suleman's clear excitement, the dollar signs practically spinning in his eyes, he would be home and hosed.

'Not in this case, Your Highness. It would be the women's council. It may sound unconventional, but this project has been the domain of the women all along. In deference to your position, they asked me to be their representative today.'

'Unconventional indeed,' he said. Not to mention disappointing. But hopefully the council of women might be influenced by the most senior of the village elders, just the same.

'It stems back to how the project began,' the elder continued, sounding apologetic. 'One of the women in the village, an aging widow, inherited some money from a family member in Shafar. She could simply have moved back to the city, but she had been in the village a long time and wanted to stay. She did not need the money for herself, so she elected to do something that would benefit the village as a whole, creating an ongoing income stream for all the women.'

Rafiq's eyebrows lifted in appreciation. 'A remarkable thing to do,' he said, and Suleman nodded sagely.

'Indeed. Already the women had been experimenting with off-cuts from the emerald mines, using the chips in all kinds of endeavours—the necklace from Abizah, for example...' he gestured towards the choker at Sera's neck '...and the lamp. They devised a method of using the emerald chips, of fracturing off tiny shards that would work like beads upon the fabrics. The inheritance supported the purchase of sewing machines and fabrics—the satins and silks that are the base of the finished product like those you see around you.'

'And because it is the women's endeavour, they are the ones who get to select the buyer—is that right?'

Suleman nodded, somewhat apologetically. 'They will listen to the advice of the council of elders, but ultimately, yes, it is their decision.'

'Could I meet with them, do you think? I would like to commend them on their endeavours.'

'They would most certainly be honoured, Your Highness. They are all working in the workshop nearby. Although...' Suleman coughed into his hand, his face serious, as if deliberating over his words carefully.

'Is there a problem?'

Suleman wavered, the creases at his brow deepening as he took a thoughtful breath. 'It is indeed the decision of the Marrashi women to make—and they will, of course, be honoured to meet you and show you their workroom—but I must warn you, the women do not feel confident in negotiating with a man. *Any man.* I am sorry, but it would be best if you left the negotiations to your companion.' He nodded towards Sera.

It was as his mother had said. She had advised him he would need a woman to negotiate any deal with the villagers.

He looked over to where Sera stood meekly at his shoulder, her dark eyes wide with concern, as if terrified by the prospect of speaking to the women's council on his behalf. But he saw beyond that too, stirring once again at the near perfection of her features, the perfection he would find if only she would smile again.

Need curled around him like a viper and tugged tight. At her throat the necklace of emerald chips winked and glinted in the light like a living thing, perhaps given life by the beating pulse at her throat that continued to fascinate him.

And he was suddenly consumed with the need to touch her, to slide his body along hers, to attain completion inside her slender form.

Release.

That was what he needed. That was what he wanted.

Release, and that secret smile she used to give him that gave an even warmer glow than the sun.

He breathed deep, knowing that one would come this night, perhaps, and, if he were lucky, both.

He turned back to Suleman, if only to remind himself that he was still here, and so as not to take Sera right now where she stood.

'Sera is here,' he managed to growl through a throat thick with need, 'for just that purpose.'

The older man nodded. 'I am glad you understand. I should also warn you the women's council likes to deliberate over its decisions, and it is highly unlikely that you will have a decision today, despite your generous offer.'

'I am not in Qusay for long,' Rafiq stressed, trying to impress upon Suleman some kind of urgency. 'I must return to Australia after the coronation, and it would make sense to have any deal nutted out before then.'

The older man nodded. 'I understand. However, the council of women has waited this long. It will most likely not choose to be rushed.'

The slow lamb, Rafiq thought. They would want a rich and plump beast, with meat enough for all to share. He doubted the other party would match his offer, but there was a possibility they would want to go back to find out. And then what? How long would the council of women keep waiting in order to get the fatted lamb?

Damn. If he was permitted to be the one to negotiate, he had no doubt he'd be able to turn them around—even if it was an entire roomful of women he was facing. He had a wealth of experience at negotiating mammoth business decisions behind him. It was the stuff he dealt with every day.

But Sera? She had no experience with such matters. No background in negotiating that he knew of.

Most important of all, she had no stake in the outcome. Apart from putting his offer to them, why should she argue for anything more—especially now she'd heard the women would probably want to take their time? Why should she rock the boat? It was no skin off her nose if he missed out on the deal.

Besides, how did he know she wouldn't deliberately sabotage him as payback for being forced to come out here with him?

But there was nothing he could do. So instead he growled out his understanding, already feeling the buzz of discovery waning with the possibility that the deal he'd felt so close to making might yet slip away.

Most likely would, now that it was in Sera's hands.

CHAPTER EIGHT

'How did you do it?' They'd not been long settled, or as settled as one could be, in the car that now rattled and lurched its way away from Marrash and down the mountainside, the sun slipping to the west on one side, its slanted rays colouring the cliffs an even more vibrant red. In the front seat one driver was offering the other his unappreciated advice from the passenger seat as to which set of ruts to follow, while Rafiq stared disbelievingly down at the paper in his lap—the paper Sera had provided him with after her meeting, and the paper that guaranteed him exclusive rights to the Marrash Collection, as the women's council had decided to call it.

Of course the lawyers would have to convert the hastily written scrawl into something resembling a legal document, with all the 'i's dotted and 't's crossed, and there would be signatures and counter-signatures required before it was all done and dusted, but the guts of it was done, the basic contract terms agreed.

But he still didn't understand how. Three hours or so ago they'd entered the sweetly perfumed building that housed the women's workshop to the whir and hum of a dozen sewing machines and the sound of the chatter and laughter of a score of women. Through it all had come the melodic tones of a lullaby, as a young woman soothed a baby in a corner of the room set up as a crèche. All had fallen silent at the arrival of the visitors, even the baby stopping its fussing as the room descended into an unexpected hush.

It hadn't lasted. The women, initially shy but more than delighted to accept their prince's compliments on their endeavours, had proudly showed him and Sera around their workshop, and then into the adjoining room, where another small group of women polished the tiny flakes of precious stone and transformed them into the shimmering beauties that would adorn fabrics or other souvenirs.

After the tour the women had apologised and begged Rafiq and Suleman to leave them with Sera while they deliberated. Suleman had done his best to distract the prince with a further walk through the village, relaying its long and ancient history and introducing citizens of interest along the way, but Rafiq had found it impossible to focus. Even knowing that there was little chance of any kind of agreement today, just knowing Sera was negotiating in his place was akin to having an iron chain knotted tight around his gut. What was the point of leaving someone else negotiating in his place? Especially when that woman was Sera.

It did not bode well.

'How long will they take?' Rafiq had asked, when they'd been an hour already, when already the wait had seemed interminable, but Suleman had merely smiled and shrugged his shoulders sympathetically.

'We are talking about a council of women,' he had replied, and Rafiq had taken his point even while the knotted chain around his gut had drawn tighter.

What was happening in there?

Until finally the women had emerged, smiling, from their meeting, and to his surprise Sera had presented him with the paper and the done deal. In relief, nothing more than relief, he'd picked her up and spun her in his arms and kissed her, to the cheers and whoops of everyone around.

But there had been no time to talk to her then, no time to check the details or to question how it had come about, for suddenly it had seemed the entire village had come out to celebrate the good news. And if he had thought the coffee pot had been constantly refreshed before, this afternoon it hadn't just been bottomless, it had been damn near eternal. Even if he'd wanted to get back to Shafar tonight, to make Kareef's state banquet, it would have been nigh on impossible to leave the celebrations in time.

Which gave him the perfect excuse. Now there was no choice but to stop at the coastal encampment a second night.

Amazing that fate had played into his hands so conveniently. Now his task would be so much easier. Sera could not be surprised when he made his move. Now they had something to celebrate. *Together.*

But still he didn't understand how this twist of fate had come about.

'How did you make it happen?' he asked again of the woman sitting alongside him in the back seat. Sera looked composed and serene, as always, but if he wasn't mistaken another layer of that cloak of sadness was gone, he was sure, and the corners of her mouth were turned up just the slightest fraction, as if she were just the tiniest bit pleased with herself as she contemplated his question.

She gave a tiny shrug. 'I liked meeting them. Strong women, determined to make a difference in their lives, working hard to achieve it.'

They had to be, Rafiq decided, for them to be doing what they were doing. But that still didn't answer the question that was uppermost in his mind. 'But Suleman said the women's council would most likely take its time. How did you manage to get their agreement to go to contract today?'

And Sera almost smiled, the merest shadow of a smile, and it was more than just the sloping rays of the sun's setting light playing upon her perfect features.

'You made it easier, to start with, for the women were almost beside themselves with your offer,' she told him. 'The previous offer had seemed a dream come true for all of them, a validation of everything they had hoped for, but your offer to double it was like a gift from the gods. They would be doubly blessed, and Abizah's pleas to wait seemed to have been vindicated.

'Yet still,' she continued softly, 'some thought that perhaps they should seek a counter-offer from the other party, to see if they could increase the offer even more.'

He nodded. *The fatted lamb.* Hadn't Suleman warned him of just such a likelihood? 'But they decided not to go that route. What happened to change their minds?'

'It was a close decision. The first vote was tied, and for a while all seemed to be at a stalemate. I guess they might have been waiting for me to offer more money, I don't know, but I felt that was not my place as you had given me no such authority to do so. So instead we left behind the thoughts of contracts and we just talked, as women do, about the recent developments in the royal family: of Xavian's—*Zahir's*—unexpected abdication, and about Prince Kareef and the upcoming coronation.'

Rafiq battled to find an answer to his questions in what she was saying. If there was one to be found, it eluded him. But he did find satisfaction, and a grudging degree of respect, in the fact she hadn't tried to increase his offer. It would have been easy enough for her to do so. After all, it wasn't her money she'd be spending, and she knew how much he wanted the deal wrapped up. 'And then what happened?'

And this time she did smile. Her hands crossed in her lap, and her eyes slanted ever so slightly towards him, as if sharing a secret joke. She was wearing an enigmatic smile that would have made the Mona Lisa proud. 'I was thinking about that bolt of fabric sent to the palace and of what that meant to the people of Marrash.'

He scrambled to make sense of the connection. 'And?'

Her smile broadened. 'Because it's one thing—a wonderful thing!—to be able to sell your goods to businesses that can afford them, wherever they are based in the world, but it seemed to me that there was a lingering disappointment in that room. Nothing would have been more important for the women of Marrash, nothing more satisfying while the eyes of the world were upon Qusay, than their fabrics being showcased during the coronation ceremony itself.'

'But it's too late to change that!' Rafiq growled, raking one hand through his hair in frustration, turning his face to the window in disappointment mingled with disgust. The ceremony was just a few short days away. If Sera had offered the Marrashi fabrics a place in the coronation the contract would be unstuck before it could even be drawn up by the lawyers and he would be back where he started. Worse. He would have a disappointed and no doubt uncooperative business partner into the deal. 'You can't expect them to change the arrangements for the coronation at this short notice.'

'I don't!' she came back, her reaction so vehement after all her meekness of before that he was suddenly reminded in one instant of how she once had been, years ago. Vibrant, and filled with life and laughter. And he swung his head back, the offence she'd taken at his words so plain on her features that he felt it like a slap to his own face.

She sat up, impossibly stiff and rigid against her seat, the smile he'd waited for and celebrated when it had finally arrived now vanquished. 'It just seemed, from what was said while the women talked, that the women would really value their work

being recognised and admired in their own country. They knew
the collection would be sold to the highest bidder, and that made
good economic sense to them, but they also needed to have their
work showcased and celebrated by their own. The coronation
seemed to them the perfect time that this might happen, while
the eyes of the world were upon them. But, as you say, it is too
late for that to happen now.'

'So what did you suggest?'

She bit down on her lip, and looked out of her window
for a second before swinging her head back. 'I merely suggested that if—*if*—they accepted your offer, that one day,
when you married, with the eyes of the world upon a royal
wedding, you might wish your bride to wear a gown fashioned from the most glorious fabrics that the Marrashi
women could provide.'

He blinked, slow and hard. 'You promised *what*? A royal
marriage? A wedding gown? But I have no plans for marriage—*ever!* Which means no bride for the women of Marrash
to dress. What kind of position do you think that puts me in?
What the hell were you thinking?'

She snapped her head around, her dark eyes flaring like
coals. 'I was thinking you wanted the deal closed today!'

'But to promise them a wedding. *My* wedding!'

'I could hardly promise them Prince Kareef's! He will no
doubt have to marry soon, to provide the kingdom with an heir,
but I could hardly commit him to the same arrangement when
the deal is purely to benefit you!'

She dragged in a breath as she cast her eyes downwards, and
when she resumed her voice was softer, more controlled, reminding him of how she had sounded, so meek and docile,
when they had started this journey. He hated how it sounded.

'I did not say that a marriage would definitely take place, or
when, but I thought you, at least, would understand my reason-

ing. It is important to the women that their fabrics and their expertise be recognised in their own land. And what else did you give me to negotiate with?'

'I never gave you a wedding!' But even as he said the words he realised how churlish he sounded. He growled in irritation and turned his head away, knowing the cliff at his side had more cracks and faults than her logic. She'd got the women's agreement. She'd got the contract in the space of one not entirely short meeting.

And yet marriage…?

Sera had built into the negotiations an expectation from the women of the village that he would marry. The women would expect it now. The women would be waiting for any hint…

And his mind reeled back to the cheers and whoops that had met his impulsive reaction when Sera had emerged with the news.

He had kissed her.

Sera.

And the women had cheered and laughed and cried their blessings. Their laughter had made him remember he wasn't in Australia, that it wasn't the usual thing to pick up any unmarried woman, even if a widow, and kiss her in public.

But still he'd thought they were merely celebrating the contract.

But they wouldn't be delighted, would they? They'd normally be shocked at such bold behaviour.

Unless…

And suddenly the chains that had worked their way so tightly around his gut this day started tightening their grip around his neck. The women of Marrash expected that Sera would be his bride. Hadn't Abizah already assumed that she was?

He turned to her. 'The women think I'm going to marry you. It is *our* wedding they are contemplating. It is you they see wearing the bridal gown of Marrash.'

She was shaking her head, her eyes swirling with panic.

Because she'd been caught out? 'No, I'm sure they don't think that.'

'I kissed you.'

Still her head shook from side to side. Her cheeks flushed, as if the very idea was anathema to her too, and that only made him more annoyed. *She should be so lucky!*

'You didn't mean anything by it. You didn't know. You weren't to know. It meant nothing.'

And even he, who wanted it to mean nothing, who needed it to have meant nothing, had to question her words. *Had* it meant nothing? Then why had it felt as if he had poured everything into that kiss? His frustrations at waiting, at not being permitted to negotiate himself. His relief when Sera had emerged victorious from the meeting. All of it he had poured into one impulsive kiss as he had spun her around, the feel and taste of her lush lips giving him a thirst for more, a thirst he intended to slake tonight.

So maybe that kiss *had* meant something—a physical need, an itch that had never been scratched. But it still didn't mean...

He leaned across the seat and put his arm around her shoulders, drawing her close, murmuring in her ear so that those in the front seat could not hear, so close that in other circumstances his words might almost be interpreted as a lover's caress. He touched the fingers of his other hand to her cheek, drinking in the softness with the pads of his fingers until she shuddered under his touch.

'I won't marry you, Sera. It doesn't matter what the women of Marrash think. It doesn't matter what anyone thinks. I won't marry you. *Ever.* Because there is no way I could marry you after what you did.'

There was a pause. A slowing of the earth's rotation while he heard her hitched intake of air, while he waited for her eyelids to open after they'd been jammed so firmly shut, before finally she acknowledged his words with a slow nod, her smile once again reappearing in a way that rubbed raw against him.

'Don't you think I know that?' Her voice was hushed but the tone was rapier-sharp. 'Don't you think I've lived with the knowledge that you must surely hate me for what happened all those years ago? I realise that. I understand it. And what makes you imagine for a moment that I need another man in my life? What makes you think I need or want *you*? I came up with the idea of the wedding gown for your bride so that you might win the deal. Not because I was somehow trying to engineer a wedding between the two of us.'

And his barb of irritation grew sharper and more pointed, working its way deeper into his flesh. She was a widow and he was now a prince—a wealthy prince. He could give her everything she wanted: status, money and privilege. And now she was saying she didn't want him.

She did. Of that he was sure.

So he didn't let her go. Instead, he toyed with her hair with a playfulness he didn't feel, weaving his fingers through its heavy silken curtain, trying hard not to pull it tight, trying hard not to pull her face against his. 'That's not how it looked to the Marrashis.'

She kicked up her chin, glared at him, resentment firing her eyes. 'And whose fault is that?'

His fingers curled and flexed with aggravation before they would relax enough for him to be able to stroke her neck, and he felt the tremor under her skin even as she tried to suppress it. 'I'm not the one who put the wedding idea into their heads.'

'And I'm not the one who kissed you!'

His eyes dropped to her lips, slightly parted. Her breathing was fast, her chest rising and falling with the motion.

Maybe not, he thought, but she hadn't been an unwilling

party. He remembered the feel of her mouth under his own, her delight at her success right there to be tasted on her lips, and the way she had so easily melted into his kiss. Neither would she be an unwilling party now—he'd bet on it.

All it would take would be to curl that hand around her neck and draw her closer.

He breathed deep, looking for strength but instead filling himself with her beguiling scent, the herbs that she used to rinse her black hair, the soap she used against her satin skin.

Twice now he'd kissed her—impulsive, unplanned kisses that had ended abruptly, leading nowhere but to frustration— kisses that had been doomed to come to nothing from the very beginning because they had not been alone.

But still those kisses had given him something. Two things. A taste for more, and the knowledge that she wanted him. She might say she didn't want to marry him, but she wanted him. He'd as good as read her confession in the tremors that plagued her skin when he touched her—he'd read it in the way her mouth opened under his. Her melting bones had told him. She wanted him. Of that he was sure.

And right now that was the only truth that mattered.

He smiled at her, finally tearing his eyes from her lips to see her looking uncertain, bewildered, almost as if she had expected he was going to kiss her again, almost as if she had anticipated the press of his lips against hers.

And his smile widened.

'Don't be disappointed,' he whispered, so close to her ear that he could feel the soft down of her earlobe, his lips tickled by the cool gold of the hoop that circled through it. 'I will kiss you again. But not now. Not yet. For the next time I kiss you it will be somewhere we cannot be interrupted.'

And this time she trembled in his embrace, her dark eyes conveying surprise. More than surprise, he noticed. For there was the smoke of desire there too, turning them cloudy and filled with need.

He breathed deep, dragging in more of the air flavoured with her signature scent, letting it feed his senses. For now, in the back seat of a car, descending a mountain track, it would have to be enough.

He squeezed her shoulder one last time before sliding his arm out from behind her, stretching back into his own seat, for the first time noticing the sunset that blazed red and gold in the distance as the vehicle wound its way down the switchback road. Soon it would be night, and they would stay once more at the encampment by the sea. Which meant that soon he would have her.

He took another desperate gulp of air, suddenly needing the oxygen, needing to shift in his seat to accommodate his growing tightness. Maybe he should concentrate on the sunset for now, instead of what might come after. But knowing that made no difference. For it was near impossible to drag his mind away from thoughts of Sera in his arms, her long limbs naked and wound around him as he plunged into her silken depths.

How long had he dreamed about this night? How long had those visions plagued him? Tonight, though, the dreams would become reality. Tonight she would be his.

He growled on an exhale, trying to dispel some of his burgeoning need. Admiring the sunset would be safer. For it was a stunning sunset: the sun a fireball sinking lower, the sky awash with colour.

Colour.

Which reminded him of the package he'd brought with him—the only purchase Suleman had permitted him to negotiate himself. He reached behind the seat for it, but stopped when he saw Sera huddled alongside, pressed tight against the door, her eyes lost, her expression bleak as her hands twisted first at her necklace and then in her lap.

And something shifted in his gut: guilt, emerging in an unfamiliar bubble. What had caused her sudden misery when so recently she had been warm for him? Had he provoked this slide into desolation?

He almost reached out to her. Almost lifted a hand to touch her. To reassure her.

But just as quickly he snatched his hand back, snuffing out the notion. Because that would mean he cared. And he didn't care. Not really. He wanted her—there was no doubting that. But caring? He had long since given up caring about Sera.

Besides, he thought, shrugging off the unfamiliar sense of guilt, what evidence did he have that he had upset her? For all he knew she could be thinking about Hussein and wishing he were still here.

He swung his head away, disgusted with himself. That thought was no consolation. Hussein might have been her husband for a decade, but he did not want her so much as thinking about the man.

Not that it would last. Tonight he would drive every memory of Hussein from her thoughts.

Tonight she would discover what she had missed.

CHAPTER NINE

It was impossible. Sera shrank further back into the leather of her seat, not understanding what had just transpired. There had been brief moments today when Rafiq had seemed different, when they had seemed to be able to share the same planet without sniping at each other. But they had gone from discussing the day's success to suddenly being at each other's throats—before the atmosphere had changed again and suddenly become more charged. More intense.

More dangerous.

She fingered the emerald choker at her neck as she stared out of her window, remembering the feel of Rafiq's fingers as he had secured it around her neck—more a lover's caress than that of a man who abhorred her. She despaired of the inconsistency, wishing she could focus on the glorious sunset instead of having these thoughts constantly thrashing through her mind. Wishing even more that she could control her own wayward emotions. But there was no focus. No control.

For every time he had looked at her today, every time he'd been near, she had felt the increasing pull between them, the flare of desire that charged the air with a shimmering need, a force that served to draw them together.

And when he touched her—the pad of his fingers against

her neck, the lacing of his fingers through her hair—it was simply electric.

Had anyone else around them felt it? Could anyone else tell?

She sighed against the glass. Of course they could. They all could. The women had seen him kiss her. Everyone had seen the way she'd spun in his arms as if she belonged there.

Everyone knew—even, it seemed, a woman whose cataracts had nearly blinded her. And was it any wonder, when she felt her own need so badly?

For how had she reacted when he had told her he would kiss her again? Not with outrage or anger, or even offence at his arrogant statement. No! Instead she'd looked at him with big puppy eyes, sad because she'd missed out on the treat of him kissing her then, suddenly excited because he'd given her the promise of a kiss later, *when there was no chance they would be interrupted.*

Tremors ran down her spine anew, shooting out laterally through soft tissue to find nerve-endings too receptive, too ready to surge into life. She squeezed her eyes shut, dragged in air, trying unsuccessfully to deny the sensory assault. Why did his promise fill her with such fear and such anticipation at the same time? Why was she so suddenly conscious of her swelling breasts, her nipples, and the insistent yearning between her thighs? How could he reduce her to this when she felt so ashamed?

She had to stop herself from crying out with the unfairness of it all. Why should she feel so much, so intensely? She was no teenager any more. She was a mature woman. Perhaps not as experienced as most, but she'd been a wife, a married woman, for almost a decade. She'd long since buried her teenage hopes and wishes, just as she'd buried her body's needs and desires under a public face that aimed for serenity. Control. Cool composure.

Why, now, should her body betray her?

For ten years she had felt nothing, suppressed all her desires and wishes and needs until she was sure they were banished for ever. And now, instead of serene and cool and calm, she felt hot and agitated, her skin tingling in places she'd thought long since devoid of feeling, as if all the emotions and unrecognised desires of the past ten years were welling up to engulf her in one tidal wave of emotion.

She was like that teenager all over again—the girl who had fallen head over heels in love with a tall, golden-skinned Qusani, with piercing blue eyes and a magnetism that had bound her to him from the first instant they'd met.

Even then she'd felt this way around him—this heightened sense of awareness, as if he was caressing her without even touching her. But why, more than ten years on, should he still affect her this way? It wasn't as if she was still in love with him.

And she gasped, a new realisation slamming through her like a thunderbolt.

She couldn't be!

Surely there was no way?

She squeezed her eyes shut, prayed she was mistaken. She was taken aback, that was all—taken aback at his sudden re-appearance. Thrown off-balance at their forced proximity these last few hours.

It could be nothing more than that, surely?

For once before she had lost him; once before she had seen him go. And once before it had all but ripped her heart from her chest.

Soon he would return to his business in Australia and she would watch him leave once again.

No, she could not love him. She dared not.

Oh, no, please not that!

But there came no denials, no safety ramp to save her as the brakes failed on her reason. Instead came only the constant thrum beat of her heart, pounding out what she had denied for so many years, what she had hoped to suppress for ever.

She loved him.

The rest of the journey down the mountainside passed in a blur, a jumble of confused emotions and tangled thoughts. None of them helping. None of them sorting out the morass that had become her mind. But at least Rafiq left her to her despair. She could not have handled conversation when her mind was in such turmoil, her thoughts in such disarray, disbelief the only continuous thread. They'd stopped at the campsite before she'd even realised.

It was Rafiq who opened her door, his blue eyes moving to a frown as he took in her startled face. 'What's wrong?' he growled.

She blinked and took a deep breath of the warm sea air, unlatching her seat belt, realising that even by merely drifting off she had annoyed him. Although maybe sleep was what she needed? Maybe it would make some sense out of the tangle of her thoughts.

And then she put her hand in his to climb down, and felt the charge like a shockwave up her arm. She gasped, and his eyes snagged hers, and the hungry gleam in his eyes told her that he'd felt it too.

So much for making sense.

She moved away as soon as she could, putting distance between them, confused when she saw the drivers already unloading things from the back of the car. Other servants who had stayed at the camp today were coming to assist, making long shadows against the tents in the light of the torches. She was further confused when she detected the aroma of lamb mixed with herbs on the breeze.

'How long are we stopping?' she asked, as she stood on a dune overlooking the long, pristine beach, under a sky emblazoned with stars. But they did not hold her attention—not when she became more concerned as more and more was unloaded from the car.

'Until morning. We are camping here again overnight.'

She turned, surprised to find that he was so close, surprised even more by his answer. She'd hoped they'd be back in the palace tonight. She'd hoped she'd be once again tucked away in her room in the Sheikha's apartments, where she could lie in her bed and try to forget about Rafiq all over again. But another night out here with him, after what he'd told her...

Would he kiss her tonight? Here in the camp? Was that his intention, before she could be tucked safely away in his mother's quarters at the palace?

She swallowed. She remembered last night, when he'd hijacked her peaceful swim at the end of the beach and refused to give her back her *abaya*. She remembered the way his eyes had seared a trail over her skin—how it had made her breasts come alive, her senses buzz and quicken with expectation. No way would she risk that tonight! For tonight she wouldn't trust herself to coolly walk away.

'I thought you wished to return to Shafar as soon as possible once the deal was done.'

'It is not safe to drive through the desert at night with only one vehicle.' He raised an eyebrow, the flickering torches turning his golden skin to red, making him look more dangerous than ever. 'Some might say it is not safe even to drive through the desert during the day.'

Heat flooded her cheeks at the reference. Was it only one day ago that she'd driven the other car into the sinking sands? So much seemed to have happened since then. So little time, but enough to throw her entire world upside down.

'But is there not a state banquet at the palace tonight? We should press on, return to the palace as soon as possible, surely?'

He shrugged, unmoved by her need to return to Shafar. 'It is too late to get there, even if we left now. Besides, it will not be the first or the last time that I miss a state banquet. After all, I am merely—what did you call me?—a tourist prince…'

This time she gasped, her hands flying to her mouth. 'Rafiq, I was so wrong. I saw you with the people of Marrash. I saw how you related to them and how they took to you. I should never have said such a thing. I had no right.'

He hushed her words by holding two fingers to her lips, enjoying the way they parted underneath his fingers, as if she were shocked by his touch. 'No. You had no right. But you did make me think. Last night at the beach, for the first time you made me think about what kind of prince I could be. I have not lived here for many years. I know nothing of politics, or the things that matter to the people. But I have not got to where I am now without knowing that I will succeed at anything I turn my hand to. I will be a good prince of Qusay, Sera, a strong prince.'

She swallowed. 'I can see that.'

'And I will start now, with my first royal command. You will dine with me tonight, in my tent.'

His voice was gruff and low, his command scraping against her senses, and his eyes, his blue eyes, were heavy with want. The combination sent vibrations deep down inside her. 'Is… Is that wise?'

And he smiled—a lean, hungry smile. 'It is what I command. That is all you need to know.'

She dropped her eyes to the ground. 'Of course.'

'And Sera?' He retrieved a package from the back seat of the car and returned to where she stood, almost invisible in her dark gown, knowing if just for that reason that he was right about this.

'What is it?'

'Open it and see for yourself. Suleman would not let me negotiate on anything but this.'

She slipped the tie binding the package slowly off its ends, unwrapped the paper, and gasped as a burst of blue, bright and sparkling in the flare of the torchlight, met her eyes. For a second she thought it was merely fabric, and then she recognised it.

'The dress,' she cried, recognising one of the gowns she'd seen on the models in the small corner display. She lifted it by one shoulder, admiring how the stones winked at her in the light from the torches, before noticing the flash of red below it. The weight of the package told her there was more. She dug deeper and caught a hint of sunset-gold. 'You bought all three?'

'I wanted all three.'

'They're so beautiful.' Suddenly she frowned. 'But will such garments sell well in your country?'

He shook his head. 'These garments are not destined for my stores.'

The smooth skin between her eyes creased a fraction more. 'For the Sheikha, then?'

'I'm sure she would love them, but no.'

'Then why?'

'They are a gift. For you.'

And once again he had taken her unawares; once again he had sent her spirits into confusion.

She pressed the package back, the silken fabric heavy with gems sliding downwards. 'Rafiq, I cannot accept such a glorious gift.'

He pressed the package to her, scooping up the ends and bundling them into her hands. 'You can, and you will. For too long now you have buried your beauty under the colour of mourning. I knew it the moment I saw the emerald-green choker at your neck. It is time for you to reveal your beauty once more.'

His words hit a nerve she'd thought long buried. He knew that? She'd worn black initially out of the respect she must show for her dead husband, but then it had come to suit her, reflecting the dark hole her life had been, the dark hole her life had become. It had become a dark hole too deep, too convenient, to climb out of.

'But Rafiq…' She tried to hand the package back. She couldn't accept anything from him. No gift. Nothing.

'Take them, I command you.'

Her head tilted, the heavy curtain of black hair sliding over her shoulder with it, so sleek and shiny that he was tempted to run his hand through its weight, to feel the slide of its silken length through his fingers.

She had no choice but to accept the package. What was the point of objecting? How could she object? He was a prince.

But *colour*. She stroked the fabrics, drinking in their feel with her fingertips. For so long her life had been black and white, her feelings neutral to numb the pain. But now her senses had been reawakened, along with a yearning for the things she'd missed. Colour was one of them.

'Tonight you will wear the blue gown.'

She looked up at him, uncertain, her dark eyes wide. The stars in the night sky were reflected in their depths, he noticed, a galaxy of stars that along with the flicker of torchlight gave her eyes a molten glow. Soon, he knew, it would be him who turned them molten.

Later, in her tent, bathed but still shaking and breathless from the unexpected encounter, Sera held the blue gown up in front of her. What would it be like to wear such a bold colour? As much as she was tempted, after so many months of covering herself in black the idea of colour seemed somehow daring. Provocative.

Or was it just because of the way Rafiq had looked at her, with hunger in his eyes and a wicked smile curving his lips?

She dragged in air, needing the burst of oxygen. How could she decide when she could not so much as think rationally?

So, instead of thinking, she shrugged the gown over her shoulders, letting the weight of the stone-encrusted fabric pull it down over her skin. She felt the whisper of silk, the weight of tiny stones, and the close-fitting gown moved against her like the slide of a thousand fingers. And then it was on, and she looked once more in the small mirror and she saw someone else—a stranger, a woman she hadn't seen for more than a decade—standing before her. A few years older, maybe, but not so markedly different that she couldn't recognise the girl who had come before.

For a minute or two she just stared, before realising that it wasn't just the colour of her dress that made her look so different and turned back the clock. It was her eyes that had changed also. They looked alive, somehow. Excited. As they had so many years before. As they had when they'd been filled with love—and desire—for Rafiq.

The desire was still there.

Her heart fluttered in her chest and she gasped, unused for so long to feeling the heat of need, surprised by its power. She'd once put this feeling down to adolescence and the stirrings of the first tender buds of first love.

But it wasn't that now.

She'd tried to deny it because it was beyond modesty to think of such things—forbidden territory for a woman in her position to feel such raw, potent need.

She'd tried to deny it because she was so ashamed of her past. So ashamed of the things her body had been used for.

But there was no denying it.

She did want him. She did need him. And it didn't matter what happened after this—for destiny seemed determined to keep them apart—it didn't matter that she'd married another when she'd loved Rafiq, it didn't matter that he'd sworn he'd never marry her now. There was no denying it. She wanted him.

Star-crossed they might be, destined never to be together, but maybe tonight, *this night*, they would become lovers.

She brushed her hair, giddy with anticipation, her blood fizzing in her veins at the recklessness of her thoughts. She'd never known the pleasure a man could give. She'd never known the magic she'd heard newly married women giggle about in muffled whispers to each other in the hallways of the palace. She'd never known the delights of the flesh.

Rafiq, she was sure, could supply them.

And why shouldn't she take advantage of this beachside encampment, just as Rafiq intended? Why should she not use it for her own purposes, to assuage her own desperate longings and desires?

Just one night, with a man who would never love her, never marry her. It was wrong on so many levels. And yet on so many more it was right.

She smoothed down her dress, garnering her resolve in the process. If he did intend to kiss her again tonight, if he did want them to be uninterrupted, she would not be the one to interrupt.

This night was like a gift from the gods. People said you didn't get a second chance, that you couldn't go back, and maybe they were right. Maybe there *was* no going back to the days when she had believed she and Rafiq would one day marry and share their lives together for ever. Those days were surely gone.

But one night—this night—was something. A glimpse, perhaps, of what might have been. A bittersweet reminder of what she had lost.

And something to hold close to her when he had gone from her life again. For he would leave soon, return to his business in Australia, forget about her all over again.

She would have this one night to remember for ever. She took one last, steeling breath of air, recognising the effort was futile, that she would never settle the butterflies that even now jostled for air space in her stomach, before she stepped from the tent.

All was prepared. Rafiq waited patiently. The table under the stars was prepared; the food was ready to serve. All that was needed was Sera.

Away from the tents he could hear the men talking around their campfire, the burble and fragrant scent of the *shisha* pipe carrying on the night breeze. A perfect evening, neither too hot nor too cool, with the blanket of stars a slow-moving picture overhead.

And then Sera appeared, and the night became even more perfect.

Shyly she approached the table, her eyes cast downwards. *Like a virgin*, he thought. A shy and timid innocent, on her way to be sacrificed. But she was no virgin, he knew. And it was not white that she wore. Nor even black, he acknowledged with relief. The blue gown skimmed her curves, fitting without catching anywhere, the shimmering gem-encrusted silk bringing her body alive in light and shadow as she moved, the jewels around her neck turning her into a glittering prize.

His prize.

'You look beautiful,' he said, his voice thicker than usual, and for the first time her eyes lifted, only to widen with shock when she saw him. 'Rafiq!'

And he smiled. 'A fair trade, wouldn't you say? My robe for your gown.'

'Rafiq, you look— You look…' *Devastating.* Her eyes drank him in—this man who wore Armani and turned it into an art form, this man who lifted a mere suit and made it an extension of his lean, powerful self, who looked like a god in the robes of his countrymen. The snowy-white robe turned his olive skin to burnished gold, turned his black hair obsidian.

And his eyes—what it did to his eyes! They were like sapphires warmed by the light of the moon. Penetrating. Captivating.

He looked taller somehow, and even more commanding, and she had no doubt he was indeed a true prince of Qusay!

Finally she managed to untangle her useless tongue. 'I mean, you look different—almost like you belong here.'

And he laughed as she hadn't heard him laugh for so long, the sound rich and strong, his face turned up to the heavens and showing off the strong line of his throat. 'My mother will be delighted to hear it. She has been on at me to wear the traditional robes from the moment I arrived. But now come. Sit. Eat. For we are far from the palace, and tonight…' he swept his arm around in an arc '…this is our palace.'

His eyes seemed to glitter more brightly than any jewels she was wearing, his teeth shining white in his smile.

Staff appeared from nowhere, ready to serve and fill glasses and dishes, to perform every wish of their master, before fading back into the darkness of the night as the sea provided music, its endless swoosh and suck of the waves curling over the shore. Here, this night, she could believe he had embraced his role as prince. Here she could see the man had become more than a prince in name only.

'Doesn't it frighten you?' she asked softly, when the staff had edged back into the night. 'Knowing your brother will be king? To know that you are but one step from becoming king yourself?'

His face tightened. 'Nothing will happen to Kareef. Before long he will marry and have the heirs he needs and I will no longer be second in line to the throne. Besides which,' he said, attempting a smile, 'there is always Tahir.'

'Your younger brother? But nobody even knows where he is.'

Rafiq shook his head, not for the first time wondering where his wayward brother had got to. Maybe there would be some news when they returned to the palace. He shrugged. 'It is all academic. Kareef will make a fine King.'

A servant bowed and approached the pair then, asking if they needed anything more. Rafiq waved the intrusion away. Neither of them seemed to be hungry, merely picking at their food despite the tender herbed meat and freshly spiced vegetables. Instead they seemed content to drink each other in with their eyes, as if that was all the sustenance they needed.

It was all Rafiq needed. To see her like this, her beauty emblazoned in colour, for once highlighting instead of dragging down her dark beauty, was enough to sustain him.

Almost enough.

'Why did you do it?' he asked softly, when it was clear both of them were finished with eating, even though their plates were still full.

'Why did I do what?'

'Why did you bother to make a deal with the women's council? You could have accepted their position when they said they'd like to seek a counter-offer. You could have walked away then, knowing that Suleman had predicted such an outcome, knowing I'd half expected it. You could have walked away from the negotiation. After all, why should you care whether or not I got the deal? The way I've spoken to you, dragged you halfway across the desert against your wishes, why wouldn't you want to sabotage my chances?'

She leaned back in her chair, her eyes thoughtful, though it was the way the fabric tugged across her breasts that captured his gaze, and he felt his hunger building—though not for food.

She paused before answering, as if measuring her words, wanting to make each one count. 'I know it's hard for you to believe, Rafiq, but I was hoping to make up a little for the pain I caused you in the past. I am truly sorry for what happened, and for the way you found out about my wedding.'

He growled, cursing himself for bothering to make conversation when all he wanted was to bury himself in her body. He wasn't interested in hearing her lame excuses again. 'You didn't look sorry at the time! You didn't sound sorry.'

'I don't… I can't expect you to believe me.'

'And how *can* I believe you? You keep saying you had no choice.'

If she'd looked away he might have felt differently. If she'd looked away he might have thought she'd had something to hide. But she held his gaze from under lids slumberous with intent, her eyes fixed level upon his. 'I had a choice,' she started, and he flinched and wished she had said something different. 'A choice that was made plain to me. I could protect my family's honour, with the promise of a plush job for my father, or he would ruin them for ever.'

'*He* would ruin them? Who do you mean?'

'Who do you think? Was he not there, gloating at the wedding, knowing it had all gone even more perfectly than he'd imagined?'

'What are you talking about?'

'Your father, Rafiq. Your own father threatened me, told me that a match between you and me would come to nothing. I already knew how badly Kareef had suffered, but when your father visited me, told me that he had plans for you, plans that included better than me, and that my entire family would suffer if I did not marry Hussein, what choice did I have? Do you really think I could have married Hussein otherwise? Do you really believe that?'

But Rafiq was still reeling from the discovery his father had had a hand in his betrayal. That it was his father who had been the one to force them apart. His own father.

Ever since their argument at the oasis yesterday it had bothered him. Sera had said then that she'd had no choice, that she couldn't bring the shame of Jasmine's family on her own, and in the white-hot heat of his fury he had refused to listen, refused to see her point of view.

But he had lived in Australia a long time. He had forgotten what life was like here—had failed to remember the expectations a father had for his daughters, had disregarded what it must have been like to live with the ever-present risk of shaming one's family by one's actions.

And he had never for a moment considered a father's expectations for his sons. His father had wanted to control every aspect of his sons' upbringing, had made every decision, and he had been beyond furious when Kareef had been rescued in the desert with Jasmine.

Of course he had wanted to choose their wives. Of course he would have considered it his choice. He had wanted to control their lives. Instead, he had driven them all away, one by one.

It made some kind of sense. Even his own mother taking Sera in. No wonder she felt responsible. No wonder she wanted to make amends.

Rafiq dragged fingers through his hair, nails raking his scalp. He had been blinded by his own hurt. His own pain. Rendered himself incapable of seeing anything else.

And while his mind reeled with his own inadequacies, another snippet managed to filter through. His mind spun backwards, desperate to replay the words…

'…when your father visited me, told me that he had plans for you, plans that included better than me, and that my entire family would suffer if I did not marry Hussein, what choice did I have? Do you really think I could have married Hussein otherwise?'

A tidal wave could not have hit him with more force. 'You didn't want to marry him. You didn't love him.'

And this time she did turn her head away, as if she couldn't bear to look at him while she spoke of her husband. 'I never loved him!'

There was a chill in her words that he didn't understand, couldn't compute, but there was no time to analyse that now, no time to think of anything but the incredible satisfaction of knowing she had never loved her husband. 'And when you told me, in front of everyone, that you had never loved me…'

She dropped her face into her hands. 'I lied.' Her voice was as thin as the golden thread that held the tiny gems to her gown, and he felt her words run ice-cold through his veins.

He thrust his hands once more through his hair, the pain of his nails raking his scalp nowhere near enough to wipe away the pain in his heart. He wanted to believe her. So much. But still it wasn't enough. Because it hadn't just been the words she'd spoken. It had been the evidence of his own eyes that had damned her, and still did.

'But it wasn't just what you told me, was it? I saw you at the reception! I saw him pull you to him. I saw him practically thrust his tongue down your throat, his hand mauling your breast. And I saw you reaching out your own hand to his lap, squeezing him like you'd never touched me! Everyone was busy watching the dancers, but I witnessed it all. And I wanted to tear him limb from limb. It was only Kareef who managed to talk sense into me, holding me back and telling me to go, to leave you, to get out while I still could.'

'And you would have seen me run out to be sick, but you had already gone!' Her voice was but a whisper, a thin thread that sounded as if at any moment it might snap. 'Hussein liked you watching. He revelled in the jealousy he saw in your expression.'

'Why did you do it? How could you do it?'

'He threatened me. Said if you kept coming after me he would hurt you. Not enough to enrage your father, but enough to teach you a lesson.' Her head sagged further towards her lap. 'I couldn't let that happen. I had to convince you that we were over. If you wouldn't believe my declaration that I'd never loved you, there was no other way but to do as he said.'

Mechanically he left his chair, crossed to her side, all without consciously thinking about what he was doing. He knelt at her side, took her wrists in his hands, and peeled her hands away. Moisture clung to her closed lashes; her lips were jammed together.

'You did that to protect me?'

Her eyelids parted on dark eyes filled with pain. 'I was afraid—too afraid of what might happen if I did otherwise. He scared me.' She shuddered where she sat, her teeth biting her bottom lip white, the involuntary action telling him more than any words could.

'It's okay,' he said, taking her by the shoulders, coaxing her to her feet. 'It's all right.'

But she was shaking her head. 'It's not okay. You were supposed to be away for a year. I thought you might forget about me in that time. I thought it might not be so bad. When you turned up unexpectedly at the ceremony I had to do something to make you hate me. Something to make you accept what had happened. And so I lied. I acted like I loved him, like I wanted to be with him. But I never did, I swear.'

Her liquid eyes looked too huge for her face, the misery they contained too much for any one person to have to bear. 'And so you did love me. All along.'

Slowly she nodded, her lips tightly clenched between her teeth, tears once more flooding her eyes.

And he wanted to roar with possession, howl at the moon. For she had always been his. He had known it. She had been his from the very first moment they had laid eyes on each other.

And tonight he would take what had been rightfully his— would take what he had been denied, so long ago.

CHAPTER TEN

HE TOUCHED two fingers to her lips, smoothing away their tightness, taking her chin in his hand and guiding it higher. She was afraid, he could tell, her dark eyes filled with trepidation, her breathing jerky.

And her fear was no doubt his fault too, because every time she had tried to explain, to make amends, he had been blinded to her words and had refuted her every argument. He was the reason she had fled into the desert. It had been his words that had put her very life at risk.

'I'm sorry,' he told her, and her fear turned to confusion as he slid both hands over her slim shoulders into her thick black hair. 'I would not listen to you yesterday when you tried to explain. I made no attempt to understand. And it was from me you felt you needed to escape. It was me who put you in danger. Is there any chance you might forgive me?'

Her eyes wavered with uncertainty, colour rising like a tide in her cheeks, and her lips parted, closed, parted again, as if she were searching for words. 'I might,' she managed tentatively, pausing for air. 'If you… Do you think there is any chance you might still want to…kiss me again?'

And his lips turned into a smile as his eyes were drawn to her mouth, to her lips, lush and ripe, just as his body was drawn to hers, as it had been every single moment since they'd passed each other outside his mother's suite. 'You know that I want you,' he whispered, his mouth hovering scant millimetres above hers.

This time when her eyes widened, their dark depths stirred with something other than fear. 'I know.'

'And you want me.'

A pause, a blink, and then came the halting response, 'It's…true.'

'Because, like I said before, the next time I kiss you I won't stop.'

A hitch in her breath, a flare of her nostrils. 'I know. I'm scared, Rafiq. I'm scared I can't do this.'

He had her in his arms before his blood had stopped its tidal surge through his veins, his lips on hers before the crashing had stopped in his ears.

And this time it was neither a kiss of anger, wrenched from her, nor a kiss of spontaneous relief, but a deliciously anticipated act that spoke of mutual need and mutual pleasure, a journey of rediscovery and shared desires and ten long years. His lips moved over hers in an unchoreographed dance that she somehow knew, matching him move for move. Fitting him perfectly. Suiting him perfectly. Hot breath and the sweet taste of Sera filled his senses and he could not get enough, could not think straight beyond wanting her. Except for knowing they could not stay here.

He growled, low in his throat, the vibrations rumbling into the kiss as he untangled his hands from her hair, battled to untangle himself from the kiss. Sera felt them through the hard wall of chest, rippling through her as he swept her into his arms. 'Come,' he said, 'tonight you need not be afraid.'

And, suddenly uncertain, she felt the first seeds of panic worm their way into her bliss. 'Rafiq, there is something—'

But he had no use for words. Not any more. Not when he

had seen they could be used to distort and corrupt and crucify with such devastating effect. 'Shh,' he whispered as he parted the curtains to his tent with his elbow. 'Enough of words.'

And so she fell silent. Except for the tiny mewls of pleasure that escaped unbidden when his mouth descended once more, this time to plunder hers with an even greater hunger.

He was right, she thought in one fleeting moment of clarity amidst a whirl of sensation. Why ruin this perfect moment, this perfect night? For maybe, just maybe, he wouldn't even know.

He lowered her to a bed, plush and welcoming, and richly adorned with pillows of satin and brocades in Bedouin shades, a combination rich in texture and colour. A lamp at the bedside was turned low, casting shadows around the room, turning colours deeper, accenting both the blue-black of his whiskered cheeks and the glint in his sapphire eyes.

He looked massive standing above her, tall and impossibly good-looking, and she caught her breath at the look in his eyes, at the raw desire she saw there.

Desire for her.

Desire that ramped up her own need tenfold.

It was surreal that after everything between them, after all the years and the angst and the pain of coming together again, this day had finally come. It would only be for a night. She knew it couldn't last. But neither did she know what she had done to deserve this moment.

'Beautiful,' he growled, and it wasn't just the word or the gravel-rich tones of his voice that moved her, but the way his eyes, dark with desire, drank her in, and the rigid set of his jaw and throat, as though it was taking every bit of control he possessed not to throw himself on top of her.

Time lost all meaning as he stood there. It could have been just a minute. It could have been an hour. But it was a moment of connection she recognised, a moment that had been inevitable from the very first moment they'd set eyes on each other.

I do love him, she acknowledged, in that one crystal-clear moment. And this time there was no fear to accompany it, no shame, just a rolling tide of heat that coursed through her. For she was with Rafiq, and it was right.

He smiled then, a tight, hard-won smile, as if he enjoyed the way her body reacted to him, before he pulled the pristine robe over his shoulders and tossed it unceremoniously aside.

Her brain shortened.

Her mouth went dry.

For he was magnificent.

Once upon a time she'd known him, ridden horses with him, swum with him. He'd been fit, his body muscled and toned, but he'd been a youth then, still a teenager. Whereas now...

Now he was a man in his prime. He had the same rich golden skin that she remembered, but the shoulders were broader, and dark hair patterned in whorls across his chest, circled his navel and sent an arrow pointing down his hard-packed stomach before disappearing under the band of his boxer shorts.

She swallowed.

His *massively distended* boxer shorts.

She shuddered, suddenly unsure, a new fear assailing her even as the prospect of taking him—*that*—inside her body thrilled her at some primeval level she couldn't quite comprehend. She wanted him—oh yes, she wanted him—but what if she couldn't? What if he was too big?

'Rafiq,' she started breathily, caught between nervousness and heady excitement, her voice no more than a gasp as she contemplated the impossible. 'I'm afraid.'

And he smiled the smile of a man who was used to being complimented. 'There's no need to be afraid,' he said, before he placed one knee on the bed beside her, slipping the sandals from her feet and sliding one hand up her foot from toe to ankle, so slowly, so intimately, that she almost cried out with the sheer pleasure of his touch.

Pleasure or need? Both, she decided, as he trailed a line along her calf through the silk of her gown, the heat from his fingers warming her flesh and igniting fires under her skin as his voice washed warm like velvet over her. 'I know it's been a while, but it's like riding a bicycle. You never forget.'

Assuming you'd ever learned. Should she tell him outright? And then his long fingers swept over her thigh, his thumb perilously close to touching her *there*, and the sensations he generated, the raw hunger that met her touch, made her think that maybe she might just be able to bluff her way through it after all. The flesh she'd hitherto been so ashamed of, the flesh she'd numbed into non-existence for so long, was willing, even if she herself was weak.

The bones at her hip had never felt so special, nor had the dip in her waist felt so curved as his hand slipped past, and she was breathless now, breathless with his slow ascent, and through it all he watched her, blue eyes on black, his smile like a victor about to enjoy the spoils. And then his thumb grazed one tight breast and she cried out with the unexpected and unfamiliar pleasure, her spine arching against the bed. He dropped himself over her and smiled. 'You see? Like riding a bicycle.'

She blinked up at him and her brain shorted, with not a clue why he should be talking about bicycles, knowing only that Rafiq's mouth was descending again, knowing that he would kiss her again and that it had already been too long since the last one.

The touch of lips, the nuzzle of noses, the rasp of whiskered skin against her cheek—how could such simple things feel so good? Even the heat emanating from the man hovering over her warmed her soul and pleasured her senses, driving her need.

She mewed and sighed as sensation rippled into sensation,

her fingers curling into the coverlet as he kissed her throat, suckled at her flesh, turned her inside out with desire. Why had nobody warned her it could be like this?

And then his mouth ventured lower, his lips closing over a breast, his tongue circling her aching nipple. Two thin layers of cloth were no barrier. The shockwaves were spearing down to her core.

Or had she just forgotten how good it could be to feel?

All those years when she'd buried everything. Her needs. Her desires. And especially her memories of a dark-haired youth who'd made her feel like a woman. Beautiful. Desirable. The woman he had promised not to take until a wedding night that would never be.

Even then he had set her alight with his touch, just the trail of his fingers down her arm, the feel of his hand in hers. Even then, in her youth, she'd known how good one special man could make her feel.

One special man.

That was Rafiq.

And he was here now.

She shrugged off her inexperience as Rafiq peeled away the layers of her shame and his hot mouth devoured her breasts, her stomach, and then moved back to suckle at her rock-hard nipples. Gasping, breathless, she let her useless hands find a purpose after all. She reached for him, found him, felt the jolt that moved through him as her fingers spread, taking the measure of his chest and sliding down his sides before letting her fingers trail back up the sleek wall of muscled flesh.

Air whooshed out of him as her fingers found the tight nubs of his nipples, hard as pebbles on the beach, and flicked over them with her thumb, and there was something empowering knowing that she had caused his reaction. Oh, he felt so good—

the sculpted planes of his chest rippling under her hands so perfect! She thought briefly about all those wasted years when she'd felt nothing but humiliation. Nothing but shame. Then she thought fleetingly about all those wasted minutes and seconds when she'd been lying here, too tentative to reach out and touch the man above her who was making her feel again. Making her blood fizz.

Wasted years. Wasted moments, every one of them.

She would waste no more.

Starting now.

Drowning under his kisses, she let her palms follow the sculpted arch of his back, finding the band of his boxers and pressing her fingernails beneath, her fingers tracing the line that circled his firm hips, until her hands were almost between them and the only place to go was down…

A hand snared her wrist.

'Not so fast.' She blinked up at him, wondering if she'd done something wrong, wondering if she'd just revealed the extent of her inexperience, to see eyes wild with want, his features taut with control. 'If you're going to touch me there, I really need you out of that dress.'

He was just the man to peel it from her. He rocked back on his knees, his hands at her ankles before they started the slow ascent once more, each leg getting the special treatment, skimming the fabric of her gown from her skin and gathering it at his wrists as he went.

He peeled the silken fabric away, uncovering her, exposing her inch by slow inch, and yet still his eyes never strayed from hers. When his thumbs grazed her inner thighs, and her muscles clenched and jerked, he simply smiled with satisfaction—and she understood, because of the moment her hands had grazed his nipples and he had started, and she had realised the power of her own touch.

He wanted her to feel good. He delighted in it. There was no need to feel apprehensive or afraid. She was in safe hands.

She lifted her hips before he had to ask, allowing the swish of bunched stone-encrusted silk to slide past her until his hands gathered at her waist, his thumbs performing lazy circles around her navel.

Lazy circles that felt anything but. Lazy circles that turned her insides to jelly.

He leaned over then, pressed his mouth to the physical reminder of her birth and kissed it reverently before he rose. 'We need to get this off,' he muttered, sounding strangely troubled, his voice as thick as the sinking sands that had swallowed her car. And then leaned down and drew her into his embrace as he kissed her again, and she let him draw the garment over her head.

She heard a sound like a waterfall as the bejewelled gown pooled on the rug, felt one brief moment of regret for its unfair fate—and just as swiftly forgot it as Rafiq chose that same moment to look down upon her body.

'I thought you were beautiful last night, in the moonlight, emerging from the sea,' he said. 'But tonight you are perfection.'

Her heart swelled in her chest. She was so close to tears— but tears of euphoria and not of sadness. For he was a god and he was calling her perfect! She thanked whatever kind fortune had brought her this moment, this night. For she would remember it for ever.

He lowered himself over her, so that their bodies met length to delicious length, their mouths enmeshed, their tongues tangled, their bodies skin to skin apart from the underwear they both wore—the underwear Rafiq was already intent on removing. He kissed the line of her bra straps, sliding them from her shoulders in the process. And then, with a skilful hand, the reason for which she didn't want to dwell on, he snapped open the closure at her back. With a flick of his wrists, even that scrap of material was gone.

The lamplight threw crazy shadows across the room—crazy shadows that merged with the crazy ideas in her mind and the crazy feelings in her heart. She had loved Rafiq once. He had loved her. Could he love her again?

Then his hot tongue circled one nipple, sending spears of pleasure down to her very core, and she didn't care what he felt.

She loved him. She wanted him. He was here now.

That was enough.

His hot mouth was at her breasts, his teeth and tongue combining in their unmerciful assault against one tight nipple and then the other, and her spine was arching with the delicious pleasure, so that she was barely aware of the downward slide of her underwear, or of his.

Until his tongue circled a nipple and she felt his hand cup her mound, felt his long fingers separate her, heat into molten heat, driving her head into the pillows with the sheer force of it. With the wonder of it. With the near agony and ecstasy when he zeroed in on that tight nub of nerves and circled it, the flick of a fingertip turning her inside out.

'Rafiq!' she cried, not entirely understanding what she was so desperate for, only knowing that his touch, her very delight, was suddenly her torture.

'I know,' he whispered, and he suckled at her throat on the way to reclaiming her mouth, 'I feel it too.' And he lay atop her and she felt him, naked and wanting, hard and heavy against her belly. 'I can't wait either.'

And this time her stab of fear at what was to follow was blunted by his hot kisses and the knowledge of his own desire and the hot rush of moisture between her thighs. She wanted him. That thought was paramount. She wanted him more than anything in the world, wanted to feel him inside her. Deep inside her, where her body ached so very much to receive him. And she wanted him *now*.

'Look at me,' she heard him urge. 'Open your eyes.' And, when finally she had complied, 'Keep them open. I want to see your eyes when you come.'

He'd sheathed himself and was already between her legs, his thickness nudging at her slick entrance, and her breath hitched, the internal muscles she'd never known already participating, trying to draw him in to their own dance of seduction.

She was burning with need, burning with fire, and the weight of him was heavy against her flesh. Heavy and yet compelling. And still she could feel his control, his tension, as the muscles bunched in his arms around her head, as his body seemed drawn tighter than a bowstring, waiting to release the arrow.

And she looked for him then—because if he was going to see her come, she wanted the very same. Their eyes connected, fused, and the circuit was complete.

And then he moved.

His hips swayed against hers, once and then again. She felt the push and the power, his masculine force against her feminine core, and feared for a moment the impossibility of it ever happening. But he must have read her panic in her eyes, because he slowed and kissed her. Slowly, thoroughly, soul-deep. So deep she melted into him even as he angled her higher.

She looked up at him in that moment and loved him. With her eyes and her heart and her very soul. Loved him for waiting, for hesitating, and for not rushing her. Loved him for the youth he had been. Loved him for the man he was now.

Loved him as he drove into her in one mind-blowing lunge that had her screaming his name.

It couldn't be possible. Rafiq was immobilised, buried to the hilt inside her. Buried tight.

Surely it wasn't possible.

And she opened her eyes and looked up at him, a tear sliding from each eye and scampering for her hair, wonder and astonishment meeting his questioning gaze, telling him that it was.

'Please,' she pleaded, her voice husky with sex. 'Don't stop. I want you.'

And even inside her he felt himself swell against the press of her tight, slick walls.

She was a virgin. *Had been* a virgin.

'Please,' she repeated impatiently, tilting her hips in a way far more persuasive than any words.

One hundred questions raced through his mind, one hundred answers eluded him, and yet he knew this was no time for explanations. The moment he had waited for in vain so many years ago, the moment he had been cheated of, was now his. Totally, exclusively, gloriously his.

And she *was* glorious.

With her black hair splayed across his pillow, her breasts firm and hard-tipped, the sensual curve of waist to hip where they joined.

She was his. *Only his*. And he was glad.

He moved inside her, testing her depths, and she cried out—this time in pleasure—her head pressing into the pillow, before he slowly withdrew, her fingers curling into the bedcover even as her inexperienced muscles clung desperately to him, as if afraid he would not return. She didn't know him well, for there was no way he could not.

He could take it slowly, in deference to her inexperience. He could try to be gentle. But something told him she wanted neither slow nor gentle. Whatever had been the problem in her marriage, she didn't want pity. She wanted him, all of him, and she would have him.

Poised at the very brink, his body screaming for completion, he wrapped her long legs around his back. 'Look at me,' he said. 'Feel me.'

And then he lunged into her again, felt her stretch and hug around him, and recognised somewhere amidst the shower of stars in his brain that he was a fool for even thinking he might be able to go slowly, for there was not a chance.

Each lunge became more desperate, each withdrawal became more fleeting, and she moved with him in the dance, welcomed him, clung to him, driving him mad with the demands of her own pulsing body.

Until her pulses turned into red-hot conflagration and she came apart around him, her eyes wild and wanton, and it was so satisfying that he had no choice but to follow her into the raging inferno.

'Did I hurt you?' She was bundled in his arms, their bodies spooned together, as slowly they wended their way down from that mountaintop.

'Only for just a second,' she admitted hesitantly. 'But I didn't mind. It was wonderful.'

'It *was* wonderful,' he agreed, remembering just how good as he pressed his lips into her hair, breathing her in deep for the space of three long breaths before asking the question that had been uppermost in his mind.

'Why didn't you tell me?'

CHAPTER ELEVEN

SHE stilled in his arms, suddenly so rigid it was a wonder she didn't snap. So he had worked it out. She'd wondered when he'd hesitated, been afraid he would stop. And yet blessedly, thankfully, he hadn't stopped, hadn't expressed surprise or demanded explanation. Instead he'd taken her to a place she'd never been, had shown her a world where she was a stranger, a place of miracles and wonder and magical new sensations.

But he must have been curious. The question had been bound to come. She swallowed back on the lump in her throat and sniffed.

'Ten years of marriage and still a virgin. It's not exactly the kind of thing you want to admit to anyone.' Her voice sounded flat, even to her own ears, and the wonder and delight of her previous words was long gone. 'It's not exactly the kind of thing you can be proud of.' Her voice caught, half a hiccup, on that last word, and she jammed her eyes together to stop the memories and the tears that accompanied them. But the pictures remained; the endless humiliation persisted.

'Sera?' She felt herself tugged around to face him. 'Look at me, Sera.' Reluctantly she prised open her flooded eyes. 'You were wasted on him—do you understand me? A man would be a fool not to want to make love to you. Hussein was that fool.'

But her lips remained tightly clenched. Rafiq didn't understand. Hussein had wanted to, had even been desperate to, she was sure. Why else make her strip in front of him and make her perform like some cheap nightclub dancer as he tugged on himself futilely? And why else would he have been so angry, so bitter, when nothing worked?

'He said I wasn't beautiful enough or enticing enough. He said it was my fault that we would never have children—that because I was so undesirable my womb would remain forever empty.'

Blood heated in his veins, reached boiling point in the time it took to take his next breath. 'Hussein told you that? But you didn't believe him? You couldn't have believed him?'

She shrugged. It wasn't just because of Hussein, but there was no reason to tell Rafiq that. He had discovered she was a virgin and she felt she owed him some kind of explanation. But there was no need to tell him anything else. No need to reveal any more humiliating truths.

'Why else could he not make love to his own wife? His own wife, Rafiq! For ten years. Why else would he say such things if they were not true?'

'Because he was using you as an excuse for his own inadequacies! I swear that if Hussein weren't already dead, I would kill him myself.'

'Rafiq, you mustn't say that!'

'Why not? It would not be murder. He was not a man. He was barely a cockroach. So why do you rush to his defence when he fed you nothing but lies, when he brainwashed you into thinking it was you with the problem?'

'But you were not there. You don't know—'

'I know this. That you have no problem, Sera. You are the most desirable woman I have ever met and I have had no trouble wanting you from the moment I saw you outside my mother's apartments.'

He kissed the last of her tears from her eyes, pushed her hair behind her ear with her fingers and followed the movement down her neck to shoulder and below, cupping one breast in his hand. She trembled, her breast already swelling, her nipple budding hard against his palm.

'Why is it so hard to believe, Sera? You are a beautiful woman. A desirable woman. Can you not see what you do to me?'

She felt the nudge of him against her belly and looked down, gasping to see him already swelling into life again. A sizzle of anticipation coursed through her. 'You want to do it again?'

And he smiled. 'And again, and again, and again.'

His words shocked her, thrilled her, confused her. 'But I thought you… I thought this was all about revenge. Because of what you thought you'd been cheated out of. You were so angry before. You said you hated me—'

And he pulled her to him, cradling her head against his chest, aching because she was so right, and had just cause for thinking it. 'I know, and you're right. It *was* revenge in the beginning. It was a desire to get even that drove me. I wanted you to accompany me to Marrash to spite you, because I could see you were afraid.' He paused, retraced his words. 'It was hate. I'd had more than a decade to do nothing but build a shrine to hatred, and I worshipped there every chance I got. Seeing you again brought the hatred back tenfold. In my own perverse way, making sure you came seemed the perfect way to punish you. I wanted you to suffer in my company if you hated it that much. But I had no idea how much I would suffer in yours, purely because of wanting you.'

She looked up at him with wide eyes. Was it possible he was telling the truth? Was it possible? 'You really did want me?'

'I never stopped wanting you,' he confessed, running his fingers through the thick black weight of her hair to cup her neck and draw her closer into his talking kiss. 'As you know I want you now. If you feel ready.'

Her lips tingled as she felt his words on her lips, as his teeth nipped at her for an answer. 'If I feel ready?'

'I know you might feel too tender.'

Parts of her did feel tender. Deliciously, lusciously tender. But definitely ready. 'Make love with me, Rafiq.' *Make love with me and blot out the memories of Hussein and his cronies and the men who looked at me as if I was dirt.* 'Make me come apart again.'

Three more times she'd come apart before, utterly exhausted, she'd fallen asleep in his arms. Three more times he'd marvelled at her responsive body, at the way she fitted him so perfectly. She stirred in her sleep and sighed, nestling back into him like a kitten.

But, unusually for Rafiq after a night of sex, sleep eluded him. He lay there in the dark, listening to the sound of her breathing, slow and even, wondering what it was that felt different.

He still wanted her. That felt different. Usually he could discard a woman as easily as he'd picked her up, his desire slaked. But Sera? How many times before his interest waned now that he had had her?

They would be back at the palace tomorrow. He would go back to doing the job he was supposed to be doing—supporting his soon-to-be-crowned brother. Sera would go back to playing companion to his mother.

Sera, who had never slept with anyone but him before.

A gentle breeze stirred up from the desert sands—a warm, unsettling breeze that whispered around the tent, rustling around the edges and whistling low through the tiny gaps.

Sera slept on—despite the steadily building wind and the flapping of canvas somewhere outside, despite the noises of his own mind that were too loud to let him sleep.

And then the coronation would be upon them, and Kareef

would be King. His duty here would be done and he would be free to return to Australia.

Why did that thought suddenly leave him cold? And he looked down at the woman nestled into his shoulder and knew.

It would be justice in a way to leave her cold now that he'd had her. He could walk away, abandon her just as she'd done to him all those years ago. And nobody would blame him.

But he didn't want that. Whatever this was—this obsession he'd had with her ever since he'd arrived, this need to have her, to possess her—he didn't want it to end just yet. Maybe he should talk to Kareef. There might be something he could do here, to give him a reason to stay a few days longer. After all, his business was fine. It wasn't as if he needed to rush back.

Something crashed outside, blown over by the wind, and the woman in his arms stirred, her sleepy eyes blinking in the first grey fingers of dawn. She smiled that secret smile he'd so missed when she saw him, and stretched, pushing deliciously against him as she arched her back.

'Good morning,' he growled, kissing her tenderly on her forehead. 'How do you feel?'

'Excellent,' she said, sliding one hand over his belly, her fingers stretched wide. 'How do *you* feel?' And then she encountered him and answered her own question, following it with a short, 'Oh…'

Not that she took her hand away. For the first time she did a little tentative exploration of her own, while his hardness danced and bucked under her inquisitive fingers. Rafiq was forced to grit his teeth as she tried and failed to complete a circle around him, before deciding that stroking him up and down was a more satisfying option. She flicked her thumb over the moist end and it was his turn to gasp.

'So smooth,' she said in awe, her teeth at her bottom lip. 'Like satin. Do you think…?'

'Do I think what?' Rafiq groaned, only a few short seconds shy of forgetting *how* to think.

Her cheeks flushed dark. 'I liked it when you flipped me over that time. Do you think it would work if this time *I* started on top?'

'I think,' he said, grinding the words out between his teeth, 'that would work just fine.'

She straddled him, and the sight of her over him, her breasts firm and dusky, nipples peaked, her black hair in riotous disarray over her shoulders and her gold-skinned body the perfect hourglass, more curvaceous and beautiful than any statue, was nearly enough to bring him undone. She took him in both hands, lifting herself to guide him to her entrance, and he wanted to weep with the pleasure of it.

And then, with a sigh, she slowly lowered herself, and he watched as he felt himself disappear deep into her honeyed depths.

He closed his eyes, using his last remaining brain cell to make a decision while there was still time. He would talk to Kareef. Find any excuse. But he was *definitely* not leaving Qusay or Sera any time soon.

The return trip to Shafar was uneventful, if you didn't count the innumerable unspoken messages that passed between Rafiq and Sera, and if you didn't count the number of times one or other of them found the flimsiest excuse to touch the other, to help locate a wayward seat belt buckle, or to brush a strand of hair from the other's eyes. She was wearing the sunset-coloured gown today, and the colour suited her even more than last night's ocean-blue—not that she'd actually worn that one for long. If he played his cards right tonight, and managed to shoehorn Sera out of his mother's apartments as he intended, this gown would no doubt meet the same fate.

He could hardly wait.

The trip back felt much quicker, and it seemed hardly any

time at all before they were through the desert and once again eating up the wide highway as they neared Shafar.

Rafiq would have preferred them to stay another night at the beach encampment, but the dawn wind had blown itself out and come to nothing, and the day that had followed the dawn was still and bright. Besides, the coronation was tomorrow. Missing a state banquet was one thing. Missing his brother's coronation would be inexcusable. But he wasn't looking forward to their return. The palace would be heaving with preparations, the walls bulging with visitors and guests, and he cared for none of it. He was pleased for his brother, but he did not really feel part of the celebrations, more an interested onlooker. The only person he really wanted to be with right now was here, in this car, the one who had so aptly labelled him the tourist prince.

So it would not hurt to play tourist a little while longer. His mother would approve of his staying longer, at least. She could hardly disapprove of his relationship with Sera—she had practically forced them together after all. Plus, if Tahir ever bothered to make an appearance, it would be an opportunity for all three brothers to catch up properly.

But his plans to run the idea past Kareef when they arrived at the palace would have to be deferred.

Akmal greeted them in the buzzing forecourt with the news that there was still no sign of Tahir, and that Kareef had taken himself down to Qais for the running of the Qais Cup. The fact that it apparently also had something to do with tonight's wedding of Jasmine, Kareef's former lover, surprised Rafiq—although Sera seemed strangely unaffected by the news.

'I thought from what you were saying that Jasmine was a friend of yours,' he said, as they retrieved their personal belongings from the car.

'She is.'

'Then how is it that you aren't going to her wedding?'

'Maybe I don't enjoy seeing a friend forced to marry someone she doesn't love.'

And the way the shutters slammed down over her features, as if she was trying to shut out something she'd rather forget, told him it was true. He grabbed her hand across the seat as she reached for her purse. 'You never loved him at all, did you?'

Her eyes didn't lift from the upholstery. 'There was only one man I ever loved.'

And before he had a chance to digest what she had said, let alone work out how to reply, she'd slipped her fingers from his and disappeared in a glide of sunset-coloured silk into the palace.

'Did everything at Marrash go to your satisfaction, Your Highness?' asked Akmal, who had suddenly reappeared at his elbow.

Rafiq's eyes were still on the doorway Sera had disappeared into. 'Very well, thank you, Akmal.' *On all counts.* Except one… He swung his head around. 'Although I'm afraid we lost one of the cars.'

'It broke down?' The older man looked sceptical.

Rafiq grimaced. 'More like got bogged down. The last time I saw it, it was up to the windows in sand.'

'Sinking sands!' Akmal's eyes opened wide, and for the first time Rafiq saw the unflappable Akmal, the man who oversaw the goings-on of an entire palace with the calm confidence of a born leader, actually look shocked—as if the prospect of losing one of Qusay's princes was clearly not on his agenda. 'I will speak to the drivers. I must apologise—it is unthinkable that something like that should happen.'

Rafiq put his hand to his wiry shoulder. 'They weren't driving. It was my fault, Akmal. But we are all safe. It ended well—apart from the car, that is.'

The vizier bowed slightly, and regained his calm demeanour. 'I am pleased to hear that.'

'Oh, and Akmal?' he said, suddenly remembering something else. 'I need you to arrange something as soon as possible. But first, do you know if my mother is in the palace today?' The older man nodded. 'Good. Perhaps you might pass word that I'll visit her after we've had our chat.'

Rafiq allowed himself a smile as he slung his overnight bag over his shoulder, waving away the offers of assistance.

Given Kareef was away, once his meeting with Akmal was finished there was little other choice left to him but to visit his mother. And if visiting his mother meant that he might also run into Sera, all the better.

An hour later, the Sheikha greeted him with a smile and a song in her voice. 'My son, you are home. And how did it go in Marrash? You must tell me everything.'

Not a chance. He had no doubt she had already extracted what relevant details she could from Sera, and now it was his turn, so she could see if the pieces matched. It was a game they were playing, and who was he to throw the board into the air? At least until he knew exactly how much she knew...

'It went well, Mother,' he said, trying to deflect any underlying questions with an easygoing answer meant to show he had nothing to hide. The last thing he needed his mother knowing was that he had slept with Sera. *Several times*. And intended to sleep with her again. *Several times*.

'And you have your contract?'

'We made a deal, yes.'

She clapped her freshly hennaed hands together in delight. 'You did? How wonderful! This calls for a celebration.' The ubiquitous coffee pot made another appearance, and while his mother was busy pouring, Rafiq was busy checking out the doors. Which one led to Sera? Where was she?

He was about to take his cup when he remembered the small package he had brought. 'I brought you a gift from Marrash,' he said, handing it over. 'Actually from Abizah, an old woman who refused to take payment. A gift for you, she said.'

'For me? Thank you.' His mother took the package, as delighted as a schoolgirl. 'And thanks to Abizah.'

'It's just a trinket,' he warned.

'It's beautiful,' his mother exclaimed, holding the tiny lamp up high, letting the encrusted gems catch the light. 'It's perfect! Thank you.'

'Sera chose it. She said you would like it.' He looked around. 'Where *is* Sera?'

His mother put the gift down, took a sip of her coffee, and looked nowhere in particular in the process. 'I thought you might be more comfortable without her presence here. The last two days must have been difficult for you both.'

'Most considerate,' he replied, hooded-eyed, and sipped from his own cup. 'But unnecessary. As it happens, Sera and I have come to an—amicable arrangement. In fact...' he coughed '...Sera is the one who negotiated the deal.'

'Sera did that? Well, didn't I tell you that you would need a guide?'

'You did, and you were right. I couldn't have done it without her. She won the contract all by herself.'

'Did she now?' the Sheikha asked, clearly more delighted than surprised, and Rafiq could see she was already settling against her cushions for a long Q&A session. 'She didn't tell me that. How exactly did she do it?'

Rafiq coughed again. 'Just as you said might be the case, Sera was asked to negotiate with the women, of course.'

'Of course,' said his mother with an I-told-you-so shrug. 'So what did she do to ensure you the deal? I told you there were others interested. I'm surprised the tribespeople made up their minds so quickly.'

He hesitated, wondering if he wanted to reveal everything,

but then it was a contract, the terms would soon be known far and wide, and then his mother would wonder why he hadn't just come clean and told her in the first place. It wasn't as if he had anything to hide.

'Sera picked up on their being disappointed about it being too late to use the fabric they had sent down in the coronation. To sweeten the offer I was prepared to make, she suggested that at my wedding my bride will wear a gown made of their best golden fabric, for the eyes of the world to see.'

His mother's blue-grey eyes grew wide as she drew herself up straighter, and Rafiq was in no doubt that Sera had chosen not to share this particular snippet of news with her. To protect him from his mother's over-active imagination? Or herself?

'But you're never getting married. At least, that's what you told me. Have you changed your mind?'

He had said that. He'd meant it. And he hadn't changed his mind—although right now he just couldn't summon the same level of absolute certainty. 'I'll have the lawyers look over the terms, see if there's something else we can't offer them instead. It's too late for the coronation, but no doubt Kareef will have to marry soon…'

But even as he said the words, a vision formed unbidden in his mind, of a black-haired, kohl-rimmed dark-eyed woman in a robe spun with gold and laced with emeralds, and he wondered where the image had come from—because there was no way *that* woman was marrying Kareef. So why…?

He barely heard the door open, and his mother's exclamation was just a spike in his thoughts until he caught her sudden movement as she uncharacteristically jumped to her feet. He glanced around to see what the problem was—only to see Sera standing inside the door, her eyes wild and wet, her skin an unnatural shade of grey.

CHAPTER TWELVE

DESPITE his mother's head start, Rafiq had swooped her into his arms in a heartbeat. 'Sera, what's wrong? What's happened?'

His mother looked on, asking the same questions herself, but with more than a tinge of curiosity mingled with the concern. He couldn't care less about his mother's curiosity right now. All he knew was that Sera was hurting.

'What is it?' he said. 'Tell me. Let me make it right.'

'You can't,' Sera replied, her head rocking from side to side in his swaying arms. 'No one can fix it. She hates me.' And then, in a hollow breath, 'She will always hate me.'

And from his mother came the unfamiliar sound of air sucking over teeth. 'Cerak has had the nerve to show her face here, at the palace?'

'She has an invitation, she claims,' Sera assured her, the colour returning to her cheeks, though she was still clinging to Rafiq's arms. 'There is no way she would miss the social event of the decade.'

'Who is this woman and what did she do to you?' Rafiq demanded, impatient with his own lack of knowledge, feeling excluded from the conversation. His voice growled with his dissatisfaction. 'What did she say?'

And Sera's beautiful dark eyes shut down, her face as bleak

as the deepest, coldest winter's night. 'She said that I had poisoned her son. That he would not be dead but for me, a barren woman with a poisoned womb, who had been like poison to his very soul.' And her tears came, at first silently, her body buckling against his with the pain, but then giving way to sound as her sobs found voice.

And even as he held her, even as he comforted her, his anger boiled and raged inside him. *Hussein's mother.* He turned to his own mother then, his desire to find this woman and ram home a few home truths about her precious son paramount. 'Where will I find this witch?'

'No, Rafiq,' said his mother, putting one hand to his forearm and one to Sera's hair. 'I will find Akmal and ensure the woman leaves immediately. You are needed here, with Sera.'

She was at the door, almost gone, when he called to her. 'Make sure she is told, when they find her, that there is recorded in history just the one virgin birth, and that if she dared to look more closely she would find that any poison was the product of her own fetid womb.'

His mother did not blink. She looked from Rafiq to the woman nestled against his chest and nodded, before slipping silently from the room.

'You told her,' Sera said much later, after he had carried her to his room and laid her down on his wide bed, after he had kissed her hurt away with a thousand tiny kisses as he stripped her bare, after making slow, deliberate love to her. 'With that message for Cerak you told your mother about us.'

And he shrugged as he ran one finger down her arm, relishing the way she shivered into his touch, her glorious dusky nipples peaking once more. 'She would have found out soon enough. She was already wondering when you didn't reel from my arms.'

'Yes, of course.'

He leaned over, unable to resist, his tongue circling that budded temptation, 'Besides, even if that hug had never happened she would have put two and two together when she found out I was planning on staying a few extra days and spending them and the nights that followed in your company.'

A pause. 'You're staying longer?'

He heard the delighted note in her voice, how it rose at the end, her words delivered just a fraction faster, and it pleased him. 'I was thinking about it.' He targeted the second nipple, feeling spoiled for choice, loving the way she gasped as he suckled, drawing her in tight. 'But I changed my mind.'

'Oh.' Exit delighted note.

He slid first one leg between hers and then the other, pressing his lips to her softly curved belly and then lower, his hand sliding down, parting her, circling that tight bundle of nerve-endings that knew only his touch and which was guaranteed to have her arching her spine.

'I had a better idea.'

He dipped his head, working his teeth around a nipple, gnawing, nipping, laving with his tongue while his hand worked his magic below. She was panting now, her breath coming in ragged, frantic breaths as her fingers clutched at his hair, his shoulders, her nails digging into his skin. But some part of her brain must have still been functioning.

'Which was?' she asked. And he had to switch gears in his mind to work out what he'd said before.

Although his first priority right now was not with words but with actions. She was ready for him, and he could not wait. He sheathed himself in an instant and waited at her very cusp, his muscles bunched and readied as he sought her eyes. Only when he had them did he answer. 'I want you to come back to Sydney with me.'

Her eyes opened wide. With pleasure? Or shock? But the

time for conversation was long gone, his ability to converse gone the same way, his focus required elsewhere.

He lunged into her, filling her in that heated way he did, and her mind swirled to get hold of the words he'd uttered, battling to hold onto them even as he lunged again, deeper this time, faster, more ferocious. And then his mouth was on hers, his slick body bucking into hers again and again, and she was lost. She spun away, or so it seemed, wild and out of control and weightless, his cry of triumph her trophy.

'Come back with me,' he urged through breath still uneven, after they'd collapsed together, heavy-limbed and exhausted.

'I can't,' she replied, confused and unsure, and not knowing what it was he actually was asking of her, what it meant. 'Your mother—'

'You cannot stay now. Everyone will know the truth—that you have been with me. In Australia it would not matter, but here in Qusay…'

She put a hand to her head. He didn't have to finish the sentence. He was right. Here she would pay for her recklessness, in sly looks and whispered innuendo. Hussein's mother alone would guarantee there was a steady stream of gossip about her failed daughter-in-law after the humiliation of her ejection from the palace. But Australia?

'Besides,' he continued, pushing himself up on one arm, using the other to emphasise his points, 'there is nothing for you here. Nothing but the ghosts of your past. And you will love Australia, Sera. There are deserts and endless skies, like here, but there are snow-capped mountains and tropical islands, and rainforests and cities that sprawl along the coast.'

It sounded wonderful, and she longed to see it all, especially at Rafiq's side, but still she didn't understand, didn't want to read too much into his offer. It didn't mean what her heart wanted it to mean. It couldn't. Not given this was the man who

had so recently professed his hatred for her. But maybe he
didn't hate her so much any more—at least not when they were
in bed. Or maybe that was how he'd redirected all that energy…

'You mean, like a holiday?'

'Live with me! I have a house in Sydney that overlooks the
cliffs and the sea. You should see the surf when it storms, Sera,
it is spectacular—like the passion unleashed in you when you
come apart in my arms.'

'But I don't understand what you're saying. I thought…
You said before that you would never marry me. Yet now you
are asking me to live with you?'

He raked a hand through his hair. He was struggling to make
sense of it too, she could tell.

'How could I ever contemplate marriage after what happened?' His eyes appealed to hers, the pain of her betrayal laid
bare in their blue depths, and then he reached out and laced her
fingers in his. 'But I didn't understand. I thought you wanted to
marry him. I thought you wanted a rich husband and the lavish
lifestyle to go with it. But I was wrong. I couldn't see past my
pain. I understand now why you acted as you did back then. I
understand you had no choice. I want you, Sera, and if having you
in my bed has shown me anything, it's that whatever this attraction is between us isn't going away any time soon. A few nights
longer here won't be enough. I want you in my bed at home.'

His words swirled and eddied in her mind. She was scared
she was imagining it all. She was almost too scared to breathe.

'Anyway,' he continued with a shrug, his thumb making
lazy circles on the back of her hand, 'when it all boils down to
it, live with me or marry me—what's the real difference?
Maybe we *should* get married. Then you can make a start on
those six children you always wanted.'

'What are you talking about? You said you'd never marry
me. *Never!*'

'That was before. Before I knew the truth. My father treated you abysmally—everyone treated you abysmally—and I was so wrong. Why not marry me and let me make up for the wrongs of the past?'

It was too much to take in, and her mind was spinning with the possibilities. *Marriage to Rafiq. Bearing his children.* Her heart thudded against her ribs, echoed loud in her veins, his words her every fantasy come true. Did he understand what he was offering? What an unbelievable gift he was holding out to her?

Could it mean the impossible?

Was there a chance his love for her had been revived after the crushing weight of years of hatred?

It was crazy, just crazy to imagine it. Crazy to think that after all this time they could be together, could wipe away those painful years and start over. But if he loved her…? Maybe it could work. But he hadn't said he loved her, had he? He'd given her no inkling that love was any part of this crazy plan. No inkling at all.

'It doesn't work like that, Rafiq. You don't just marry someone and have their babies because you enjoy the sex. What if you change your mind in a week or a month? What if you've had enough by then and we're stuck together? It doesn't make sense.'

He didn't understand it either. He only knew that he wasn't about to let Sera go. Ever. And if the best way to do that was to marry her, he'd do it. Gladly. And then he hit on the perfect way to convince her.

'Don't you see?' he added, his eyes suddenly alive with excitement as he sprang up on the bed. 'It makes perfect sense. The Marrashis want a royal marriage. We'll provide them with one. Save all the legal hassles of renegotiating the contract terms. It's the sensible thing to do.'

The contract. Sera felt her fledgling hopes take a dive. Rafiq was nothing if not a consummate businessman. Of course it would all be about the contract. Of course he didn't love her.

The Marrashis had tied his hands. He could marry or face some kind of renegotiation and possibly risk the entire contract in the process. Marrying her was clearly the lesser of two evils. *Sensible.*

'Sera, what do you think? Isn't it perfect?'

Perfect? Nowhere near.

'Aren't you taking a lot for granted?' She had to say something. She could not just let him steamroller her into this—not when it was for the wrong reasons. 'You seem to assume I'd be happy to marry you.'

He frowned. 'Would it be such a chore…?' He ran his hand down her side, a featherlight touch all the way from her shoulder to one knee that made her quiver. 'Putting up with me every night?'

'But it's not just about sex, surely?'

And his eyes took on a glacial hue, as if he was annoyed she was not falling in easily with his ever so *sensible* plan. 'Who was it who came up with that condition, Sera? Who was it who led the Marrashis to believe there would be a wedding and that it would be mine? Who had those women believing that you would be that bride?'

She swallowed and looked away. 'I didn't tell them that—'

'You might as well have, because that's what they expect. You owe me, Sera. Marry me. It's the least you can do. Say yes, before I am forced to command you.'

He was serious. He was actually serious. The concept of merely living together was forgotten. Now he was demanding she marry him as if he was calling in a debt. She swallowed down on her disappointment.

Maybe it wasn't all bad. Okay, so he might not love her— she could hardly expect that from a man who had so recently expressed his hatred of her—but he did want her. Of that she had no doubt. Could she settle for marriage with Rafiq, bearing his children, loving him, even knowing he didn't love her?

And she looked up into the waiting eyes, the beautiful blue eyes in the beautiful chiselled face of the man who had a place in her heart and her soul for ever, whether or not he loved her, now or ever, and she knew her answer.

'You don't have to command me. I'll do it. I'll marry you.'

Coronation morning dawned bright and beautiful. Rafiq knew this because he'd been awake and had watched the silvery-grey morning light spear through the drapes and turn Sera's gold-tinged skin to satin. He'd lain there, watching her sleep on a pillow of her own black hair, the curve of her long lashes resting on her cheek, her lush mouth an invitation, her lips, slightly parted.

When would he get sick of looking at her? When would he get sick of making love to her? Never, if the hunger he felt for her even now was any indication. Never, if she remained so responsive to his touch.

Sleep had confirmed last night's brainwave. Marriage would solve everything. Sera would be safe away from here. She would be free from the ghosts of her past, able to make a new future.

But most of all she would be his.

And nothing and nobody was ever going to steal her away from him again.

He pressed his lips to hers, unable to resist their silent invitation any longer, and she stirred and stretched into sleepy wakefulness so deliciously that he could not resist kissing her again, finally groaning as he pulled away, knowing there was no time for them to make love this morning.

'I'm having breakfast with Kareef before the coronation, and from there we'll go to the ceremony together. I will have Akmal assign you a seat next to mine, and I will join you there after the official entrance.'

Sleep slid from her eyes like a coverlet slipping from a bed, exposing emotion so naked he almost flinched. 'But I wasn't planning on going to the coronation.'

He sat back. 'Of course you are. It's Kareef's coronation. Why wouldn't you be there?'

She was shaking her head, clutching her bedclothes in front of her like a shield. 'There's no need. Or…I can stand at the back. Because you'll be right up at the front with your family. I don't need—'

He took her shrouded hands in his. 'Sera, what's wrong?'

'There's just no point. I don't need to be there, to take someone else's seat.'

'Sera, Cerak will not be there. She cannot hurt you now. She has been banished.'

But still Sera's eyes looked panicked and turbulent. 'I will go with you to Australia. Didn't I agree to that? I'll go today, if necessary. Oh, Rafiq,' she said, clutching at his shoulder, 'could we not go today? Why not leave right after the ceremony? Just slip away in all the commotion? Your plane is still here. It would be easy.'

His patience was wearing thin. Last night she'd made it seem as if marrying him would be some kind of imposition, and now she was suggesting they leave today—before the crown was barely warm on Kareef's head, before the event he'd specifically flown all the way from Australia to attend had barely concluded?

'Now you're being ridiculous. It's not as if you don't have anything to wear.' He headed for the bathroom. He'd wasted enough time on this meaningless discussion. If she'd played her cards right, they could have used their time much more productively. He turned at the door. 'This is my brother's coronation. You are going to be my wife. There will be no standing at the back. You *are* family now, and I expect you by my side. Is that understood?'

* * *

The conversation troubled him, even as he breakfasted with Kareef, even as he should have been focusing on his brother's words and his needs. But Kareef seemed strangely at odds with himself too, and uninterested in Rafiq's half-hearted talk of contracts with the tribespeople of Marrash. Or was that just because he found it hard to regain the enthusiasm for his own success after this morning's strange conversation with Sera? It was certainly not the way he intended waking up with Sera again.

News of their impending marriage would have snagged Kareef's attention, he was sure. But today was Kareef's day, and there was nothing he would do to deflect attention from that. There would be time for that announcement later. Not that Kareef didn't look as if he could do with some cheering up. Maybe if Tahir had managed to make it in time, as he'd promised? But their younger brother was nothing if not scrupulously unreliable, and, sadly, there seemed scant possibility he'd show up now.

An onshore breeze caught them as they crossed the courtyard, whipping at his robes as he walked side by side with his brother, and the cries of the crowd outside the gates interfered with his tangled thoughts. Once again he'd made the decision to don the robes of his countrymen. It was not so much to ask, he'd decided. Not so much of a stretch as he'd imagined. Maybe there were some parts of Qusay he didn't need to forget.

Sera had turned out to be one of them.

He frowned. Would she be waiting for him inside the ancient ruin? Or had whatever had been troubling her this morning swung her mind, and she was hiding somewhere in the cloistered shadows, as she'd clearly been intending?

It didn't make sense. Cerak had been taken care of. So what was her problem?

* * *

Today Sera had reluctantly chosen the peacock-blue gown from Marrash to wear. She had fingered her black *abayas* lovingly, wishing she could hide under one of those, and hopefully go unnoticed and unrecognised, but Rafiq would be upset, she knew, and already today she had angered him. And now there was colour all around her, a multitude of guests dressed in finery from one hundred nations, and still she felt achingly conspicuous as she sat in the seat Akmal had arranged for her, so close to the front that she could feel a thousand eyes at her back, a butterfly for each pair flitting inside her. She kept her own eyes to the front, not wanting to meet any of them, managing an awkward smile only when the Sheikha caught her eye. Her lover's mother! What must she think? She wished Rafiq would get here, so that she could at least hide herself against him. He had defended her against Cerak, made sure she could not hurt her again. He made her feel safe.

She took a deep breath, tried to settle her jittery stomach and cool her damp palms. Soon he would take her away from here. Far away from Qusay and the palace and any chance of running into someone from her past. She could hardly wait.

The sound of trumpets filled the air and the crowd hushed, heads swivelling around to where the official party gathered at the back. Relief quelled her flighty stomach. Rafiq would be among them. Soon he would be here. But for now she resisted the temptation of turning her head, waiting until the party had made their way almost to the front before she dared glance behind her.

Her gaze never made it to the official party. He was staring at her, the ambassador from Karakhistar, his burgundy sash stretched across a white dress shirt that looked a size too small for his spreading paunch. But it was the sneering look of contempt on his face that turned her stomach. The nervous butterflies were now massive moths, writhing in their death throes inside her. And she remembered the night when Hussein had ordered her to sit alongside the ambassador, her breasts practically spilling from the near-transparent top Hussein had insisted she wear, and how he had reached for her greedily, with pudgy fingers, thinking she was the entertainment, before Hussein had bundled him unceremoniously out—only to make her watch while he had tried and failed to achieve the same level of arousal as his guest, cursing her for her failure to stimulate him.

She dropped her head, her hand going over her mouth, sweat beading at her brow. She was so glad now that her heaving stomach was empty, that there was nothing to lose, nothing to further humiliate herself with. And suddenly Rafiq was there alongside her, his arm around her back.

'What's wrong?' he whispered, even as the voice of Akmal could be heard as the ceremony began.

'Take me away,' she managed. 'Take me away from Qusay.'

'I will,' he promised, his voice thick with questions that she could not answer, *dared not answer*, in case he changed his mind and left her here after all.

There was a stir amongst the guests, a ripple of astonishment that had heads turning once again, and a feeling that things were going off the rails. Even in the depths of her misery, Sera heard Rafiq's muttered, 'What the—?'

And she looked up, her mind not believing the picture her eyes were telling her. Jasmine? In Kareef's arms? *Kissing?*

'What's happening?' she said.

But Rafiq only scowled as Akmal uttered the fateful words, 'Kareef Al'Ramiz has renounced the throne. Long live King Rafiq!'

CHAPTER THIRTEEN

'WHAT the hell just happened in there?' Rafiq wasn't pacing the room, he was devouring it, with giant purposeful strides that ate up the carpet and spat it out again. 'Akmal, tell me—what the hell happened? One minute my brother is supposed to be crowned King, the next he is renouncing the throne. He cannot *do* that.'

'Yes, Akmal,' his mother added, sitting alongside a sick-looking Sera on a couch, 'what does it mean?'

Akmal stood, eerily composed, his hands knotted in front of him, the only one in the room who seemed to have recovered from the pandemonium of the last few minutes. 'Kareef can renounce the crown and has done so. He did that when he decided to marry Jasmine Kouri, a woman unable to bear him children.'

Rafiq was shaking his head, but there was no shutting out the crashing sound of the chains and bars of responsibility clanging shut around him. 'But I am a businessman. I am flying home to Australia tomorrow. I cannot be Qusay's king.'

'You are the second son. The first has abdicated. That makes you first in line to the throne now.' Akmal's voice was patient and deliberate as he set out the facts, each one hammering home Rafiq's fate.

'But it makes no sense,' he railed. 'I know nothing of Qusay's affairs. I have not lived here for more than a decade.' He turned to Sera then, noticed her wide eyes and still ashen skin and felt himself frown. 'Some might even call me a tourist prince…'

Instead of a smile, as he'd hoped, she winced and shrank back further into the sofa, and he remembered she'd been upset even before the ceremony. Had she known, even then, that her old friend would marry Kareef? Yet the dramatic turn of events had taken everyone by surprise, including Kareef and Jasmine, it seemed. So what was bothering her?

Akmal's steady voice hauled his attention back. 'It matters neither what you did before nor what you know. For it is written in your blood. Kareef has stepped aside and it is your place to become King.'

And even though he still shook his head, he knew Akmal was right. He had no choice. His blood had spoken. So much for his fly in, fly out visit—so much for being relaxed about being second in line for the throne, smug in the knowledge that soon Kareef would marry and provide the heirs that would distance him from the throne. Kareef had fairly and squarely dropped him right in it.

And yet how could he damn his brother for snatching this chance at happiness with the woman he had loved for ever? How could he blame him, when he knew what it was like to find that woman again after so many years—the woman of your very heart and soul?

The woman you loved.

And a wave rushed through him, a tidal wave of realisation that felt like pure light coursing through his body, finally illuminating the truth.

He loved her. *Sera*. And he would marry her. He looked at her now, huddled into the seat, and he yearned to take her into his arms and soothe away whatever pain was hurting her. Something had upset her and upset her deeply, and he needed to find out what it was.

He turned back to Akmal, hauled in a deep breath. 'I understand,' he said, even when his mind was still reeling from his
recent discovery, still connecting the dots. 'We have a palace
full of dignitaries we have already inconvenienced. How long
can we wait before this coronation will proceed? There is much
I must do beforehand.'

The vizier nodded, clearly pleased to see that order might
once again be restored. 'No more than a few days, I am sure.
Many guests were planning on staying longer to tour the
emerald mines. They should not be too inconvenienced.'

'Good. And be sure, when you tell them, to say that they will
see a double celebration. For they will also witness my marriage
that day to Sera.'

A wail of distress, a cry of absolute agony, rent the air, and
she was on her feet and at the door in a moment, her black hair
swinging crazily as she hauled it open and disappeared before
anyone knew what was happening.

'Sera!' he shouted, as he wrenched the door open behind her,
but the passageway was empty and she was gone. He turned
back to the room, confused, wondering just when it had been
that he had started losing control of this day—when his world
had tilted sideways and everything he'd known, everything he'd
held precious, had somehow slipped out of his grasp.

'I'll find her,' his mother assured him, her hand soft on his
forearm. 'You have things to discuss with Akmal.' And he
blindly nodded and let her glide from the room. Let his mother
talk to Sera. Let his mother soothe her fears and doubts.
Because if he could be King, surely she could be Queen?
After being an ambassador's wife for so many years, how
hard could it be?

'Akmal,' he said, getting back to business, trying to forget
Sera's impassioned cry, the tortured look on her face as she'd
fled, 'have you had any luck with my other request?'

The older man nodded. 'The team arrives later today, and the procedure is scheduled for tomorrow morning.'

Rafiq sighed with relief. At least *something* in his world was going to plan.

His mother told him where he would find Sera: down the carved steps that wound their way down from the palace to the small, secluded private beach. 'Sera will talk to you there,' his mother had said, 'away from the palace and prying eyes and ears. 'She will explain.'

He didn't understand what there was to explain. She'd agreed to marry him less than twenty-four hours previously. What was there to explain—unless it was her erratic behaviour of today?

She stood at the far end of the small cove, looking out to sea as the sun settled low on the horizon, her blue robe fluttering in the breeze, her black hair lifting where the breeze caught it over her shoulders and her breasts imprinted on the fabric by the kiss of the wind. So beautiful, he thought, as he crunched his way through the warm sand of the tiny cove, and yet so very forlorn.

This beach had seen so much, he thought, wondering if that was a good omen or bad. For it was here that Queen Inas had found Zafir, the Calistan prince, washed up half-dead on the shore. It was in this place that, drunk with grief, she'd taken him for her own dead child, Xavian, and denied Rafiq's own father the crown.

This was a beach that had seen a lie perpetrated that would come majorly unstuck some three decades on. And now the unbelievable events of the past weeks had taken a more dramatic turn and the unimaginable had happened. Now, instead of his brother, Kareef, he himself would be King.

And the woman he wanted for his queen stood looking out to sea, lost and alone.

She looked around as he neared, and again he was struck by

her pallor, and the look of dread that filled her eyes. 'What is it?' he asked, wanting to take her in his arms, but she held him away and he had to settle for taking her hand, and even that slipped from his fingers as she turned to walk along the shore. 'Sera, what's wrong?'

She shook her head, turning her black hair alive. 'Everything's wrong.'

'What do you mean?'

'Do you ever think that we were not meant to be together? That the fates were against us from the very beginning, that destiny was against us?'

Her words made no more sense than anything else that had happened today. 'But we have been together—these last nights. We are good together.'

She smiled a smile that told him she agreed, a bittersweet smile that curled her lips and came nowhere near her eyes. 'That's destiny playing tricks again, giving us each other for a few magical hours before twisting the knife in a final, savage act of fate.'

She went to turn away again, but before she could he grabbed her shoulders, wheeling her around. 'What are you talking about? Fate? Destiny? We are together now. You are a widow. I am free to marry whoever I choose. And I choose you, Sera, above all others. I want you to be my wife. I want you to be my queen.'

She pressed her lips together, but he could already see the moisture seeping from her eyes, turning her eyelashes to spikes.

'But I can't marry you, Rafiq.'

Her softly spoken words tore at his heart like razor-sharp claws. 'Can't? Or won't?'

'I can't! And you can't marry me. Not now. Not ever.'

'This makes no sense! Last night you agreed. Last night you said yes. What is the difference now?'

'Because now you will be King!'

He wheeled away. 'This is ridiculous. How do you think I feel about becoming King? Unprepared, raw, inexperienced. Don't you think I could do with someone by my side who has some experience? You were an ambassador's wife for a decade. Don't you think that would help me? God knows I will need help if I am to perform anywhere near what this country needs.'

'No.' Her voice sounded little more than a squeak, with her head bowed low, her chin jammed against her chest. 'I could not help you. Not if you married me.'

The day that had started so badly was getting progressively worse. What could she want? Once upon a time he'd thought her a gold-digger, thought she'd married Hussein for glamour and prestige. He'd accepted that she'd been forced to marry him, and that she'd found a cold marriage bed, but now any lingering thoughts that a rich and opulent lifestyle might somehow still appeal to her died a swift death. Nothing could be more glamorous than the life of a Qusani queen, and yet she was turning that down flat.

'Can you tell me why?'

But she just shook her head. 'I'm sorry. I'm so sorry.'

He wheeled away, his hands tugging at his hair, relishing the sudden pain of it, wishing he could understand what was happening. What the hell did she want? Hadn't he offered her everything last night?

But, no, he hadn't. He hadn't offered her everything because he hadn't realised it then, not until today, when he'd tried to damn Kareef for his actions and found himself justifying them instead. When he'd realised… When he'd *realised*! And it was not too soon to tell her. She felt something for him, he knew. She melted into his touch, became liquid fire in his arms. She must feel something. He just hoped it was not too late to convince her.

He slowly turned back, found her clutching her arms across her belly, tendrils of black hair dancing loose across her wild-eyed face.

'But you have to marry me, Sera, because nobody else will ever do. I love you.'

And her beautiful face crumpled, her keening cry of agony carried away by the wind as she buckled onto her knees in the sand.

'Sera!'

She sobbed without tears into her hand. It was so unfair! He'd spoken of contracts and convenience and sense and sensibilities. He'd made no mention of love when he'd asked her to marry him last night. And she'd agreed, because she wanted him more than anything and it didn't matter if he didn't love her because she would be starting fresh, in a place nobody knew her, and she would have him by her side for ever.

But now to learn he loved her, when she knew she had no choice but to lose him again! There would be no escape, no fresh start, no having Rafiq by her side for ever.

Her lungs squeezed so tight it was near-impossible to breathe. Could this possibly be any harder to bear?

'You can't love me,' she uttered, low and defiant, when the agony in her chest allowed her to continue. 'You mustn't. There's no point.'

'But why?' he asked at her side. 'I know you feel the same. I can feel it.'

And the seeds of escape planted themselves in her mind. Poisoned seeds, perhaps, but not out of character for a woman who was supposed to have poisoned her own husband. Useful in fact, given she had to poison this relationship too. 'That's where you're wrong,' she lied, straightening herself up to stand and dusting off the sand, knowing it would never be so easy to brush memories of this man away. Not after what they'd shared together. 'It was nice to have sex with a real man, I admit—it was definitely a bonus to be relieved of my virginity at last—but I'm frankly surprised a man like you would confuse sex with romance. Because I don't love you, Rafiq. Though I have no doubt there are plenty of women who are already lining up for the opportunity to say they do.'

'You're lying! Tell me you're lying. I command it!'

And somehow, above the shame and hurt and despair, she found the strength to laugh. 'You will make a good king. That much is certain.'

'Tell me!'

'I have told you all I need to hear. I don't love you, Rafiq.'

'Then why did you agree to marry me yesterday?'

She shrugged, her lies tearing her heart apart even as she forced hardness into her features. 'Australia sounded fun. But you'll be stuck here in Qusay now, won't you? I'd be mad to tie myself to you, and you'd be mad to tie yourself to me—given I don't love you, that is.'

Blood crashed in his ears, turned his vision red. It could not be happening again! But he was back there, transported by a thunderbolt through the years, there in that gilded, perfumed hall, a youth with a dream of love for a woman who was his every ideal of perfection.

An ideal that had come crashing down when she had declared to all and sundry that she had never loved him. *Never.*

He was that young man again.

History was repeating itself. His world had once again been split apart. Cruelly. Savagely.

By a woman who didn't deserve his love.

There was a reason you learned from your mistakes, he told himself after he had spun blindly away towards the shell-lined steps to the palace. It was so you wouldn't make the same mistake again. He'd always been proud of his record on that score, always been proud of his ability to learn from his mistakes.

And yet he'd just blown that record, in spectacular style, by begging Sera to marry him—the same woman who had rejected him publicly more than a decade before, the same woman who had just rejected him and his love out of hand once again.

So much for learning from his mistakes.

The sand beneath his feet was too soft, too accommodating to the pounding of his feet. He needed something he could smash, something he could crush under his feet, something he could slam into pieces with his fists.

How could he have been so stupid? How could he have been so blind?

But even as he climbed the stone steps back to the palace, even as the setting sun reflected bright off the shell-rich stone, something sat uneasily with him. For ten years ago she *had* loved him—hadn't he learned as much? And she had said what she had because she'd been forced to marry Hussein and forced to make it look like she actually wanted to.

So why was she saying she couldn't marry him now?

His right foot wavered over a step, the gears crunching in his mind. They were good together—they both knew it—and this time they had more than proved it. And he'd been her first lover, as he'd always intended. Didn't that prove something? That they were meant for each other?

That it was fate that had brought them together again, not fate that was forcing them apart?

Damn it all! Whatever she said, whatever she claimed, this time he wasn't just walking away bitter and twisted and waiting another decade before he found out why. There were enough wasted years between them. There would be no more.

Maybe he had learned from his mistake after all.

He spun around and launched himself down the stairs,

sprinting across the sand to where she sat slumped with her head in her hands.

'Sera!' he cried, and before she could respond he had pulled her to her feet and into his arms. Her eyes were swollen, her cheeks awash with tears and encrusted with grains of sand, but without a doubt she was still the most beautiful woman he'd ever seen. But just one look was enough to make him sure. Enough to let him know he was right.

'Tell me,' he said. 'There is no father this time to intimidate you, no other man you need be afraid of. This time there is only me. So tell me, truthfully this time, why you say you cannot marry me.'

CHAPTER FOURTEEN

SERA collapsed into his arms, her sobs tearing his heart apart, her tears seeping into the cloth of his robe, wetting his skin.

'Oh, Rafiq, I'm so sorry. I...I love you so much!'

They were the words he most needed to hear—so much so that he wanted to roar with victory as he spun her around, his lips on hers a celebration of love shared and hard earned. But he knew there were other words that needed to be said, that he needed to hear, before the way would be clear between them. But it *would* be clear, of that he was sure. He would make damn well sure of it.

'Sera, you must tell me what has been troubling you. I will not leave you another time without knowing. I could not bear it.' His hands stroked her back, soothing, gentling. 'Tell me what's troubling you, and then I can make it right.'

She shook her head. 'There is no righting this. You will want to have nothing to do with me when you know. You will not be able to afford to.'

And he felt a frisson of fear in his gut. *How bad was it?* 'You have to tell me. Everything. Come, sit with me. Explain.' He drew her gently down to the sand, settling her across his lap so he could hold her like a child and kiss her tears away while she spoke.

'Hussein found a use for me,' she began, and Rafiq's blood

ran cold. 'He thought if I was good for nothing else I could help "persuade" visiting delegates to see his point of view. He made me dress like some kind of courtesan, and all the time he was negotiating he would make lewd innuendoes about sex, and how he liked to share what was his.' She stopped, and Rafiq hugged her tight to his chest, wanting to murder the man who had done this to her, who had treated her with such little respect.

'Most of the men were as embarrassed as me. They were family men, they said. They loved their wives. They would leave, barely able to look at me, and Hussein would later say it was because I was not good enough, not pretty enough, that nobody found me attractive enough to sleep with. That I deserved to remain untouched, barren, when I could not even arouse my own husband. And then he would make me try…'

She shuddered, and he sensed her revulsion. 'You don't have to talk about it.'

'You need to know. You need to know it all to understand.' Her voice sounded hollow and empty, as if it was coming from a long, long way away. 'He made me dance, if you could call it that. He watched me from the bed, where he lay naked, and while he— Oh, God, while he tried and tried, and it was my fault that he couldn't—my fault that every time he failed.'

'It's okay,' he soothed, stroking her jet-black hair. 'It's not your fault.'

She blinked up at him, her watery eyes desolate. 'It's not okay. Because by the end I wanted so much for him to succeed I tried to make him come. I thought that maybe then he would be happier. Maybe then he would not be so angry all the other times.'

His hand stilled in her hair, and despite the warmth from the sun a chill descended his spine. 'What other times?'

She buried her head in his chest again, as if too ashamed to look at him. 'There were men who were not such family men, vile men, who believed Hussein was simply being generous, who were only too happy to agree to whatever Hussein wanted for a piece of his wife. But once he had that agreement he would get angry and pretend to take offence, and have them thrown out.'

She jerked in his arms as she gulped in air.

'The ambassador from Karakhistar was one of them. He tried to touch me, brushing his fat fingers through my hair, breathing his ugly hot breath on me, before Hussein had him ejected. He was there today, at the coronation.' She shuddered in his arms. 'I saw him watching me, hating me…'

Rafiq felt sick to the stomach. The enormity of the wrongs against her was inconceivable, and he hugged her closer, trying to replace the hurt, the humiliation. No wonder she'd looked so stricken when he had arrived to take his seat. And no wonder she'd been a shadow of herself when he'd first seen her outside his mother's apartments, unsmiling, her whole body leaden with the abuse Hussein had subjected her to.

Anger simmered in his veins. Because, for all the indignity inflicted upon her, she had remained in the marriage until Hussein had died. 'Why did you do the things you did? Why did you stay with him?'

Again came the quiet, chillingly flat voice. 'I had a kitten he had given me as a wedding present—a perfect Persian kitten, as white as snow. The first time I tried to say no he took it from my hands. He was so angry. I thought he just wanted to get it out of my hands so he could hit me. But he didn't hit me. He didn't need to. One minute he was gently stroking the kitten's fur. The next he had snapped its neck.' She squeezed her eyes shut, her teeth savaging her lip. 'He told me it could just as easily be someone I loved, a friend or one of my family, and I believed him. And then he gave me another kitten the next day.' She looked up at him. 'I tried to save it, Rafiq, I tried to protect it. Believe me, I tried.'

He curled his arms more tightly around her, feeling sick to his stomach. 'What happened?'

'I found it on my pillow, the day Hussein discovered one of the security guards had secretly given me driving lessons. The guard was taken to hospital, bashed senseless. Two lessons! Only two, and that innocent man suffered so much. But Hussein never gave me another kitten after that. He didn't need to.'

Tears flooded her beautiful eyes and he held her close and rocked her, not knowing what else to do, what else to say, until she pushed herself up, swiping tears from her cheeks with the back of her hand. She took a deep breath and then sighed it out.

'And even though Hussein's gone, that's why you can never marry me now. Because as King you will be expected to entertain some of the same people Hussein met, whether it's the ambassador of Karakhistar or any one of a hundred other dignitaries who saw me being offered in exchange for deals and favours. How can they be expected to meet me? For even if they refused, why would they not believe that someone, some time, *would* have taken advantage of Hussein's generous offer? How could such a woman ever be Queen? People will talk. And sooner or later the story will get out. The tabloids would love it. Qusay's Queen, no more than a harlot. The monarchy would become a joke.'

And he pulled her to him, crushing her head to his chest, pressing his lips to her hair, wanting to tell her that she was wrong, wanting to tell her that there was a way out, but finding nothing he could say, nothing he could do.

Because she was right.

The gossip rags would have a field-day.

Damn his brother! For, as much as he had a grudging respect for the strength of character that had seen him choose the woman he loved over a responsibility borne of blood, in doing so his brother had ruined Rafiq's own chance of love.

If Kareef hadn't abdicated they could even now have slipped away to Sydney to live in relative anonymity. But as the Queen Sera would be forced to move in the same social circles as she had with Hussein. It was inevitable that she would run across some of the same men Hussein had offered her to. And, as much as he wanted her as his wife, he had seen her reaction today at the ceremony, and he could not do that to her. And, similarly, he could not expose the monarchy to such scandal.

It would be unworkable. Their marriage would be unworkable. Sera was right. There was no way he could become King, as was his duty, *and* take Sera for his wife.

It didn't stop him trying to work out a way. Lap after lap that evening his swinging arms and kicking legs ate up the pool. Ten laps, then twenty, then thirty, until he had lost count, wanting the pain in his muscles and lungs to overtake the pain in his heart, finally emerging from the pool weak-limbed, with lungs bursting and his mind going over and over the possibilities.

Qusay needed a king to rule over it.

Sera needed a man to love her.

Qusay deserved a king after the hell of the last few weeks.

Sera deserved a lover who could make her forget the hell of her previous marriage.

He fell onto a lounger and dropped his face into a towel. How could he be both lover to Sera and King to Qusay?

And the answer came back in his own fractured heartbeat. *He could not.*

But neither was he afforded the ultimate choice Kareef had decided upon: to give up the throne for the woman he loved. With no sign of Tahir, no sightings of his helicopter after days of fruitless searching in the seas around Qusay, he had no option to walk away. He was duty-bound to assume the mantle Kareef had flung in his direction.

This was no mere game of last man standing or pass the parcel. This was about duty and responsibility. The future of a kingdom was at stake and he had no choice.

But why did it have to come at such a cost? Why should he have to give up Sera?

Akmal called for him after a restless night during which he had tossed and turned alone until the early hours, before finally sinking into a fitful sleep. He was being asked for at the hospital, came the message, and, knowing who would be making such an enquiry, Rafiq reluctantly dragged himself from bed and towards the shower.

Sera had refused to sleep with him now that there was no chance they could be together. The sooner they parted, she'd said, the better chance he had to find someone new, someone befitting the title of Sheikha. She would not even accompany him to the hospital. He appreciated her logic even while he doubted it, resenting the thought of having to find another woman when he had her. When he'd *thought* he had her. How exactly was he supposed to sleep with another woman? How could he give that woman children when it was Sera he wanted in his bed, Sera he hungered to see ripe with his child?

'Any news of Tahir?' he asked Akmal as they climbed into the waiting limousine, but Akmal merely shook his head. There was no need for words. Each passing day made the likelihood of his younger brother showing up even slimmer. Rafiq felt the noose tighten ever so slightly around his neck.

Her eyes were closed as he entered her hospital room, but he had the uncanny feeling that even so she missed nothing.

'Prince Rafiq.' It was a surprisingly clear gaze that met his, the curtains gone from her eyes—eyes that shone a startling green, the colour of the very emeralds the women of Marrash worked wonders with. Set amidst her deeply creviced face, they made her look years younger.

'Abizah. It's good to see you again.' He took her gnarled hand. 'Did the operation go well?'

'Thank you so much,' she said, with grateful tears in her eyes, clutching his hand between her own papery-skinned fingers. 'I was hoping you would come, so I could thank you for your generosity. I cannot tell you how wonderful it is for an old woman to see colours and shapes and the beauty of her surroundings.' She looked around, saw only Akmal standing by the door. 'But where is your lovely wife?'

Rafiq drew a sharp breath. Tossed a look at the poker-faced Akmal and wished he'd been in the mountains with them, to hear what Suleman had said about some people thinking she spoke rubbish so that he might understand and not think them both crazy.

'Sera… Sera will visit you later.'

Abizah looked at him with her unclouded eyes, and Rafiq got the impression she could see all the way into his very soul. 'I am sorry. I have caused you sadness by asking when I merely wanted to let you know how much I appreciate your kind gesture.'

'My mother loved your gift,' he said, deflecting the conversation, and at this she smiled.

'Your mother is a fine Sheikha,' she said with a decisive nod, 'as will be our next Queen.'

He turned away. Coming here was pointless. He didn't want to hear about the next queen, no matter how fine she might be, not when it could not be the woman he loved.

'Prince Rafiq, before you go…' He stopped and looked back to the woman on the bed. 'Do not give up hope. Believe. Have faith. There is always an answer.'

Breath whooshed into his lungs as he took a step forward,

his insides flushed with sensation. 'How…? How is it that you see the things you see?'

And she smiled at him, a lifetime of wisdom shining forth from her green eyes. 'Sometimes we look with our eyes and we see only that which is in front of us. Some people have perfect vision but will never see.' She folded her arms and patted her chest. 'For sometimes we must look beyond the pictures our mind presents as fact. Sometimes we need to see what is in our hearts. Only then do we see what is really true.'

He wasn't sure it answered his question. He wasn't sure he understood—but he held onto her words as they made their way back to the palace.

'Sometimes we have to see what is in our hearts.'

Was that what Kareef had done? Listened to his heart and not to his brain? Believed what he felt, rather than what he saw as his duty?

He knew what his brain told him he must do. It was his duty, his responsibility. A king for Qusay.

And yet he knew too what his heart wanted. A black-haired woman with dark eyes and golden skin. The woman who possessed his heart.

Sera.

He had loved and lost her once before. Why should he lose her again?

But who would be king? Who would rule Qusay?

'Believe,' Abizah had said. *'Have faith.'*

He pushed back into the buttery leather upholstery and took a deep breath. The old woman was right. By the time the car pulled up outside the glistening palace he knew what he had to do.

'Akmal,' he said, stopping the vizier from alighting with a hand to his arm. 'There's been a change of plans.'

CHAPTER FIFTEEN

HE RAN through the palace, along the long cloistered walkways fragrant with citrus and frangipani and a thousand exotic flowers whose heady scent perfumed the air. He ran up the steps to the wing that housed his mother's apartment, scattering cooing pigeons in a flurry of feathers and flapping wings.

'Sera!' he called, banging on the door. 'Sera. I need to talk to you.'

And then the door opened and she was there, her eyes confused, still puffy. 'What's happened, Rafiq? What's wrong?'

He spun her in his arms. 'Nothing is wrong. Everything is wonderfully, perfectly right.'

She laughed uncertainly. 'What are you talking about? Have they found Tahir?' For a moment he faltered, but only for a moment. 'They will,' he said, believing it in his heart, 'but this isn't about him. This is about you and me. We're getting married.'

'But, Rafiq, we can't. You know we can't. There is no way—'

'There *is* a way, Sera. There is one way, and I am taking it.'

Shock transformed her face. 'You can't renounce the crown! Not after Kareef. You would be denying your very birthright.'

'Is it my birthright? I have never once in my life thought about taking over the reins of Qusay. It was a thought as foreign to me as this very land became when I adopted another as my home. And now, to find that circumstances have thrust me into this position—how is that a birthright?'

'But, Rafiq, you would be throwing away your future.'

'No, Sera, I would be reclaiming it. For *you* are my future and always have been. Because from the moment we met we were meant to be together—as surely as the sand belongs to the desert and the mountain peaks to the sky. We are part of each other and always will be.'

'Rafiq, think of what you are doing…'

'I know exactly what I am doing. I lost you once before and I will not lose you again.' He went down on one knee before her. 'I love you, Sera. Marry me. Be my wife. Live my future alongside me.'

Tears welled in her beautiful dark eyes, but there was love there too, love that swelled his heart and gave him hope. For if she denied him he would be a broken man. A king with no queen. Adrift and alone.

'Oh, Rafiq, I love you so much. You have given my life colour again when I thought there would be none. You have given me back my heart.'

'Then you'll marry me?'

And she nodded, her lips tightly pressed. 'Yes, Rafiq—oh, yes, I'll marry you!'

He was still kissing her when his mother bustled in, calling for Sera. She stopped, wide-eyed, when she found them, the excitement in her eyes masked by questions for no more than a second. 'You're both here, how wonderful. Have you heard the news? A helicopter's been found in the desert. Akmal's gone straight there. They think it might be Tahir's!' She wrung her hands nervously in front of her. 'And to think that all this time we thought he just hadn't bothered to come. Do you think…? Is there any chance…?'

And Rafiq wondered if this day could get any better as he put an arm around her shoulders and brought her into his embrace—the two women he loved most in the world held within the circle of his arms. 'Believe,' he told her, remembering the words of the wise woman, the woman their firstborn daughter would be named for. 'Have faith.'

EPILOGUE

SYDNEY society had seen nothing like it. The dress was made of a spun gold fabric laden with emerald chips, the best the craftswomen of Marrash had to offer, and the design an ancient Qusani pattern that meant, so Rafiq had been assured, prosperity, long life, and—most important apparently—fertility. Fitted to the waist, it fell in skilfully constructed folds to the ground. The gown was both elegant and timeless, a blend of the best of the east and the west, and with a veil of gold over her black hair she looked like a gift from the gods.

His gift from the gods.

Rafiq tried to contain his joy as she neared. Others could not. The group of tribespeople flown in especially from Marrash to one side, Abizah among them, called blessings as she passed, remarking on her beauty, sending their good wishes in voices that sounded in this place of worship like song.

Other guests, thinking this some quaint Qusani custom, joined in, so that Sera joined his side not to the sound of organ music but to the sound of a thousand blessings ringing out through the chapel.

It was a wedding the likes of which Sydney had never seen before, he thought, and nor was it likely to see again. It was a wedding where the guests responded spontaneously and the whole world rejoiced as it was transmitted around the globe. The guest list had been carefully handpicked, so there could be no embarrassment, no humiliation on either side.

It was the wedding, as far as he was concerned, to end all weddings.

Rafiq smiled down at her as she drew near, curled her hand in his, and she beamed up at him with what looked like her whole heart.

'I love you,' he said, knowing those words were more true in this very moment than ever before.

His black-haired beauty looked up at him, nothing but love shining out at him from her dark eyes. 'As I love you, Rafiq. Forever.'

And his heart swelled. Who needed to be king, he wondered, when you already had your queen?

Scandal: His Majesty's Love-Child

ANNIE WEST

Annie West spent her childhood with her nose between the covers of a book—a habit she retains. After years preparing government reports and official correspondence she decided to write something she *really* enjoys. And there's nothing she loves more than a great romance. Despite her office-bound past she has managed a few interesting moments—including a marriage offer with the promise of a herd of camels to sweeten the contract. She is happily married to her ever-patient husband (who has never owned a dromedary). They live with their two children amongst the tall eucalypts at beautiful Lake Macquarie, on Australia's east coast. You can e-mail Annie at www.annie-west.com or write to her at PO Box 1041, Warners Bay, NSW 2282, Australia.

Carol, Jennie and Trish.
It was terrific working with you.
Thank you!

CHAPTER ONE

'PLACE your bets, *mesdames et messieurs*.'

Sheikh Tahir Al' Ramiz glanced around the gaming table, at the crowd watching him with rapt attention, eager to see his next move. His gaze trawled past the stack of chips he'd won in the last hour.

A waiter hovered with a fresh bottle of champagne. Tahir nodded and turned to the woman pressed so eagerly against his side. Blonde, beautiful, accommodating. She'd turned heads from the moment they entered Monte Carlo's opulent old casino.

She moved and the fortune in diamonds encircling her throat and dripping down her superb cleavage flashed in the chandelier's mellow light. Her stunning evening dress of beaded silver was testament to the effect wealth and a world-class couturier could achieve.

She smiled, the sort of intimate, eager smile women had been giving him since adolescence.

He passed her a flute of France's finest champagne and leant back in his seat, finally acknowledging what he'd felt all evening.

He was bored.

Last time it had taken him two days to tire of Monte Carlo. This time he'd just arrived.

'Last bets, *mesdames et messieurs*.'

Stifling a sigh, Tahir caught the croupier's eye. *'Quatorze,'* he said.

The croupier nodded and moved Tahir's chips.

A hush fell as the crowd sucked in its collective breath. People on the other side of the table hurried to follow his lead, placing last-minute bets.

'Fourteen?' said the blonde, eyes widening. 'You're betting it *all* on one number?'

Tahir shrugged and lifted his glass. Idly he noted how the faint tremor in his hand made the surface of the wine ripple.

How long since he'd slept? Two days? Three? There'd been New York, where he'd finally closed that media deal and stayed to party. Then Tunisia for some all-terrain racing, Oslo and Moscow for more business, then here to his cruiser in the marina.

Was his lifestyle finally catching up with him?

He tried to dredge up some interest, some concern, and failed.

With a flourish the croupier set the roulette wheel spinning.

Slender fingers gripped Tahir's knee through the fine wool of his trousers. His companion's breathing quickened as the wheel spun. Her hand slipped up his thigh.

Did she find the thrill of gambling, even by proxy, so arousing?

He almost envied her. Tahir knew that if she were to strip naked and offer herself to him here and now, he'd feel nothing. No desire. No excitement. *Nothing*.

She flashed him another smile, a sultry invitation, and leaned close, her breast pressing against his arm.

He really should remember her name.

Elsa? Erica? It eluded him. Because he hadn't been interested enough to fix it in his mind? Or because his memory was becoming impaired?

His lips quirked briefly. Unfortunately his memory still functioned perfectly.

Some things he'd never forget.

No matter how hard he tried.

Elisabeth. That was it. Elisabeth Karolin Roswitha, Countess von Markburg.

Clamorous applause roused him from his thoughts. A cushioned embrace engulfed him as the Countess von Markburg almost climbed onto his lap in her excitement. Soft lips grazed his cheek, his mouth.

'You've won again, Tahir!' She pulled back, her eyes glittering with excitement. 'Isn't it marvellous?'

He moved his lips in what passed for a smile and raised his glass.

Tahir envied her that simple rush of pleasure. How long since he'd experienced that? Gambling didn't do it for him any more. Business coups? Sometimes. Extreme sports? At least he got an adrenalin rush when he put his neck on the line. Sex?

He watched another woman approach. A dark-haired seductress wearing ruby drop earrings that brushed her bare shoulders and a dress that would have her locked up for indecency in a lot of countries.

And he felt not a flicker of response.

She stopped beside him, leaned down, giving him a view right down her dress, past unfettered breasts to her navel and beyond.

'Tahir, darling. It's been an age.'

Her lips opened against his and her tongue slicked along the seam of his lips. But he wasn't in the mood.

Fatigue suddenly swamped him. Not physical tiredness, but the insidious grey nothingness that had plagued him so long.

He was tired of life.

Abruptly he pulled back from her hungry kiss. It was only months since they'd been together in Buenos Aires yet it felt a lifetime ago.

'Elisabeth.' He turned to the blonde still glued to his side. 'Let me introduce Natasha Leung. Natasha, this is Elisabeth von Markburg.'

He nodded to the waiter, who produced another champagne flute.

'Ah, it's my favourite vintage,' Natasha purred, standing closer, so her thigh slid against his. 'Thank you.'

Over her shoulder Tahir caught the croupier's expressionless gaze.

'Place your bets, *s'il vous plaît.*'

'*Quatorze,*' Tahir murmured.

'*Quatorze?*' The croupier's impeccable reserve couldn't hide the astonishment in his eyes. '*Oui, monsieur.*'

'Fourteen again?' Elisabeth's voice rose shrilly. 'But you'll lose it all! The chances of getting the same number again are impossible.'

Tahir shrugged and, alerted by a discreet ring tone, dragged his mobile phone from his pocket. 'Then I'll lose.'

At the look of horror on her face Tahir almost smiled. Life was so simple for some.

He looked at the phone, frowning when he didn't recognise the number displayed. Only his lawyer and his most trusted brokers had his private number. This wasn't one of them.

'Hello?'

'Tahir?' Even after so long that voice was unmistakable. Tahir surged to his feet, dislodging both the women clinging to him.

'Kareef.'

Only something truly significant would make his eldest brother call him out of the blue and after so long. He turned his back on the table, gesturing to his companions to stay where they were. The crowd around him parted, as it always did, and he strode across the room to the privacy of a quiet corner.

'This is an unexpected surprise,' he murmured. 'To what do I owe the pleasure?'

Silence. It stretched so long the back of his neck prickled.

'I want you to come home.' Kareef's voice was as calm and familiar as it had always been.

But the words. They were words Tahir had never thought to hear.

'I don't have a home any more. Remember?'

A tiny part of long-dormant conscience told him he took out his old bitterness unfairly on Kareef. His brother wasn't to blame for the disaster that was Tahir's past.

He clamped his mouth shut.

'You do now, Tahir.' Something in his brother's voice sent a tingle of premonition down his spine.

'Our revered father would have something to say to that.'

'Our father is dead.'

The words rolled like thunder in Tahir's brain.

The brute who'd ruled his people and his family so corruptly was gone for ever.

The tyrant who'd betrayed his wife with a string of whores and mistresses. Who'd ruled his tribe by fear. Who'd thrashed Tahir time and again to within an inch of his life. Then had his thugs take over when Tahir grew old enough to defend himself against his father.

The man who'd exiled his youngest son when he'd finally done what the old Sheikh had probably secretly wanted and overstepped the mark completely.

Tahir had never been able to please his father, no matter how he tried. He'd spent his boyhood wondering what fault of his inspired such hatred.

But he'd long ago given up caring.

Tahir turned to look across the elegant room and its throng of late-night pleasure-seekers. In his mind's eye it wasn't the glamorous crowd he saw, the flirtatious and curious glances or the opulent display of wealth. It was Yazan Al'Ramiz's blood-shot eyes, his bristling moustache flecked with spittle as he ranted and bellowed. The violent pounding of his clenched fists.

Surely Tahir should feel something, anything, at the news his tyrant father was dead? Even after eleven years' absence the news must evoke some response?

A yawning void of darkness welled inside where once emotions had lodged.

He supposed he should have questions.

When? How? Wasn't that what a child asked about a father's death?

'Still, I don't feel a burning desire to return to Qusay.' His tone was as blank as his mood. There was nothing for him in the land of his birth.

'Damn it, Tahir. Stop playing the arrogant unfeeling bastard for a moment. I need you here. Things are complicated.' Kareef paused. 'I *want* you here.'

Something unfamiliar roiled deep in Tahir's belly.

'What do you need?' Kareef had always been his favourite brother. The one he'd looked up to, in the long-ago days when he'd still tried to emulate his elders and betters. 'What's the problem?'

'No problem,' Kareef said in a curiously strained voice. 'But our cousin has discovered he isn't the rightful king of Qusay. He's stood aside and I'm to take his place on the throne.' He paused. 'I want you here for my coronation.'

Tahir walked slowly to the roulette table.

Kareef's news was momentous. To discover their cousin had been made King in error was almost unbelievable. He was no blood relation to the old King and Queen, but had been secretly taken in by them while they grieved the death of their real son. If it had been anyone other than Kareef telling the story Tahir would have doubted the news.

But Kareef would never make such an error. He was too careful, too responsible. He would make the perfect King for Qusay. Either of Tahir's older brothers would.

Thank merciful fate their father wasn't alive to inherit the throne! As brother to the old King and leader of a significant clan he'd been too powerful as it was—too dangerous. Having him rule the whole nation would have been like letting a wolf in amongst lambs.

A heart attack, Kareef had said.

No wonder. Their father had liked to indulge himself and hadn't limited himself to one vice.

Tahir approached the gaming table. He saw his barely touched champagne and the two women waiting for him, both undoubtedly eager to give him whatever he desired tonight.

His lips curled. Perhaps he was more like the old man than he realised.

'Tahir!' Elisabeth's voice was a shriek of delight. 'You'll never believe it. You won! Again! It's unbelievable.'

The babbling crowd hushed. Every eye was on him, as if he'd done something miraculous.

Before him, piled high, were his winnings. Far larger than before. The croupier looked pale and rigidly composed.

Eager feminine hands reached for Tahir as his companions sidled close. Their eyes were bright with avarice and excitement.

Tahir slid some of the most valuable chips to the croupier. 'For you.'

'*Merci, monsieur.*' He grinned as he scooped his newfound wealth safely into his hand.

Tahir lifted his glass, took a long swallow and let the bubbles cascade from the back of his tongue down his throat.

The wine's effervescence seeped into him. He felt buoyant, almost happy. For once fate had played things right. Kareef would be the best King Qusay had known.

He put the glass down with a click and turned away.

'Goodnight, Elisabeth, Natasha. I'm afraid I have business elsewhere.'

He'd taken but a few steps when the babble of voices stopped him.

'Wait! Your winnings! You've forgotten them.'

Tahir turned to face a sea of staring faces.

'Keep them. Share them amongst yourselves.'

Without a backward glance he strode to the entrance, oblivious to the uproar behind him.

The doorman thrust open the massive doors and Tahir emerged into the fresh night air. He breathed deep, filling his lungs for the first time, it seemed, in recent memory.

A hint of a smile played on his lips as he loped down the stairs.

He had a coronation to attend.

Tahir skimmed low over the dunes of Qusay's great interior desert.

Alone at the helicopter's controls, he put the effervescence in his blood down to the freedom of complete solitude. No hangers-on. No business minions seeking direction. No women with wide eyes and grasping hands. Not even paparazzi waiting to report his next outrageous affair.

Perhaps the barren glory of the desert had lifted his spirits? He even, for this moment, put from his mind what awaited him in Qusay.

His family. His past.

Yet he'd visited deserts in the last eleven years. From North Africa to Australia and South America, motor-racing, hang-gliding, base-jumping—always searching for new extreme ways to risk his neck.

Finally he recognised his mood was because he flew over the place he'd called home for the first eighteen years of his life. The place he'd never expected to see again.

But this realisation came as an almighty gust buffeted the chopper, slewing it sideways. Tahir grappled with the controls, swinging the helicopter high above the dunes.

The sight that met him sent adrenalin pumping through his body. The growing darkness filling the sky wasn't an early dusk, as he'd thought.

If he'd been flying by the book he'd have noticed the warning signs sooner. Instead he'd been skylarking, swooping dangerously low, gambling on his ability to read the topography of a place that changed with every wind.

This was the mother of all sandstorms. The sort that claimed livestock, altered watercourses and buried roads. The sort that could whip up a helicopter like a toy, whirl it round and smash it into fragments.

No chance to outrun it. No time to land safely.

Nevertheless, Tahir battled to steer the bucking chopper away from the massive storm. Automatically he switched into crisis mode, sending out a mayday, knowing already it was too late.

Calmness stole over him. *He was going to die.*

The prodigal had returned to his just deserts.

He wasn't dead.

Fate obviously had something far worse in store. Dehydration in the heat. Or, going by the pain racking him, death from his wounds.

The preposterous luck that had seen him win several fortunes at the gaming table had finally abandoned him.

Tahir debated whether to open his eyes or lie there, seeking the luxurious darkness of unconsciousness again. Yet the throbbing pain in his head and chest was impossible to ignore.

Even opening his eyes hurt. Light pierced his retinas through sand-encrusted lashes. It dazzled him and he groaned, tasting heat and dust and the metallic saltiness of blood. His hands and face felt raw from exposure to whipping sand.

He had a vague recollection of sitting, blinded by dust and strapped in a seat, hearing the unearthly yowl of wind and lashing sand. Then the smell of petrol, so strong he'd fought free of both seatbelt and twisted metal, stumbling as far as he could.

Then nothing.

Overhead the pure blue of a cerulean sky mocked him.

He was alive. In the desert. Alone.

Tahir passed out three times before he dragged himself to a sitting position, sweating and trembling and feeling more dead than alive. His brain was scrambled, wandering into nothingness and then jerking back to the present with hideous clarity.

He sat with his back against a sandbank, legs stretched out, and tried to ignore the brain-numbing pain that was the back of his skull in contact with sand.

He was drifting into unconsciousness when something jerked him awake. A rough caress on his hand. Gingerly he tilted his head.

'You're a mirage,' he whispered, but the words wouldn't emerge from his constricted throat.

The animal sensed his attention. It stared back, its horizontal pupils dark against golden-brown irises. It shook its head and a cloud of dust rose from its shaggy coat.

'Mmmmah.'

'Mirages don't talk,' Tahir murmured. They didn't lick either. But this one did, its tongue tickling. He shut his eyes, but when he opened them the goat was still there. A kid, too small to be without its mother.

Hell. He couldn't even die in peace.

The goat butted his hip, and Tahir realised his jacket pocket had something in it. Slowly, so as not to black out from the pain, he slipped his hand in and found a water bottle.

A muzzy memory rose, of him grabbing bottled water as he stumbled from the wreckage. How had he forgotten that?

It took for ever to pull the bottle out, twist off the lid and lift it to his lips. The hardest thing he'd ever done was drag it away after one sip.

Guzzling too much was dangerous. He risked another sip then lowered his hand. It felt like a dead weight.

Something nudged him and he opened his eyes to see the goat curled up close. In the whole vast expanse of desert the beast had chosen this place to shelter.

Gritting his teeth as he brought his left hand over his body, Tahir poured water into his palm.

'Here you are, goat.'

Placidly it drank, as if used to human contact. Or as if it too was on its last legs and had no room for fear.

Tahir had just enough energy to recap the bottle before it slid from his shaking hands. His head lolled.

Beside him the warmth of that tiny body penetrated his clothes, reminding him he wasn't alone.

It was that knowledge that forced him to focus on surviving Qusay's notoriously perilous desert.

Annalisa drew water up in the battered metal scoop and sluiced it over her face. Heaven.

The huge sandstorm had delayed her journey into the desert. Her cousins had tut-tutted, saying it was proof this trip was a mistake. The sort of mistake she wouldn't survive. But they didn't understand.

Just six months after her granddad's death, and her beloved father's soon after, it meant everything that she come here.

Annalisa was keeping her last promise to her father.

It was wonderful to be here again, though sadness tinged the experience as she remembered previous trips with her dad.

She'd arrived this morning, spending the afternoon cleaning her camera and telescopic equipment. A day out here meant a day of heat and dust, and the luxury of having the oasis to herself was too much to resist.

She lifted another scoop of water and tipped it over her head, shivering luxuriously as the water slid through her hair, over her shoulders and down her back. Another scoop sluiced over her breasts and she smiled, revelling in the feeling of being clean. She wriggled her toes in the sandy bottom of the small pool.

The sun was setting and she should move to build up the fire before darkness fell.

She was just turning to get out of the water when something on the horizon caught her attention. She narrowed her eyes against the setting sun.

A shadow. More than a shadow. A man. She made out broad shoulders and dark clothes. Remarkably, for this place, he was wearing what looked like a suit as he took a step down the dune, letting the slip of sand carry him several metres.

Automatically Annalisa reached for her towel and wrapped it close, her actions slowing when she registered his strange gait. He didn't use his arms to keep his balance on the treacherously steep slope and his movements were oddly uncoordinated.

Caution warned her to take no chances with a stranger.

No local would harm her. But this man clearly didn't belong. Who knew how he'd react to finding a lone female?

But as she knotted the towel and watched his slow progress she realised something was wrong. Instincts honed by years of helping her father tend to the sick overrode her wariness. The stranger was no threat. He looked as if he could barely stay upright.

Moments later she was racing up the other side of the *wadi* towards him.

Her steps slowed as she neared and took in the full impact of his appearance.

Her breath hissed in her throat. Disbelief filled her. She blinked, but the image was clear and unmistakable.

A tall man, dark-haired, wearing a tuxedo and black leather shoes, was slipping down the dune towards her. His dress shirt was ripped open and filthy, revealing bronzed skin and the top of a broad chest. A dark ribbon, the end of a bow tie, fluttered against his collarbone.

His face was long and lean and so caked in sand she could barely make out his features. Yet the solid shape of his jaw and the high angle of his cheeks hinted at a devastating masculine beauty. His temple was a mass of dried blood that made her suck in a dismayed breath.

But it was his eyes that held her still as he slithered down the slope. Piercing blue, they mesmerised her. Such an unexpected colour here in a desert kingdom.

Even as he staggered towards her his tall frame looked improbably elegant and absurdly raffish. As if he'd drunk too much at a society party and wandered unsteadily off.

Then she registered the way he cradled his arms across his torso and fear escalated. Chest wounds? She could deal with cuts and abrasions. She was her father's daughter after all. But they were days away from medical help and her skills only went so far.

Clumsily Annalisa raced up the dune, hauling the flapping towel tighter. Her heart thudded painfully as she fought to suppress panic.

She'd almost reached him when he stumbled and dropped to his knees, swaying woozily.

He stretched out his arms and looked up from under a tangle of matted dark hair.

'Here, sweetheart.' His voice was a hoarse whisper, thick and slurred, as if his tongue didn't work properly. She leaned closer to hear. 'Take care of it.'

His arms dropped and something, a small scruffy animal, rolled out as the stranger pitched to one side, seemingly lifeless, at her feet.

CHAPTER TWO

ANNALISA sat back on her heels and pushed a lock of hair behind her ear with shaky fingers. She trembled all over, her arms weak as jelly from exertion. Her pulse was still racing from shock and the fear she mightn't be able to save him.

After a quick check she'd decided to risk moving the stranger to her campsite. His temperature was dangerously high and a night on the exposed dune could prove fatal.

But she hadn't reckoned on the logistics of transporting a man well over six feet and at least a head taller than her.

It had taken an hour of strained exertion and all her ingenuity to get him down, dragging him on a makeshift stretcher. Most frightening of all he'd been a dead weight, not stirring.

'Don't you die on me now,' she threatened as she checked his weak pulse and began cleaning the wound on his temple.

Head wounds bled prolifically. It probably wasn't as bad as it looked, she told herself. Yet she found herself muttering a mix of prayer and exhortation in mingled Arabic, Danish and English, just as her dad had used to when faced with a hopeless case.

The familiar words calmed her, made her feel slightly more in control, though she knew that was an illusion. It would be a miracle if her patient pulled through.

'It's okay.' A slurred voice broke across her thoughts. 'I know I won't survive.' His eyes remained closed, but Annalisa watched his bloodied, cracked lips move and knew she hadn't imagined his voice.

Hope surged, and a spark of anger born of fear.

'Don't be ridiculous! Of course you'll live.' He'd echoed her fears so precisely she lashed out, heart pounding in denial.

After a moment his lips moved again, this time in a twitch that might have signified amusement.

'If you say so.' Now his voice was weaker, a thready whisper. 'But don't fret if you're wrong.' He drew a shaky breath that rattled in his lungs. 'I won't mind at all.'

The words trailed off and he lay so still in the lamplight Annalisa couldn't make out his breathing. Frantically she fumbled for his pulse. Relief pounded through her when she felt it.

She told herself it was better he'd slipped into unconsciousness again. He wouldn't feel pain as she tended his wounds.

It was only later, as she placed a damp cloth on his forehead, trying to lower his temperature, that she realised the man had spoken to her in perfect English.

Who was he? And what was a lone foreigner doing in Qusay's arid heartland dressed like some suave movie star?

Tahir ached all over. His head hammered mercilessly, as if a demolition squad had started work inside his skull. His mouth and throat were parched and raw. Swallowing felt like his muscles closed over broken glass. His body was stiff and weighted, bruised all over.

It was one hell of a beating this time, he realised vaguely. *Had the old man finally gone too far?*

Tahir couldn't bring himself to struggle out of the blackness to take in his surroundings. Instinctively he knew the pain would be overwhelming when he did. Right now he didn't have the strength to pretend he didn't care.

His only weapons against his father were pride and feigned unconcern. To meet the old man's eyes steadily and refuse to beg for mercy.

It drove his tormentor wild and robbed him of the satisfaction he sought from lashing out at his son.

No matter how bad the thrashing, how prolonged or vicious, Tahir never begged for it to end. Nor did he cry out. Not a murmur, not a flinch, no matter how remorseless his father's ice-cold eyes or how explosive his temper. Even when Yazan Al'Ramiz brought in thugs to subdue Tahir and prolong the punishment, Tahir refused to give in.

There was triumph in facing down the man who'd hated him for as long as he could remember. That was little recompense for not knowing *why* Yazan loathed him, but it gave him something to focus on rather than go crazy seeking an explanation the old man refused to give.

Obviously Tahir wasn't the sort to inspire affection.

Far better to be alone and self-contained.

He was stubborn and contemptuous enough never to give in. It was a matter of honour that every time, when it was over, he gathered his strength and walked away. Even if his steps were unsteady and his eyes clouded. Even if he had to haul himself along using furniture or a wall to keep upright.

Sheer willpower always forced him on. He refused to lie broken and cowed at the old Sheikh's feet.

Tahir drew a shaky breath, awake enough to register the constriction in his chest and the pain ripping across his side. Broken ribs?

He couldn't walk away this time. The realisation tore at his pride and ignited his stubbornness.

Something fluttered at his neck. A touch so light that for a moment his dazed brain rejected the notion.

There it was again. Something cool and damp slid from his jaw down his throat, then lower, in a soothing swipe over his chest. And again, from under his chin, the caress edged down, tracing blessed coolness across burning skin.

It stopped and, straining his senses, Tahir heard a splash. A moment later the damp cloth—he was aware enough now to realise what it was—returned, trailing across his pounding forehead and brushing damply at his hair.

He swallowed a moan at the pure pleasure of that cool relief against the searing ache in his head.

Was this some new torture devised by his father? A moment's respite and burgeoning hope to rouse him enough only so he could feel more pain when the beating recommenced?

'Go away.' He moved his lips, worked his throat, but no sound emerged.

The cloth paused, then slid down his cheek in a tender caress that was almost his undoing. He couldn't remember feeling weaker.

His skin burned and prickled, as if stung by a thousand cuts, yet the bliss of that touch made him suck in his breath. That sudden movement scorched his battered torso with a fiery ache.

'Go away.'

He didn't have the strength to withstand the lure of this gentle treatment. It would break him as the pounding fists never could.

'You're awake.' Her voice was a whisper, soft as a soughing breeze. He racked his brain to place it. Surely he couldn't forget a woman with a voice like that? Low and sweet, with a seductive husky edge that set it apart.

He didn't know her. In his foggy brain that fact stood out.

She must be one of his father's women. A new one.

Bitterness flooded his mouth, ousting even the rusty taste of blood. He should have guessed Sheikh Yazan Al'Ramiz would try something new to break his obstinate son. What better than the soft touch of a woman?

'Leave me,' Tahir ordered. But to his shame his voice emerged as a hoarse whisper. Almost a whimper.

'Here.' A firm hand slipped beneath his shoulder and a slim arm supported his skull, lifting him slightly.

Instantly pain shot through him. A stabbing spike of lightning shattered the blankness behind his closed lids and he stiffened against the need to gasp out his agony.

'I know it hurts, but you have to drink.' He heard the voice vaguely, as if through a muffling curtain. Then water, blessedly cool, trickled over his lips. Thought fled as he gulped the precious fluid.

Too soon the flow stopped.

He opened his lips to ask for more, heedless now of pride. But she forestalled him, her voice soothing.

'Be patient. You can have more soon.' She leaned close. He felt her warmth beside and behind him as he lay in her lap. Her scent, wild honey and cinnamon and warm female flesh, teased his nostrils and unravelled his thoughts. 'You're dehydrated. You need fluids, but not too fast.'

'How long before he returns?'

'He?' Her voice was sharp. 'There's no one else. Just you and me.'

Tahir listened to her husky voice, a voice of untrammelled temptation, and suppressed a groan of despair. How could he hold out against the promise of that voice, those gentle hands?

In his weakened state Tahir had no reserves of strength. All he wanted was to have her hold him, nurse him against her undoubtedly soft bosom and pretend there was no such thing as reality.

How long before he begged for the first time in his life?

Damn his father for finally finding a way to break his resistance. She'd sap his willpower as no beating could.

'Tell me.' He struggled to sit higher, but was so weak the press of her palm against his bare chest stopped him. 'When will he be back?'

'Who? Was there someone with you in the desert?' Urgency threaded her voice.

'Desert?' Tahir paused, his brows turning down as he fought to remember. Sheikh Yazan Al'Ramiz enjoyed the luxuries of life too much to spend time in the desert, even if it *was* the traditional home of his forebears.

She was trying to distract him.

'Where is my father?' he whispered through gritted teeth, as pain rose in an engulfing tide. 'He'll want to gloat.'

'I told you, there's no one here but us.'

His face hurt as he grimaced. 'I may have been beaten senseless but I'm not a fool.' He raised a hand and unerringly encircled her wrist where her palm rested against his chest.

She was young, her skin supple and smooth. He felt her pulse race against his fingers, heard her breath catch in the resounding silence that blanketed them.

'Someone *beat* you? I thought you'd been in an accident.'

Finally, against his better judgement, he forced his weighted eyelids open. The world was dark and blurred. It took a long time to focus. When he did his breath seized in his lungs.

Damn the old man. He knew Tahir too well. Knew him better than Tahir knew himself.

She glowed in the wavering light, her smooth almost oval face pale and perfect. Her nose was neat and straight. Her lips formed a cupid's bow that promised pure pleasure. His pulse leapt just from looking at it and, despite his pain, heat coiled in Tahir's belly when she furtively swiped her tongue along her top lip as if nervous.

The slightly square set of her jaw hinted at character and a determination that instantly appealed to Tahir. And her eyes… He could sink into the rich sherry-tinted depths of those wide eyes. They looked guileless, gorgeous, beguiling.

Glossy dark hair framed her face. Not a stiff, sprayed coiffure but soft tresses that had escaped whatever she'd done to pull her hair back.

She looked fresh, without a touch of make-up on her exquisite features. She blinked, eyes widening as she met his gaze, then long lush lashes lowered, screening her expression.

She was the picture of innocent seduction.

His poor battered body stirred feebly.

If he'd had the energy Tahir would have applauded his father's choice. How had he known that façade of innocent allure would weaken his son's resolve more than the wiles of a glamorous, experienced woman?

Tahir remembered the first time he'd fallen for the mirage of sweet, virginal womanhood and scowled. Who'd have thought after all this time he'd still harbour a weakness for that particular fantasy? He'd made it his business to avoid falling for it again.

His hand firmed around hers, feeling the fragility of her bones and the thud of her pulse racing. Her face was calm but her pulse told another story.

Did she fear his father? Had she been coerced?

He grimaced, searching for words to question her. But his

eyes flickered shut as the effort of the last minutes took its toll. His fingers opened and her hand slid away.

'Go! Leave before he hurts you too.' Even to his own ears his words sounded slurred and uneven. Tahir groped for the strength to stay awake.

'Who? Who are you talking about?'

'My father, of course.' Walls of pain rose and pressed close, stifling his words, stealing his consciousness.

Annalisa lowered his head and shoulders to the pillow.

Shock hummed through her.

Looking into his searing blue eyes was like staring at the sun too long. Except watching the sky had never made her feel so edgy or breathless.

Even the sound of his deep voice, a mere whisper of sound from his poor cracked lips, made something unravel in the pit of her stomach.

Belatedly she looked around, past the lamp and the low-burning campfire, towards the dune where he'd appeared.

Had he been attacked? If so, by a stranger or by his father, as he'd claimed? Or was that a figment of a mind confused by head wounds? As well as the gash at his temple Annalisa had found a lump like a pigeon's egg on the back of his skull.

For hours she'd been checking his pupils. Though what she'd do if he had bleeding to the brain she didn't know. She couldn't move him. It would be days before the camel train returned and this part of the country's arid centre was a tele-communications black spot.

Fear sidled down her spine and she shivered. All night she'd told herself she'd cope, doing her best to rehydrate the stranger and lower his temperature.

Now she had more to worry about.

She got to her feet and searched her supplies. Her hand closed around cool metal and she dragged it out.

The pistol was an antique. It had belonged to her mother's father, been presented to Annalisa's father on the day he'd wed. A traditional gift from a traditional man. All the men of Qusay knew how to shoot, just as they knew how to ride, and many still had skills in the old sports of archery and hawking.

Annalisa's father, an outsider, had never used the gun. As a respected doctor he'd never needed to protect himself or his family. But she felt better with it in her hand.

She'd brought it for sentimental reasons, remembering how he'd carried it on their trips into the wilderness.

Once more that dreadful sense of aloneness swept over her, pummelling her stomach and stealing the calm she'd worked so hard to maintain.

What if someone else was out there, lost and injured or angry and violent? She bit her lip, knowing she couldn't search. If she left the oasis her patient would likely die of dehydration and exposure.

She returned to his side. His temperature was too high. She picked up the cloth but was loath to touch him again.

Despite the nicks and abrasions marring his face he was a handsome man. More handsome than any she'd met before. Even with deep purple shadows beneath his eyes and the wound at his temple. Dark stubble accentuated a lean, superbly sculpted countenance. Even his hands, large and strong and sinewed, were strangely fascinating.

Annalisa remembered the feel of his fingers encircling her wrist and wondered at the sensations that had bombarded her. She'd felt wary yet excited.

Her gaze slipped to his bare chest. She'd spread his shirt open to bathe him and try to reduce his fever.

In the mellow light from the lamp and the flickering fire he looked beautiful, despite the bruises marring his firm golden skin. His chest was broad and muscular but not with the pumped-up look she'd seen on men in movies and foreign magazines. His latent strength looked natural but no less formidable for that. As for the way his powerful torso tapered to a narrow waist and hips… Annalisa knew a shameful urge to sit and stare.

Even the fuzz of dark hair across his pectoral muscles looked appealing. She wanted to touch it. Discover if it was soft or coarse against her palm.

Her gaze strayed to the narrowing line of hair that led from his chest down his belly.

Annalisa's pulse hit a discordant beat and staggered on too fast. Heat washed her cheeks and shame burnt as she realised she'd been ogling him.

Determined, she squeezed the cloth, took a fortifying breath and wiped the damp fabric over him.

She refused to think about how her hand shook as it followed the contours of his body, or about the alien tingle in her stomach that signalled a reaction to a man who, even asleep, was more potently virile than any male she'd encountered.

Tahir woke to pain again. At least the throb in his head didn't threaten to take the back off his skull, as it had before. Only one jackhammer was at work there now.

His lips twisted in a rueful smile that felt more like a grimace from scratched, sore lips. He stirred, opening his eyes a fraction. Not darkness. Not bright daylight either. The light filtering through his lashes was green-tinged and shadowed.

He heard the soft stirring of the wind, breathed deep and inhaled the unique scent that was Qusay. Heat and sand and some indefinable hint of spice he'd never been able to identify.

A searing blast of confused feelings struck him, roiling in his gut, rising in his throat.

'I'm not dead, then.' The words, hoarse as they were, sounded loud.

'No, you're not dead.'

His muscles froze as he heard a voice, half remembered. Soft, rich, slightly husky. The voice of a temptress sent to tease a man too weak to resist.

She spoke again, 'You don't seem particularly pleased.'

Tahir shrugged, then stiffened as abused muscles shrieked in protest.

He didn't explain his innermost thoughts to anyone.

'Why is it green? Where are we?' He kept his head averted, preferring not to face the owner of that voice till he had himself in hand. He felt strangely at a loss, unable to summon his composure, as if this last beating had shattered the brittle shell of disdain he used to maintain distance from the brutality around him.

Tahir blinked, amazed at how vulnerable he felt. How weak.

'We're at the Darshoor oasis, in the heart of Qusay's desert.' Her voice slid like rippling water over him and for a moment his hazy mind strayed.

Till her words sank in.

'The desert?' He whipped his head round then shut his eyes as a blast of white-hot pain stabbed him.

'That's right. The light's green because you're in my tent.'

A tent. In the desert. The words whirled in his head but they didn't make sense.

'My father—'

'He's not here.' She broke in before he could cobble his thoughts together. 'You seemed to think he was here too but you're confused. You were…disturbed.'

Tahir frowned. None of this made sense. His father lived in the city, with easy access to his vices of choice: women, gambling and brokering power and money corruptly.

'You seemed to think you'd been beaten.'

Instantly Tahir froze. He would never have admitted such a thing, especially to a stranger! Not even to his closest friends.

Who *was* this woman?

He forced his eyelids open again and found himself sinking into warm sherry-tinted depths.

By daylight she looked even better than she had the first time. For he remembered her now, this woman who'd haunted his thoughts. Or were they dreams?

'Who are you?' A swift glance took in hair scrupulously pulled back from her lovely face, an absence of jewellery, a long-sleeved yellow shirt and beige cotton trousers. She didn't dress like a local in concealing skirts. Yet surely only a local would be here?

From where he lay, looking up, her legs looked endless. She moved and he watched the fabric pull tight over her neatly curved hip and slim thighs. A moment later she sat on the floor beside him, her faint, sweet fragrance tantalising his nostrils. Her shirt pulled across her breasts as she leaned towards him.

A jolt of sensation shot through his belly.

No. He wasn't dead yet.

Perhaps there were some compensations after all.

'My name is Annalisa. Annalisa Hansen.' She paused, as if waiting for him to say something. 'You arrived at my campsite days ago. Just walked out of the desert.'

'Days ago?' How could he have lost so much time?

'You're injured.' She gestured to his head, his side. 'My guess is you were in the desert for quite a while. When you reached me you were seriously dehydrated.' She lifted a hand to his brow. Her palm was cool and curiously familiar.

He had a jumbled recollection of her touching him earlier. Of blessed water and soothing words.

'You've been drifting in and out of consciousness.' She leaned back, lifting her hand away, and Tahir knew a bizarre desire to catch it back.

'Your little friend has been worried.'

'Little friend?' Automatically he looked past her, taking in the cool interior of the tent, the neatly stowed gear in one corner. A ripple of pages as a furtive breeze played across a book left open a few metres away.

'You don't remember?' She surveyed him seriously.

'No.' He remembered just in time not to shake his head. He was no masochist and the pain was already bad enough. 'I don't recall.'

It was true. His thoughts were fluid and incomplete. He was unable to fix anything in his mind.

'That's all right,' she said with the calm air of one who'd perfected a soothing bedside manner. Vaguely he wondered who this woman was, caring for him at a desert oasis. 'You've taken a nasty knock to the head so things could be jumbled for a while.'

'Tell me,' he murmured, forcing down rising concern at his faulty memory. He recalled a casino. A woman all but climbing into his lap as the chips rose before him. He remembered a

cruiser in a crowded marina. A party in a city penthouse. A
meeting in a hushed boardroom. But the faces were blurred.
The details unclear. 'What little friend?'

The woman…Annalisa, he reminded himself…smiled. A
shaft of sunlight pierced the interior of the tent, or so it seemed,
as he stared up into her calm, sweet face.

'You were carrying a goat.'

'A goat?' What nonsense was this?

'Yes.' This time her smile was more like a grin. Her dark
eyes danced and she tilted her head engagingly. 'A little one.
Obviously it's a friend of yours. It's been foraging for food but
it keeps coming back to sleep just outside the tent.'

A goat? His mind was blank. Frighteningly blank.

'What else?' he murmured. There must be more.

She shrugged and he caught a flash of something in her eyes.
Distress? Fear?

'Nothing else. You just appeared.' She waited but he said
nothing. 'So, perhaps you could tell me something.' She lifted
a hand and tugged nervously at her earlobe. 'Who are you?'

'My name is Tahir…'

'Yes?' She nodded encouragingly.

A sensation like a plummeting lift crashed through the
sudden void that was his stomach. Blood rushed in his ears as
he met her gaze. The kaleidoscope of blurry images cascaded
through his brain into nothingness.

'And I'm afraid that's all I can tell you.'

He forced a smile to lips that felt stiff and unfamiliar. 'I seem
to have mislaid my memory.'

CHAPTER THREE

FOR a man who couldn't remember his name Tahir was one cool customer.

Annalisa read the shock flaring in his eyes and the way he instantly masked it. Ready sympathy surged but she beat it down, knowing instinctively he'd reject it.

Despite never having left Qusay, Annalisa had seen a lot in her twenty-five years. As her father's assistant she'd seen the effects of accident and disease, the way pain or fear could break even the strongest will.

Yet this man, traumatised by wounds that must be shockingly painful, smiled at her with a veneer of calm indifference. As if he were one of her father's scientist friends and they were conversing over a cup of sweet tea in her father's study.

Yet none of her father's friends looked like Tahir. Or made her feel that warm tingle of awareness deep inside.

Years ago, with Toby, the man she'd planned to marry, she'd known something like it. But not so instantaneously, nor so strong.

There was something about Tahir that she connected with at the deepest level. More than his extraordinary looks or the innate sophistication that had nothing to do with his beautiful clothes. Something that set him apart. She was drawn by his core of inner strength, revealed as intensely blue eyes met hers with wry humour, ignoring the unspoken fear that his memory lapse was permanent.

He comes from another world. One where you don't belong.

She'd do well to remember it.

A pang shot through her and her calm frayed at the edges. *Just where did she belong?*

All her life she'd never fitted in. She was a Qusani but didn't live as other Qusani women or fit their traditional role. She was poised between two worlds, belonging to neither. She'd been part of her father's world, his assistant, his confidante.

But he'd gone, leaving her bereft.

'What's wrong?' Tahir's deep voice roused her from melancholy reflection. 'Are you all right?'

Despite herself Annalisa smiled. Lying flat on his back, bruised and barely awake, his memory shot, yet this man was concerned for *her*?

She laid a reassuring hand on his arm. His muscles tensed beneath the fine cotton of his shirt. His warm strength radiated up through her fingertips and palm.

A zap of something jagged between them as she met those piercing eyes. His nonchalant half-smile disappeared, replaced by frowning absorption.

'Nothing's wrong,' she said briskly, slipping her hand away. It tingled from the contact and she clenched it at her side. 'Your foggy memory is normal. It should come back in time.' She drew her lips up in a smile she hoped looked reassuring. 'You've got two head wounds. Either would be enough to knock you about for a couple of days.'

Or do far worse. Ruthlessly she pushed aside the fear that he might be more badly injured than she realised.

'You speak as if you have medical experience.'

'My father was a doctor. The only doctor in our region. I helped him for years.' She turned away, horrified by the way memories swamped her again, and the pain with it. 'I don't have medical qualifications but I can set a sprain or treat a fever.'

'Why do I suspect you've done much more than that for me, Annalisa?'

The sound of her name on his lips was strangely intimate. Reluctantly she turned back, meeting his warm gaze, feeling his approval trickle through her like water in a parched landscape.

'You've saved my life, haven't you?' His voice dropped to a low rumble that vibrated along her skin.

Annalisa shrugged, uncomfortable with his praise. Uncomfortable with her intense reaction to this stranger. She'd done all she could but he wasn't out of the woods yet. Fear edged her thoughts.

'You'll be okay, given time.' Fervently she prayed she was right. 'All you need to do is rest and give yourself time to recuperate. And try not to worry.' She'd do enough worrying for the pair of them.

Even now she couldn't quite believe he was holding a sensible conversation. He'd drifted in and out of consciousness since he'd stumbled into her life, leaving her terrified but doggedly determined to do what she could.

'I want to check your reactions.' She moved to kneel at the end of the mattress. 'Can you move your feet?'

She watched as he rotated his ankles and then lifted first one foot then the other. Relief coursed through her.

'Excellent. I'm going to hold your feet. When I tell you, push against my hands. Okay?'

'Okay.'

Gently she lifted his heels onto her knees and cupped his bare feet with her palms. A curious jolt of heat shot through her from the contact. She blinked and tried to concentrate.

His feet were long, strong and well shaped. For a moment she knelt there blankly staring, absorbing the sensation of skin on skin.

She'd never before thought of feet as sexy.

Annalisa's brow puckered. She felt out of her depth.

'Annalisa?' His voice yanked her mind back and heat seared her cheeks. She kept her head bent and concentrated on what her father had said about head injuries.

'Push against my hands.' Instantly she felt steady pressure. She smiled and looked up, meeting his narrowed stare. 'That's good.'

Carefully she lowered his feet and moved up beside him, leaning over so he didn't have to twist to face her.

'Now, take my hands,' she said briskly, adopting a professional manner. But it was hard when eyes like sapphires fixed unblinkingly on her. She wondered what he saw, whether he read her trepidation and uncertainty.

Large hands, powerful but marred by scratches, lifted towards her.

Not allowing herself to hesitate, Annalisa placed her hands in his. She told herself the swirling in her abdomen was relief that he was well enough to cooperate.

'Now, squeeze,' she murmured, ignoring the illusion of intimacy engendered by their linked hands.

Again the pressure was equal on both left and right sides. Her shoulders dropped a fraction as relief surged. For now the signs were good.

She moved to pull back, slide her hands from his. Instantly long fingers twined with hers, holding her still.

Her heart gave a juddering thump as their gazes meshed. She realised how she leaned across him, the heat of his bare torso warming her through the thin fabric of her clothes. The way his eyes flashed with something unidentifiable yet disturbing. Her breathing shortened. She felt vulnerable, though he was the injured one.

'What are you checking?' The words were crisp. Not slurred like when he'd called out in his sleep.

'Just making sure your reactions are normal.' She met his gaze steadily, refusing to mention the possibility of bleeding to the brain. 'They are. You should be up and about in no time.'

'Good. I find I have a burning desire to bathe. You said this is an oasis?'

'Yes, but—'

'Then there's no problem getting water.' He paused. 'I'll need someone from your party to help me get upright.'

'There's only me. And I don't think bathing is a good idea yet.'

His eyes darkened in surprise. 'You're alone?'

She nodded.

'You're a remarkable woman, Annalisa Hansen.' His grip loosened and she found herself free. Belatedly she remembered to straighten so she didn't hover over him.

'Do you do this often? Camp alone in the desert?'

She shook her head. 'This is the first time I've been here alone.' Stupidly her voice wobbled on the last word and his eyes narrowed. Abruptly she looked away.

It was almost six months to the day since her father died. Maybe it was the looming anniversary that sideswiped her, dredging up such grief sometimes she thought she couldn't bear it.

Abruptly he spoke, changing the subject. 'If you knew how much sand I've swallowed you wouldn't begrudge me your help to get clean.' He levered himself up on one elbow, then pushed himself higher to sit, swaying beside her.

He ignored her protests, setting his jaw with a steely determination and clambering stiffly to his knees. Finally she capitulated and helped him, realising she couldn't stop him.

It was only later she remembered the look in his bright eyes as grief had stabbed her out of nowhere.

Had he read her pain and decided to distract her?

No, the idea was absurd.

Tahir cursed himself for being every kind of fool as he sat in the pool and let water slide around his aching body. He'd known moving was a bad idea, but he refused to play the invalid.

Bad enough that his brain wasn't functioning. The more he tried to remember the more the ache in his skull intensified, matching the searing pain in his ribs. He let his thoughts skitter from the possibility the damage was permanent. He wouldn't accept that option.

It made him even more determined to conquer his physical weakness.

Then there was the memory of Annalisa's soft brown eyes, brimming with distress as she avoided his gaze.

Despite her brisk capability he sensed pain, a deep vulnerability. Looking into her shadowed eyes, Tahir had felt an overwhelming need to wipe her hurt away.

Enough to brave getting to his feet.

Fool! He'd almost collapsed. Only her support had kept him upright the few metres to the water. Now he sat waist-deep, naked but for the silk boxers he'd kept on in deference to her presence, wondering how he'd summon the strength to return to the tent.

Wondering how long he could keep his eyes off the woman who sat watchfully beside the stream.

It had been torture of a different sort, allowing her to undress him. Her soft hands fumbling at his trousers had been a torment that had made him forget for a brief moment the pain bombarding him. The sight of her kneeling before him, drawing his trousers off as he leaned on her shoulder, had evoked sensations no invalid should feel.

Then she'd waded into the water, supporting him. She'd been heedless of the way their unsteady progress had sent up sprays of water that soaked large patches of her trousers and shirt.

But Tahir hadn't.

When he shut his eyes he still saw her lace bra outlined against transparent cotton, cupping voluptuous breasts that strained forward as she steadied him. He remembered the neat curve of her hip, the narrow elastic ridge of bikini underwear where her trousers plastered her skin, then the long supple line of her thigh.

Tahir's mouth dried and it had nothing to do with the arid air.

He should be frantically trying to remember who he was. Trying to piece together the fragments of memory, like snippets of disjointed film, swirling in his head.

Instead his thoughts circled back to Annalisa. Who was she? Why was she here?

Despite the cool water, his groin throbbed as he watched her patting a spindly-legged goat.

Was he like this with other women? So easily aroused?

He remembered the woman at the casino. The one in beads and diamonds and little else, who'd been so amorous. The memory didn't spark anything. No heat. No desire.

Tahir frowned. He had an unsettling presentiment he should be very worried by his reactions to Annalisa Hansen.

Bathing in the *wadi* had been a huge mistake. Annalisa bit her lip as Tahir mumbled in his sleep, his dark brows arrowing fiercely in a scowl. These last hours he'd grown unsettled and she'd feared for him, giving up her position by the telescope to sit at his side.

He rolled, one arm outflung, dislodging the blanket and baring his chest to the rapidly cooling night air.

She strove not to think about the fact that he was naked beneath the bedding. He'd barely made it back from bathing when he'd collapsed on the makeshift bed, shucking off his wet boxers with complete disregard for her presence. She doubted he'd even realised she was there.

But to her chagrin she had perfect recall. *Detailed recall*. A blush warmed her throat at the memory of his tightly curved buttocks, heavily muscled thighs and—

'Father!' The hoarse groan yanked her into the present.

Tahir's head thrashed and Annalisa winced, thinking of the lump on his skull.

'Shh. It's all right, Tahir. You're safe.' Whatever nightmares his injuries conjured, they rode him like demons. He sounded desperate.

She leaned across, touching his forehead. His temperature was normal, thank God, but—

A hand snapped around her wrist and dragged it to his side. The movement caught her off balance. She tugged, but the harder she fought, the more implacable his hold, till she leant right across him. His frown deepened, and his firmly sculpted lips moved silently, the muscles of his jaw clenching beneath dark stubble.

He pulled. With an *oof* of escaping air she landed on him. Frantically she tried to find purchase without digging her elbows into his ribs, but his other arm came round her. There was no escape.

'He sent you, didn't he?' The words were a low growl.

'No one sent me.' She tried to slip down out of his grip but he simply lashed his arm tighter round her back, dragging her till she lay over him, her legs sinking between his when he moved.

Heat radiated up from tense muscles and she stiffened. With each breath she was aware of his chest, his hipbones, his thighs like hot steel around her.

'He knew what he was doing, damn him.' Tahir's voice was rough and deep, resonating up from his chest and right through her.

Annalisa struggled to ignore her fascination at being so close, encircled by him. Even with Toby, even when he'd taken her in his arms and talked of a future together, she had never been this close. This…intimate. He'd respected that in Qusay a woman's chastity was no light gift to bestow. He'd promised to wait. Except their bright future had never eventuated.

'Houri…' Tahir mumbled, and his searing breath feathered her scalp. Tremors ran down her spine and spread in slow-turning circles through her belly. 'Temptress.'

His grip eased and he smoothed a hand down her back. It felt so good she fought not to arch into his touch, like a cat responding to a caress. Spread across him, in full-length contact as he stroked her and murmured in her ear, Annalisa felt an unravelling in the pit of her stomach. A heat that was unfamiliar and edgy and worrying.

His hand moulded her buttocks, dragging her closer. The unmistakable ridge of male arousal against the apex of her thighs grew pronounced and she bit her lip as his caress rubbed her against it.

He didn't know what he was doing. Yet the pulse building between her legs and the heat there proved that didn't matter. She shuddered in horrified excitement at her own arousal.

Who'd known a man's body could feel so very good?

'Mustn't…' His voice died as his hands stopped their trawling caress. He drew a shuddering breath that pushed his chest to her breasts. Annalisa shut her eyes, willing herself not to react even as her nipples peaked in delight.

She waited a few moments then tried to ease away. Instantly his embrace hardened, imprisoning her.

Tahir grew quiet, his mutterings less vehement.

Annalisa waited ten minutes then tried again. Even in sleep Tahir held her tight, refusing to release her.

Telling herself she had no choice but to bide her time till he was completely relaxed, she gave up the unequal struggle to hold herself even marginally away. Her head sagged and her muscles went limp as she sank into him. She was going nowhere yet.

* * *

A shaft of early-morning light woke Tahir. Instantly the familiar low-grade hum of abused muscles, torn flesh and a battered head roused him to full wakefulness.

And something else. Sexual awareness.

More than awareness. Delight drenched him as he absorbed the full extent of his good fortune.

He lay on his side with Annalisa in his embrace. Her head was on his arm, her knees bent, allowing his bare legs to spoon in behind her. He breathed deep and the sweet fragrance of her hair filled his nostrils, shimmering there like a promise of pleasures to come. She was warm and curved, slim but rounded, exactly where it counted.

Not daring to breathe, Tahir gently flexed his fingers, cupping the exquisite ripeness of her breast. He'd pushed her shirt aside and her bra was soft, a thin layer of lace between his fingers and her feminine bounty.

His breath whistled out from contracting lungs and he cursed silently, not ready yet for her to wake and move away. It was clear that whatever had led to them sharing the narrow mattress, it wasn't sex. Annalisa was fully clothed.

But clothes provided little protection. Not when he lay flush against her.

He shut his eyes, realising exactly how aroused he was. The sweet curve of her buttocks pressed against him in unconscious invitation. Her warmth enclosed him and he fought rising lust. Fought the need to thrust against her and appease the hunger eating at his belly. Or better yet, to tear those light trousers away and bury himself deep within her pliant, lush body.

Pain shot through him and Tahir realised he'd locked his jaw so tight it felt as if he might dislocate it.

Slowly he breathed, telling himself to move. He had no right to hold her like this. But he wanted...how badly he wanted her.

For long minutes he lay, tense and still, his instincts at war. His palm pressed against her breast and he couldn't help tightening his grip, his fingers encircling her budding nipple.

Was this the sort of man he was? To take advantage of a

sleeping woman? A woman who'd shown him nothing but kindness and not a hint of sexual interest?

His breath shuddered out, riffling her dark unbound hair.

He didn't even know if he was married. Committed to a woman far away and worried about him.

The notion sliced like ice-cold steel through the searing heat of sexual excitement. Moments later he slid away, drawing back carefully so as not to wake her.

Every movement was torment.

The sun was high when Annalisa woke.

She remembered Tahir holding her with a strength that belied his injuries. Remembered realising she needed to wait till his nightmare subsided before escaping.

She recalled the unfamiliar but unmistakable response of her body to Tahir's embrace. Her skin flushed all over as she remembered how she'd revelled in his hardness, his masculine power, even the musky spice scent of his freshly washed skin.

Hastily she tugged her shirt closed, grateful he wasn't there to see how it had come undone during the night.

She suppressed panic that he wasn't there. Surely that was a good sign—that he had enough energy to get up without assistance.

Nevertheless she didn't linger. Despite his strength and his formidable determination he was far from well.

She saw him immediately she left the tent.

He sat with his back against a palm tree, long legs outstretched. He wore the trousers she'd washed and set aside for him. He wasn't naked, as when he'd clasped her close. Yet Annalisa shivered as awareness trickled through her middle, igniting a scorching heat.

Memories of last night and her burgeoning physical responses swamped her. Guilt rose that she'd reacted so to a man who was vulnerable and in her care.

And confusion. In twenty-five years she'd never responded so to any other man.

With his broad bared chest and shoeless feet he looked

untamed, elemental, despite his tailored dress trousers. Annalisa
recalled the texture of that fine fabric. Even to her untutored
touch she knew it to be of finest quality. Proof that Tahir came
from a place far beyond here. That he belonged in another
milieu.

Yet, sitting with the sunlight glancing off the golden skin of
his straight shoulders, he looked at home. Like a rakish
marauder taking his ease. Only the bruises mottling his ribs and
the gash at his temple belied the image.

She followed the play of muscles across his chest as he
leaned sideways. Annalisa tried and failed to ignore a disturbing new sensation deep in her abdomen.

It felt curiously like hunger.

'Here.' He hadn't noticed her, but spoke instead to the tiny
goat he'd carried into the oasis. It stood beside him, stretching
up towards a scanty green bush. Tahir reached out an arm and
drew a slender branch low enough for the animal to reach.

She didn't know another man who'd bother. Here in Qusay,
except for prized horses, animals weren't cosseted.

Despite his outrageously potent masculinity, there was a
softer side to him.

Had she imagined Tahir's motives last night? She'd been
almost convinced part of his abrupt determination to wash
was because he'd seen the stupid tears misting her eyes when
she thought of her father. Could he really have sought to
divert her thoughts?

It seemed ludicrous, and yet…

'Ah, Sleeping Beauty awakes.' Eyes bright as the morning
sun gleamed under straight dark brows. With his burnished skin
and black-as-midnight hair those light eyes should have looked
wrong somehow.

Yet Annalisa knew with a sinking certainty, as her pulse
sped, that she'd never seen a more handsome man. His half-
smile drove a deep crease up one lean cheek and her gaze fixed
on it with an intensity that appalled her.

'I hope you didn't need me earlier,' she murmured. 'I can't
imagine why I overslept.'

'Can't you?' This time he smiled fully, and Annalisa reached out to grab the tent post as her heart kicked and her knees loosened.

What was happening to her?

All her life she'd been sensible, responsible, dutiful. Never, not even on the brink of marriage, had she been swept away by the sheer presence of a man.

'From the little I recall I'd guess you've been running yourself ragged caring for me.'

Annalisa blinked and made herself move from the tent. It felt absurdly as if she was stepping away from safety. But the only danger lay in her reckless response to those piercing blue eyes.

'I packed up your telescope, by the way.'

Swiftly Annalisa turned to the place where her father's telescope had been last night. The location hadn't been ideal, close to the lights of the camp, but she hadn't liked to move too far away in case Tahir needed her.

Swiftly she knelt to undo the battered case.

'Thank you,' she murmured, frantically trying to remember whether she'd covered the lens before going last night to sit with Tahir through his nightmare. If the wind had risen and blasted sand across the lens—

'It seemed okay when I packed it up.'

He was right. There was no damage. Relieved, she sank back on her heels. 'You know about telescopes?'

He shrugged. Unwillingly Annalisa followed the fluid movement of his shoulders.

'Who knows?' His lazy smile slipped and for a moment he looked grim, his eyes cooling to an icy blue.

'I'm sorry.' How could she be so clumsy? 'I'm sure you'll remember soon.' Impulsively she stood and walked towards him, only to stop at his side, self-conscious.

'No doubt you're right.' His easy smile belied the gravity of his expression. 'Sit with me?'

Wordlessly she complied, settling out of arm's reach.

'I remember some things,' he said. 'More than before.'

'Really? That's fantastic. What do you recall?' If he noticed her too-bright tone he said nothing. She'd spent days wondering who he was and how he'd got here. How much worse for him not to know?

Again that shrug. Annalisa slid her gaze from the play of muscle and tanned skin, forcing her breathing to slow.

'Just vague images. A party. Lots of people, but no faces. Places I can't identify.' He paused. 'And a sandstorm, big enough to block the light.'

She nodded. 'That was just before I came out here.'

'I remember the vastness of the desert.' His eyes snared hers. 'Which leads me to wonder how we get out of here and if you've got enough food to keep us both in the meantime.'

'There's plenty.' Out of habit she'd catered for two. 'As for transport, there's a camel route through the oasis.'

'And a camel train is coming back soon?'

Annalisa's bright smile faded. 'Not straight away. In a few days.'

She'd prayed they'd return early and take Tahir to hospital. Now her desperation was edged with other emotions.

'A few more days?' he repeated. 'Maybe more?' His voice was disturbingly deep, his scrutiny so intense it was like a touch, and Annalisa sucked in a quick breath.

'You and me, alone in the desert.'

She met his unreadable eyes. Her stomach dipped. She lifted her chin, battling emotions she didn't understand.

Last night's intimacy had changed everything.

For the first time their enforced solitude felt…dangerous.

CHAPTER FOUR

ANNALISA needn't have worried. Even now he was up and about Tahir didn't encroach on her personal space. If anything he seemed to prefer distance. The idea stabbed her with ridiculous regret.

Occasionally she caught a look, a blaze of azure fire from under half-lowered lids, that stole her breath and set her pulse racing. But she knew it was imagination, her own guilty craving.

The only danger came from her wayward thoughts. They drew blushes to her cheeks and brought a twist of awareness deep inside her.

Meanwhile she was forced to keep an eye on him. Annalisa thought he was out of danger, but he still slept a lot and occasionally his temperature spiked worryingly. Nor could he recall more than disjointed images.

She almost wished she'd followed her father's urgings and studied medicine. Then she'd know what to do. But, though she'd been proud to act as her dad's assistant, medicine wasn't her dream.

'How long have you been an astronomer?'

Annalisa's gaze jerked up from the meal she was preparing over the fire. Tahir sat in his usual place by the palm tree, reading in the fading light—one of the astronomy books she'd brought.

The question was innocuous. But it struck her that this was the first time he'd asked anything personal. His questions were always about the desert and Qusay. She'd enjoyed their discussions and his quick intelligence. She wasn't used to talking about herself.

'I'm not an astronomer. But my father was an amateur one. I grew up looking at the stars.'

Tahir tilted his head consideringly. 'It's your father who usually comes into the desert with you?'

She busied herself lifting the pan from the fire. 'That's right.' Those treks had been special, precious time out from her father's busy practice.

'But he couldn't come this time?'

She forced herself to concentrate on dishing up the couscous flavoured with nuts, spices and dried fruits.

'My father is dead.' It sounded bald, almost aggressive. But Annalisa found it hard to speak of him. He'd been the centre of her life, her mainstay and friend.

'I'm sorry for your loss, Annalisa.' The simple words flowed like soothing balm over raw-edged nerves, at odds with the shivery excitement evoked by the rare sound of her name on Tahir's lips.

'Thank you.' She paused, feeling she should say more. 'It's been six months but still it's hard.'

'And you have no one else?'

Her shoulders stiffened. His words reminded her too much of her family's urgings for her to marry. They meant well, but it grew increasingly difficult to avoid their offers to arrange a marriage to a respectable man who'd take care of her.

She'd grown up with all the freedoms her father had taken for granted with his foreign background. Even her dear, traditional grandfather had understood an arranged marriage wouldn't work for her. She'd be stifled, living the more restricted life of a traditional Qusani wife.

But her grandfather was gone, like her dad. Her lips tightened as grief hollowed her chest.

She didn't need taking care of. Instead she had plans to see the world she'd only heard about. The places her father and his friends had spoken of. To build her own life.

'My mother died when I was young. But I'm not alone.' She smiled ruefully as she ladled their food. 'I have aunts and uncles, cousins and their children.' She was a cuckoo in her mother's family, never quite fitting in.

'Thank you.' Tahir took a plate from her hands and sat with easy grace beside her. 'So how did a doctor called Hansen come to be in Qusay? It's not a local name.'

'It's Danish.' Annalisa sat on the matting, overly conscious of the big man so near. 'My father was half-Danish, half-English. He came here years ago to look at the stars. He loved the place and decided to stay.'

She didn't add the old family story about him taking one look at Annalisa's mother and falling in love on the spot. How she'd loved him at first sight too and they'd waited years for family approval before marrying.

'So you're carrying on a family tradition with your stargazing?' She caught his bright stare and felt absurdly as if she were falling. It unnerved her.

'Sort of. My father believed he'd found a comet. He and various friends around the world hoped to prove its existence.' She dragged in an uneven breath, remembering the promise she'd given to her father. 'I'm hoping to see it. The Asiya Comet.'

'Nice name.'

She nodded, swallowing hard. Her mother's name. She barely remembered her mother. It was her father's grief she recalled, and his love, steady after all those years. He'd fought debilitating illness to live long enough to prove the comet existed and name it. His body had failed before he'd got to see it himself.

Annalisa blinked to clear her vision. 'I promised I'd be here to see it.' One last pilgrimage before she left.

Scientists around the globe were looking out for the comet this week. She'd be here in Qusay, her mother's home, to watch it for her father.

'Tonight?' At her startled look he gestured to the meal she'd prepared. 'We're eating earlier than usual.'

Annalisa nodded abruptly, reminded again of how much this man of few words noticed.

Had he also noticed the way her gaze followed him? Hastily she looked away, unnerved by the bewildering feelings that plagued her.

'All being well, yes.' She breathed deep.

'Then what will you do?' His voice was soft, like silk brushing her skin. 'Once you've seen your comet?'

Annalisa pushed aside her nervousness at what came next. It was what she wanted, what she'd always planned.

'Then I leave Qusay.' Even saying the words it didn't seem real. After years of wanting to see the wider world, suddenly the time was here. 'I'm going to travel, for a few months at least. Meet the scientists my father and I have corresponded with for so long. Play tourist.' She smiled as she imagined herself in Copenhagen, Rome, Paris. 'Then I'm going to university.'

'Medicine or astronomy?'

'Neither. This time I'm following my own star. I'm going to be a teacher.'

Tahir paced, so restless tonight he couldn't settle. His skin was too tight, his senses on edge, his head throbbing. He told himself it was impatience with his slow recovery, with his scattered memory.

But he knew the cause lay elsewhere. *With Annalisa.*

He'd kept to himself as much as he could. But thrown together as they were in one campsite, one tent, distance didn't account for much. Especially when he only had to close his eyes to see the sweet curve of her lips, the delicious bounty of her breasts and hips.

The scent of her skin, sweet as honey, wafted on the very air. The sound of her voice, soft and throaty, made him aware of her femininity and his own masculine need for her.

Yet it wasn't her exquisite body alone that made his blood hum. There was some indefinable quality that tugged at him. Her calm, capable demeanour, so at odds with that seductress's mouth. Her gentle touch. Her quick mind. And the intensity of her pleasure: when she'd laughed at the antics of the unkempt goat that still hung around the campsite, or tonight when she'd

spoken of travelling. Her whole heart shone in her smile and
Tahir basked in its radiance. More than anything he wanted her
to turn that smile on him.

He picked up his pace, plunging into the darkness at the far
end of the oasis where the shrubs grew thick.

Too late he realised his mistake, as his eyes widened and his
libido roared into unfettered overdrive.

The sound of splashing reached his ears just as he saw
moonlight silver a sinuous form in the stream. A form that was
all lush curves and elegant lines. A figure that would make a
man get down on bended knee and plead for the privilege of
simply stroking that satiny skin.

Only the belief that he was sleeping off another bout of
fatigue would have tempted Annalisa into total nudity.

Tahir sent up silent thanks for his wakefulness.

His gaze slipped hungrily along her body, traced the evocative darkness at the juncture of her thighs, dwelt on the supple
twist of her spine.

She lifted her hands to smooth water off her hair and the
movement raised her breasts invitingly high.

The impact of the sight was like a series of juddering im-
plosions through his body. Arousal was instantaneous. Heat
speared him as every muscle hardened. His breathing was an
uneven rasp, his hands clenching desperately at his sides.

So focused was he on reining in the need to reach for her
that it took a moment for his brain to kick into gear.

To realise he'd seen her like this before.

She'd stood gloriously naked in the afternoon light, like a
nymph, perfect, sweet and utterly seductive in this very stream.

He put a hand to his head as the stars wheeled above him.
The scattered images in his mind took on a sharp new clarity.

Staggering over that sand dune to the oasis, a warm weight
in his arms.

Lying in the sun, his mouth as dry as the great Qusani desert.

His pleasure at the dangerous game of low flying over the
sandhills.

Ragged shreds, but enough to give him a sense of identity.

* * *

'You see it?' Annalisa's voice rose in excitement. Soon the comet would disappear, but for now its tail was clear. 'My father was right.' Pride rose, curving her lips.

'I see it.'

Tahir sounded subdued as he bent over the telescope. He'd been that way since he'd emerged from the tent a short time ago. Annalisa hadn't liked to wake him, knowing how important it was that he rested. But finally he'd emerged and picked his way through the unlit campsite to where she'd stood by the telescope. The way he'd moved, with a sure, cat-like grace, had distracted her from the comet.

But she was glad he'd come. Glad there was someone with whom to share the moment. Glad it was Tahir.

He lifted his head and she felt his scrutiny.

'Congratulations. You must be very proud.' He paused and shoved a hand back through his hair. The moonlight showed it rumpled and far too appealing.

Annalisa pulled her jacket tighter, telling herself it was the chill desert night that made her skin prickle, not the insane desire to copy his movements and furrow her own hand through his thick hair.

She forced herself to turn back to the starry sky. 'It's marvellous, isn't it? Now it will be officially recorded, just as he wanted.'

Side by side they watched the comet track towards the horizon. To the naked eye it was just visible.

When it was gone they stood a moment longer, alone in the vast silence. Then Annalisa began to dismantle the telescope.

Emotions flooded her, too many to name. But as she worked on her father's precious equipment she realised that rising above them all was a sense of loss. Her fingers faltered at the task she'd done countless times. Her breath hitched.

Since her father's death she'd focused on this night. On fulfilling his dying wish.

Now it was done. Time to move on. Yet suddenly her plans for the future seemed insignificant in the face of the emptiness engulfing her.

She felt…bereft. Her father truly was gone. Her past life, so busy and organised and full, was over.

The future yawned before her like a dark void. A shudder ripped through her.

'Here,' said a warm voice in her ear. 'I'll finish, if you trust me.'

Annalisa watched his deft movements. How easily he stowed the telescope and hoisted the case, leading the way to the tent.

'Just like that and it's all over.' Her voice sounded stretched and brittle.

'Until the next time Asiya passes by.'

'Of course.' She entered the tent and fumbled inside for the lantern.

It was ridiculous to feel this way. Her grief seemed as fresh as on the day her father had died. She pursed her lips, striving to conquer the raw pain of loss.

She had everything to look forward to. Travel. A career. New friends. New experiences.

Yet at this moment she felt so alone.

Finally the lamp glowed reassuringly. She turned away, only to find Tahir unexpectedly close, his warmth enveloping her.

Their eyes met and held.

'Ah, Annalisa, don't weep.' His hoarse whisper scraped across her skin.

'I'm not—' Her words stopped as he reached out and brushed her cheek. Hard, callused fingers against wet flesh.

Amazement froze her.

She didn't cry. She had no time for tears.

Though her father was gone the locals still came to her for advice. It was she who'd reassured them. Who'd lobbied for a doctor to replace her father. Who'd taken the new medic to meet the community and help build acceptance for him. Who'd ensured her father's comet got official recognition.

Now it was all done and she was no longer needed.

She felt…adrift.

Horrified at her weakness, she stared up into eyes as clear and pure as those alpine streams she'd dreamed of seeing for herself. Tahir's brows furrowed as if in concentration while his long fingers smoothed her cheek.

She swayed forward to the rhythm of his touch then, startled, drew back.

Dark lashes veiled his eyes. His face was expressionless, still, waiting. He cupped her jaw and the pulse beneath her chin throbbed against his touch.

'You should be proud,' he murmured. 'And happy.'

'I am.' She fought back a self-pitying sniff. She was stronger than this. Her sudden weakness was inexplicable.

'You miss him.' He paused, letting the silence lengthen. 'It's difficult being alone, but you're strong. You'll survive.' The words were whisper-soft, barely audible. Yet the timbre of his voice, like a desert zephyr at daybreak, heralded something new.

More than just pity. Understanding. A precious sense that she wasn't alone. That he knew all she felt.

Abruptly Tahir dropped his hand and stepped back.

The distance between them made her shiver anew. Instinctively she moved forward, only to halt as his eyes blazed with sudden heat.

Ever since falling asleep in his arms Annalisa had known this man was dangerous in ways she barely comprehended. But she'd shoved that knowledge aside, trying to be grateful when he kept his distance.

Now, reading the glittering hunger in his eyes, she knew a reckless desire to walk straight into danger.

Not giving herself time to think, letting instinct drive her, she stepped close, lifting her hand to the hard line of his jaw.

Sensation shot through her as her sensitive palm scraped his shadowed chin. His days-old growth of beard tickled and teased. Darts of fire scorched through her, making her belly cramp and her legs quake.

His mouth firmed to a severe line and he drew a slow breath. Did he too notice the suddenly heavy scent of musk and heat on the night air? His hand clamped hers.

'You're not thinking straight.' His words were harsh and she read tension in his shoulders.

'Please, Tahir.' She didn't know what she pleaded for, yet she knew she couldn't bear him to turn away.

'What is it you want, Annalisa?' His deep voice sounded strained and his pulse hammered beneath her touch. That reminder of his vulnerability gave her the courage to meet his gaze head-on.

Mutely she shook her head, unsure how to answer, yet sure she needed *something* from him. Just the warmth of his living skin against hers was balm to a heart that hadn't been allowed time for grief.

The sense of connection felt so real, so profound, she couldn't turn away.

Annalisa raised her other palm and pressed it against the lapel of his dark jacket, absorbing the rhythmic thud of his heart against her hand. So strong. So alive.

'Annalisa.' His deep voice turned gruff with warning—or displeasure. 'Don't.'

Yet he didn't move away. He held her gaze with glittering eyes half-veiled by long lashes that somehow emphasised his utterly masculine features.

'Please...' It was a whisper of sound as she raised herself on tiptoe so her breath feathered his neck, his chin. His warmth enfolded her, drew her.

This near, his mouth was an implacable line, his jaw a study in tension, but the compulsion to touch him, as a woman touched a man, was too strong.

Just this once.

Her eyes flickered shut as she pressed her lips to his. His mouth was soft. Surprised, she pushed closer, enjoying the slight friction as her lips slid along his, revelling in the tickle of stubble against her cheek. She felt daring and powerful and anything but lonely.

She pulled back and opened heavy lids. Her breathing had quickened—or was that his? Their bodies touched in intriguing ways she wanted to explore.

But, looking into his tense face with its brooding angles, Annalisa realised she'd overstepped the mark.

The fluttering excitement in her chest died and her stomach plunged. Heat scalded her cheeks and she looked down at the lapel of his tuxedo.

Some tiny part of her mind told her if she lived to be a hundred she'd never see a man look so good in formal attire. But mostly she just wanted the earth to open and swallow her whole.

She bit her lip, an apology trembling on her tongue. Kissing a man wasn't as easy at it seemed. Especially when he hadn't invited a kiss.

Hastily she stepped back, only to find her way blocked. An arm like iron barred her way.

Startled, she raised her head. His face was set in grim lines yet the burning heat was back in his eyes.

'Is this what you want?' He dipped his head so the words feathered her lips.

Without giving her time to respond, he slanted his mouth across hers. His lips moved, caressed and stroked, and bliss reverberated through Annalisa's body. She trembled and sank against him.

Her hands slipped up to hang on to his broad shoulders, lest she collapse. She felt as if she was falling.

His tongue slicked her bottom lip and she drew a surprised breath. Before she realised what he intended Tahir was stroking the inside of her mouth.

Startled, she stiffened. Then her muscles went lax as he caressed her tongue, inviting her to meet him kiss for kiss.

Tentatively she responded, and was rewarded with a throaty grumble of approval like the purr of a sleepy lion. His other arm lashed round her, drawing her in as he delved deep, leaning over her as if he couldn't get close enough. As if needing to dominate and protect.

The idea thrilled and terrified her.

Powerful thighs surrounded her legs as he tucked her close. Her mind whirled in overload at the intimacy of being held like this. Of sharing a sensual kiss that shattered the boundaries of her experience.

A dull throb pulsed in her stomach and she shifted to ease

it. The movement brought her in contact with Tahir's pelvis and a telltale hardness.

A quiver rocked his body and he hauled her nearer.

Annalisa gasped. Not with shock or disgust.

With delight.

It was all she could do not to slide forward against that exciting bulge.

What sort of wanton had she become?

She was panting, her chest heaving, when he broke the kiss and straightened. His eyes were narrowed slits she couldn't read. But she had no trouble reading the rapid tattoo of the pulse in his neck. It mirrored hers.

Did he feel like this? All warm and jittery and lax? Trembling and dazed and hungry for more?

If anything he looked more in control than ever. His face was as still as a wooden mask. His body rigid but for the rapid rise and fall of his chest.

'Tahir?' She slid a hand from his shoulder up the side of his neck, cupping hot skin. Pleasure skittered through her at that simple contact.

His eyes flickered shut and he bit back a sound that could have been a groan. Instantly she was alert.

'Did I hurt you? Are you in pain?' What had she done? Her hands skimmed the back of his skull, his temple, then down over his wide shoulders. 'Where does it hurt?'

Suddenly she found both hands clasped together in his. Still he didn't open his eyes.

His head was thrown back and she watched the long burnished column of his throat as he swallowed hard.

'Tahir!' Panic edged her voice. 'What's wrong?'

His lips quirked up in the half-smile that always melted her insides. A long crease furrowed his cheek. She wanted to press her lips against it and taste his skin.

'Nothing's wrong, little one.' He looked at her now and his expression held her immobile. Her breath jammed in her throat. 'You didn't answer. Is that what you wanted?'

Jerkily she nodded, eyes fixed on his.

'Say it, Annalisa.' His voice was harsh, but somehow she knew it wasn't anger or disgust that roughened his words. It was the same ribbon of excitement that threaded her body, drawing each muscle and sinew tight.

'I want you to kiss me,' she whispered, spellbound by what she saw in his eyes.

'Is that all?' He leaned forward and she felt his words, small puffs of breath on her ear. She shuddered and his hands firmed around hers. Surprised, she realised they were unsteady. 'What else do you want?'

'I…' How could he ask questions? She didn't want to think and talk. Just wanted to feel.

'Is it this?'

Long fingers brushed the bare skin of her neck, trailing down to the V of her shirt.

Her breath snagged as she willed him to continue. Was that a flicker in his darkening gaze?

Finally his hand slid down, skimming the fabric of her shirt till his palm warmed her breast. She almost cried with frustration as he stood, watching her, almost, *almost* touching her as she wanted, *needed* to be touched.

It rose in her like a tide—a yearning she didn't fully understand, a craving for more, much more.

Annalisa pushed forward into his waiting palm.

His hand closed convulsively around her. It was bliss. It was more than she'd thought possible. Her breath sighed out as he rubbed his thumb over her burgeoning nipple.

Instantly heat jolted through her, right down to her belly. Lower. Where it felt as if she melted.

'Please, Tahir.'

He shook his head, a single jerky movement. 'You need to tell me.' His voice was raw and uneven, as if he held on to control by a thread. 'You want me to touch you like this?' His palm circled and pressed and her knees gave way.

Abruptly his hands closed on her arms, tight enough to hold her steady.

'Annalisa.' Just the sound of him saying her name was too much pleasure to bear. 'We should stop now.'

'No!' She wrenched herself from his hold and plastered herself against his tall frame, no thought now of shyness or distance.

'I don't want to stop. I want…everything, Tahir.' She drew a shuddering breath and forced herself to think of the words, not just the sensations. 'I need you. Please.'

CHAPTER FIVE

THE words were barely out when strong arms brought her down on the bed. Tahir's lips met hers as he peeled her clothes away.

The heat of his body against hers and the fervour of his kisses incited a heady recklessness that didn't allow second thoughts.

Annalisa wanted him so urgently; her need was overwhelming. She shuddered with the force of it as she helped him with clumsy fingers.

Then cool air caressed her skin. Tahir sat back on his heels. His eyes glowed, devouring her in a way that sent flickers of fire racing through her body. He was so intent. Utterly absorbed. Like a hungry man sighting a banquet laid out just for him. Her heart leapt against her ribs.

Annalisa reached for his shirt, needing him close. That scorching scrutiny made her feel vulnerable as never before. She was excited yet nervous, desperate for Tahir but not wanting time to examine what was happening.

For once she wanted to *feel*, not think.

'No.' He clamped his fingers around her hand. 'Not yet. Let me look at you first.'

His trawling gaze moved across her naked breasts, her waist and thighs. It should have made her ashamed or indignant. Qusani women were modest and demure. Annalisa had always thought in that at least she was like her peers.

Now she discovered potent proof that she was different.

Instead of feeling disgust she was *excited* by the flare of lust in Tahir's gaze. She revelled in his unsteady breathing, the pulse throbbing in his neck, and wondered at the reckless woman she'd become.

'Take your hair down.' His whisper grated over her nerves.

Obediently, not taking her eyes from his, she raised her hands to the pins securing her hair. She fumbled, all thumbs, and his gaze dipped to her breasts.

Annalisa barely had time to register the tumble of long tresses on bare skin before Tahir was over her, pushing her into the narrow bed with his body. Solid thighs tangled with hers, the fine weave of his suit slid against her bare flesh and she'd never felt anything so wonderful.

She trembled in delight tinged with anxiety, realising she was utterly in his power.

Then his hands cupped her breasts and he lowered his head. Every nerve in her body centred on that exquisite point of contact.

He touched her nipple with his tongue and she froze. He opened his lips over her areola and she sank into indescribable pleasure, clasping him to her. He settled closer, the unfamiliar weight of his body, his potent masculinity, anchoring her to the mattress.

He suckled, gently at first, then more strongly, and Annalisa cried out in shocked delight, arching convulsively. Her body zinged and sparked with sensations she'd never felt.

How had she lived so long without this? Without him?

'Tahir,' she gasped, 'don't stop.'

With the words Tahir's restraint shattered. His hands roved ceaselessly. He skimmed, stroked and teased till her cries of pleasure grew hoarse. He touched her everywhere, nuzzled the back of her knees, kissed her inner elbow, even sucked her fingers, till it seemed there wasn't one part of her body that didn't sing out with need for him.

She'd never realised physical love could be so consuming. Maybe, if she had time to think, she'd be scared by this intensity. But Tahir didn't permit her time to question.

Restlessly Annalisa shifted, barely noticing the way her

thighs opened wider, letting him sink the full weight of his lower body against her.

What she felt there, the long, solid proof of his virility, made her blood pump faster even as shock filled her. This was *real*, unfamiliar yet compelling.

Gently he bit her ear and her body softened, her breath sighing out.

She responded to Tahir's touch with an eagerness that left her light-headed. Her fingers dug into the soft fabric of his clothes with growing desperation.

She wanted…more.

Whether he sensed it or whether she'd cried it aloud Annalisa didn't know, but finally Tahir let her undo his shirt. Or begin to. Halfway down her hands clenched uselessly against the fine cotton, when his hand arrowed between them, touching her intimately.

Her gaze clung to his heavy-lidded eyes as long fingers slipped to a place no man had touched. The light brush against one tiny, sensitive bud made her whole body jerk as if from an electric shock. A blush seared her throat and cheeks as he watched her.

Part of her wondered at her boldness, letting him caress her so. Yet she couldn't deny her need for him.

His touch circled and there it was again. Unmistakable. High-voltage pleasure at his lightest caress.

She heard her breath loud in her ears, felt her ribcage expand with the desperate need to draw oxygen.

Her breath whooshed out as his touch moved down and into slick heat. Without conscious thought she clamped her muscles around that tiny invasion.

For what seemed for ever Annalisa hung suspended, aware only of the pleasure of his caress and the grim stillness of his face. Tahir looked as if he concentrated every effort on control.

His hand moved fractionally, building a gentle rhythm: along, down, in. And back. And with each stroke she felt herself slip further from the rational world.

She might have no direct experience to draw on but Annalisa

understood what her body told her. What Tahir was doing, the pleasure his caress promised.

Her voice was a raw gasp when it finally emerged. 'No, Tahir. Stop.'

For a moment it seemed he didn't hear. Her body was moving against his touch, her hips rising when his probing fingers stilled. Annalisa bit down a cry of disappointment, her body still throbbing to the beat of his making.

'No?' The single syllable sounded strangled, so foreign she barely recognised it.

'Not like this.' She lifted a shaky hand to his shirt, but was too unsteady to grapple with buttons. 'I want you, not...'

Her words petered out under the weight of sudden shyness and the incendiary flare in his eyes. They blazed like burning sapphires.

Before she had time to gather her thoughts he was gone, rolling off the bed to stand on the matting.

Her instant protest died in her throat as he ripped open his shirt, shrugging out of it and his jacket in one rapid movement. Before she could catch her breath he'd discarded the rest of his clothes.

Breathing became impossible.

Despite the bruises and cuts marring the symmetry of his body, Tahir was the most beautiful being she'd seen.

He moved, and the lamplight caught a line of old scar tissue low on his back. Then he turned and Annalisa's mind atrophied. She'd never seen a naked aroused man. She'd never known one could look so magnificent. Wonderful and slightly frightening at the same time.

He didn't give her time to think. Tahir lowered himself, his bare flesh against hers, hotter than fire. His thighs rubbed hers; the soft hair on his chest abraded her nipples. She welcomed the weight of him pressing her down, took his roughened jaw in her hands and planted a fervent, clumsy kiss against his lips.

A deep rumbling growl vibrated through his chest. Teeth scraped the sensitive skin at her neck and she arched, burying her fingers in the rough silk of his hair. Then she felt pressure where he'd caressed so intimately. Tahir shifted his weight, pushing her legs wide.

She stiffened and the caress at her neck became a tender bite, sending lush waves of pleasure through her. At the same time Tahir moved, pushing up in a slow surge of power.

Pleasure splintered as a ripple of something like pain shot through her, a stinging discomfort that made her catch her breath and stiffen in his hold.

But before she did more than register the sensation Tahir withdrew, lowering his mouth to her breast and laving it until she shivered with renewed desire. She held him near, overwhelmed by the emotions stirring as she watched him, felt him.

When he pressed close again Annalisa rose to him. The feel of his big body against hers held a magic she couldn't resist. Urged by large hands at her thighs she lifted her legs, clasping him close, revelling in the feel of his hot satiny skin.

He raised his head, eyes meeting hers.

There was movement, that bombarding of curious new sensations, and through it all his gaze didn't waver. It held her steady and safe, connected in a way that made her heart swell in her breast as their bodies joined.

This time there was no pain as he pushed deep.

Her body opened to his as if it was meant to be.

He stilled.

There was no sound except a riffle of night breeze against the tent flap and the discreet chirrup of an insect down by the *wadi*. Annalisa didn't breathe. Nor did Tahir. The moment stretched long and portentous between them.

Their gazes meshed as she absorbed the full weight of what they'd done. She read the grim tension drawing his lean features. The strained muscles of his shoulders and neck. The flare of his nostrils. The fact that his gaze had turned utterly unreadable.

Was he regretting this?

She should be shocked to be in this position. Yet it felt *right*. *They* felt right together.

Warmth welled in her chest, filling the place pain had hollowed.

Tentatively she smiled, clasping his face in her hands. The tickling caress of his beard felt better than velvet under her palms. She reached up to bestow a brief breathless kiss on his lips.

Tahir pulled back just far enough that she could see the light blaze in his eyes. His mouth turned up at one side, creating that sexy groove in his cheek she so adored.

The air smelt of the desert night, of the spicy musk of Tahir's skin, and of happiness.

Then he was kissing her, open-mouthed, slow yet passionate, as he moved within her. She gasped at the feel of his hard length sliding against her, igniting ripples of extraordinary pleasure.

He smiled against her mouth, his movements building to a steady pace that stole her breath all over again.

Then, abruptly, she began shaking. She was overloading on physical delight. Fire licked her belly, ecstasy sizzled along her nerve-ends and a quaking started deep inside.

'Tahir?' Her voice cracked as wave after wave of pleasure broke over her. She clung, suddenly scared.

His lazy smile was gone. But his look reassured her. 'Trust me, little one. Just let it happen. I promise you'll be safe.'

Not allowing her respite, he moved faster, harder, further, till she couldn't bear any more. Suddenly, gloriously, the volcanic force exploded into a starburst of euphoria. Wave after wave buoyed her up, till she floated high above the earth, suspended in utter bliss.

She heard his breath quicken, a groan as if of pain, then an exultant shout as he rocked faster, out of control, and suddenly the stars exploded again.

Through it all Annalisa held tight to the man in her arms, sensing for the first time a feeling of true belonging.

He felt like hell. Every bone and muscle ached. His head pounded sickeningly. He drew a slow breath and exhaled pain. The ribs he was pretty sure he'd bruised or cracked in the chopper crash hurt like the devil.

Yet he'd do it all again for the pleasure of seeing Annalisa experience orgasm for what he was pretty sure was the first time.

Heat ignited and his blood headed south at the memory of her gasping his name as she climaxed.

She'd been gorgeous. Glorious. Addictive. And the feel of her! The exquisite pleasure of being inside her!

He couldn't remember the last time sex had been that good. He doubted it ever had been.

Even though his memory had now returned, he could barely remember the last time he'd been with a woman. For months his libido had been non-existent. But he hadn't cared enough to worry about it. He'd given up caring about anything much these last years.

Too many years abusing his body with too little sleep, too many parties, too much alcohol, far too many women. Pushing the limits as he sought new challenges and pleasures. Anything to divert him from the grey pall that threatened whenever he stayed in one place too long.

Yet he'd been anything but bored in the dead heart of Qusay! With a woman who had no notion of how innately sexy she was. Who'd trusted and cared for him as no woman ever had.

An unfamiliar sensation slithered down his backbone. Regret? A pang of conscience?

It was so novel he concentrated his meagre energies on pinning it down. *Was* it conscience?

People thought Tahir Al'Ramiz didn't possess a conscience. He'd cultivated that view since he'd given up trying to be a perfect son and yielded to the weight of his father's hatred.

If you can't beat them join them.

Tahir had emulated his father in developing a taste for sybaritic decadence. By the time he was eighteen his family hadn't been able to stomach the sight of him. There'd been no tears shed at his exile.

But, despite his reputation for dissoluteness, he had some standards, even if he didn't broadcast them. He never harmed the innocent. He'd even privately helped a few of those who didn't have the benefits of wealth. Casual charity was easy. It didn't make him a good man. It was simple to give away what you didn't care about.

And he had never stooped to deflowering virgins.

Until last night.

That cold sensation was back again, slipping like ice down his spine and cramping his belly.

He didn't even have the excuse of amnesia. He'd known who he was last night: the sort of man who had no business consorting with innocents. He'd known his past, his present and, fate preserve him, his future.

Tahir hated thinking about the future. Other people dreamed of it. Like Annalisa. She'd been incandescent with delight about travelling and seeing the world. He'd been riveted by the sight of her excitement.

He couldn't remember ever feeling that happy.

His future would be the same as his past. Nothing significant enough to hold his attention.

Boredom.

Yet he hadn't been bored with Annalisa. The feral thought lodged in his brain.

Despite the pain and the infuriating slowness of his recovery, he'd enjoyed being here.

The realisation sideswiped him.

Talking with an inexperienced girl who'd never left Qusay about astronomy, the need for local schools, the latest plans for irrigating the edge of the desert. About customs he remembered from another life and people he'd never met, about the small communities that made up her world. Even about the care and feeding of an orphan goat. And he'd been content!

For days the bounds of this oasis had circumscribed his world and he hadn't hankered for more.

An image of Annalisa's smile appeared: the way her eyes softened when she laughed, the way the sun brought out gold and bronze highlights in her rich brown hair. The way her slim fingers felt as she tended his wounds. The scent of cinnamon and honey that haunted his sleep.

She was the reason he'd been content.

More than content. He'd been happy!

A sound interrupted his thoughts. Soft humming, off-key yet delightful.

He slitted open his eyes, seeing daylight. He'd slept late. He might even have been unconscious after the sheer stupidity of having sex despite cracked ribs and head wounds.

Ripping off his shirt last night had almost killed him. But he'd have died for sure if he hadn't felt Annalisa's hands on him, her sweet body against his.

His erection was instantaneous and achingly powerful, just at the memory of her.

The humming ceased and the tent flap lifted. His heart banged painfully against his ribs as she entered, wearing her hair down for the first time. Tendrils curled invitingly around her full breasts. She turned and a shaft of sunlight caught her back. Her hair rippled like finest silk, spun with threads of mahogany and gold.

She bent and retrieved something from the ground and his gaze fixed ravenously on the perfect peach shape of her bottom. His mouth dried.

Yet her movements weren't as graceful as usual. When she stepped across to tie up the tent flap he was sure of it.

She moved as if it hurt to walk.

As a woman might walk after a stranger had stolen her virginity. Then followed it up with a second bout of sex that had been far less restrained and even more desperate.

He'd been so needy. Despite his pain and her exhaustion he hadn't been able to resist kissing her awake and taking his fill of her again. He'd ensured she'd climaxed again, not once but twice. Yet he should have controlled himself. He should have known.

Hell! What did *he* know about virgins?

And, frankly, what did he care? Once he'd had Annalisa under him he hadn't been able to wait to have her again.

She turned and sunlight fell across her face.

What he saw there made his pulse thump out of kilter.

The cold feeling at his spine crept through his body, turning his organs to leaden lumps of ice.

Her once flawless skin was marred by angry reddened rashes. Around her mouth, on her cheeks and neck.

Whisker-burn.

More, there was a purpling mark on her throat. Another just visible at her neckline.

Where his teeth had grazed her.

Tahir's stomach swooped as it had the day his chopper crashed. But this time it didn't stop falling.

He shut his eyes against nausea as a vision from the past rose. His father staggering from a banquet with his closest, must corrupt cronies, his newest mistress tucked close beside him. Except his mistress had been a scared teenager who'd cringed at Yazan Al'Ramiz's touch.

His father had swatted him away like a fly when he'd tried to intervene, a skinny thirteen-year-old without the skill to tackle a full-grown man who knew every dirty trick. Tahir had gone down hard, cracking his head and coming to far too late to intervene again.

But he'd seen her the next day. Pale, with a livid bruise along her cheek. She hadn't seen him. She'd been too absorbed in misery to notice anyone.

The sound of Annalisa's off-key humming broke across the memory.

Last night hadn't been the same.

Annalisa had wanted him. Pleaded with him.

Except he'd used his sexual expertise to make her beg for something she didn't fully understand. He'd wanted her and set out to get her, even to the extent of having her admit it was *she* who wanted *him*.

As if that exonerated him.

Nothing changed the fact that he'd stolen her innocence.

Now she looked at him with stars in her eyes. Even through barely opened lids he saw her innocent wonder.

As if he was some fairytale hero.

As if he was the answer to a maiden's prayers.

The knot of glacial ice in his belly had sharp edges. It ripped his guts when he tried to breathe. It cut through his self-satisfaction and his excuses about last night.

It reminded him he was his father's son. Decadent. Self-interested. A man obsessed with pleasure.

The fact that Tahir found pleasure almost nowhere these days didn't alter the truth that he was as flawed as Yazan Al'Ramiz. He was the last man on earth she should be building castles in the air over.

For that was what she was doing. He could see it in her eyes. Annalisa was so refreshingly transparent.

Regret lanced him, so powerful it was a physical pain even stronger than what he already suffered.

He ignored it.

Annalisa would *not* be a casualty of his vices. She'd forget about him and get on with her life with never a backward glance.

He'd cure her of her romantic daydreams.

He owed her that much.

CHAPTER SIX

HE WAS awake. She caught a glimpse of his eyes, glinting like sunlight on the ocean. Her heart gave an awkward thump then settled into something like a steady beat, albeit far too rapid.

'I've made you breakfast.' She knelt beside him, eyes lowered, wishing she had the nerve to reach out and touch him as she had last night. But in the bright morning light she felt shy. It would be easier soon, when he smiled, caressed her. Maybe even tugged her down to him.

Heat sizzled in her stomach.

She wasn't sorry it had happened. Stunned, yes. Amazed at how beautiful it had been. But not regretful. It had been the single most wonderful experience of her life.

Tahir had been exquisitely tender and generous. She'd heard enough matrons gossiping about wedding nights to know not all women enjoyed their first time with a man.

Annalisa had done more than enjoy. Tahir had given her ecstasy. Warmth and connection and unbelievable pleasure. More, he'd bestowed something she couldn't name. Something glowing and positive that countered the pain of these last months. Something that made the future look sunny and wondrous.

'Not sweet tea again.' There was a petulance in his voice she'd never heard. 'Is that *all* you have?'

Her head jerked up and she met his frowning stare. His eyes were hard, almost febrile, his expression tight and unfamiliar.

The grooves around his mouth had deepened and his lips were pursed in a disgruntled line.

'Are you in pain?' What had she done, demanding so much last night? He was still far from recovered. Guilt slashed her and she reached out to him.

A sinewy forearm blocked her move. His eyes glittered and his nostrils pinched as if in displeasure.

'Of course I'm in pain. Having sex with these injuries was a fool's game.'

'I know. I've been wondering how you are.'

She waited for him to smile and say their night together had been worth the pain. That they'd shared something momentous and special.

The silence grew.

Tahir's gaze was unreadable. Something about his raised eyebrows and tight mouth made her sink back on her heels, her certainty suddenly on shaky foundations.

He *had* enjoyed it, hadn't he?

Of course he had. There'd been no mistaking his pleasure.

But maybe…maybe what had been a special, out of the world experience for her had been something else for him?

She clasped her hands, fighting the doubt roiling in her stomach. How she wished she understood.

Had he *nothing* to say about their night together? Even simply lying in his arms, tucked up against his large, powerful body had been bliss.

'I feel like you'd expect me to feel after a chopper crash, dehydration and over-exertion. I feel like death. Far worse than yesterday.'

Over-exertion? Annalisa frowned. That was what he called their lovemaking?

Over-exertion?

The churning in her stomach intensified even as a shaft of indignation hit her.

She tried to ignore it. Tahir was ill. By the look of him far worse than he'd been last night, and that was her fault. If she hadn't been so needy…

'I'll just…' She paused, his words sinking in. 'Chopper crash? You remember an accident?'

His mouth curved in a smile that held none of the rakish charm she'd grown used to. Instead he looked sarcastic.

'I wouldn't have said so if I hadn't remembered.'

'Were there others? On the helicopter?' The thought of people lost in the desert had haunted her for days.

'No. No one else to practise your precious nursing skills on.' The way he spoke made it sound as if she'd done more harm than good. Hurt and bewilderment curled inside her. Even as she heard his cutting words and saw his supercilious expression she didn't believe it. Tahir would never speak to her like that.

'But—'

'But nothing.' He paused. 'I had an important cargo, just not people. Crates of the finest champagne and the best caviar money can buy. I was bringing it here for the coronation, but I've missed the party now.' He lifted his shoulders in a stiff movement that confirmed his pain had worsened. 'A pity. If there's one thing I enjoy it's a good party.'

The way he said it, and his leer, implied something seedy and distasteful. No doubt he meant the kind of celebration no well brought up Qusani woman should know anything about.

She blinked, staring in disbelief at the changeling before her. Where was the stoic, witty, sociable man she'd cared for these past days? The one who'd been engaging and friendly, compassionate and even…loving?

He reached out an unsteady hand for the tea she'd brought. The way he clenched his jaw and the white line around his mouth told her his pain was extreme. Automatically she reached to help him, blaming herself for being so weak as to beg for sex from an injured man.

'Don't!' The single syllable was a harsh command. 'Don't touch me.'

Wide-eyed, Annalisa stared at the stranger before her.

Even in the extremity of his pain, even delirious, Tahir had never spoken to her in that tone of voice. As if she weren't worthy to breathe the same air as him.

Her heart squeezed in a spasm of acute distress. Pain, sharp as her grandfather's treasured sword, transfixed her.

'You've done enough.' His gaze slid from hers and he lifted the cup to his lips, grimacing in distaste. 'Let's hope they can at least make decent coffee in the palace.'

'In the palace?' Annalisa sank away from the mattress, lifting her knees and looping her arms around them, suddenly desperate for warmth, despite the hot shafts of sunlight illuminating this corner of the tent. She was cold on the inside. She felt as if she would never be warm again.

'Didn't I say I was heading to the palace?' He rolled his eyes as if in disgust at her ignorance. 'I'm a relative of the new king, Kareef. That's why I'm back in this god-forsaken country. To see him crowned, enjoy the celebration, then head back.'

'Back?' Annalisa felt absurdly like a parrot, repeating what he said. But her brain didn't work properly. She was still coming to terms with this shocking stranger.

It was as if, with the return of his memory, Tahir had undergone a personality transplant. From charming companion to the rear end of a camel in the blink of an eye.

The thought of her little cousin's favourite insult normally made her grin. Not this time. She tightened her grip on her legs, rocking slightly, as if seeking comfort.

There was no comfort to be found today.

If the pain lacerating her was any indication, she was bleeding internally—from the shattering of foolish, barely formed hopes.

How had she ever imagined she had anything in common with a man from another world? Who wore a tuxedo as if born to it? A man of obvious education and wealth and power?

A man, moreover, who had all the arrogance and none of the generosity that riches could breed.

She blinked hard, telling herself it was a speck of grit that made her eyes water.

'Back to civilisation,' he murmured. 'To the bright lights of the city. To business and sophisticated entertainment.' He lingered lovingly on the final words and bile rose in Annalisa's throat. She saw the glint in his eyes. There was no mistaking his meaning. Sophisticated *women*, he meant. With his looks and apparent wealth he'd have his fill.

The notion cramped her stomach.

What had she been? A passing whim? A novelty?

'No doubt you're eager to return to your friends,' she said, as brightly as she could. Unfortunately the words tumbled out rushed and uneven.

'You can't imagine how much.' He didn't even look at her, just picked at the carefully prepared food on the plate.

Annalisa's scalp prickled as nausea rose.

How had she been naïve enough to mistake last night for anything like tenderness or caring? She couldn't blame Tahir for taking what she'd offered—no, what she'd *begged* for so blatantly.

Shame suffused her, burning her cheeks and every place he'd touched last night.

But she couldn't forgive him for treating her with disdain. Did he think her lack of sophistication and experience a reason to view her with contempt? Was this her first taste of life in the big wide world?

Abruptly she raised her head, surprised to find him watching her.

She skewered him with a glare and lifted her chin, refusing to let him think she was humbled by his presence. Carefully she rose, ignoring the protest of aching muscles, then pinned on her best bright bedside smile.

'I'll leave you in peace. You'll want to make plans for your return to civilisation.'

When Annalisa's transport out of the desert arrived before noon, Tahir was ready to leave. He'd made himself thoroughly obnoxious all morning and could no longer stomach watching the effect on Annalisa.

At first she'd looked on in dazed bewilderment, her soft brown eyes brimming with disbelief. His conscience had smitten him like a hot branding iron across his already burning ribs.

Then, when she'd taken her measure of the 'new' Tahir, scorn and pride had made her lift her head and meet his jibes levelly. She'd looked regal and aloof and utterly lovely, confirming his belief that this was for the best.

But that hadn't stopped him craving her, like an addict needing just a little more. A smile, a touch, a caress. It had been hell, drawing her displeasure instead of her embraces with his arrogant nonsense.

Yet it was no more than he deserved.

He hadn't even thought of protection! Of pregnancy.

At the last moment, as the camel driver announced he was ready to go, Tahir cornered her. She'd decided to stay another few days. To study the skies, she'd said.

To lick her wounds, he was sure.

This was his last chance to talk to her.

'Annalisa.' Her head jerked up. She'd already said her goodbye, brief and stilted.

Her eyes widened and a flash of emotion warmed them for a moment. Her lips trembled open. In surprise or doubt?

Tahir clamped his hands behind him, battling the urge to reach for her. To soothe the hurt he'd inflicted. His voice when he found it was rougher than he'd intended.

'If there are consequences from last night...' His words petered out as the shocking image of Annalisa, blooming with good health and ripe with his child, blasted his mind.

'Impossible.' She shook her head. 'There won't be consequences.'

Tahir hadn't been born yesterday. If she tried to convince him she'd been taking contraceptives on the off-chance she'd let a stranger seduce her, she'd never succeed.

'If you're pregnant...' his voice dropped on the word '...I want you to tell me.' He held her defiant gaze so long that eventually she looked away. 'You can reach me via the palace.'

Silence. He cupped her chin, pulling her round to face him. The contact sizzled and he could almost swear he heard electricity crackle and spark as her eyes clashed with his.

How he wanted her! Even now, on the brink of farewell, his

body swayed forward and his hand tightened on her soft skin. Hunger gnawed at his belly, eclipsing even the burning pain that encircled his torso at every breath.

The temptation was almost too strong. Just one taste.

He dropped his hand as if burned. Took a step away.

'Promise me you'll let me know if—'

'So you can fund an abortion?' This time there was only scorn in her flashing eyes. She looked proud and dismissive as she eyed him up and down. 'There won't be any consequences. But if there were,' she hurried on before he could speak, 'I'd tell you.'

He nodded and turned away.

Minutes later he was seated on a camel. Its extreme motion, rocking perilously forwards then back as it rose to its feet, seemed expressly designed to torture a man with damaged ribs and a pounding head.

At least it took his mind off the contempt he'd seen in Annalisa's eyes.

The camels swayed out of the oasis, each step sending pain screaming through him. Even so, he mustered the willpower to turn and see Annalisa for the last time.

He needn't have bothered. She hadn't waited to watch him go. She'd already disappeared from view.

By the time they reached the coast Tahir was barely clinging on. Travelling through the heat of the day hadn't been sensible. If he'd been fit, perhaps, but with his injuries each kilometre was torture. The pain wrapping round his torso worsened and his head swam.

But he'd needed to get away while his determination held good. Before he did anything stupid like scooping her close and kissing her senseless.

He was surprised and grateful when his guide called a halt in a small fertile valley. They were still several hours from the capital, but Tahir could feel the last of his stamina draining away and he had no wish to slide off the camel in an ignominious heap.

It was only as they stopped in a pool of blessed shade that he realised the grove wasn't empty. A four-wheel drive and an ambulance were parked there.

He shot a questioning glance at his guide, already standing beside his mount.

For the first time his dour companion met his gaze directly, watching as Tahir's camel settled, lurching him sickeningly first one way then another.

'I called for assistance when we got within mobile phone range,' he said. 'Annalisa insisted.' His unblinking stare radiated disapproval. If he was a friend of Annalisa's he wouldn't have missed the undercurrents between her and Tahir.

Did he have a personal interest in Annalisa?

Tahir stiffened. His fists clenched and hot, scathing words hovered on his lips, ready to scare off this upstart.

Till he remembered he had no rights where she was concerned.

The realisation slammed into him so hard he reeled, and almost toppled over as nausea rose.

Finally, summoning the last of his strength, he lifted one leg over the saddle and slithered off. He stood, swaying drunkenly on ground that seemed to roll beneath him. His companion merely watched, arms folded.

'Your Highness?' A voice made Tahir turn, frowning.

'No. I—'

An older man, vaguely familiar, moved forward with a formal bow. For the life of him Tahir couldn't reciprocate. It was all he could do to stay upright on legs that shook mercilessly.

'Your Highness, let me express our heartfelt thanks that you've been delivered to us safely. We thought your helicopter went down over the coast and we've been searching the sea for days.'

At his nod two ambulance officers hurried forward with a stretcher.

Tahir opened his mouth to say he wasn't anyone's highness, then realised perhaps he was. With Kareef as king, that made him and their brother Rafiq princes.

The ludicrous notion of the black sheep of the family scoring a royal title pulled him up short. It was so outrageous, so bizarre, he barely noticed when his surroundings blurred around him.

He heard a shout, saw serious faces shift in and out of focus, then the world faded into oblivion.

He had to stop making a habit of passing out. He didn't have the patience for being sick. There was no amusement in it.

Even the soothing stroke of a soft, feminine hand at his brow lost its attraction when he came to enough to realise he'd dreamed it. What woman would sit patiently worrying at *his* bedside?

He'd had enough motor racing accidents to know nurses didn't caress their patients. And Annalisa, the only woman whose touch he desired, wasn't here. On the contrary, she'd be thanking her lucky stars she'd seen the last of him.

Still foggy from dreaming she was here, still weak enough to be plagued by regret that she wasn't, Tahir was in a sour mood when he woke.

He wasn't used to being dependent on anyone. Yet as he stirred he knew a craving for *her* by his side. He who'd never craved any woman! Who'd been alone so long he couldn't remember what it was like to wake up with the same woman twice.

He was in no mood to find himself hooked up to all sorts of machines. He was disengaging himself when the doctor arrived.

'No, sire. Please!'

Tahir ignored his protests. 'I don't need all this. I just need to get out of here.' Not that there was anywhere he wanted to go—unless it was an isolated oasis inhabited by the dark-eyed beauty he couldn't get out of his head.

The thought made him even more impatient.

There must be *somewhere* he should be. *Something* he should be doing. Something to keep him busy.

'I need to see my brother. I have business at the palace.' Tahir looked down in disgust at the hospital robe he wore. 'If you want to be useful, bring me clothes.'

'But, sire, you can't—'

Tahir waved aside his protests, ignoring the sharp stab of pain through his chest at the movement. 'Of course I can.'

'You don't understand, sire.' The doctor stood his ground and reluctantly Tahir focused on him. 'You need treatment and further observation. I can't take responsibility for releasing you yet.'

'I'll take responsibility. Just hurry up with those clothes.' Tahir forced himself to sit up and not sink back into the tempting comfort of the pillows. He felt absurdly weak.

'But, si—'

'And don't call me sire,' he snapped, ignoring the other man's hand-wringing. 'Just get me something to wear; that's all I ask.'

'Practising your fabled charm on the medical staff, little brother?' A deep drawl from the doorway drew Tahir's attention. He stiffened warily.

A tall man stood inside the door, his big frame suave in a hand-made Italian suit. His short black hair was brushed back severely and familiar ice-blue eyes surveyed Tahir.

After a moment Tahir saw the gleam of humour in his expression and the tension cramping his shoulders eased a fraction.

'Rafiq!' He hadn't seen his family in eleven years. Not since his father had banished him. The potent shot of delight that surged through him was a complete surprise.

He'd been so busy getting on with life, pursuing pleasure and business in equal measure, he hadn't let himself think about family. About resurrecting old ties. Even flying here he'd concentrated on the need to support his eldest brother, Kareef, as he ascended the throne, rather than on reviving personal relationships.

But the feel of Rafiq's solid hand gripping his, his other palm at Tahir's shoulder, as if to make sure he was actually there, evoked a blast of unexpected emotions.

'You're really here,' Rafiq said, his sombre expression transforming with a grin of real pleasure. 'Air control got your mayday, but there was interference and they misheard your coordinates and identification. They'd been searching the sea.' He shook his head. 'Why am I not surprised to hear you came out of the desert instead?'

Tahir felt an answering smile tug at his lips. He hadn't

allowed himself to think what sort of welcome the family would extend to the prodigal son, but he hadn't expected genuine warmth.

He returned Rafiq's grip with his own.

When he was a kid Rafiq and Kareef had been his role models. He'd striven to be as quick and as strong and as clever as they were. Particularly Rafiq, their father's favourite. But where Rafiq had been able to do little wrong in Yazan Al'Ramiz's eyes, Tahir had done nothing right. The unfairness of it had haunted him.

For a while Tahir had resented Rafiq bitterly, until he'd realised his brother had nothing to do with their father's favouritism. Or his frightening rages. In fact Rafiq had done his best to protect his little brother.

'You know I was always the contrary one,' Tahir murmured.

Rafiq shook his head. 'You were always a survivor. And I'm glad.' He nodded a dismissal to the hovering doctor, then pulled up a chair and sat, surveying Tahir with mingled amusement and consternation. 'You've been incredibly lucky, you know.'

'I know.' Even now, after days drinking all the fluids Annalisa had insisted on, he could taste the desert sand in his mouth. The flavour of death.

He'd been far luckier than he deserved.

Rafiq's grin faded. 'Do us all a favour, Tahir, and stay here. You need to recuperate.' He shook his head. 'You've got broken ribs and severe bruising, possible concussion, plus what the doctors warn is a severe chest infection. They say you're not in a good way. In fact they seem to think you're not as fit as you should be even without the injuries from the accident.'

Tahir shrugged. 'I've never cosseted myself.' And lately, as the darkness had closed around him more often and more swiftly, he'd pushed himself to the limits, seeking new thrills. He'd been careless of his health.

'Well, for pity's sake do it now. Just this once. Our mother has been frantic.'

Tahir's eyes widened. 'Our mother?'

Of all the people he'd left behind in Qusay she was the one

who'd weighed heavily on his conscience. Before his exile he'd tried to convince her to leave with him, lest Yazan Al'Ramiz turn his violence on her once he didn't have his scapegoat son to vent his anger on.

But she'd refused to see him, refused to take his calls. At first he'd thought it was fear of her husband that prompted her. But even after he'd left the country she'd wanted nothing to do with him. His calls and e-mails had gone unanswered. He'd assumed he'd alienated her too.

'You must be mistaken.'

Rafiq looked at him keenly. 'No mistake. She's been here since you were admitted, sitting by your bedside. She's only just left.'

Tahir remembered the comfort of a feminine hand soothing his brow and stroking his hand. He'd dreamed it was Annalisa.

Was it possible his mother, the woman who'd cut off all ties with him, was the one whose touch he'd felt?

It seemed preposterous. Yet Rafiq's concerned expression was real. Tahir frowned, trying to make sense of the impossible.

'I'm not imagining you, am I?' He'd suffered enough delirium in the last few days.

Rafiq huffed with laughter and settled more easily in his chair. 'Am I that ugly?'

Tahir's mouth pulled in a one-sided smile. 'You expect me to answer that?' He waved a hand in a gesture that encompassed the hospital room. 'This is just a bit much to absorb. And what's with these royal titles? "Sire" and "Your Highness" and so on?'

'Ah. I'm glad you mentioned that.' Rafiq leaned forward in his chair, his face suddenly serious. 'There's been a complication.'

'That's what Kareef said when he told me our cousin is no longer King of Qusay and that he would be taking the crown.' He watched Rafiq steeple his fingers and felt premonition spider its way down his spine. Something was wrong.

'Kareef has renounced the throne.'

'He's done what?'

'He and Jasmine… You remember Jasmine?'

Tahir nodded. His eldest brother had been besotted by her when he was eighteen.

'He's given up the throne to marry her and they've gone back to Qais to live.' At Tahir's stare he continued. 'Jasmine can't have children, and Kareef knows it's the King's duty to produce an heir.' He shrugged. 'You know how seriously he takes matters of duty.'

Tahir sank back against his pillows, absorbing this astonishing news. 'Looks like you've got a change of lifestyle ahead of you, big brother.' He'd seen a few articles about Rafiq's phenomenal business success in Australia. 'You'll have to move back here permanently. When do you take up the role of monarch?'

Rafiq paused before replying. He paused long enough to make Tahir frown again. That inkling of something wrong was back again, stronger than ever.

'That's one of the things I need to talk to you about.' There was no laughter lurking in his eyes now. 'I'm refusing the crown too, and moving back to Australia. Giving up the crown for love seems to be a family trait.'

'I don't believe it.' What sort of mess had he walked into?

'Believe it, Tahir. And as for the reason the doctor keeps calling you sire…? That would be because you're now King of Qusay.'

CHAPTER SEVEN

TIREDNESS took its toll and Annalisa's pace slowed as she walked along the wide esplanade in the capital, Shafar. She'd started out briskly from her aunt's house, needing to walk off her excess energy.

Her lips twisted ruefully. It wasn't excess energy but shock at the news she'd just received.

Yet part of her had expected it. Ever since she'd missed her period. Lately there'd been nausea, and a slight tingling in her breasts when she crossed her arms.

She'd thrust from her mind hints that her body was changing, telling herself it was the whirl of organising her overseas trip that had thrown her system out of balance.

What other cause could there be for her unaccustomed moping, her keen sense of distress?

A shudder marched down her spine at how wrong she'd been about Tahir. She'd known they were from separate worlds. Yet she'd believed herself...*connected* to him.

She told herself grief had made her turn to him for comfort. Wasn't she glad he'd shown his true colours? The return of his memory had revealed a man vastly different from the one she'd thought she'd known.

Demanding, dissatisfied, selfish.

She swallowed a knot of rising pain and stared dazedly towards the huge ornate gates set in the wall just ahead.

It didn't matter that their night together had been the most wonderful experience of her life. Was one night with an arrogant stranger, albeit a heart-stoppingly magical lover, worth the price she paid?

Her hand slipped across her flat stomach. It felt hollow because she'd been unable to face breakfast.

She'd imagined having children after marrying a man she loved. She mightn't be a traditional Qusani woman, but neither had she dreamed of being a single parent.

More than ever she felt the loss of her beloved parents and her grandfather. Her cousins were kind and caring, but they'd be shocked to the core by her news.

She shook her head, rocked by the emotions bombarding her. Excitement, fear, confusion and renewed grief.

Putting a hand to the wall beside her, she braced herself, fighting nausea as her stomach roiled.

It will be all right. Women have babies all the time.

Yet Annalisa felt bereft and shockingly alone.

'Are you all right, my dear?' The gentle voice made her turn her head.

A few metres away a silver limousine had stopped across the pavement, before turning into the massive open gates. In the back seat sat an older woman, with a severe yet chic hair-style, gentle eyes and a fortune in pearls.

Hastily Annalisa straightened.

'Thank you,' she said, a flush scorching her throat. She felt exposed, as if she'd inadvertently displayed her private fears and worry. 'I'm fine.'

The woman regarded her carefully. 'If you'll forgive me, you don't look well. You're pale. Were you on your way to the palace? Did you have an appointment?'

Annalisa's head jerked round at her mention of the palace. She'd been so absorbed she'd barely noticed which way she'd walked. Now, through the ceremonial gates, she saw the royal enclosure's majestic gardens and the massive domed palace roof.

Her stomach tumbled over. Had she subconsciously come this way because of Tahir? What were the chances of him still being here? It was more than a month since…

Hastily she looked away.

If you're pregnant I want you to tell me. Promise me.

Tahir's voice was so real Annalisa shivered, her arms automatically wrapping around her torso.

'Are you here to see someone?'

'No!' The word shot out instantly. Then she paused.

She'd have to tell him. Even though she was almost certain he'd expect her to terminate the pregnancy. A father had a right to know he had a child. That much she knew.

And the fact that she wanted this baby, come what may.

The certainty warmed her, strengthening her weary body. Of course she wanted this child! She'd barely absorbed the news of her pregnancy, but that one fact tugged her lips wide in a smile of pure joy.

'That is…' She looked again at the woman in the car, so patiently awaiting her response. Was she a diplomat, or a friend of the royal family?

Tahir was connected to the King. Perhaps she knew him?

Annalisa took a few diffident steps forward, feeling gauche, yet impelled to follow this opportunity. 'I'm sorry, I'm a little…' What? Confused? Upset? Pregnant? She stifled a bubble of hysterical laughter.

'It's kind of you to ask,' she started again, pinning a polite smile on her face. 'I was hoping to contact someone at the palace. He's called Tahir. I don't know his family name. Tall, lean, bright blue eyes? He was injured in a helicopter crash.'

The woman's expression didn't alter and Annalisa's hope waned. It was foolish to expect he'd still be here. 'But it doesn't matter. He's probably not—'

'You met Tahir after his accident?' The woman's voice held a curious inflection.

'I… Yes. In the desert. I did what I could to nurse him, but—' Annalisa stiffened, alarm jolting through her at the woman's arrested expression. She moved up to the car, would have gripped the door if a burly guard hadn't stepped in front of her.

But she had to know.

She peered round him. 'He did get better, didn't he? He's

all right?' Tahir hadn't fully recovered. 'His head wounds—they weren't…?'

Fatal. She couldn't say the word, could only stare mutely and hope for reassurance.

For all Tahir had revealed an unpleasant side to his character, she *knew* there was more to him. He'd been kind, funny, likeable through those days at the oasis. And he'd been an exquisitely tender lover. The idea of him—

'No, no. Of course he's not dead.' A reassuring smile played on the other woman's lips. 'He's recovered now. According to the doctors, he owes his life to you.'

Annalisa's heart gave a great thump of relief and she lifted a hand to it, surprised at how shaky she felt.

The woman said something Annalisa didn't hear over the pounding in her blood. The guard moved, taking her elbow and ushering her to the far side of the vehicle. A chauffeur stood to attention, holding open the rear door.

The interior smelt of leather and expensive perfume. Annalisa's eyes widened as she took in the full impact of the elegant woman inside. She wore indigo silk exquisitely embroidered with silver. High-heeled silver sandals. Pearls at her wrist as well as her throat.

Annalisa froze, suddenly fully aware that this was someone very important indeed. The limo, the guard, her clothes, her air of understated refinement…

'Don't be shy,' she said, gesturing for Annalisa to enter the vehicle. 'You want to see Tahir, don't you?'

Mutely Annalisa nodded. She told herself she *needed* to see him. She had more sense than to *want* to see him. That madness had passed.

'Thank you,' she murmured. 'But if he's here I'll come back later, when I'm tidier.' She gestured to her clothes. Shoes dusty from hours of wandering. Loose trousers and her favourite green shirt: comfortable, but hardly appropriate for calling at the palace.

'Nonsense. Tahir will want to see you and thank you personally. I know he's here at the moment.' She beckoned, and this time Annalisa complied, gingerly settling herself on the wide seat.

The door clicked shut and she jumped, unable to stifle the

notion she'd committed herself to more than she'd intended. The car slid forward and Annalisa turned to her companion, wondering if it was too late to back out. She could talk to Tahir by phone.

'Your name, my dear?' The woman forestalled her.

'I'm Annalisa Hansen.'

'How do you do, Annalisa? I'm Rihana Al'Ramiz, Tahir's mother.'

Annalisa opened her mouth to reply, then snapped her jaw shut as she absorbed the name.

Al'Ramiz. It couldn't be...

Yet, taking in the other woman's attire, Annalisa realised with a sinking sensation it could very well be. Al'Ramiz was the name of Qusay's ruling family.

'How do you do?' Her voice emerged as a hoarse whisper. She paused, unsure how to proceed. 'Tahir said he was coming for a coronation.'

Rihana Al'Ramiz nodded, her mouth curving wryly. 'His brother, Kareef, has just inherited the throne.'

'But…' Annalisa shook her head, unable to take it in. Tahir was a member of the royal family! He'd said he was related to the King, but she'd thought he meant a distant connection. She was sharing a seat with the dowager Queen of Qusay! 'I had no idea…' she blurted out.

Her skin prickled and tightened and her vision blurred around the edges. Annalisa gripped the seat with shaking fingers as the world pitched and heaved out of focus. This was one shock too many.

'It's all right.' A gentle hand on hers tugged her back to reality. 'You'll feel better when you've had some refreshment. Come.' Her tone grew brisk as the door opened and a servant gestured for Annalisa to get out.

Shakily Annalisa stood, concentrating on staying upright. Her legs were like jelly and her bones felt hollow, as if a breeze might blow her away.

She watched Rihana Al'Ramiz gesture towards the beautiful old palace. Sunlight glinted off semi-precious gems set in decorative patterns around the entrance and servants stood to attention, waiting to usher them inside.

The sense of unreality grew. And with it the worrying suspicion that life was about to get even more complicated.

'Thank you for your advice, Akmal. The views of the Council are always of interest to me.' Tahir prowled to the huge window facing the sea and reminded himself for the hundredth time that patience was required.

Patience wasn't his style.

Ruling a country wasn't his style!

He couldn't believe after all these weeks he hadn't found a way out of this bind. Or that the Qusanis wanted *him*, the reprobate son of a vicious father, to succeed to the throne. But despite his best efforts he'd yet to uncover a distant relative who could take the royal role off his hands. As far as the Council of Elders was concerned he was King, and they expected him to rule.

He couldn't begrudge his brothers their decision to give up the throne. He'd do the same himself if he could. But he was trapped till he found a viable alternative.

'A suitable marriage would be timely, sire,' his vizier said in a measured tone. 'After the…turmoil of the last months it would be a perfect way of demonstrating the stability of the royal lineage.'

Tahir's mouth kicked up at one side. 'Turmoil' was Akmal's diplomatic way of saying the Al'Ramiz brothers had caused enough sensation for several lifetimes.

After his cousin Zafir had discovered he wasn't the legitimate ruler and stepped aside, Tahir's eldest brother had inherited. But as both Kareef and then Rafiq had since renounced the throne, the country now lay in Tahir's hands.

A man who'd been exiled at eighteen. The brother with the wildest reputation. Who hadn't set foot here for eleven years. He clenched his fists.

Hell! He couldn't stay as King. He wasn't into responsibility, or settling in one place long-term.

No wonder they wanted him to marry. They hoped it would make him settled and stable. *Tied down*.

'The Princess is—'

'Thank you, Akmal.' He spun around to face his advisor. 'I'm sure she's a paragon of virtue and would make a perfect queen.' He clasped his hands behind his back, remembering the old man was only doing his job in pressing for a wedding. 'However, it's too soon to consider marriage.'

'But, sire—'

Akmal broke off as a knock sounded and a servant entered, apologising. He was sorry to intrude, he knew the importance of the King's private meeting, but he—

'What is it?' Tahir was only too grateful for the interruption.

'The Lady Rihana asks if you would join her for tea, Highness.'

Tahir froze in mid-step.

His *mother* had invited him to tea?

It was unprecedented. Since he'd been back he'd seen her, of course. She'd expressed relief that he was safe. She'd welcomed him and offered her support. All with a distant courtesy that spoke of good breeding and duty.

Not a trace of maternal love.

He'd shattered that by the time he got kicked out of the country, after being found with his father's naked mistress.

It didn't matter that it had been the mistress trying to seduce *him*. Nor that Tahir had an ingrained distaste for the notion of sharing his father's women. But he hadn't protested his innocence. His father's fury had been worth the price.

Tahir had become a son no parent could be proud of. His mother's distance made it clear he'd long ago destroyed any vestige of parental devotion.

And now? Perhaps she needed something.

That was why people got close: for what he could provide. Money, sex, publicity, the excitement of walking on the wild side with a man whose reputation was notorious.

'I'd be delighted to join her.' Tahir turned to his vizier. 'If you'll excuse me?'

Akmal was already bowing. 'Of course, sire.'

* * *

He pulled up short in the doorway. Afternoon sunlight slanted through the deep-set windows. It caught golden highlights in a woman's rich brown hair.

His stomach clenched as memories stirred. Long silken tresses tangling round him as he shivered in pleasure and release. Smiling dark eyes looking shyly up at him. Lush red lips tentatively kissing his flesh. His heart had leapt at that gentle caress.

She turned and his heart ricocheted against his ribs, beating out of kilter.

'Annalisa!' He was halfway across the room before he remembered himself and took note of the situation.

Annalisa, the girl he'd left angry and hurt but well, looked far too pale. Her face was thinner, and her brow puckered as if she were in pain. Her lips were compressed in a nervous line and her eyes skittered from his.

He started forward again.

'Tahir. I'm glad you could join us.' His mother rose from a nearby divan and he slammed to a halt.

Swiftly he bowed. 'Mother.'

He sent her a searching stare, but she met his regard blandly. What was going on?

'Ms Hansen.'

Annalisa looked up, eyes wide with surprise. Last time they'd been together the circumstances hadn't been so formal.

Curling heat in his belly testified to just how *informal* they'd been. Blood pooled low in his body, a precursor to the heavy weight of arousal.

He stood straighter, stunned by his reaction. For months his sex drive had been absent. Till Annalisa. Since recuperating he'd felt not a twinge of interest in any of the local beauties. Yet one glance at her and…

Quickly he took the seat his mother indicated.

An antique tea service was laid out on a low table. A gold salver held syrupy cakes and figs. A laden plate sat before Annalisa, untouched.

'Ms Hansen has come to see you, Tahir. I met her at the

palace gates.' His mother regarded him steadily, her look now razor-sharp.

His skin tightened. What had Annalisa said?

'I knew you'd want to thank her for what she did in the desert.' She turned, smiling at her guest. 'We owe you an enormous debt of gratitude, Annalisa.'

Tahir accepted a glass in a filigree holder and murmured his thanks, his gaze straying to Annalisa's silent form.

Despite the Queen's hospitality, she was uncomfortable, her shoulders hunched defensively. He knew a burning need to reach out and gentle her, as he would a nervous filly. Instead he curled his fingers around his tea.

Where was the confident woman who'd nursed him? Who camped alone so self-sufficiently?

'How are you?' he asked, willing her to meet his gaze. She stared at a point near his left ear.

'I'm fine, thank you.'

The husky edge to her voice caught at his midriff, drawing muscles tight.

Something was wrong. He knew it with a gut-deep certainty even this stifling formality couldn't quell. He put the tea down with a click on the inlaid table. Had someone hurt her? The hairs rose on the back of his neck as unfamiliar waves of emotion washed through him.

The shrill ring of a phone intruded and Tahir got to his feet, eager for an excuse to move.

'It's for you, Mother,' he said moments later. 'Some crisis with the reception you're planning.'

His mother rose gracefully. 'If you'll excuse me, I'd better take this.' She paused, turning to Annalisa. 'If you'll be all right, my dear?'

Fiery colour flared in Annalisa's cheeks, yet her hands clenched so tight her knuckles shone white. 'Of course, ma'am. Thank you.'

Tahir waited till his mother took the phone into the next room. Then he turned, every sense on alert as foreboding chilled his blood.

* * *

She should never have come.

Afternoon sun highlighted the strong contours of Tahir's face, gifting his glossy hair with a luxurious blue-black sheen. His eyes were vivid and probing under straight brows.

He was more imposing than she remembered. She thought she'd imagined that potent allure, that heady male strength and the lazy sexuality of his smile. But one look, just the sound of her name on his lips, and she was in danger of falling for him all over again.

Even knowing how cold and callous he really was!

Had she lost her grip on reality as she struggled with one shock after another?

She stumbled to her feet when he approached and he stopped. Her heart pattered an unfamiliar rhythm.

'It's good to see you, Annalisa.'

She wished she could say the same. The traditional robe he wore emphasised his height and rangy power. He was too big, too confronting, too attractive.

Her breath expelled in a silent hiss as she realised her weakness for this man hadn't ended.

'Are you all right?' Her body came alive under his roving gaze. How did he do that?

'Yes,' she lied. 'I'm okay. And you?' The words were stilted but she had to know.

'Fighting fit.' His lopsided smile squeezed her heart and she looked away, frightened by the intensity of her feelings. She should be over him. He wasn't the man she'd first thought him. Besides, he came from a different world. He was royalty.

'I didn't expect to see you here.' He paced closer and she forced herself to stand her ground.

'I got to Shafar last night. I'm booked on a flight to Europe tomorrow.' But should she go? This morning's news changed everything. She bit her lip, wondering what to do for the best. A doctor's appointment was her first priority now.

'Something's wrong. What is it?'

His concern drew her gaze to his. If she didn't know better she'd think he cared.

She shut her eyes for a moment, willing herself to be strong. To snap the curious hold he had over her. When she opened them he was closer, a pace away. She swallowed at the illusion of warmth she read in his eyes.

Annalisa darted a look at the closed door the Queen had used. How long would they have in private?

'I needed to see you.' Only to herself did she admit she'd *wanted* to see him, craved it. She couldn't drag her eyes from him.

His brows tilted down. 'So this isn't a social call.' He paused. 'And it's obviously important. Not about the care of our stray goat?'

'It's gone to a good home. The youngest daughter of one of my cousins has made a pet of it.' Annalisa paused, aghast at her nervous babbling.

She shook her head, feeling her hair swirl from her ponytail, wishing she'd put it up so she looked more in control.

'You said…' She swallowed and made herself go on, lifting her chin to meet his gaze head-on. 'You said if there were…consequences I should let you know.' Something inside shattered as his expression remained cool and aloof.

'Well, there are consequences. I'm pregnant.'

Her words echoed in growing silence. His brilliant blue gaze grew laser-sharp but no warmer.

If she'd needed proof she meant nothing to him it was there in his shuttered expression and tightening jaw. The only sign of life was his throbbing pulse. Otherwise he might have been carved from stone.

She told herself it was what she'd expected.

Abruptly she turned, blinking at the view of a manicured courtyard bathed in the glow of afternoon sun.

'What are your plans?' His voice was harsh, grating her frayed nerves.

No talk of *our* plans or *his* involvement. What had she expected? For him to sweep her close and say he'd missed her? That leaving her was the biggest mistake of his life?

Bile rose in her throat as she realised some forlorn part of her had wanted just that. Had clung to the mirage of the man she'd fallen for before he'd shown his true self. As if it was possible to fall in love like that!

Annalisa shrugged, anger surging at her foolishness. 'I don't know. But I *am* having this baby.' Her hand inched protectively across her abdomen.

Silence.

Her lips twisted as she imagined his horror. He wouldn't want this complication. Unless he already had a trail of illegitimate children. The things he'd said that last morning made it possible.

She hunched as pain battered her.

'How convenient you found me here.' Something in his tone made her swing round. He looked more commanding than ever. Daunting.

'You told me to contact you.'

'And how could you pass up the opportunity when you found out who I was?' His lips thinned.

'Opportunity?' Annalisa groped for understanding.

He shrugged. 'To cash in on my position.'

For a full thirty seconds Annalisa stared into a face grown harsh with suspicion. Then his meaning registered and fire exploded in her bloodstream, rippling through every artery and vein.

She drew herself up straight.

'That doesn't deserve an answer.' Yet an outraged response bubbled up. 'You have some ego! A woman comes to tell you you've fathered a child and it's all about *you*?'

How gullible she was. Even after his treatment of her, she'd expected better.

'You deny my situation has anything to do with your claim to be pregnant?'

'Claim?' Annalisa remembered the days she'd fretted that pregnancy was possible. The fatigue and nausea. The panicked knowledge that she had to make decisions not just for herself now, but for her baby. Her hands clenched as she resisted a never before felt urge to slap someone.

'I'm pregnant. It has nothing to do with you being rich or the brother of the King. I only found that out when your mother told me.'

'And you couldn't resist sharing your juicy news with her, right?' His dark scowl was furious.

'I told her nothing!'

One eloquent eyebrow rose in disbelief and he crossed his arms over that broad chest, the epitome of male scorn.

Suddenly she felt dreadfully small and powerless.

'Then why was she so solicitous?' he pressed. 'Why leave us alone against every rule of protocol?'

Horrified, Annalisa widened her eyes. Had the Queen guessed? Her stomach lurched in dismay. Bad enough sharing the news with Tahir. She wasn't ready for the Queen's censure too.

'I was sick when we arrived. Morning sickness…'

'You didn't drop any coy hints?'

His words lashed her, his distrust stinging like the blast of a sandstorm on bare skin.

Annalisa wouldn't stay to be insulted. She'd done what she must.

But as she marched past he reached out and snagged her wrist. His touch was shocking heat against her flesh, making her pulse gallop.

'Let me go. Or am I supposed to make obeisance to such an important person first?' She'd never been one for sarcasm and her furious words surprised even her.

Tahir peered down into her face. 'Where will you go?'

'To my aunt's house. I have to pack for my flight.' She tried to tug free but his hold tightened implacably.

She breathed deep. 'Please, let me go.' His closeness confounded her outrage, weakening her fragile composure.

'You can stay here,' he said abruptly.

'No! There's no need.' She stepped back but he followed, crowding her. His scent invaded her nostrils and to her consternation she felt a flicker of response to its subtle allure.

'There's every need,' he assured her. The glint in his eyes

sent a shiver of doubt racing down her spine. 'We have things to discuss.'

Annalisa looked away. 'I won't stay where I'm not wanted.' He'd made it clear he thought she was inventing the story of her pregnancy.

'Oh, I wouldn't put it that way.' His voice dropped to a silky burr. His thumb stroked her sensitive inner wrist, brushing back and forth till her pulse raced unevenly.

Startled, she met eyes turned bright with desire.

Her breath caught in her throat as an answering tide of warmth spread out from her womb. One look from half-lidded eyes, one word in that bedroom voice and she melted!

'I'm going.'

Tahir shook his head, that flash of hunger doused as if it had never been. He looked grim.

'My family and I owe you hospitality for saving my life. Besides…' his long fingers tightened on her wrist '…I'll only have you brought back. Far easier if you stay.'

'Brought back?' Indignation warred with fury. 'Just who do you think you are?'

He inclined his head, sketching a graceful gesture with one hand.

'I'm Sheikh Tahir Al'Ramiz, King of Qusay.' His eyes flickered in grim amusement. 'I'm your sovereign lord.'

CHAPTER EIGHT

FOR the first time Tahir relished the fact he was King.

Because Annalisa couldn't escape till he was ready to let her go. He could demand her obedience.

Because he revelled in the power it gave him over this one woman. He felt a ripple of primitive pleasure any civilised man should abhor.

What did that say about him?

He scrubbed a hand over his face. Why couldn't the elders and citizens of Qusay understand they supported a flawed man as their monarch?

He remembered the dismay on Annalisa's face when she'd learned who he was. Busy in her outlying province, with her packing and her goodbyes, she'd heard Kareef had renounced the kingship, but not what had followed.

She hadn't known Tahir's identity.

The doubts that had swarmed on hearing her revelation had disintegrated in the face of her shock. Cynicism engendered by grasping lovers and false paternity suits had melted as he'd watched her struggle with the gravity of her situation.

Pregnant with the monarch's child.

No wonder she'd paled. She'd swayed, the dazed look in her velvet eyes evoking a protectiveness he'd known only once before. When he'd deliberately invited her scorn at the oasis so she could be free of him.

If only he still had such strength of mind.

He stared across the shadowed bedroom, past billowing curtains drawn aside to let in sweet night air. Moonlight covered the wide bed, gleamed on pale bare arms, caressed the dark fall of long hair across the pillow.

What sort of man was he?

One who couldn't master himself to keep away from a woman who despised him. Had he no shame? No scruples?

Yielding to temptation was a speciality of his.

Unable to sleep after hours working on official documents, he'd given in to restlessness and prowled the corridors. Only to find himself outside the suite set aside for the woman who was officially his mother's guest.

Here he was, a voyeur, rooted to the spot by the sight of her, fast asleep. She didn't wear silk or lace like his usual lovers. Just a white cotton nightshirt. Yet she looked utterly seductive and he was hard with wanting.

Tahir passed his hand over his face again. An honourable man wouldn't have entered her chamber.

He'd given up being honourable a lifetime ago.

His lips twisted in a savage grimace. What irony he should be named Tahir: 'pure'. He hadn't been pure in thought, word or deed since adolescence.

What business had he in this woman's chamber? A woman who was decent and trusting.

'Who is it?' Her voice was a thready whisper.

He stepped forward into silvery light.

'It's only me.' His mouth tightened derisively. That was meant to reassure her?

'What do you want?' She curled higher in the bed, drawing the sheet to her chin. Her defensive move amused and annoyed him. He hadn't yet stooped to attacking unwilling women.

'To see you.' It was simply the truth. But the need that had dragged him from the other side of the palace was neither simple nor straightforward.

In the dark he felt her regard, saw her lift her chin belligerently. 'You shouldn't be here.'

Once, the knowledge that he broke the rules would have

been an incitement, prompting him to outrageous action. But he'd barely given the proprieties a thought, simply yielded to his need to be with her.

'Your flight has been cancelled,' he said. 'The money will be refunded to your account.'

'You had no right to do that.' She sat up, propping a pillow behind her, and he caught sight of her lush, round breasts, outlined by fine cotton. His groin tightened.

'We need to discuss our options. We can't do that if you're in Scandinavia.' He should be grappling with the issue of her pregnancy, not this potent lust.

She folded her arms. 'You still had no authority.'

He stepped nearer, drawn by her sleep-husky voice. 'I've arranged for you to see an obstetrician.'

'I can organise that. You have no right to take over my life, forcing me to stay here.'

She sounded huffy. He was relieved to hear the spark of energy in her voice. She'd been so wan earlier. Was it normal for a pregnant woman to look worn to the bone? Or was it shock at discovering his identity that had sapped her strength?

'As far as the world is concerned, you are my mother's guest. What could be more pleasant?' He paused, acknowledging the need to keep Annalisa close was about his own desire as much as necessity. 'Now it's done, and you can reassure yourself everything's all right.'

'Or is it that you still don't believe I'm pregnant?'

He shook his head. When he'd heard her news he'd thought the worst, remembering the lengths women had gone to in order to snag his attention and his money. But within minutes he'd realised she wasn't bluffing. Annalisa was light-years from the sort of women with whom he usually consorted.

That was why the memory of their night together had burned indelibly into his consciousness. His gaze followed her lush curves under the pale sheet.

'I believe you, Annalisa.'

'Good.' Her voice was strained. 'Now you'd better go.'

'You wouldn't like me to stay and soothe you back to sleep?' One step took him to the bed. If he reached out…

'No!' Her voice held a telltale breathlessness that stirred the devil inside him, heating his blood.

'Perhaps I should persuade you.' He paused to drag in a surprisingly unsteady breath. 'I could, you know.'

He'd been taught by the best. Even his first sexual partner, the gorgeous girl he'd yearned for in his gullible teens, hadn't been the innocent he'd imagined. She'd enthusiastically shown him a myriad of ways to share pleasure before he'd discovered she'd bedded him not for affection but for his father's money.

And that he'd shared her with the old man.

The taint of that discovery had left him determined never to fall for anything approximating female innocence.

Until Annalisa.

'Is that why you're here? You want a change from your glamorous lovers?' Her voice dripped disdain.

She couldn't know how right she was. He yearned for her as he'd never yearned for any of the seductive beauties he'd bedded.

He couldn't recall feeling so *hungry* for a woman.

He stroked a finger along her bare arm, feeling her shiver in awareness. Instead of yanking her arm away she stilled. Tahir stiffened, iron-hard in arousal.

'How many have there been, Tahir? Dozens? Hundreds?'

'I'm no saint,' he growled, annoyed at her insistence on talking.

'I gathered that,' she murmured. 'I looked you up on the Internet this evening, since I had a name to search for.'

He froze at her frigid tone.

'Is it true you dated *all* the finalists in that Caribbean beauty pageant last year, in between closing a major business deal?' He watched her shift beneath the sheet and imagined his hands on her.

'The reports were exaggerated,' he murmured. A little.

'So is there a chance you've given me anything else, as well as a baby?'

For an instant he didn't follow her logic. Then his head reared back. 'You really are a doctor's daughter, aren't you?'

Annoyance warred with reluctant admiration at her temerity. No one spoke to him like that—ever. 'I may be reckless, Annalisa, but I'm not completely foolhardy. I have a clean bill of health.'

'I'm glad. For the sake of our child.'

Our child.

The reminder was a cold douche to his libido and he straightened away from the bed. He'd spent the last half-hour ignoring that complication. Far easier to focus on the delicious Annalisa than face the reality of a ready-made family.

Tahir didn't do family.

Couldn't do family.

He was a loner. Had been all his adult life. He had nothing to offer a child or a long-term partner.

He'd probably take after his unlamented father when it came to parenting. What if that defective gene had passed from the old man to him? Certainly he'd followed the old devil's footsteps in courting vice. Had his father seen that flaw in Tahir's personality from the first? Was that what had inspired such hatred of his own son?

The notion sent an icy shiver through his gut.

He'd never inflict his father's brand of paternal discipline on any child. Never risk that tainted strain appearing and harming an innocent.

He turned on his heel and strode for the door, his stomach churning. 'We'll talk later.'

'But not here,' she said quickly. 'I don't want you in my room. Ever.'

Tahir paused, the muscles across his back and shoulders tightening as if in response to a blow.

It was a sensation he hadn't felt for years. He couldn't remember it hurting this much.

'As you wish, Ms Hansen. I won't set foot in your room unless invited.'

Annalisa watched him go, her hand at her mouth to stop herself calling him back. She *didn't* want him here.

So why had she waited, quivering in anticipation, to see if he'd do more than stroke her arm? If he'd caress her properly?

Properly! There was no properly between them. She was pregnant with what would be his illegitimate child. She was a commoner and he a king.

He'd probably gone to meet some glamorous woman who'd be at home in the bed of a spoiled, aristocratic playboy.

What she'd read on the web had ripped the scales from her eyes. If a quarter of it was true Tahir was a man she couldn't begin to understand. A financial marvel, reckless gambler and lover of epic reputation. He strode through the ballrooms, boardrooms and bedrooms of at least three continents, taking what he wanted and moving on.

Stories about him were legion, but there was one common thread. He was a loner, never linked for long with any lover, not burdened with close friends or business partnerships. A man who needed no one.

And the man she'd met in the desert?

He hadn't been real. He'd been the product of Tahir's weakened state and extraordinary circumstances. He'd bedded her for the novelty of it. She couldn't be more different from the sexy women draped on his arm in the media reports.

The knowledge cramped her chest and she drew her knees up tight, curling into a ball.

Pregnancy was an enormous responsibility. Add to that the fact that she couldn't quash this craving for a man who saw her as an amusement and she was in deep trouble.

She'd even imagined something dark and troubled behind Tahir's careless demeanour. Had his nightmares in the desert been proof of that, or simply a fantasy brought on by delirium? She wanted to probe, uncover and confront the bleakness she sensed beneath his casual, sexy attitude.

She wanted to believe he cared.

Annalisa shook her head. She created excuses where there were none. She was out of her depth with Tahir.

In future she'd remember it.

* * *

'This way, please.' The footman bowed and Annalisa hesitated on the threshold of her suite. For days it had been a haven as she struggled to absorb the implications of her situation.

This period of peace and quiet had been what she'd needed. Sheikha Rihana, Tahir's mother, had been a daily visitor and, contrary to Annalisa's fears, she'd remained friendly rather than judgemental. The older woman must know of the obstetrician's visit yet she hadn't mentioned it. Did she guess at the fraught relationship between her guest and her son? That it was his child Annalisa carried?

They talked of everything but Tahir, and it felt as if a rapport had developed between them. Something more than good manners and hospitality. As if Rihana was as grateful for Annalisa's company as she was for Rihana's.

As for Tahir, after invading Annalisa's privacy that night, and hinting he'd seduce her, she'd expected to confront him the next morning.

Instead he'd left the capital on urgent business.

Only his personal intervention had saved regional diplomatic talks from foundering. Everyone sang his praises. But Annalisa suspected he'd found it a convenient reason not to face her.

Each day she braced herself to see him but he remained absent. *That told her all she needed to know about the importance of this baby to him. Her importance.*

'Madam?' The footman waited, his face expressionless. Did he wonder about her presence here? 'If you'll follow?'

Annalisa straightened her spine and stepped forward, following obediently down the wide arched corridor.

She couldn't hide for ever. Especially from her own kin. Yet when news had arrived that her uncle Saleem was here, her stomach had knotted. She'd never liked her aunt's husband. If there'd been an alternative to staying in his house when she'd arrived in Shafar she'd have taken it.

What did he want?

He'd never approved of her 'western' ways. Unlike the rest of the family, his relationship with her and her father had never been good. This couldn't be a social call.

Her tension increased as they progressed through the palace. Past sumptuous apartments and breathtakingly beautiful courtyards. Each inch was exquisite, from the inlaid floors to the luxurious furnishings and the view over a perfect indigo sea. They reached the public reception rooms where solemn visitors watched her with thinly veiled interest. Anxiety skated up her spine.

At every step she felt like an interloper in a world of privilege, prestige and protocol.

'Here you are, madam.' The servant opened gilded double doors. 'Refreshments have been provided. Please ring the bell if you need anything.' He stood back so she could enter, then shut the doors with quiet precision.

Saleem stood, feet wide, in the centre of the room. If he was awed by his surroundings he didn't show it. Instead he stood proud, a tall man, lantern-jawed and swarthy.

'Hello, Uncle. It's good of you to visit. My aunt hasn't come with you?' Annalisa kept her tone light, despite the chill that enveloped her as he scrutinised her like a beetle under a microscope.

'I came to see the King.' He paused on the word, investing it with distaste. 'I'm told he's not in, so I asked to see you instead.'

Annalisa stiffened at his bristling disapproval. This wasn't going to be good.

'Would you like a seat?' She gestured towards a group of elegant couches around a low table groaning with delicacies.

'You make yourself at home here, miss. As if you have every right to do so.'

'I'm a guest of the Sheikha Rihana. This is her hospitality and I—'

'Don't give me that! I wasn't born yesterday.'

He strode across to loom over her, eyes flashing.

Clasping her hands before her, Annalisa stood her ground. She'd seen him bully her aunt and refused to be cowed. Yet her pulse raced at how vulnerable she felt in face of his fury.

'You may put that story out for the gullible public but I know why you're here. You're *his* guest, aren't you? His mistress. His whore!'

Despite her resolve, Annalisa stumbled back, frightened by the violence in his snapping dark eyes and his bunched fists. Her heart thrashed against her ribs and the oxygen rushed from her lungs.

'I wonder he's got the gall to install you in the palace for all to see—but then, with his reputation, nothing should surprise me. A fine man you've chosen to give yourself to!'

Spittle flecked her cheek as he ranted and Annalisa cringed, the blood draining from her face. This was worse than anything she'd expected. Horror froze her to the spot.

'I'm nobody's whore,' she said breathlessly when she found her voice. 'You have no right—'

'I have *every* right. You're my responsibility now your father and grandfather are dead.'

Annalisa shook her head. 'No! I'm responsible for myself.'

'Not when you bring shame on the family.' His jaw thrust forward aggressively. 'I should have expected something like this, considering the freedoms you were given growing up. That father of yours—'

'Don't you *dare* say a word against my father.' It was Annalisa's turn to step forward and she saw surprise flash in Saleem's eyes. 'He was worth ten of you.'

For a moment there was silence. Blood pounded so hard in her ears she felt light-headed with the force of it. Distress, fear and fury were a sour mix on her tongue.

And guilt. Guilt at the way she'd fallen so easily for Tahir's facile charm.

'What would your precious father say if he could see you now?'

Annalisa swayed as if from a body-blow. Her father would be on her side. But how disappointed he'd be. He'd taught her the value of love. She'd fallen for its pale shadow.

'Don't you realise what you've done?' Saleem pressed on. 'The gossip about you and the King alone together in the desert for days?'

'What was I supposed to do? Ignore him when he stumbled into camp and leave him to die?' Annalisa planted her hands on her hips, finding relief in anger. She glared. 'If there's gossip, I don't have far to look for the source, do I?'

She guessed any such news hadn't come from the palace. The Queen didn't need to give reasons for inviting a guest to stay. Nor would it be from her other relatives, or the camel driver, who was an old friend of her father's.

Her suspicions were confirmed when Saleem spluttered, his gaze sliding from hers.

'You never liked me and you wanted an excuse to blacken my name.'

'Excuse?' he bellowed. 'What need for an excuse when you're pregnant? Ah, you didn't know I knew, did you?'

A sneer distorted his face and he grabbed her elbow in a merciless grip. Annalisa felt the walls close around her as shock and fear crowded close.

'You little slut. You were so caught up in your affair you didn't even have the sense to hide the evidence. Your aunt found the pregnancy test, clearing out your belongings when your lover sent his servants for them.'

Annalisa shrank from the hatred in his face.

'She was so upset I knew something was wrong. It didn't take much to get the truth out of her.'

Annalisa closed her eyes, praying fervently he hadn't used violence on her poor aunt.

A savage wrench of her arm made her flop like a rag doll. 'Now what have you got to say for yourself?'

'She'll say nothing to the likes of you.' The deep voice came from somewhere behind Annalisa, penetrating the haze of shock. 'Let her go. *Now*.' Tahir's voice dropped to a lethal rumble, like thunder on the horizon.

Instantly Saleem released her arm and she staggered a couple of steps away.

He'd heard the threat in Tahir's voice, for all the newcomer hadn't raised his voice. The air thickened, heavy with a menace more powerful than any of her uncle's taunts.

Swiftly she turned. Tahir stood feet wide, fists clenched. The sheer aggressive energy radiating from his tall frame was at odds with the urbane sophistication of his tailor-made suit. Never had she seen him so forbidding. His jaw was razor-sharp, his sensuous mouth firm. Tahir's face was austerely calm, but the light in his eyes was bloodthirsty. As if he wanted to tear her uncle limb from limb.

Relief swelled, buckling Annalisa's knees so she sagged against the back of a couch. She slid a shaking hand protectively across her abdomen.

'Your Majesty.' Her uncle bowed stiffly.

'Are you all right?' Tahir ignored him, turning to look at her. Even the concern in his tone didn't obliterate his distant, inflexible expression.

She wished he'd sweep her into his arms and hold her tight, till the trembling and the sick distress passed.

'I'm all right.' Annalisa was so shaken she didn't care that her voice wobbled with relief.

He swung round to her uncle, closing the space between them in a few strides. 'If I ever hear you've used violence on a woman, any woman, I'll make you wish you'd never been born.' The softly spoken words had the force of a cracking whip. 'And I'll know. I'll make it my business to know.'

'It wasn't violence, sire.' Saleem cowered back. 'It's a matter of honour.'

'You have a quaint understanding of honour.' Tahir's scorn was knife-edged. He turned his head again, looking over his shoulder at her. 'Can you walk?'

'Of course I can!' She stood up, away from the couch.

'Then go now. The footman outside will see you to your rooms.'

A cowardly part of her wanted to do as he said, escape from her uncle's ugly accusations. But she stood her ground. 'This is my business.'

For long seconds his deep blue gaze held hers, till tendrils of heat curled inside her, warming the chilled numbness. Finally he nodded.

'It is. Do you trust me to deal with it?'

Deal with Saleem? She had no doubts Tahir could do that more effectively than she.

Instinct overrode every doubt she had about his character.

He hadn't even acknowledged the baby was his, yet in this moment she knew no one could be a stronger champion for herself and her child.

'I trust you,' she murmured.

CHAPTER NINE

ANNALISA breathed deep of fresh, salty air, her hands twining restlessly. After that appalling scene she'd sought the garden overlooking the King's private beach. A quiet place to think.

But she hadn't been able to decide what to do. She'd been too caught up in reliving the horror of her uncle's accusations, and her overwhelming relief when Tahir had appeared. Just his presence had steadied her nerves.

Should she leave? Where would she go? To the village that had been her home? Could she expect the same treatment from the rest of her family?

Salty tears clogged her throat. Surely not. Surely they'd be more charitable. But right now she didn't want to test that.

She had to find a safe home, where her child would be welcomed, not scorned. She hugged her arms around herself, feeling more alone than ever.

Tahir had asked her to trust him, at least with Saleem. It confused her that she had. Shouldn't she be wary of the man who'd been shallow and callous? Yet now he'd stood up for her so forcefully.

'Annalisa?' A deep voice spoke as gravel crunched underfoot. She sat straighter and turned.

Her breath escaped in a sigh of appreciation as she devoured the sight of Tahir. Commanding nose, chiselled jaw and sapphire eyes that glittered under heavy lids. Sensation flared inside her. Desperately she told herself it was from gratitude that he'd dealt with Saleem.

Long legs ate up the distance separating them and she stood, feeling at a disadvantage sitting.

Besides, he was her king. She had to remember that.

'Thank you for dealing with…' she swept her arm wide '…with him. If you hadn't come—'

'Don't think about that.' He reached out, enclosing her hand in his. Heat engulfed her fingers and spread wondrously. 'It's over. He's gone.'

Was that satisfaction she heard in Tahir's voice? Surely he hadn't strong-armed Saleem into leaving?

'I'm sorry.' She shook her head miserably. 'You shouldn't have had to witness that.' Embarrassment fired her cheeks as she recalled all Saleem had said. Her skin crawled at his filthy outpouring of venom.

'Look at me!'

Tahir's abrupt tone jerked her head up. She met his bright, unblinking eyes. Somehow that steady regard strengthened her still-trembling body.

'You have nothing to apologise for. I'm just sorry I didn't arrive early enough to deal with him before you were called.' His lips curled in a tiny piratical smile. 'He won't bother you again. Ever.'

Annalisa didn't care how Tahir had done it; she simply basked in the knowledge.

'Thank you.' Profound relief coloured her voice and he inclined his head.

'How are you?' His grip tightened. 'Do you need a doctor?'

'Of course not.'

'You've been unwell.' His expression was sombre. Her pulse gave a shaky little jerk at his concern. 'The obstetrician was at pains to stress you need rest.'

She frowned. 'How do you know what she said?' At Tahir's bland expression futile anger spiked. 'So doctor-patient confidentiality doesn't apply at the palace?' She pulled her hand free and paced, restless at the discovery her privacy had been overridden.

Annalisa had never felt more powerless than in these last days, when her life had been turned upside down.

She was used to making decisions, being useful and active. Now she was in limbo, unsettled and unsure of herself. She'd thought today's interview with Saleem the final straw. Now she discovered she didn't even have exclusive rights to information about her own body.

She felt caged, no longer in control of her life.

'I was concerned for you.'

'Really?' She met his eyes. Fervently she wished she couldn't remember how they'd glowed with approval as she'd climaxed beneath him. Such memories underscored a weakness she couldn't conquer.

'It was unpardonable to leave you at such a time. I'm sorry.'

Her surge of indignation deflated abruptly with his apology. He was the monarch. He had other responsibilities.

'You were needed elsewhere. I understand.' Suddenly she felt exhausted.

'That's no excuse. My presence at the negotiations was more or less symbolic.'

Why did he brush off his vital part in the treaty talks? She frowned. Surely a shallow man who revelled in his prestige would brag about his pivotal role?

'You should rest.' A hand at her elbow propelled her to the seat and she subsided, Tahir beside her. His body warmed her even where they didn't touch.

It felt as if he drew her close with an unseen force field. Annalisa breathed deep and told herself she imagined the zap and crackle of electricity between them.

'It's time we resolved this,' he said finally.

'What?' she said wearily. 'You want a DNA test to prove the baby is yours?'

His fingers flexed and his hand dropped away.

'I know it's mine.'

Annalisa swung to meet his gaze head-on, plunging into clear depths that glinted with an expression she couldn't name.

'You've changed your tune.' It didn't matter that an hour ago he'd championed her against Saleem. It still rankled that Tahir had doubted her word.

His nostrils flared and he straightened, as if unaccustomed to being challenged. 'The news came as a shock.'

'You thought I was lying.'

'It wasn't the first time a woman had said she carried my child.' His gaze bored into hers. 'But it's the first time it was true.'

Bile rose in Annalisa's mouth. She was simply one in a long line of women. A notch in his belt. Only she hadn't been sophisticated enough to prevent her pregnancy.

'So you believe me now?'

'I believe you. I know you.'

Fervently Annalisa wished she could say the same. Tahir confused her. Was he a careless, selfish hedonist, or a man of sense and compassion? He altered each time she saw him. No wonder she felt disorientated.

'Unfortunately your uncle's visit changes things. There's no chance now of keeping our relationship private.'

Relationship? It was on the tip of her tongue to say they *had* no relationship. Just a one-night stand.

'What do you suppose he'll do?' She felt sick, thinking of the vitriol he'd pour into waiting ears.

'Nothing. He won't say a word to anyone.'

Annalisa opened her mouth to protest that Saleem would surely continue gossiping. Then she saw Tahir's expression and a chill pierced her. She wouldn't like to be in Saleem's shoes.

'But he's already said enough. When your pregnancy starts to show people will remember his words and put two and two together.'

Stupid, but she couldn't prevent a fillip of pleasure that Tahir had accepted she'd have the baby. That he hadn't tried to push for a termination.

'They'll know the baby is mine.'

'If I'm in Qusay.' Yet she couldn't imagine raising her child anywhere else.

'It doesn't matter.' His voice was terse. 'The damage is done. Wherever you are this will catch up with you. There's no escaping.'

His words carried the weight of a judge delivering sentence. The hairs on her nape stood up at his bleak tone.

'There's only one option.' He drew in a slow breath, as if delaying the pronouncement. 'We must marry.'

The words echoed in her disbelieving ears.

'You've got to be kidding!'

'You think I'd joke about this?' He shot to his feet to pace before her. 'You think I *desire* marriage? That I haven't considered every alternative?'

Annalisa read disdain in the proud lines of his face. A bone-deep distaste that shrivelled something in the pit of her stomach.

What he meant was he had no desire to marry *her*.

The fact that she wasn't ready for marriage either didn't ease the pain of his rejection.

Tahir's eyes were glacier-cool and her heart plunged. Did he think she'd tricked him into this? What other reason for that terrible distant look?

'I didn't know Saleem would come here. I didn't intend for anyone to know.'

He swatted aside her protestations with a slicing gesture. 'I know. That's immaterial. What matters is our solution to the problem.'

He didn't sound like a man proposing marriage.

She pressed shaking hands together, painful memories resurfacing. Dreams she'd spun years ago when she'd begun to fall in love with Toby.

Annalisa had expected a marriage proposal then.

It had never eventuated. Toby had gone back to Canada, taking up a new job as a geologist. Instead of returning for her, as promised, news had arrived months later that he'd married someone else. Someone 'from home'. Who fitted his world, his expectations.

Not someone like Annalisa, who straddled two cultures and was viewed as alien to both.

Was she doomed always to be an outsider, unworthy of love?

'Marriage isn't the only solution.'

When she married it would be for love. Like that her parents had shared. Her father had loved his wife till the end. His whole focus those last days had been surviving long enough to name the Asiya Comet for her.

A cold-hearted marriage to a cold-hearted man would be disaster. Even with her inexperience Annalisa knew that.

'What else is there? For you to bring up my illegitimate child under my nose?'

She raised her chin. 'Would it be the first?'

'I've already told you.' Tahir bit out the words with a restrained savagery that made her shrink back. 'No other woman has carried my child.'

Spoken like a man with a soft spot for the woman he planned to marry!

'It needn't be under your nose.'

'You intend to emigrate?'

Silently she shook her head, feeling harried. This was too much, too soon. What should she do for the best?

'You *want* our child born illegitimate?'

'No,' she said miserably. 'But I don't want…'

'What don't you want, Annalisa?'

She bit her lip, not daring to voice the fears crowding close. How could she tie herself to a man she barely knew? A man she'd naïvely believed she…cared for, only to discover she didn't know him at all.

Could she trust a man of his reputation? Give herself and her baby into his keeping? In Qusay a husband had real power over his wife. His word was law.

If that husband was also King… They were poles apart, separated by an unbreachable gulf.

'Annalisa, look at me. Talk to me.'

Slowly she turned. He leaned close, broad shoulders blocking the view. His powerful presence pinioned her as if he held her in his arms.

If only he *would* hold her. Sweep her into his embrace as he had in the desert. She wanted to lean in and let him comfort her, care for her. But allowing herself to trust him in such a way would pose a dangerous threat to her already vulnerable heart.

She looked up into eyes bright as gems, at a mouth firm and decisive, a chin that jutted just a little aggressively as he waited for her to speak.

'Thank you for the offer,' she said in a low voice. 'No...' She looked away. 'I don't know. I need time.'

She needed time!

How much time did she think there was before her pregnancy became obvious? Before she became the subject of cruel jibes? Before she was shunned for her liaison with him?

Did she want that for herself and her baby?

Guilt punched hard in his gut. This was his fault. He'd given in to temptation and she'd pay the price.

Annalisa was so proud, so obstinate, and she wouldn't let him help her. Couldn't see how much worse the scandal would be because of who he was and what he'd been. The memory of that scene with her uncle curdled his stomach. He couldn't let her face such prejudice alone.

Or his child. Tahir had experience of being hated as a boy. He refused to give anyone the chance to hold *his* child in contempt.

He raked a hand through his hair as he paced his vast apartments, a sullen mix of emotions boiling over as he recalled her hesitation.

Since when had any woman said no to him? Women fell like ripe peaches into his open palm. Yet *this* woman hesitated. This little mouse, unsophisticated and innocent.

At least she had been till Tahir met her.

He had to make this right. Even if she didn't want him to. Even if she didn't want *him*.

The absurdity was that, with beautiful women put forward daily for his approval by those hoping he'd marry, it was Annalisa he wanted.

He felt a stirring in his groin and pounded his fist against the wall. It didn't matter what he *wanted*.

This was about necessity.

The thought of becoming a husband and father made him break out in a cold sweat. As usual, his desires were less honourable. It was sexual gratification he dreamt of, night after night. He hungered for Annalisa as he hadn't hungered for any woman.

Yet he couldn't leave her to cope with pregnancy and child-rearing alone. Not with *his* child. He might have lived the life of a reprobate, but he wasn't a complete moral vacuum.

Qusani society wasn't designed for unmarried mothers. The scene with her uncle had reinforced that. She'd never fit in and nor would the child—especially when it became known that Tahir was the father. They needed protection, even if the idea of acquiring responsibility for a family left a chilled lump in the pit of his belly.

He remembered his father, presenting an acceptable face to the public. Yet in private he'd been a cruel brute. Such a man shouldn't have children.

What if Tahir shared that same taint?

He didn't have his father's taste for violence. He didn't get kicks from bullying those weaker than himself. Yet, with his family history, who knew what sort of husband and father he'd make?

Rafiq and Kareef were brave men, embarking on married life with enthusiasm. But the taints of character had been Tahir's, not theirs. Their father's rage had always been directed at him, not his brothers.

When Tahir had recently visited his brother, in his new kingdom of Qais, Kareef and Jasmine had been ecstatically happy. Marriage suited Kareef. But he and Tahir were poles apart.

Tahir's lips flattened derisively at the notion of himself protecting Annalisa. Yet it had to be done.

He was tempted simply to organise the wedding despite her protests. He wasn't used to waiting. Yet he'd seen how shaken she was. She really did need time. He'd make one more attempt to make her see reason.

Heat kindled in his belly and he smiled at the thought of *persuading* her.

CHAPTER TEN

THE royal reception ran smoothly: the hum of conversation was steady, guests were smiling as they enjoyed the honour of being in the gilded audience rooms.

Tahir nodded to an ambassador.

Strange how easily he fitted this role. He worked long hours. But his talents for turning a deal, weighing situations and acting decisively were assets that made his royal role easier.

Except with Annalisa.

She'd managed to avoid him for days. Frustration gnawed at his belly.

He wanted this settled. Not because he wanted Annalisa, he assured himself, ignoring the nightly erotic dreams that kept him sleepless.

He stared past a cluster of businessmen and found her instantly. He'd been attuned to her presence since she'd entered the reception with his mother.

One look at Annalisa in shimmering amber silk and he couldn't concentrate on anything else. He imagined he heard her soft laughter over the noise of the exquisitely dressed throng.

She was smiling.

The sort of smile she hadn't given him since their night together. The sight punched a hole through his gut.

She smiled at a man: young and good-looking.

Tahir stiffened.

She tilted her head, as if to hear what her companion said. The man moved closer, cutting her off from the crowd.

Like a man with a woman he wanted, separating her so she could concentrate on him. Tahir knew the manoeuvre, the subtle shift of posture, the intimate tone, the extended arm gesture that made it seem they were alone.

He'd used that tactic himself, countless times.

Fury vibrated along every nerve. A proprietorial anger that demanded instant action.

'Pardon me.' He bowed to his companions with rigid decorum. 'I'll look forward to exploring this project in more detail with you. My staff will arrange a meeting.'

His companions murmured their thanks, and then he was striding across the room, deliberately not meeting the looks of those trying to catch his eye.

His attention was riveted on the woman in amber. Her gown was demure, yet the tracery of gold embroidery at its neckline drew the eye to the sweet swell of her breasts. When she moved the fine silk slithered over luscious curves that made his mouth water.

His fingers curled possessively.

She was his. No matter how she denied it.

The knowledge beat a primitive tattoo in his blood.

For hours he'd done his duty. It was time to act as a man, not a king.

'Really? That's fascinating,' Annalisa murmured, surreptitiously shifting back half a pace.

She'd enjoyed this conversation until her companion had closed the distance between them and the atmosphere had suddenly become intimate. Had she unwittingly encouraged him to think she was interested in him, not in his plans for dry land farming?

Annalisa was so used to sharing her father's discussions with visiting experts she'd responded openly and enthusiastically when Rihana had introduced them.

She should have followed her instinct and stayed away

tonight, despite Rihana's persuasion. Circumstances were different now. She didn't have the freedom of her father's protection to chat with strangers like an equal.

The scene with Saleem had reinforced that. She had to fit Qusani expectations. *Something she'd never been able to do.*

Distress and regret stifled her. She turned her head, seeking Rihana's reassuring presence. Instead she discovered searing blue eyes staring at her from under disapproving dark brows.

Annalisa caught her breath on a gasp and her companion swivelled, stammering, 'Your—your Majesty.'

Tahir inclined his head briefly. 'I'm not interrupting?'

The look in his eyes said he didn't give a damn if he was.

'Of course not, sire,' the young man replied hurriedly. He looked from Annalisa to the Sheikh looming beside them, then scuttled away, murmuring excuses.

At Tahir's blatantly disapproving look Annalisa felt a surge of anger rise. She hadn't done anything wrong.

Demurely she bowed her head. 'Your Highness.' She let her tone tell him what she thought of his attitude.

For one heady moment she'd thought he'd searched her out because he wanted her company. How pathetic could she be? The reception included plenty of sophisticated, beautiful women and Tahir had talked with all of them.

'Don't *Highness* me, Annalisa. It's too late for that.'

The acid in his voice jerked her head up. Thank goodness he was speaking so softly no one else could hear.

'And don't look for anyone else to rescue you.' He bit the words out through gritted teeth. 'No one will interrupt.' His mouth twisted wryly. 'That's one of the perks of being King.'

'I wasn't looking for rescue.' She tried to still her galloping pulse and slow her breathing. Her weakness for him horrified her. 'Why would I need rescuing?'

'If you flirted with me the way you did with him, I'd be tempted to flirt back. And, believe me, I wouldn't be as easy to shake off.' His lips drew wide in a feral smile.

Something fluttered deep inside her. Excitement.

'I wasn't flirting.' Annalisa lifted her chin, but she couldn't prevent a guilty flush staining her face. It wasn't her fault her companion had misunderstood. Was it?

One step brought Tahir close. His warmth enveloped her. If she moved a fraction they'd be touching.

Around them she heard a ripple of speculation sharpen voices, then an expectant lull as conversation ebbed.

Her heart thudded against her ribs and she felt again that curious tightening in her womb. Her body recalled too well the delights they'd shared, no matter how she tried to forget.

She sucked in a deep breath, then wished she hadn't as the movement brought her breasts close to his torso. Heat zapped between them and the air crackled.

Annalisa stepped back, pulse skittering.

He followed, closer than ever.

'Don't,' she whispered.

'Why not?' One eyebrow arched.

'Everyone is looking.' She felt the stares, heard the whispered speculation.

'So?' His mouth twisted in a cruel smile. 'Shouldn't you get used to it? If you're going to bear my bastard you'll always be the focus of gossip.'

Annalisa gasped, her body stiffening as if under a blow. She shuffled back another step, hand spread over her juddering heart. How could he be so…merciless? There was no sympathy in that proud, powerful face. Just disdain and a shadow of anger.

'Don't speak of it that way,' she whispered.

'Can't face the truth, Annalisa?'

Pain sheared through her. It *would* be the truth. Because she'd been foolish enough to give herself to him. Because, despite the threat of scandal, she was scared to marry Tahir. Such a union would stifle her. She and her baby needed love. Could they get that from a convenient marriage?

'This isn't the place to discuss it.' She dredged up her battered self-respect and met him stare for stare.

'Then we'll go elsewhere.' He paused. 'I warn you, if you're thinking of staying to snare another man it won't work. I'll make sure of it.'

Outrage doused her pain. 'Don't be absurd,' she hissed. 'You're mistaking me for someone else. I have no interest in *snaring* any man.'

'Not even to find a gullible, alternative father for—?'

'Not even for that!'

How could he *think* it? Had he *no* notion how momentous their short relationship had been for her? Did he really think she'd scheme to marry another man?

That she'd give herself so easily to another?

Annalisa's anger grew white-hot, and with it a hurt that stabbed her to the core. Tears burned her eyes and she turned to stare, blinking, across the room as if absorbed in the colourful scene. The depth of her pain appalled her.

'I wasn't flirting.' She drew a shuddering breath. 'I was just…talking. He was interesting, okay? And I've missed…'

'What have you missed, Annalisa?' His voice had lost its accusatory edge. It sounded almost regretful.

She shook her head. Tahir wouldn't understand. The man she'd shared so much with in the desert was no more. She couldn't bring him back, no matter how she wished it.

'Annalisa.' He moved close, stepping into her line of sight. 'I'm—'

'There you are, my dears.' At the sound of Rihana's voice Annalisa blinked furiously and pasted on a shaky smile. She turned to find her hostess bearing down upon them. The dowager Queen smiled, but the smile didn't reach her eyes.

Annalisa's heart sank. Did Rihana think she'd caused the disturbance?

'You mustn't monopolise our guest,' she scolded.

To Annalisa's surprise the older woman slipped her hand through Annalisa's arm and turned to face Tahir. A look passed between mother and son that she couldn't decipher, but she felt tension hum in the air.

'Especially,' Rihana continued, 'when you're the centre of attention. Whatever you have to say can be said in private. Our family has already provided enough gossip.' Her smile belied the steel in her tone.

Astonished, Annalisa realised the Queen was warning her son off. She was protecting Annalisa from Tahir.

Annalisa felt a surge of gratitude. How would she react when she realised the true situation between Annalisa and Tahir? Annalisa dreaded to think.

'As always, Mother, you're right.' Tahir sketched an elegant bow, then turned to Annalisa. 'As you said, this is neither the time nor the place.' He paused. 'We'll finish our conversation later.'

With a smile that would have fooled most people into believing he was in high good humour, Tahir left them.

Annalisa exhaled shakily, torn between relief and regret that they parted on such terms.

Rihana patted her hand. 'I hope you can forgive Tahir. He hasn't yet learned patience. He's been getting his own way for too long.' She turned, and Annalisa was struck by the sadness in her eyes. 'But it wasn't always that way. And the shame of it is he never got the one thing he wanted above all. The one thing that really counted. All the rest meant nothing.'

What was it? That one thing Tahir wanted most? Annalisa needed to know—to understand the man who stirred such strong, conflicting emotions in her.

For a moment she thought she saw a glimmer of tears in the other woman's eyes. But it must have been an illusion, for now Rihana was perfectly poised. She patted Annalisa's hand again.

'If you give him time I know you'll find him…' she paused '…worth the effort.'

When Annalisa went to her room later a tall shadow detached itself from an alcove near her door.

Though she'd expected him, her pulse jittered nervously as she followed Tahir. His silence in the empty passageways and the set of his broad shoulders increased her awareness of him as a man, powerful and potentially dangerous.

They emerged into the garden where he'd announced they'd marry. Had he chosen it deliberately? She twisted her hands together, her nerves close to shredding. Moonlight on the bay gave the scene a romantic feel. Or would have if she didn't recall Tahir's words stripping her to the bone.

She ignored his invitation to sit.

Silvery light threw one side of his face into shadow, emphasising the strong lines and aristocratic planes of his face. And the grim set of his mouth.

Annalisa stood straight, ready to counter more accusations.

'Your mother thought I'd enjoy meeting your guests tonight, and I did.' She refused to apologise. It wasn't she who'd created a scene.

'As for the gown...' She plucked nervously at the exquisite outfit she'd adored from the moment Rihana had produced it. 'Your mother kindly provided it because I didn't have anything suitable. Of course I won't keep it.' She refused to be accused of mercenary ways.

'My mother has taken a shine to you.' His voice revealed nothing.

Annalisa shrugged. 'She's lovely. And so lively, so interesting.' She watched one sleek black eyebrow climb. Did he doubt her sincerity?

'She's been very kind to me.' It emerged as a challenge.

'I can see that.' He surveyed her from head to toe and heat sizzled through her at his leisurely inspection. He had the lazy air of a pasha inspecting a new slave.

She stiffened, crossing her arms.

'There's no need to justify yourself,' he murmured. 'Of course you'll keep the dress.' He raised a silencing hand when she opened her mouth to protest. 'And you were welcome at the reception.'

His mouth quirked in a shadow of the lopsided smile she knew so well and her stomach gave a disturbing little jiggle. 'I've had two diplomats, the Chair of the Literacy Commission and countless others remarking how they enjoyed your company.'

'Really?'

Then what was his problem? She hadn't pushed herself forward, trying to embarrass him. Why had he been angry?

'Really.' Tahir lifted a hand, then paused, before spearing

his dark locks in a gesture of frustration. Abruptly he turned and paced away, then back again.

'I'm sorry for my behaviour tonight,' he said finally, his voice a low rumble. 'It was inexcusable, especially in public. I saw you with him and I...' Tahir made a slashing, violent gesture.

Clearly he wasn't used to apologising. But Annalisa sensed there was more. She stared. If it weren't so preposterous she'd think Tahir was *jealous*.

Impossible! To be jealous Tahir would need to care. He didn't.

'You don't accept my apology?'

Surprised, she noticed his indignant expression. Clearly humbling himself was a new experience.

'No, I— That is, yes. Of course.'

'Good.' He met her eyes with a seriousness that reminded her of the man she'd known at the oasis.

The man she'd fallen for.

Annalisa drew a sustaining breath and told herself to stop fantasising. But she couldn't prevent the spark of warmth that look had engendered. She'd felt it when he'd protected her from Saleem too.

'You've had days to think, Annalisa. Days since I said I'd marry you. I've been more than patient.'

Her pulse thrummed a heavy beat, quickening as she met his gaze. He reached out and clasped her hand, raising it between them. He held her lightly, yet instantly longing swamped her. Indignation and hurt were forgotten.

'It's not what either of us wants. But we're trapped by circumstance.' His voice deepened. 'You know in that logical head of yours this is the only way.'

Before she could respond he lifted his other hand and brushed a strand of hair behind her ear. Her breathing faltered and her cheek tingled where his knuckles brushed.

Yearning rose, swift and undeniable. She shouldn't respond. Yet her eyelids flickered, weighted under the impact of the glint in his eye.

There were times, like now, when she longed to trust Tahir.

Forget her doubts and fears and accept his strength. Times
when her dreams sank beneath the weight of what she felt for
him. Because she was off-balance in this harsh new reality?
Because she felt so alone and bereft of friends?

Tahir's fingertips brushed her cheek again, swept to her
chin and then her throat. Annalisa swallowed hard, remembering the sweet ecstasy he'd wrought with his touch once before.

She wanted Tahir so badly.

Feather-light, his fingers trailed to her neckline. Annalisa's
heart pounded a needy rhythm even as she tried to tug herself
free of his sensual spell.

'If we marry it will be all right.' His deep voice soothed, almost
as hypnotic as his touch. 'Our child will have the protection of
my family name.' His thumb traced the line of her collarbone and
she trembled. 'You want to protect our child, don't you?'

Annalisa nodded, her throat too dry for speech. The banked
heat in his eyes mesmerised her. As did his hand, curling around
her neck, fingers sliding into her hair and tugging it down. Her
skin prickled deliciously at the sensuous caress against her
scalp. She tipped back her head, unconsciously baring her
throat. His fingers tightened in her hair and she caught the
sultry spice scent of his skin.

That magical feeling was back. Wondrous sensations only
Tahir could ignite. Tiny shudders of excitement and pleasure
shook her.

'Marriage will protect you both, Annalisa. You'll be safe and
cared for.'

She barely heard him over the clamour of her heartbeat.
What she felt was so strong surely it was *right*.

'You'll be wealthy and respected, mother of a future monarch.
There will be no public backlash or snide remarks about our child.
It will be secure and accepted. And you needn't worry I'll interfere or take over your life, apart from the necessary royal obliga-
tions. You have everything to gain from our convenient marriage.'

It took an inordinate amount of time for his words to sink
in. Annalisa looked up into that proud, stern face and wished
she hadn't heard.

She had been melting at his touch, seduced by his tenderness and her need into believing a future with Tahir mightn't be the disaster she'd feared. That perhaps they had something to build on. Something that might flower one day into the sort of love her parents had shared.

Only to discover he wasn't talking about a proper marriage. Her insides caved in as understanding hit. What a fool she'd been, deluding herself.

Convenience was the key word for him, not marriage.

Would they even live together? He'd have lovers; she had no doubt of that. How would she cope? Surely he wouldn't install them in the palace!

Something twisted inside and she hunched reflexively, fearing she'd give in to nausea. She felt hollow, a fragile shell.

Even after Saleem had flayed her with his brutal prejudice, she'd been naïve enough to believe that between she and Tahir there was hope for something precious. Something more than simply escaping sordid scandal.

'Annalisa!' Tahir's voice was sharp with concern.

She ignored him and stumbled to the garden seat, subsiding as the strength ebbed from her shaky legs.

'I'll get a doctor.'

'No!' She tried to gather her wits. 'I'm okay.'

His look told her he didn't believe her. He was poised for instant action.

Wearily she stared up at the man who offered support for her and their child for the sake of respectability. For safety. Possibly even because he feared a public backlash that might affect the monarchy.

But not because he felt anything for her personally.

Annalisa's heart clenched.

Did she have any choice?

Stupid to wish for a real marriage, a loving union, when the only man she cared for wasn't capable of love.

She ignored the pain piercing her. He offered security for her child.

His gaze held hers steadily. His look questioned.

'Very well,' she murmured, finally accepting the inevitable. This was the only option. Anything else was wishful thinking. Yet still she hesitated, drawing a sustaining breath.

'I'll marry you.' She almost choked on the words.

CHAPTER ELEVEN

'EXCELLENT.'

In an instant he was beside her on the seat. The scent of his skin mingled with fresh salt air and unthinkingly she breathed deep. Behind him stars winked in a black velvet sky. *It should have been a night for lovers.*

'I knew you'd make the sensible decision.'

Sensible. The word was a lead weight. How sensible to marry for public opinion, for show and security? It made a sham of the vows they'd make and all she believed in.

Her melancholy thoughts shattered as Tahir took her hand and bent his head. His lips caressed the back of her hand in a courtly gesture that dragged her straight into another reality. One where the needs of her body and the sentimental hopes he'd just obliterated rose tremulously once more.

No! She'd be a fool to fall for his practised charm.

Yet the sight of his dark head bent over her hand, the pressure of his mouth, ignited feelings she couldn't douse.

She almost sobbed her despair that even now, with her pride and heart in tatters, she responded.

She tugged her hand but his hold tightened.

Her breath hissed as he turned her hand and pressed an open-mouthed kiss to the centre of her palm. To the sensitive spot she hadn't known existed till he'd introduced her to physical pleasure.

Under dark lashes his eyes glittered, bright and knowing.

Her heartbeat accelerated and her fingers itched to stroke his soft hair as she had once before.

Tahir's tongue swirled against her skin and every nerve cell juddered. Bone-melting bliss stole through her.

She opened her mouth to object, but all that emerged was a sigh as floodgates opened on feelings, *needs* she'd struggled so long to suppress.

Where was her resolve? Her strength?

As if attuned to her weakness, Tahir kissed her fingers, the tender skin at her wrist, sending her pulse racing wildly out of control.

This man was dangerous.

She tugged again, surprised when he released her hand. Bright eyes met hers from mere inches away. Fear—or was it excitement?—tugged at her belly as she saw what was in his eyes.

'No, Tahir! I don't—'

The rest was muffled as his mouth claimed hers. Not hard, not recklessly, but with complete assurance. Their lips met, clung, meshed as if it was the most natural thing in the world.

Her hands wedged against his chest. She told herself to push, *hard*. Yet traitorously they clung, fingers spreading greedily across the deep curve of his muscles.

A sob rose in Annalisa's throat. Frustration at his arrogance and her instant capitulation? Or relief at the absolute rightness of it? She'd craved this so long.

Her head spun crazily as he pressed close, his kiss deepening possessively. She tried to fight, to summon strength and detachment, but his passionate mouth, his deft fingers in her hair, were exquisite pleasure.

Once this ended she'd be bereft anyway. Did it matter that for a few glorious moments she succumbed? After this she'd be strong.

She leaned into him, revelling in his fervour, in the seductive power of the one man in the world who awoke her dormant longings.

She heard a growl of approval as her hands crept to his neck. He scooped her up, settling her on his lap. His intimate heat cradled her and excitement spiralled. Her heart galloped at the feel of him surrounding her even as dimly she realised she should stop him.

Tahir didn't even break their kiss. He tucked her close, leaning her back over his arm and claiming her mouth so thoroughly her disjointed thoughts shattered.

Annalisa's fingers tunnelled through his hair as she revelled in a kiss turned hungry and urgent.

Her body throbbed in every secret place.

When his hand slid to the neckline of her dress she arched instinctively. But the tightly sewn bodice defied him and she almost cried out in frustration.

Restlessly Tahir traced the edge of the fabric, testing, then curling his fingers around it. A shocking jolt of excitement shot through her at the idea of him ripping the material, shredding the costly silk and gold so he could caress her bare skin.

She pressed higher, silently urging him.

He cupped her breast, then arrowed in on her peaking nipple. Annalisa groaned as fire flashed. That strange ache was back again between her legs and her body shook.

It was only as she dragged in a deep breath that she realised Tahir had pulled back, ending the kiss to look at her with glittering eyes.

In this light his face seemed pared down to slashing lines. Their gasping breaths drowned the roar of the surf. She shifted and abruptly stilled as she came into contact with proof of his arousal.

His lips tilted in a knowing smile that radiated masculine satisfaction. He lowered his head to her breast.

'No! Don't!' The expression on his face had cut through the glorious haze enveloping her. Harsh reality filtered in. Clumsily Annalisa pushed at his shoulders.

His mouth hovered a breathtaking centimetre from her breast. She shoved harder and he looked up from under raised eyebrows.

'No?' His voice curled around her like rich, dark chocolate. Pure temptation.

What was happening to her? Where was her pride? Her

self-control? He'd decided to kiss her and she'd let him. Shame singed her face.

He doesn't want you. For a couple of hours maybe. When it's 'convenient'.

Was this a test to see how compliant she was?

She gasped down a horrified breath. How easy it would be for him to seduce her into making this relationship more than a paper marriage. If she let him he'd tempt her into surrendering to him physically.

Presumably on the few nights when he preferred less sophisticated amusement in his bed.

Instantly strength returned to her pleasure-drugged body and she shoved harder. This time he straightened.

His eyes narrowed. In the gloom Annalisa caught a glimpse of danger in that stare. For a heartbeat she felt fear, the awareness of the hunted. Then it was gone. Tahir sat back, his hands dropping to the seat. Only the grimness around the lips hinted that she'd displeased him.

Annalisa scrabbled to her feet, reaching for a nearby trellis to keep her upright on weak knees.

'You don't want to kiss me?'

'No!'

His look told her eloquently that she lied.

Stubbornly she stared back. 'That was a mistake.' She wished her voice was steady, without that husky edge. 'I...' She put a hand to her pounding heart and searched for a suitable lie. 'I don't want you to touch me.'

His eyes held hers, as if weighing her mood, her distress. Had he any idea how close she'd come to total capitulation?

'As you wish.'

His words were so unexpected it took her a moment to process them. Could it really be so easy?

She didn't wish! That was the problem. She longed for his touch, his tenderness. For a hint that he felt something for her, even if only a pale reflection of what she still felt for him. Annalisa blinked and looked away to the rolling surf. She *would* master her feelings.

All he felt was lust. And obligation.

'I'll make the wedding arrangements,' he said, with a change of subject that left her floundering. 'You won't have to worry about anything other than resting.'

Could she marry him after what had just happened? Surely this proved he was even more dangerous than she'd thought.

'I'm not sure—'

'Be sure, Annalisa. We *are* marrying.' His tone brooked no argument. 'For the sake of the child.'

For their child. Her shoulders sagged. She had to remember they would be married for her baby, even though her body still thrummed with frustrated desire.

The fact that Tahir had taken her withdrawal so easily just proved he'd been amusing himself. He wasn't really interested. She wasn't his type. Their marriage would be a legality only.

'In the circumstances it will be a small wedding. You won't want the pomp and bother of traditional festivities.'

Annalisa's lips curved in a mirthless smile. If she married the man of her dreams she'd adore a big wedding. But the man of her dreams was a mirage who'd been the centre of her world for a few short days. Now he was no more. The real Tahir had no interest in her except for a light amusement.

'Annalisa? I asked if there's anyone you want to invite.'

She turned to meet his searching look and silently shook her head.

'No one? I know your parents are dead, but isn't there someone to support you?'

'Apart from my uncle?' Annalisa swallowed a clot of bitter regret. 'I'd rather do this alone.' At his steady look she felt compelled to explain. 'I was close to my grandfather but he died recently too. The rest of my family are on the far side of the country. They aren't like Saleem, but...'

But she didn't know how they'd react to her news. Better to break it to them after the wedding.

'My father and I were a team. We were always busy in the community and knew everyone, but there were no really close friends.' Except scientists and scholars scattered around the globe.

At his quizzical look she shrugged. 'There are people I could invite, but no one close. I live in a rural area bound by tradition. It was fine for me to help my father heal people, or represent them by lobbying for services, but I was different. I dress and speak differently. I was allowed freedoms my peers weren't.' She breathed deep. 'For all I was born and bred there, I never fitted in.'

A pang of familiar longing pierced her. The yearning to be wanted and appreciated for herself. Her father and her grandfather had, but they were gone.

'You're alone.' Tahir's voice held a curious note. Not gushing sympathy, but an understanding she hadn't expected.

'Hardly alone. I told you I've got cousins galore, all wanting to organise a wedding for me with some local man.' Her words petered out. That was in the past. What would her relationship with them be now?

'And you are marrying a local man.'

'What about you?' She needed to divert her thoughts. 'Will all your family and friends be here for the wedding?' The idea of facing resplendent royal relatives and VIPs petrified her. She was enough of an outsider already.

'Hardly.' The single word held a bitterness so deep she stilled.

'But you're the King,' she prompted, glad to talk about him instead of herself.

'I'm the prodigal, the outsider,' he countered, with a twist of his lips that held no humour. 'I haven't been in Qusay for eleven years. Since my father banished me for scandalous behaviour.'

Banished? She hadn't read that in the press reports.

His father. The father he'd dreamed about. The one Tahir had imagined, in his delirium, beating him.

Surely that had just been a disturbing fantasy? Yet his sombre expression distressed her.

'You didn't know?' he murmured, watching her face so closely she was sure he read her every thought.

'No.' She couldn't imagine being cut off from the people she loved. 'But you must have kept in contact with your family, even if your father…'

At the look on his face her words disintegrated. Hauteur froze his features in an expression of disdain that she hated.

'There was no contact. My brothers didn't know where I was, and I was too busy feeding and clothing myself for a long time to make many long-distance calls. Once I got on my feet there seemed little point. The split was a fact.'

Annalisa's head spun. He'd been exiled and completely alone since…when? Eleven years ago he'd have been only eighteen.

'But you have money.' She gestured helplessly. This didn't make sense. 'The media loves reporting your wealth.'

'Not as much as it loves reporting my misdeeds.' He leaned back and thrust his hand through his dark locks. Suddenly he looked unutterably weary.

'I left with nothing.' He rolled his shoulders as if to relieve an old stiffness. 'I built wealth through luck at the gaming tables, a talent for finance and sheer hard work. I'm sure no one was more surprised or disappointed than my father when I prospered instead of conveniently disappearing or dying.'

It was on the tip of Annalisa's tongue to protest. But what sort of father exiled his son? Or inspired tortured dreams even after eleven years?

She clenched her hands, wanting to reach out and soothe the pain in Tahir's eyes, so at odds with his severe countenance. But she wasn't naïve enough to give in to the impulse. She didn't have the right. He wouldn't thank her for guessing at his hurt.

Annalisa bit her tongue, wondering what else his demeanour of aloof control hid. He was a man of contradictions: demanding, arrogant, abrasive once his memory had returned. His record with women was appalling.

Yet she remembered earlier kindnesses. He'd understood her grief even when she'd fought to stifle it. She remembered his ready sympathy, the dry humour he'd used to lighten her mood when sadness overcame her.

He'd stumbled out of the desert, more concerned for the safety of an animal than himself. He'd treated it with easy kindness, and herself with gentle consideration.

Which was the real Tahir?

Seeing him now, ramrod-straight and wearing an implacable expression of detachment, she was convinced there was more to Tahir than the face he showed the world.

Was it possible the man she'd begun to love in the desert lurked somewhere inside?

Or was that wishful thinking?

'But your mother will be at the wedding,' she murmured, searching desperately for solid ground.

He tensed, his expression stonier than ever. 'I'll invite her. It's up to her whether she chooses to attend.' He paused, then spoke again in a neutral tone. 'My brothers are busy with their own business and their new wives. Rafiq's in Australia and Kareef in Qais. It will be a small wedding. I'll give you details in due course.'

Tahir stood, his tone making it clear their discussion was over. He gestured for her to precede him into the palace.

Her audience with the King was at an end.

'So you enjoyed talking to the guests last night,' Tahir murmured as he accepted tea from his mother.

Rihana's rooms weren't where he'd choose to meet Annalisa, but he didn't trust himself with her in private. Last night she'd looked at him with huge doe eyes and guilt had scored him to the bone.

He couldn't keep his hands off her. He'd kissed her and his good intentions had instantly collapsed. He'd have taken her then and there, on the stone seat! Only the distress in her eyes had stopped him.

He'd have to live with frustration. *Until they were wed.* By then she'd be ready to accept the passion that flared between them and give him what he wanted. What they both wanted.

'Yes.' She watched him warily. She was pale, and dark shadows bruised her eyes. 'The reception was fascinating.'

'What in particular?' Maybe guilt prompted him, but he was curious. Annalisa was such an antidote to the world of cynicism and mistrust he'd known so long.

She shrugged, the movement so jerky he caught his mother's concerned look.

Again guilt speared him. He'd stolen Annalisa's bright future with one greedy lapse of judgement. Trapped himself too, in the yoke of marriage.

A chill filled him at the idea of marrying. He had a deep-seated horror of anything that smacked of commitment. Yet it had to be done. In a couple of weeks, when Annalisa had had time to acclimatise. She looked so fragile.

He'd do his best to support her. After all, in her own way she was as much an outsider as he.

'So many people were interesting,' Annalisa murmured, her husky voice an echo of his erotic fantasies. 'Archaeologists and diplomats. Experts in health and farming.' She stopped, eyes rounding as she caught his gaze, obviously remembering his anger when she'd spoken to that agricultural advisor.

'You find all that interesting?'

'Of course.' He caught a glimpse of the passionate woman who'd entranced him in the desert. 'Don't you?'

'I...' Tahir stopped as something struck him.

He'd been busy learning to be monarch, at the same time working to divest himself of the responsibility but finding no alternative ruler. In all that time he hadn't once been bored. He'd been challenged, frustrated, even occasionally pleased when he'd made important progress.

But never bored.

'Tahir?' Two pairs of eyes stared at him.

Tahir dragged himself back into the conversation, but for the next twenty minutes only half listened.

As he watched Annalisa, so on edge with him, he realised he needed to bridge the chasm he'd created between them. She was wound so tight it couldn't be healthy for the baby or her.

But bridging that gap might leave him vulnerable.

Annalisa made him doubt himself and his certainties.

She made him...feel.

She stirred emotions he wasn't accustomed to. Like last night's jealousy. It had blasted like the desert wind, scouring away his reason. He'd become a covetous brute, lashing out when he should have looked after her.

The reception must have been overwhelming for her. He hadn't missed her wide-eyed look at walls panelled with gold and gems.

He had to protect her and ease her way.

Tahir Al'Ramiz, a champion of duty.

Would wonders never cease?

'What do you think, Tahir?' His mother interrupted his thoughts. 'Will decentralised healthcare get off the ground? Or is it rhetoric?'

He watched Annalisa blush, guessing they'd been expounding upon the problems with the current system. Just the sort of thing she *would* be interested in, he realised with something like pride.

'Since you're interested, come to the next meeting of the working party.'

Silence greeted his suggestion.

'It's not usual,' his mother explained. 'It's normally just officials.'

Didn't he know it? He felt hemmed-in by bureaucracy. It wasn't his style. Ruling a country wasn't his style! But if he was stuck with it, he'd do it his way.

Tahir leaned forward to select a date from the platter before him. He favoured Annalisa with a long look and saw her eyes grow round again. It reminded him of her wide-eyed wonder as their bodies joined. He struggled to find the thread of the conversation.

How did she do that without even trying?

'I'll have one of the secretaries let you both know when the next meeting is.'

'Oh, but I don't think…' Annalisa's words trailed off as he watched her.

'But you *do* think, Annalisa, and that's why I want you there.' Even as he said it he realised how true that was. The meetings had been a tangle of officialdom and little practical input. Besides, it would give Annalisa a chance to think about something other than her pregnancy. He guessed after living a life busy with responsibilities being cooped up here with nothing to do gave her too much time to worry.

'You have experience in healthcare in the provinces. It would be useful to hear your perspective.' He turned to his mother. 'Did you know Annalisa helped provide medical care in outlying villages?'

'I did.' His mother's look might almost have been called approving. He paused in the act of chewing. 'Annalisa would give valuable input. What a good idea.'

Tahir swallowed the date and sat back, his head spinning. His royal mother sounded almost warm in her praise. What was the world coming to?

For as long as he could recall she'd been coolly polite. During his exile she'd refused to answer his calls.

'But I couldn't,' Annalisa murmured. 'I'm not—'

'I'd appreciate your involvement. And my mother will be there.' Tahir leaned forward and fixed Annalisa with a look he knew could melt feminine resolve in under thirty seconds. He watched her blink rapidly as a soft blush warmed her cheeks and throat.

Triumph filled him. She wasn't indifferent, for all her unwillingness to wed.

If he had to marry, he intended to enjoy the benefits. Soon, very soon, she'd give him everything he desired.

CHAPTER TWELVE

Tahir leaned back in his chair and silently congratulated himself.

With Annalisa's input the working party had achieved more these last couple of weeks than he'd have thought possible. She'd done what his officials hadn't: sought advice from contacts in outlying regions. The plans for coordinated medical care promised to be a success.

His wife-to-be was talented and able. She related to people at all levels, yet was curiously lacking in ego. She was clever, caring, intelligent.

And she aroused him as no other woman.

Even the knowledge that she carried his child couldn't quench his desire. He'd found himself hungrily tracing her figure for some sign of the baby. Instead of shying from the idea, he found her pregnancy evoked urgent, possessive feelings that made his self-imposed distance almost impossible.

The fact that he barely slept, haunted by erotic dreams, was testament to his newfound strength. Once upon a time he'd have seduced her as soon as temptation rose.

Yet he'd found a strange contentment in restraint, knowing he did the right thing, allowing her time to adjust. The way she glowed and her renewed confidence proved he'd done right.

He nodded goodbye to his staff. The room emptied but for Annalisa, still poring over plans.

Silently he paced across to stand beside her.

The familiar wild honey scent of her skin filled his nostrils and sent a tremor through already taut muscles. He inhaled deeply. No scent was more evocative. His hands grew damp as he suppressed the impulse to pull her close.

He watched her graceful movements as she turned the pages. The way she pursed her lips in an unconscious pout. He wanted to bite that succulent bottom lip till she groaned with delight, then plunder her sweet depths. He wanted to see the glitter of incendiary fire in her warm brown eyes as she gasped in pleasure and fulfilment.

He wanted to be with her, possess her, have her smile at him and let him bask in her warmth.

Annalisa sensed Tahir before she saw him. Her hand trembled as she put the papers on the conference table.

Hard fingers clasped her elbow and she froze. Looking up, she sank into the blue depths of Tahir's gaze. Strange that a man with his reputation should have eyes that looked like a glimpse of heaven.

'Come,' he said, drawing her to a group of comfortable chairs. 'Sit with me.'

Automatically she looked back, but the doors were shut. She and Tahir were alone. Heat shimmied through her veins and her palms grew clammy as she remembered what had happened the last time they were alone. Did she trust him? Or herself?

'No one will interrupt,' he assured her. But, seeing the intensity of his gaze, Annalisa didn't feel reassured.

She felt…excited.

Desperately she tried to dredge up horror at her reaction. Yet all she could manage was an edgy sense of playing with fire.

Since the night he'd kissed her she'd been on tenterhooks, fearing he'd tempt her into intimacy. Her nerves were raw, waiting for him to act, and when he didn't she stifled disappointment.

Secretly she'd longed for the marauder who'd entered her bedroom without a by your leave and offered to seduce her. The man who'd only had to kiss her hand to reduce her to trembling need.

He was a puzzle, not easily understood. Yet recently she'd found so much to admire.

Tahir was a born leader who didn't need to bully people into agreement. He had a quicksilver energy that only added to his charisma. And beneath his occasional air of cynicism, despite his reprobate reputation, she suspected Tahir was a decent man.

A man she feared she cared too much for.

Yet he'd left her room that first night in the palace without a qualm. He hadn't touched her after that last searing kiss when she'd agreed to marriage. Clearly whatever allure she'd once held for him was now dead. How could *she*, without an ounce of sophistication, hold his interest?

It scared her that she wanted to.

Annalisa sat on the low divan. To her consternation he sat beside her. Close enough for her to watch his long lashes veil his gaze.

Did he notice her breathing turn shallow? Panic surged at being so close to the man she dreamed of every night, the man she couldn't stop thinking about.

'I've organised a date for our wedding.'

Our wedding.

She swallowed hard and her pulse tripped as she caught the flash of something unsettling in his eyes. Emotions tumbled through her. Relief that he hadn't reneged. Excitement she tried to stifle. Anxiety at whether marriage was the right thing.

'When will it be?' Her voice emerged husky and she reminded herself this was a paper marriage only.

But the way Tahir leaned close, hands engulfing hers, sent other, contrary signals. Fire shot through her veins, warming her all over.

'A week tomorrow.' He paused long enough for her pulse to thud slow and heavy, once, twice. 'Then we'll be man and wife.'

Heat shimmered between them. The sort of heat that ignited each time she allowed herself close to Tahir.

Dangerous heat.

Annalisa sat straighter, trying to look away from his intense gaze. She wanted to jerk out of his hold but feared she'd give away the effect he had on her.

His thumb swept an arc across her hand, sending tremors shooting up her arm. His nostrils flared and a pulse throbbed at his temple, matching the urgent beat in her blood. Deep inside desire woke.

Tahir leaned in and her eyelids flickered. She shouldn't want him to kiss her but she did. So badly.

She struggled for a distraction.

'You've told your mother about the marriage?' Annalisa forced the words out, making one last effort to resist him. 'It's been obvious she doesn't know your plans.'

Obvious Tahir wasn't eager to spread the word he was marrying. Because he didn't really want her. He was stuck with her.

He straightened, looking suddenly more distant.

'Given your hesitation, I thought you'd prefer keeping the engagement private at first.'

Was he serious? 'But she's your mother! She must have wondered what was going on.' Though the relationship between the women had grown close, Annalisa was uncomfortable with her status as a long-standing guest.

'I wished you to stay. That's all she needed to know.'

Annalisa stared. What sort of relationship did he have with Rihana? Nothing like what she'd shared with her father.

'Why don't you like her?' she whispered, then froze, horrified she'd spoken aloud.

His hands clamped round hers and every skerrick of warmth bled from his face.

'I'm sorry. It's none of my business—'

'You've got it wrong.' He paused so long she thought he wouldn't say more. He looked down at her hands clasped in his. His thumb swiped idly across her skin. 'It's my mother who doesn't approve of me.'

His face was a stony mask. Utterly still. Bereft of emotion. Yet she *felt* it, flowing from him, swirling between them.

Pain. Deep, soul-destroying pain.

Annalisa could barely breathe as the weight of his suffering bore down upon her.

Then his face changed. She watched the familiar twist of his lips, the raised eyebrow, the cool eyes. Yet despite his derisive expression she'd swear he looked haunted.

'I'm hardly a model son. I was a disappointment to my parents from an early age.'

Annalisa's heart wrenched at his arrogant attitude, certain it hid suffering.

Fleetingly she remembered he'd worn that same expression on his last morning at the oasis. Had his supercilious behaviour then been a smokescreen too?

She tugged her hands loose from his grip and dared to wrap them in turn around his powerful fists. They were rigid.

'I don't believe that.'

His glare could have frozen water in the desert sun, but she refused to look away. Annalisa didn't understand the need to champion him. She acted on instinct. On emotion so powerful it wouldn't be denied.

'You're hardly in a position to know, my dear.'

The casual endearment was laced with cool dismissal. In response she raised her chin and met him stare for stare.

'I know your mother loves you.'

He jerked beneath her hold. His big shoulders rose and dropped, as if a massive earthquake had thundered through him. An instant later he was still, his look quizzical.

'I appreciate your good intentions. But not all parents are like yours, Annalisa.'

An expression flashed in his eyes. Something so stark it stole her breath and made her more determined to persevere.

'It's there in the way she talks about you.' Annalisa refused to be cowed. 'She talks about you all the time now, did you know that?' At Tahir's amazed look she kept going. 'She talks about all three of you. She's so proud of her sons. Of what strong, honourable men they are.'

Tahir snorted in disbelief and Annalisa grasped his hands tighter, *willing* him to listen.

'It's true. She says you're all different but you have traits in common. Strength, determination, passion, pride. Honour.'

'You're confusing me with someone else.'

She shook her head. 'She said you'd taken on the kingship though you desperately didn't want it. Because you felt obligated.'

Tahir's eyes widened. She pressed on. 'She says that even while you were out of the country you anonymously funded initiatives in Qusay for abused and disadvantaged children.'

'She knew about that?' Another tremor shook his big frame. Annalisa's heart ached. She wanted to reach out and palm his cheek, stroke his hair, soothe him. He looked stunned. Shocked to the core.

Abruptly he dragged his hands from hers, leaving her bereft.

'It's easy to give money when you have a fortune.' A slashing gesture emphasised the words. 'It wasn't important.'

It was on the tip of Annalisa's tongue to say it was important to those who'd benefited from his generosity, but she bit it back.

'So you haven't noticed the way she looks at you? The way she follows your progress around a room?'

It had puzzled her at first, the coolness between mother and son, contrasted with the Queen's avid interest when Tahir wasn't aware of it. Till Annalisa had realised there was an unhealed breach between them.

Tahir's brows furrowed. He opened his mouth, then shut it again.

Finally he shook his head. 'Maybe once she cared. But that stopped long ago.' His voice was clipped, testament to his discomfort. He surged to his feet, looming over her. 'Until I returned to Qusay my mother hadn't spoken to me for years. Not during my exile. Not before.'

His eyes glittered with an ice-cold clarity that chilled Annalisa to the bone. 'She refused even to speak to me the day my father banished me.'

His voice throbbed with a passion that tore at Annalisa's heart.

'So you'll understand why I find it hard to believe you.' He turned abruptly and strode to the door.

Trembling, Annalisa stumbled to her feet. 'I'm not a liar, Tahir. You know that.' She forced the words out over a throat choking at the sight of his torment.

She didn't have explanations, but she was certain Rihana loved her son. If anything, after listening to her discuss her children, she thought Tahir might even be her favourite.

'Maybe you should ask her why she wouldn't talk to you.'

Tahir checked for a moment on the threshold. 'The subject is closed,' he growled. 'I'll hear no more.' He exited, leaving the door hanging open behind him.

He prowled the corridors and courtyards, the antechambers and audience halls. Yet Tahir couldn't shake the words haunting him.

Your mother loves you.

His strides ate up another wing of the palace.

He'd given up believing such platitudes years ago. It no longer mattered. He was a grown man. Had survived on his own—totally, completely on his own—for years.

He didn't need love.

He barely believed in it any more. He'd never had it from his father. And from his mother? He shuddered to a stop. He recalled her warm hugs and tender smiles when he was small. Only when they were alone together. As the years had passed she'd become distant.

Who could blame her? He'd striven to make his father proud. But when it had become clear nothing he did would earn the old man's approval, that in fact his father hated him, Tahir had plunged into excess with an abandon that rivalled even his sire's. Better that than driving himself crazy trying to fathom why the old man detested him.

Had he seen too much of his own weaknesses in his son?

Tahir scrubbed a hand over his face.

He wasn't the sort who inspired or sought love. That was a fool's game. Sentimental folly.

Annalisa imagined things. She was sweet and innocent enough to believe families were about caring.

What stunned him was the way, just for a moment, he'd *wanted* to believe her. He'd craved it with every fibre of his body and what passed for his soul.

He! Tahir Al'Ramiz! The dissolute son of a dissolute father. A man who cared for no one.

Except, he realised, a feisty girl with tender eyes and an indomitable spirit.

He put out a hand to steady himself as the realisation rocked him back on his feet.

He cared…

How long he stood there, unfamiliar sensations swirling through him, he didn't know. *He cared!*

Finally, shaking his head as if clearing it of a waking dream, he looked around and realised he'd stopped outside the dowager Queen's apartments.

Chance? Or a subconscious decision?

Something in his chest gave a queer little jump and his pulse settled into a jagged, staccato beat. He turned to leave, then stopped.

Annalisa's words rang in his ears.

She'd confronted him with a story too unbelievable to countenance. *Surely* it was unbelievable.

Yet eventually he lifted his fist and rapped on the massive door. A voice answered and he forced himself to push the door wide.

His mother looked up from a book. Her eyes met his and just for an instant he saw them sparkle with pleasure. Then, swift as a door slamming, her expression cleared into the familiar one of calm detachment.

Tahir swallowed hard. He stepped inside, his mind whirring.

'Annalisa's not here, I'm afraid.' Her voice was crystal-cool, like the fountains tinkling in the exquisite courtyard outside her chambers. 'If you come later, I'm expecting her for tea.'

'I know.' His voice held an unfamiliar rough edge. He cleared his throat. 'It's you I came to see.'

* * *

Hours passed and Tahir was still in Rihana's rooms.

He felt odd—something like the sensation he'd experienced the first few times his father had used him as a punching bag. As if someone had rearranged his internal organs.

His mother smiled up at him from one of her photo albums and he felt the warmth and wonder of it embrace him.

The albums were filled with photos he hadn't known about. Him on horseback. Him striding down the beach. Him stepping from a four-wheel drive after speeding over the dunes, a rare smile on his teenage features.

Annalisa was right. His mother had cared all along. He'd been too caught up in his bitter struggle against his father to understand how the old man's hatred had affected Rihana and why she'd had to hide her feelings.

He returned her smile, enjoying what he saw in her face and the way it made him feel.

He tried to analyse the sensations and couldn't. He felt too…full, as if all those emotions he'd learned to repress in childhood now pushed too close to the surface. As if it would just take one more tiny scrape of his skin to set them free.

'Mother, I—'

A crash of sound, a deafening boom, rent the air.

Tahir was on his feet before its echo died away. In slow motion he processed the sight of the walls and ceiling dipping and swaying. The decorative lanterns swung impossibly wide.

Memories of a day in Japan that he'd rather forget crowded his brain.

'Earthquake!' He hauled Rihana to her feet, taking in her dazed eyes. 'Quickly, this way.' He half carried her out into her private courtyard.

The initial eruption of sound died, but in the distance he caught an ominous rumbling. Another quake, or a building coming down? Automatically he held Rihana protectively close, well away from the decorative arches lining the courtyard. He scanned the roofline but could see no damage. Could hear no cries for help.

'Stay here,' he ordered. 'Either I or someone else will come for you.'

'Tahir!'

Her urgent tone and her grasp of his sleeve stopped him in mid-stride. He turned. What he saw in her face made him want to stay and comfort her. But he couldn't. Others mightn't be as lucky as they'd been.

'Be careful,' she murmured.

Those two simple words turned his heart over in his chest. He stepped close, gently embraced her and pressed a kiss to her cheek. 'I will. Now, don't forget. Wait here.'

It was the first time he'd kissed his mother in more than a decade.

The news was bad. No damage to the palace, but a section of the old town was devastated. Ancient structures and adobe walls had tumbled into narrow streets, making rescue difficult.

A check on the provinces brought news that only the capital was damaged. Nevertheless, Tahir set in motion national arrangements for evacuation should there be aftershocks.

Rescue and medical teams worked at full stretch. Tahir had contacted his cousin, Zafir, once King of Qusay and now ruler of nearby Haydar, and arranged for more rescue specialists to fly in. Tahir's brother, Kareef, had already sent men from the mountains of Qais to help.

As afternoon faded into night Tahir was still busy directing, reassuring, planning. He did it on autopilot. Beneath his calm façade lay a fear so potent it froze his bones and threatened to paralyse his brain.

Annalisa was missing.

Just thinking it sent dread spiralling through him.

Every centimetre of the palace and grounds had been searched. Surrounding streets had been investigated.

Had she gone home, angry after their last encounter?

Guilt lanced him. Even as he pored over city plans with engineers and officials he was alert for footsteps, lest one of his staff return with news of her. He hoped for and feared it.

It was his fault she'd gone. He'd barked at her, furious that she'd dared to pry into the most private part of his life. He'd punished her for trying to heal the rift between himself and his mother.

His stomach churned at the knowledge that he was to blame for her disappearance.

Silently he told himself over and over that she wouldn't have ventured into the old *souk*. But he didn't believe his own reassurances. He wanted to scour the streets himself, looking for her.

Already he'd been down amongst the wreckage too often for his staff's liking, hoping to find her. They'd protested he was in danger. Only the knowledge he was more useful coordinating the rescue efforts had kept him in the makeshift emergency centre on the edge of the damage zone.

The acrid scent of fear filled his nostrils with every breath. His heart drummed frantically.

Never had he felt so powerless. If anything happened to her…

He'd rather endure a lifetime of beatings than this. Waiting, trying to be strong for those needing his leadership, while terror gnawed at his vitals. If only he had some clue where she'd gone.

He'd thought himself safe in his isolated world, relying on no one, caring for nothing.

What he felt now obliterated that self-deception.

Finally he gave in to those urging him to rest for an hour before daybreak. But instead of returning to the palace he prowled the streets. People welcomed their King's presence. But it was the need to find Annalisa that kept him going.

He'd almost given up hope when he came upon a temporary triage centre on the furthest side of the disaster zone. Makeshift awnings protected the wounded and lights were set up to assist the medics.

Movement caught his eye: a spill of rich dark hair. Golden highlights glinted as the woman turned her head. Impatiently she reached round and secured the waist-length tresses in a familiar gesture.

Tahir felt a huge weight rise to block his throat and impair his breathing. He strode through the debris, past stretchers, piles of rubble and huddled figures. He heard nothing but the rush of blood in his ears.

As he approached she turned, her hand out to grasp a nearby pole for support. Her clothes were rumpled and dirty. A dark stain marred her shirt.

Terror jammed his throat as he realised it was blood.

She stumbled and he ran, just in time to scoop her off her feet before she fell.

Tahir's heart pumped out of control as his arms closed convulsively around her. She felt warm and wonderful and alive. Alive. Thank God.

He was whirling around, looking for a doctor, when her voice finally penetrated.

'Put me down. I have work to do.'

'Work?' He stared down into her exhausted face, terrified at the intensity of what he felt.

'I'm helping the wounded. You have to let me go.'

'You're injured.' He shouldered through the crowded space towards a couple of doctors bent over a patient.

'It's not my blood, Tahir. Tahir?'

But he was already talking to a white-haired medic who explained Annalisa had been here all night, helping.

Even then Tahir couldn't release her. He listened as if from a distance as the doctor reassured him that she was unharmed, heard praise for her efforts. But he couldn't trust himself to believe.

Blind instinct urged him to ignore the expert's words and Annalisa's urgings. He needed her close.

'You need rest,' he said as her voice grew strident. 'You're pregnant, remember?'

His words fell into a pool of silence. The emergency staff, patients, even his staff who'd followed him seemed to still.

Then the doctor was agreeing, saying she'd done enough and urging Annalisa to go. They were closing this centre anyway and moving to the hospital.

Tahir instructed his staff to help pack up. He'd be back

soon. His stride lengthened as he passed into the wider streets
of the new city.

'Tahir?' She didn't sound angry now. 'You can put me down.
I'm fit and healthy. Honestly.'

But he walked on, arms tight as steel as he cradled her close.

He didn't want to let her go. He wouldn't let her go.

He looked into worried dark eyes, saw a flush stain her
lovely face, the pout of concern on her lush mouth.

Tahir remembered the terror of losing her. The sense of
loss. The fear he'd never find her. Horror still trickled through
his belly at the recollection.

Realisation struck him with the force of an act of a divine
power.

He couldn't let her go.

The man who'd turned independence into an art form, self-
reliance into a way of life, had met his match.

He needed her.

CHAPTER THIRTEEN

IT WAS late in the day when Annalisa woke. She'd fallen exhausted into bed. Yet she hadn't slept for hours. Instead she'd replayed events in her mind. The quake, her work to help the wounded.

And Tahir, appearing out of nowhere and sweeping her into his arms. Her heart fluttered at the memory.

He'd been a stranger: intent, focused, all hard-muscled strength and determination. No hint of the playboy, just one hundred percent powerful, commanding male. One look at the set of his jaw had told her she hadn't a hope of escaping his hold. *Even if she'd wanted to.*

In his embrace was exactly where she'd wanted to be.

She'd been so worried for him, but had found herself in the thick of disaster and hadn't been able to turn her back on the pitifully wounded victims.

Tahir had barely heard her as he'd marched through the dark streets. Nor had he relinquished his hold when he'd reached his vehicle. He'd held her tight all the way, then carried her through the palace to her rooms.

Ignoring propriety, he'd only released her when he reached her bed. Even then he'd loomed close as servants scurried to provide food and run her a bath.

He'd looked immovable, his features a study in potent masculinity as he stared silently down at her.

Something had stretched taut between them. A tension she

hadn't been able to name but had felt with every slow breath, every tingle of awareness across her burning hot skin and in the deep, slow, coiling excitement in her belly.

When a maid had announced the bath was ready he'd abruptly disappeared, leaving her to ponder what had just happened.

When Tahir looked at her that way her doubts melted into nothing. It was like the sizzle in the air the night they'd made love. But more. Something stronger still.

Was she a fool, reading too much into his actions? Had he just been protecting his unborn baby?

And yet…she found herself hoping it was more.

She turned from her view of the sun setting in a blaze of colour. It was time to—

Annalisa's footsteps faltered as she spied the figure just inside her room. His hand clenched high on the filmy curtains that separated the entry foyer from her chamber.

'Tahir?' Her husky voice betrayed her longing.

Need rose. It had gnawed at her so long. A need that had escalated last night as he'd carried her with the stern certainty of a man claiming his woman.

She *wanted* him to claim her. *She wanted to be his.*

Every warning, every doubt, ebbed in the face of her feelings for Tahir. She'd tried to focus on the negative, to tell herself she shouldn't care for a man who didn't love her. But stern logic didn't work any more.

Flutters of excitement whirled and swooped in her abdomen. She stroked trembling fingers down the opalescent silk of the gown Rihana had given her.

His gaze followed the movement.

Heat blossomed low in her womb and at the apex of her thighs. She tried to calm herself and failed.

Last night's crisis had cut through her attempts to be sensible and careful. All that remained was raw feeling.

What she felt for Tahir was stronger than ever.

He was the embodiment of every dream she could no longer deny. Tall, suave and potently masculine in dark trousers and a black shirt, his head bare.

Tension radiated from him. His jaw was rigid, his face composed of taut angles and lines. His eyes blazed like the sky at midday. Almost too bright to watch. Yet she couldn't look away.

She took a step towards him and his hand clenched white-knuckled on the gossamer fabric. Her heart thumped out of kilter at what she read in his expression.

He looked fierce, stern, forbidding. Yet she felt no fear. For there was warmth too. Such warmth.

Surely it was real, not a product of her needy imagination?

For so long she'd wanted him to want her, really want *her*, as she did him. Now she had her wish. The force of that look almost buckled her knees.

Instinctively she realised he battled with himself. She had so little experience yet at some primitive level she understood her power over him.

For he had the same power over her. He'd wielded it from the first. She'd been blind to think she could escape its pull. Foolish to think she could walk away.

They might be king and commoner but in this they were equals. That knowledge gave her strength.

'Tahir?' Her voice was a barely audible throb of sound.

His fingers eased their grip on the fabric and his arm dropped to his side. He hefted a breath that inflated his chest and lifted his shoulders. It shuddered from him in a sigh. Annalisa felt its twin tremble through her.

He stepped forward, his long stride closing the distance between them. All she saw was him.

'*Habibti.*' *My darling.* His deep voice was hoarse and unfamiliar. The sound of his endearment crept like warm fingers up her spine till she shivered, her nipples peaking.

This close, she saw the lines of fatigue around his eyes. Had he been up all night and all day too?

Annalisa opened her mouth to ask about the rescue, but he reached out and pressed his index finger to her lips. She inhaled the warm scent of man, of Tahir, and heat pooled low in her body. She felt herself tremble on the brink of a precipice. No thought now of their turbulent past. The emotion she'd read in his ravaged features last night was more important than what had gone before.

For countless moments they stood, drawn by a force so strong the air crackled with it.

The tension was too much to bear. Annalisa swayed towards him. A muscle in his jaw worked; his eyes devoured her.

Tentatively she lifted her hand, unable to stop herself. She needed to feel him, safe and real.

Before she could touch him he hauled her close, slamming her into his rigid body. His arms wrapped hard round her, tucking her against him as if he had no intention ever of releasing her.

Annalisa trembled as his fiery heat encompassed her. Beneath her ear his heart thudded, matching her own racing pulse. She hugged him close, squeezing tight as tears she didn't even understand stung her eyes.

A hiccough escaped as she fought back surging emotion that threatened to overwhelm her.

Long fingers cupped her chin and tilted her face up. Then Tahir was kissing her, lips slanted across her mouth in stormy possession. He gave no quarter, allowed no hesitation, as he took her.

He delved deep, kissing her thoroughly, like a conquering marauder taking his fill. Yet there was a piercing sweetness to his caress that spoke of far more than easy gratification. Her heart soared at his urgency and underlying tenderness.

His hands shook as he cupped her face. For all his power and physical strength, Tahir was as needy as she.

Annalisa answered his kisses with her own, leaning on tiptoe and planting her hands in his thick, soft hair, as if to prevent him pulling away.

Tahir groaned deep in his throat as she slid her tongue into his mouth, mimicking his caresses, luxuriating in the dark mutual pleasure consuming them.

He bowed her back over his arm, his legs wide around hers as he demanded even more. Gladly she gave it, sinking into a warm tide of delight as their open-mouthed kiss grew needier, deeper, hungrier. *This* was what she'd craved.

A barely familiar throb quickened in the place between Annalisa's legs and she shifted restlessly, finding comfort in the press of his body against hers.

The pressure inside rose and she kissed him feverishly. She needed him closer even than this.

A moment later she was falling, and the air was squeezed from her lungs as he came down on her, pressing her into the cushioned mattress of her low bed.

Eyes wide now, she saw him prop himself on one arm, keeping most of his weight off her. Her eyes met his and thought fled.

Such fierce passion in his sky-blue eyes. Annalisa only had to meet his look and she spiralled towards paradise.

'Tahir.' Every scintilla of longing and hope and tremulous desire was in that one word. And she didn't care. All she cared about was having this one man who meant so much, here where he belonged. For this time it was right.

Her body softened, accommodating his hard length, readying for his possession.

A shudder racked his big frame and she saw the tendons in his neck stretch taut. Tenderness filled her at his vulnerability.

'I had to come. I need…' He shook his head, eyes squeezing shut.

She felt a spasm of sympathy clench her heart, seeing his inner turmoil, feeling the same driving force for intimacy.

'I need too, Tahir.'

At her whispered admission his eyes snapped open. Cerulean fire blazed down, scorching her face, her lips.

'*Habibti.*' The endearment was a low hum of sound that curled up and wrapped itself around her, warming every last recess of her body. Emotion shimmered in each syllable.

He lay poised above her as her heart thudded out a rhythm that spoke of desire, need, love. A love she could no longer deny for this proud, complex man.

Acknowledging her love didn't scare her when she saw Tahir at the mercy of his own emotions. Not just desire but tenderness, relief and regret. She recalled the stark fear on his face last night, the convulsive clamp of his arms around her, and wanted to soothe the remnants of his anxiety away.

She raised her hands to his face, to the strong jaw so smooth it must be freshly shaved. Over high cheekbones, feathering his brow, his ears, his nose and lips. She learned his face as a blind woman would, committing each detail to memory.

His tongue sleeked across her palm and she stilled. He clasped her hand to his mouth and kissed her there, laving and nipping and caressing till longing bubbled up inside and burst out in a throaty moan of bliss.

Then he was gone, rolling off her and leaving her bereft and wanting. Instinctively she turned towards him, but already he'd moved. He knelt, hands skimming up her legs, drawing the delicate silk she wore higher and higher.

Excitement rose as their gazes meshed. She lifted her bottom so he could push the fabric up. Then he peeled the dress over her shoulders and head, tossing it in a stream of pearly colour across the room.

Movement ceased as he loomed above, straddling her hips. His chest heaved, straining the buttons of his shirt. His gaze roved greedily.

A twinge of self-consciousness penetrated Annalisa's heady pleasure. Had her waist thickened? Her breasts seemed fuller. Too full? Instinctively she lifted her hands to shield herself, but he clamped hold of her wrists and pulled her arms wide.

She *felt* his eyes on her skin, like the graze of flesh on flesh. Tiny explosions erupted within her. Excitement reached fever-pitch just at the way he devoured her with his eyes. Her breasts seemed to swell against the lace of her bra and between her legs she felt dampness.

She revelled in his breathless regard. The way he looked at her made her feel like the most important being on the planet.

Deliberately he bent and planted a kiss to her belly, where her womb cradled the tiny new life they'd made.

Annalisa's heart turned over, undone by the reverence and tenderness of the gesture. She slipped her hands free to cup his head in her hands, cradling him to her as a flood of emotion stole her heart.

Seconds later he was moving, slipping off her bra and panties with an ease that reminded her just how practised he was with women.

Yet even that knowledge didn't give her pause. Not now. *This was meant to be.*

She welcomed his caressing hands, shifting under each sweep of his palm, each circling finger. She gasped as he bent his dark head to suckle at her breast, gently at first, then, as she held him close, tugging greedily, in a way that sent shafts of fire arrowing through her.

His hand slipped down, restlessly stroking her hip, her thigh, the secret needy place where his touch sent waves of pure pleasure rushing through her.

Annalisa's heart raced. Her skin bloomed, flushed with sexual arousal and a soaring happiness she'd never known. Her hips lifted off the bed, towards Tahir's caress. Yet he took his time, pleasuring her slowly, as if eking out every nuance of delight.

'Please, Tahir,' she gasped. 'I want…'

Hooded eyes met hers. She drank in the sight of his desire-ridden face just centimetres from the peak of her breast. Dark burnished golden skin beside pale.

Her proud lover.

A tremor shook her, and another.

'Then take what you want, *habibti*.' He ripped open his shirt and tossed it aside, revealing his powerful torso. A moment later he shoved his trousers and underwear off and onto the floor. His feet were bare, and she had no idea if he'd come to her like that or shucked off his footwear beside the bed.

Her throat dried as he stretched out beside her, propped on one arm. He looked utterly relaxed, like some long, lithe predator, resting in the heat of the day. Only the rapid rise and fall of his powerful chest gave him away. And his jutting erection.

Her eyes rounded as she took in the glory of Tahir, fully

aroused. How could she have forgotten his sheer magnificence? Or had she been so overwhelmed by her first experience of lovemaking that she hadn't looked? This time she felt no nerves, no anxiety. Just love and a soul-deep need.

His erection throbbed as she watched. 'See what you do to me?' His voice sounded curiously tight, as if he were in pain.

Her eyes roved him and hunger grew. She reached for him, curling fingers tentatively around his surprisingly soft skin. Warm silk over iron, over pure potent masculinity.

Something plunged deep inside her and she moved nearer.

His hand closed around hers, prying her fingers loose and then dragging her hand wide, to his other side, as he rolled onto his back. He held her like that, poised over him, holding her more with the searing intensity of his eyes than with his touch on her hand.

'Take what you want,' he repeated. This time the words were so slurred she wouldn't have understood if she hadn't been watching his face.

Did he mean…?

She looked down to where their bodies touched. A frisson of erotic awareness raced through her. She sank against him a fraction and his mouth tightened in a grimace that she understood too well. The pulse throbbing between her legs was a driving force, urging her to take as well as give.

Carefully Annalisa pushed herself onto her knees so she could straddle his supine form. His heavy weight between her legs, pushing against her thigh, sent a shudder of anticipation through her. As did the gleam in Tahir's eyes.

When his hands closed around her waist, adjusting her position above him, she let him, eager to ease the burgeoning ache inside.

A second later she felt pressure where she most needed it as Tahir rose beneath her. He drew her inexorably down, meanwhile pushing higher and higher, till surely any more was impossible.

One final sharp thrust of his hips and he lodged deep within her, part of her. The magic of it stunned her. She felt full, but not just physically. Her heart welled with the intensity of her emotions. With love for Tahir.

'All right?'

She nodded, bereft of speech as he massaged her breasts and sent delight coiling. He shifted beneath her, slowly at first, then to an increasing tempo that made the most of the friction between their shifting, sliding bodies.

Annalisa leaned forward, her hands on his shoulders, falling into the depths of his welcoming eyes. Long fingers clamped her hips, holding her firm against him as he thrust higher, harder.

Then with a hoarse cry she was flying, soaring above the world in exquisite delight as fire shimmered in her veins and pleasure exploded. An instant later Tahir shuddered beneath her, within her, as he gasped her name.

Greedily he hauled her close and they rode the last rocketing paroxysms together, his musky, hot skin fragrant against her, his heart pounding in tempo with hers, his body enfolding her.

Annalisa breathed deep of pleasure and peace and knew this was where she belonged. With Tahir. Always.

The white heat of cataclysmic orgasm burned Tahir's retinas. Scorched his flesh. Seared his soul.

He wrapped Annalisa closer, tangling his hand in her long hair, catching her slim leg with his knee, locking them together as if to prevent her moving.

He couldn't let her go.

He'd been right last night. *He needed Annalisa.*

Sex had never been so good. But he knew now this was more than physical satisfaction.

Tahir couldn't put a name to it. Couldn't get his mind to grapple with definitions and meanings.

But she was his. By right of conquest. By her own choice. By dint of the simple fact he'd never release her.

He'd never needed a woman as he needed Annalisa.

He'd never *needed* any woman.

He nuzzled her neck, breathing deep of her sweetness. Instantly tendrils of desire coiled within him, tightening sinews and hardening flesh.

Blood roared in his ears and rushed south. He stroked her collarbone, let his fingers trail to her breast and felt her shiver.

It was too soon. It shouldn't even be possible, not yet. But there was no mistaking the stirring in his loins.

Tentatively he moved, still lodged inside her.

He felt her grip on his shoulders tighten, reminding him how she'd scored his flesh in the throes of ecstasy. The idea of her marking him was strangely pleasing.

'Tahir?'

He shifted so he could see her, read the surprise and confusion in her flushed face. He stroked a strand of hair from her face. 'Too soon?'

Wide eyes held his for a moment, then a tiny dimple appeared in her cheek as she smiled and shook her head.

That was all the encouragement he needed. Moments later she was on her back, her hair a glossy fan beneath her as he took her slowly, tenderly and thoroughly.

This time he kissed her all the while, swallowed her small mews of pleasure and surprise, cupped her face in his hands as she gasped her completion. Mere seconds later the fire rose in him, spreading from his groin to his belly, sending incendiary flares through his whole body and setting a blaze in his lungs that made him gasp for breath.

He burned for her till the explosion blew him apart.

Yet even then the fire kept burning inside, a permanent unquenchable glow.

Tahir slid into oblivion, basking in its warmth, his arms locked about her.

CHAPTER FOURTEEN

'WHAT are these scars?' A gentle finger traced across the small of his back. 'Was it an accident?'

Tahir stilled in mid-stretch, tensing instinctively. In the past when women had asked that he'd brushed off the query, pretending the marks didn't matter. Yet each time the truth had burned his soul like red-hot coals.

The reminder of his father's 'loving' touch. Though Tahir couldn't see the scar tissue, it was a permanent brand of who he was and what his past had been.

It would be easy to demur now, to hide the shame of his past. But he didn't want to lie to Annalisa. For the first time he wanted to unburden himself. To share just a little. The realisation made his stomach clench in fear.

His reprobate reputation hadn't scared Annalisa. Nor had his position. She'd stood up to him time and again. She didn't act like any other woman he knew.

She acted as if she cared.

His mind shied from the notion even as its allure drew him. After a lifetime of believing himself unlovable, the idea of someone caring about him was too foreign.

Yet she'd been right about his mother.

'I'm sorry. I didn't mean to pry.'

'No.' He cut off her hurried apologies. 'It's all right.' He turned, and her gentle smile filled him with such pleasure it gave him the impetus to continue.

'It's a mark from a lash.'

'A lash?' Her brow furrowed in confusion, her eyes clouding, and Tahir was assailed by doubt.

He couldn't taint her with knowledge of his sordid past. The desire to talk about it was mere selfish weakness.

He rose quickly from the bed, only to feel her hand on his arm, stopping him.

Looking down, he met her questioning gaze head-on. Her expression was clear, open.

It reminded him of her extraordinary inner strength. The strength she'd needed to nurse him with no assistance in the desert. The strength to stand up to the man who was her sovereign and refuse to comply with his wishes.

For all her innocence, Annalisa was a strong woman.

'Tell me. Please?'

Finally he sank back onto the rumpled sheets and let her slip her arms about him. She leaned her head on his shoulder and her long hair blanketed him. He loved the feel of her near. It filled him with emotions he'd never felt and gave him strength to admit what he'd never told a soul.

'It's from my father's whip. He used to beat me regularly.'

So it hadn't been just Tahir's delirium. The beatings had been real. She'd wondered, but hadn't wanted to believe.

Her pulse pounded sickeningly. Not one beating but regularly. Not just with fists, but a whip. What sort of sadist behaved so?

Annalisa choked on rising bile.

Suddenly Rihana's comment about Tahir contributing to charities for abused children made perfect, horrible sense. Had he tried to save others from what he'd suffered?

Annalisa clasped him tight. She wished she'd been able to protect the boy who'd grown into this reserved man. Was it any wonder he hid his inner self? Or that he was difficult to know?

Fiercely she hugged him, sensing his unwillingness to talk.

'Don't cry, *habibti*.' He brushed her wet cheek where it pressed into his shoulder. 'It was a long time ago.'

'But you still remember it, all these years later. You still bear the scars.' They both knew she wasn't talking about the marks on his back. 'In the desert you dreamed about it every night.'

He wrapped an arm around her and she snuggled in, grateful for his acceptance. Tahir was unused to sharing anything more than his body. He was the sort of man to keep confidences to himself.

Had he ever talked of this before?

'I survived.' His tone was flat and uncompromising.

'You did more than survive,' she whispered urgently. 'You put it behind you. Look at you now.'

'Don't glamorise me, Annalisa.' His tone was sharp. 'Just because I'm Sheikh of my people it doesn't make me a good man.'

'No. But you *are* a good man.' She thought of his care for her at the oasis when grief had engulfed her. His anonymous efforts to improve the lives of children. The sensible, caring way he'd taken up the reins as ruler of a kingdom, though he didn't want the crown. The efficient way he'd mobilised every resource into a rescue effort after the quake, maintaining calm with his presence. The fact that he would marry her to make things right for their child.

'Hardly that.' His laugh was short and harsh. 'I'm too like my father. I've spent years wallowing in pleasure, seeking instant gratification, building a reputation for self-indulgence.'

'You're not like him.' She bridled at the notion. 'You're not manipulative or cruel.'

'Maybe only marriage and fatherhood will bring out my true depths.'

Annalisa reared back, staring aghast into his grim face, hearing his hollow tone. Was he serious? He surely couldn't fear that?

She'd seen him at his lowest ebb, on the edge of death, stripped of every pretence. The man she'd known then, the man she knew now, was nothing like the monster he tried to paint himself. The arrogant cynic wasn't the true Tahir.

She levered herself onto her knees and rose till their faces were level. She cupped his face in her palms and met his searing gaze.

'You're nothing like that—do you hear me?' Her voice rose with a potent fury she barely understood. 'I've never heard such rubbish in my life. Don't you *ever* speak like that again, or I'll know you're just after sympathy.'

His eyes widened in astonishment, as if the kitten he'd petted had turned into a tigress and drawn blood.

'You can't use that excuse to hide from life.'

'You don't know what you're talking about.' Before her eyes his expression chilled, became all arrogant hauteur.

'And you're too old not to face the truth.'

Her heart slammed against her ribs, fear rising that she'd pushed him too far. But the thought of him imagining himself like his brutal father was unbearable.

'Why did he beat you?' she asked before he could respond. 'Did he beat your brothers too?'

For a long time she thought Tahir wouldn't answer. His mouth thinned to a grim line and his eyes flashed with a mix of emotions. Her hands tightened on his jaw and, seeing his turmoil and pain, she couldn't stop herself leaning forward and pressing a tender kiss on his lips.

Would it be the last time he let her kiss him?

Fear catapulted through her as she realised she wanted more than anything to spend her life with Tahir. But perhaps she'd pushed him so far he'd turn his back on her.

Warm hands framed her face. Gentle thumbs scraped fresh tears from her cheeks as he drew back a fraction.

'I told you,' he murmured gruffly, 'not to cry. That's a royal command.' His mouth tilted in the lopsided smile that flipped her heart in her chest. 'I don't like it.'

Shakily Annalisa nodded, swallowing a knot of emotion.

He hadn't pushed her away. Instead his hands were gentle as they shaped her face.

'You're not going to give up, are you?'

She shook her head, her long hair swirling around her bare shoulders in a reminder that she was naked. They were both naked. But it didn't matter. Not when she saw pain shadowing Tahir's eyes.

With a sigh he lifted her up, right off her knees, and sat her on his lap, warm flesh against warm flesh. He reached for a coverlet and dragged it over her, cocooning them together under its satin comfort, hugging her close. His chin rested on her head and his heart thudded strong and familiar beneath her ear.

'No, he didn't beat Kareef and Rafiq,' he murmured at last. 'Just me.'

'But why?' Surely abusers weren't so discriminating?

Silence for another thirty seconds. 'I spent a lifetime wondering that, thinking it was a fault in me that provoked his hatred. My earliest memories are of his rage, his disapproval.' He paused. When he continued his voice was flat. 'It was because he thought I wasn't his son.'

Annalisa jerked in his hold, stunned. 'Seriously?'

He nodded. 'Oh, yes. After all these years my mother has finally explained what she didn't dare before.'

His chest expanded in a deep breath.

'My parents had an arranged marriage. My father amused himself with mistresses but he was incredibly jealous of his wife. She had a difficult birth with Rafiq, and on her doctor's recommendation she spent several months in France, recuperating. When someone made a sly remark about how she'd enjoyed herself with friends my father decided she'd taken lovers. It wasn't true, but that made no difference.'

Tahir tugged Annalisa close and she shut her eyes, grateful for his warmth as she imagined Rihana's life with a cruel brute who didn't love her.

'Then when I was born I was different. I didn't have the pale ice-blue eyes of his family. I stood out from him and my brothers.'

She stiffened, staring at his wide shoulder before her. 'Your father didn't think you were his son because your eyes were a darker blue?'

Tahir shrugged and she felt his muscles ripple. 'He wasn't a reasonable man. He was unhinged on the subject. My mother even suggested a DNA test, but he was paranoid news of it would leak. His pride wouldn't countenance anyone knowing he might have been cuckolded.'

He paused, breathing deep. 'It was no wonder I couldn't please him no matter how I tried. He didn't publicly accuse me of being a bastard. That would have reflected on his ability to keep his wife under control. Instead he made my life hell.'

'He made you his whipping boy.'

'Literally.' There was no humour in his laugh.

'And your mother?'

'No, he didn't beat her.' Tahir must have read her mind. 'He realised he could exact a more exquisite revenge by maltreating me and letting her know she was helpless to stop it.' His hand tightened on her shoulder. 'He'd shown his displeasure from the first, and she soon learnt that if she showed affection to me I'd pay for it.'

'How she must have suffered.' Annalisa shuddered at the idea of being unable to protect her own child. Short of running away and leaving her elder sons to the mercy of a vicious father, under traditional Qusani laws Rihana had had little power to stop it.

'I never realised how much,' Tahir murmured, 'till you forced me to talk to her.'

'Forced you? I—'

'I'm grateful, Annalisa, believe me.' His hand slipped down her arm in a slow caress that made her melt against him. 'If you hadn't brought up the subject I'd never have confronted my mother and known the truth.'

Annalisa luxuriated in his approving tone as much as in the sensation of chest hair and solid muscle beneath her cheek.

Grateful… It wasn't love, but surely it was a start.

'For years I thought she didn't care.' His voice was husky. 'Now I know she distanced herself from me because any sign of love on her part provoked more furious retribution for me. She tried to protect me the only way she could.'

His hold on her tightened.

'I was petrified he'd begin physically abusing her after I was exiled, but even then she wouldn't break her silence.' He paused, his breath fast and loud. 'She feared he'd kill me if she returned my calls. He knew I'd tried to contact her again and threatened violent retribution if she spoke to me.'

'Tahir!' Annalisa clung close, her arms tight around his torso. 'That's monstrous!'

She felt him shake his head above her. 'He *was* a monster. The damage he did.' Tahir stroked the hair back from her brow. 'Even when he died my mother didn't call me. She thought she'd killed my feelings by seeming to turn her back on me. She was afraid *I* didn't care for *her*.'

When all the time it had been the other way around. Tahir had believed his mother hadn't loved him.

What would that do to a child?

Annalisa's heart cracked even as fierce maternal protectiveness surged at the notion of anyone abusing *her* child like that.

Now she understood Rihana's words. Tahir had had everything he wanted: success, wealth, women. But not the one thing he'd really craved.

Love.

Tahir had been without love, or believed himself without it, most of his life.

Jagged fear shot through her. He'd found pleasure and comfort in her body. Yet he'd committed himself only to a marriage of convenience. Would Tahir accept the one thing she wanted most of all to give him?

Would he accept her love?

He'd spent so long cultivating his independence and his self-belief as a man unworthy of deep regard, maybe he was no longer able to accept love or even believe in it.

Was he capable of reciprocating? Of loving her?

Annalisa found her answer the next day.

After a night of passion beyond anything she'd believed possible, after tenderness that brought tears to her eyes more than once, Tahir left.

Words of love trembled on her tongue, her heart so full she had to share her feelings.

Yet he looked so weary after another night without sleep.

His expression settled into grim lines as he spoke of the need to oversee the rescue efforts and she didn't have the heart to burden him with more.

Others needed him more urgently. Her news, her needs, could wait a little longer.

Besides, she shied from the possibility he'd freeze when he heard her admission.

Perhaps he'd reject her. She wasn't ready for that.

Her love for him had grown so much, obliterating her doubts once she saw beneath the mask he presented the world. She wanted to stay and make him happy. Prove to him love was possible and that they could have far more than a marriage of convenience. That they could make a family together.

She was so preoccupied it took her a while to realise the stir she caused as she moved through the palace much later in the day. Everyone looked at her differently, from servants to officials and visitors waiting for appointments.

Overnight the news of where Tahir had spent the night must have spread. Or perhaps it was the way he'd blurted out news of her pregnancy in public.

People refused to meet her gaze, bowing lower than ever as she passed, yet she felt their eyes on her back. Heat crawled up her throat and into her cheeks as she entered an audience chamber to be greeted by a cessation of all conversation. No doubt they'd been gossiping about the latest royal scandal, confirmed by the Sheikh himself.

Stiffening, her pulse thudding, Annalisa paused, grateful that she'd again worn one of the beautiful gowns Rihana had pressed on her. She might feel small and insignificant, but at least she looked as if she belonged in this world of wealth and finery.

She lifted her chin, forcing down the impulse to spread her hand over her abdomen in a telltale protective gesture.

Did they assume she was simply the latest in the long series of Tahir's conquests?

Her stomach plunged. Remembering how he'd left so abruptly, and his air of distraction, maybe they were right. Was

she kidding herself that Tahir could feel more for her than duty
and physical pleasure?

He'd shared some of his past but that didn't mean he loved
her.

Yet she refused to give up her dreams without a fight. She
owed it to her baby too, to try and build a meaningful marriage.

Turning on her heel, she spun round and marched to Tahir's
offices. His senior private secretary was alone in the outer
office.

'Excuse me,' she said, approaching his desk. 'I wonder if
you can help me with some information?'

'Of course.' He stood abruptly, his expression uncomfortable as he shot a glance towards the other office.

Instantly a premonition hit Annalisa. A feeling of impending disaster. These last weeks she'd developed an easy relationship with Tahir's staff. What had changed?

The secretary's eyes dipped fleetingly to her waist and her
poise almost crumbled. Of course. News of her pregnancy and
a potential scandal changed everything.

Warily she let him lead her towards a private sitting room
partly screened from the main area.

Her lips twisted bitterly. Was she such an embarrassment she
had to be ushered from sight?

'I'd like you to look up the King's appointments,' she said as
they walked, her voice a little too strident as she fought embarrassment and anger. 'We're marrying next week and I need
details of the time and location so I can arrange some invita-
tions.'

If she was going to fight for Tahir, attempt to turn this into
a real marriage, she'd start as if it were real. She'd proudly
invite her family. Every last cousin. She refused to let Tahir turn
their wedding into a hole and corner affair, as if he were
ashamed of her.

The secretary halted so abruptly Annalisa almost walked
into him.

'I'm sorry,' he muttered. 'Pardon me.' He turned but didn't
meet her eyes. 'Won't you take a seat?'

She shook her head, watching with growing concern the way he clasped and unclasped his hands, clearly ill at ease.

'No, thanks. I'd rather stand. Now, about the wedding?'

He swallowed hard, as if clearing a constriction in his throat. Still he didn't look her full in the face.

'I'm sorry, I…' He paused, looking back to the office as if seeking help.

'You were saying? Just the time and location will do.'

'I'm afraid…' He stopped and finally met her eyes. 'I'm afraid you'll have to talk to the King. He's altered the arrangements.'

'Yes?' Annalisa's skin prickled as that prescience of trouble grew stronger. 'How did he alter them?'

'He's cancelled them.'

Annalisa heard the words echo through her, felt their impact like the slow motion force of a traffic collision.

Blindly she groped for support, clutching the back of a chair with shaking fingers.

Only yesterday Tahir had referred to their wedding. Why change his mind? Had he read her neediness and her emotions even though she hadn't voiced them? Had he understood how she felt and decided to weather the scandal rather than lumber himself with a woman so obviously in love with him?

Had he rejected her because he couldn't accept her love? Because he couldn't return it?

'Here. Please! Sit down.' The secretary grabbed her elbow and guided her into a nearby chair.

Obediently Annalisa sank, grateful for the support as her knees turned to water.

'Are you absolutely sure?' She fixed him with a look that begged him to be wrong.

Hurriedly he shook his head. 'No, I'm sorry. His Majesty cancelled the arrangements only a few hours ago. Perhaps if you talk to him…?'

What? He'd agree to marry her after all?

From the first Tahir hadn't wanted marriage. He'd felt obligated. And now…now, for all their physical intimacy, perhaps she'd got too close to that part of himself he held so private.

Her heart throbbed pure pain. No doubt he thought it easier to provide financial support for their child than entangle himself with a needy woman.

'Wait there. I'll get you some tea.' Her companion hurried away, leaving Annalisa to stare at the cluster of gilded French antique furniture in the room. It reminded her inevitably of the huge gulf between her and Tahir.

Had she fooled herself with dreams of a love-match? How had she let herself think for a moment it was possible?

She tried to tell herself it was for the best, ending things now rather than going through the emotional entanglement of a doomed marriage.

Yet she couldn't convince herself.

She was still gazing dry-eyed before her, when a door slammed and she heard footsteps on the inlaid floor of the outer office.

'…and your personal leadership during this disaster has made all the difference, sire. Without it the relief operation would not have been so effective.'

'You flatter me, Akmal. But thank you. I realise I'm not the man the elders expected to have on the throne.'

'Let me assure you, your actions these past couple of months have won their respect. As will your decision to cancel that imprudent marriage. It's gratifying you've taken the advice of your counsellors on this issue.'

Annalisa pressed her palm to her mouth.

'If I'd taken your advice, Akmal, I'd be crowned already and married to a foreign princess with blue blood and ice in her veins.' Tahir's voice was terse.

The sound of it made Annalisa twist in her seat. But they couldn't see her. She was hidden by a carved screen inlaid with mother of pearl. Her stomach fluttered in distress. She didn't want to be here, listening to their discussion. But she couldn't face him. Not yet.

'I wish you'd stop delaying your coronation, sire. It's what the country needs. Stability, proof that the monarchy is solid and here to stay.'

'You don't think marrying the mother of my child indicates a certain permanency?'

Annalisa winced at the heavy irony in his tone.

'Laudable as your intentions were, Majesty, we both know the child can be brought up out of the limelight. With sufficient money it will be well cared for and educated. And if you wish to continue a discreet relationship with the mother…'

Nausea engulfed her, and she didn't hear the rest of the sentence for the buzzing sound in her ears. She hunched over, arms wrapped around her waist, breathing slowly through her nose in an attempt to force down the bile in her throat.

'Besides…' The other man's voice began to fade, presumably as they entered the inner office. 'Such a marriage isn't possible. The King must either marry royalty or a woman of pure Qusani blood. It's written in the constitution. This woman's father was Danish. She's not suitable as your consort.'

Annalisa barely heard the thud of heavy doors closing. Her mind was filled with the brutal words she'd not been meant to hear.

Tahir's advisor proposed to pay her off with cash then set her up somewhere so she could be the King's…what? Mistress? Concubine? Even for Qusay the idea was medieval.

As for the requirement for pure Qusani blood! Right now *her* blood, pure or not, was boiling at the man's attitude. How could he take such an antiquated view of the world? Hadn't he heard of the twenty-first century?

She shot to her feet and paced the small salon.

To be discussed as if she were a problem, a *thing* to be moved or used or discarded as they saw fit! To be rejected because she wasn't royal, or because her father had been born in Copenhagen! She was as much a Qusani as Tahir and his precious Akmal. More so. Unlike Tahir, she'd lived here all her life—and, unlike his advisor, not in a gilded palace but with ordinary Qusanis.

How dared they belittle her like that?

Fury surged in her bloodstream, propelling her across the room and out of the door.

She'd wondered if Tahir could ever love her and now she had her answer. Now she knew exactly what to do.

It was time to go home.

CHAPTER FIFTEEN

TAHIR strode down the frescoed corridor, eager to reach his destination.

The day had been difficult. The cleaning-up work after the earthquake continued, and organising emergency housing and supplies for the dispossessed was a massive undertaking.

Then there was the matter of his marriage.

He'd reckoned without the obstinacy of the Council of Elders, who stuck blindly to the old ways. They wanted him married, all right, but to a woman of their choosing. It was only today he'd learned exactly how far they'd take their opposition.

Strange how they were willing to accept him, a prodigal returned, as their monarch, but quibbled over his choice of wife.

He set his jaw, remembering his recent interview with Akmal. The vizier was determined to force his hand and manoeuvre him into marrying a princess.

Tahir slipped a hand into his trouser pocket, grasping it on the weighty package there. His lips curved in a smile of anticipation.

With this gift he planned to get everything he wanted from Annalisa.

'What's the meaning of this?' Tahir strode past the suitcase lying open on the bed, half full of her clothes. He followed the sound of movement into the nearby dressing room and slammed to a stop.

Annalisa stood there, wearing nothing but lace panties and bra. On the floor at her feet lay of pool of crimson silk embroidered with pearls. He recognised it instantly: a dress he'd ordered for Annalisa to go with the pearl and ruby diadem he'd present her with when they married. He'd asked his mother to give her the dress, knowing his fiancée, with her quaint scruples, would balk at accepting it from him.

Annalisa's face was chalky, her expression mutinous as she stared back at him. No mistaking the anger sparking in her gaze, nor the hurt tightening her mouth.

What had happened to the warm, accommodating woman he'd left in bed just hours ago?

'I'm leaving. That's what it means.'

She drew a deep breath, and despite his confusion he couldn't help appreciating the way her breasts lifted in their lace cups.

'And stop looking at me like that!' Her eyes flashed. 'I'm not a plaything for your enjoyment.' She stooped and retrieved the dress, holding it in front of her.

'You're not going anywhere.' The notion was unthinkable. He strode nearer and his blood ran cold as she backed away.

She shook her head and her unbound hair swirled around her bare shoulders, reminding him of the way she'd lain in his arms through the night. The way she'd made him feel: pleasured, triumphant, whole. Curiously at peace.

'I'm leaving and you can't stop me.' Her chin lifted in the sign of quiet resolution he knew so well.

'Annalisa?' A curious sensation began deep in his gut. A roiling, unsettled feeling he remembered from another time, another life.

Anxiety. *Fear*.

The notion of her walking out of his life made a yawning void open up before him. Worse than the agony he'd endured at his father's hands. Worse even than the blank grey nothingness that had haunted him before he came here.

Pain transfixed him, froze his heart as he read her bitterness and anger.

She couldn't go. He wouldn't allow it.

'Of course you'll stay.' He tried to sound reasonable, but the words emerged brusquely.

'No! What have I got to stay for?' She lifted her chin still higher in unconscious arrogance and Tahir's certainty crumbled.

'To be with me.'

Or had she decided he was too flawed? That he wasn't worth the risk? A man with a past like his had no right expecting a woman like Annalisa to want him. But he did. He had from the first.

She blinked, and he thought he saw her eyes glaze with tears. He started forward, but again she retreated.

'That's enough, you think?'

Her words pierced him to the core. He'd finally realised what he wanted from Annalisa, only to have her reject him out of hand.

He should accept her decision. An honourable man would. But Tahir had no pretensions to honour. Not if that meant letting her go.

His eyes blazed fire as he closed the gap between them, looming over her, all male aggression and power.

A tiny part of her revelled in the fact that he wanted her so badly, even though it was only for sex. As his mistress on the side. Even now she responded to him physically, wanted him so badly.

'Don't touch me!'

But it was too late. His hands curled round her shoulders, hauling her close so he engulfed her senses, his body hard against hers, the scent of his skin sabotaging her resolve.

'You love it when I touch you.' His look told her he knew her weakness and intended to make the most of it. He slid an arm around her bare back and secured her tightly.

The air around them shimmered with tension, with sparks of electricity, with combustible emotional energy.

'No!' She couldn't afford to give in now—not when she'd gathered the strength to do what she must.

But her resistance had no effect. He slipped his other hand over her breast, moulding it in a possessive grasp that sent desire shuddering through her.

How was she meant to withstand him when she couldn't fight her own weakness?

'Please, Tahir. No.' She squeezed her eyes shut and her head lolled as she arched instinctively in his hold, pressing wantonly for more.

'*Yes*, Annalisa. You *will* be mine. Whatever I have to do. Whatever it takes.' He dragged in a rough breath. 'I gave you up once before. At the oasis I deliberately baited and insulted you so you'd turn away and not look back. I didn't deserve you and I knew it, so for that day I became the sort of shallow bastard I knew you'd abhor.'

The urgency of his words, the deep hoarse timbre of his voice, mesmerised her.

'I owe you apologies for that. You don't know how it cut me to hurt you that day, when all I wanted was to drag you close and not release you.' Searing blue eyes met hers. *'But I can't do it again. I can't force myself to give you up. You can't expect it of me.'*

Was it true? Had his loutish behaviour been a ploy to scare her off? She could barely believe it. Yet it would explain the puzzling difference between his behaviour then and since. Could he have cared so much and behaved so foolishly?

Yet what did it change? Nothing.

She shook her head in mute desperation, knowing she had to escape before she succumbed to him again. But her body already betrayed her. With Tahir she lost the will for self-preservation. He even undermined her pride.

'I can't—'

'You can, Annalisa. You will.' He mouthed the words against her neck as he swept kisses over her throat.

'For how long, Tahir?' Anguish drew the words from her. 'How long will you want me as your mistress? How long before the next woman takes your fancy?'

He froze, hands tightening on her. She felt the heavy thud

of his heart through the thin fabric. Finally he raised his head and she met his curiously blank stare.

'There will be no other woman.' The words sounded like a vow. 'I've never wanted a woman the way I want you. I never *will* want another woman.

How self-delusional could she get? She shook her head, trying to dislodge the illusion that he meant it.

'So you say.' She spat the words out. 'Will you expect to keep me somewhere conveniently close and still come home to your royal wife?'

His head reared back as if struck. Dull colour mounted his high cheeks.

'What are you talking about? *You'll* be my wife.'

If she didn't know better she'd believe the confusion on his face. Even now it was a struggle to accept the truth. Tahir had never lied to her before.

'Don't.' She pushed fruitlessly against his broad chest. 'Don't pretend. I know you've cancelled the wedding. And I know why.' She turned her head, unable to meet his piercing gaze any longer. 'I know you can't marry me. I'm not *suitable*.' The word tasted bitter on her tongue.

All her life she'd been an outsider. Never more so than now, when she wasn't deemed good enough to marry the man she loved.

Tahir swore, long and low and comprehensively.

'Who told you that?' His voice sliced the air like a cold steel blade, raising the hairs on the back of her neck. 'Give me his name, Annalisa.'

She turned her head, shivering at the deadly intent she read in his taut features.

'Who was it?' His voice burred with barely veiled threat.

'I heard it with my own ears, Tahir. You and Akmal. There's no use pretending.'

He tugged her hard against him, arms encompassing her. 'I wouldn't have had you overhear that for anything.'

'No. I'm sure.' She tried to stand rigid within his embrace but it was impossible.

'I thought you'd decided you couldn't trust yourself and the baby to a man like me.' The echo of pain in his voice drew her skin tighter. 'That you hold my past against me.'

'No!' She was aghast he'd even think it. 'This isn't about trusting you as a father.'

Her throat closed as she realised how much she wanted him as a hands-on dad for their child.

'This isn't about you, Tahir. It's about me. About the fact that I won't make a suitable queen.' She lifted her head. 'And about the fact you don't want to marry me. Now, please,' she said, summoning the last of her pride, 'don't make this harder. Let me go.' Her voice wobbled and she bit her lip hard, striving for control.

Tahir stepped back and instantly she craved his touch. She wanted to burrow herself in his embrace and say she'd take whatever he'd give her, no matter how fleeting.

He stood proud and tall. A strong man. The man who owned her heart and soul. *The man who could never be hers.*

A sob rose in her chest and jammed her throat. She wrapped her arms round herself, hugging the crimson silk close, knowing her dream was over.

'You fill my life, Annalisa. You make me whole. *That's* what matters.'

Slowly, without taking his eyes from hers, Tahir reached into a pocket and drew out a velvet pouch embroidered with gold. He opened it, plunged his hand inside and withdrew something that shimmered fire.

'You will be the finest queen Qusay has known. Not just because of your compassion and intelligence. But because I love you, Annalisa.' He held out his hand. 'Do you hear me? I love you and I want you to be my wife. Not only for the sake of our child, but because I can't imagine my life without you by my side.'

He unfurled his fingers and a thousand scintillating lights dazzled her. Emeralds and diamonds spilled from his hand in a massive sparkling web.

Her breath stopped as she realised what it was: the Queen's Necklace. A royal symbol of power and wealth dating back centuries to the time, it was said, of the first emerald mines in Qusay. It was given to each new queen as a sign of her paramount place in the kingdom and of her husband's fidelity.

Annalisa's knees crumpled, and only Tahir's strong hands stopped her collapsing. Against one bare shoulder she felt the cold touch of peerless gems. They were real.

'Annalisa! Say something.' His voice was hoarse with passion.

'But you can't—' She struggled for words as she grappled to understand. 'You don't—'

'Love you? Of course I do.' His hands tightened against her. 'Can you forgive me for not realising sooner? It's still a new concept to me. But if knowing I never want to be anywhere but by your side means love, and wanting to grow old with you, watching our children and their children, then I love you.' He dragged in a huge breath. 'You make me dare to want what I never dreamed of before: the love of one special woman.'

Her heart swelled at the look in his eyes.

'The question is, do you trust me enough to be my wife?' A shadow of doubt darkened his clear blue gaze. 'I'll do my best to be a good husband. And I'll learn to be the sort of father our child needs.'

Annalisa had never seen him so earnest. Never before felt the emotion that flowed from him in warm waves. Love, strong and pure.

'Of course I trust you, Tahir.' She raised her hands and cupped his strong jaw. 'I love you. I've always loved you.' Fire blazed in his eyes and, emboldened, she leaned close to kiss him, her heart overflowing with a happiness she'd never thought possible.

'Wait! Let me do this first.'

Bewildered, she saw him lift one hand and turn her round. In the full-length mirror on the wall she saw their reflection. Tahir behind her, raising the net of stones, massive emeralds interspersed with teardrop diamonds, over her head.

The crimson dress had already dropped unheeded to the floor and she stood, naked but for her lace underwear, as he fastened the elegant necklace, a king's ransom, around her throat.

Her eyes widened at the weight of it, the sheer magnificence. But it was Tahir's hands, slipping round to undo her bra and tug it away, that absorbed her attention. The sight of them together, of his bronzed hands moving purposefully on her paler flesh, sent ripples of desire through her.

'My perfect bride,' he murmured against her neck as he cupped her breasts with warm hands.

Fire sizzled through her and she sagged back against him, eyes fluttering shut.

'But I'm not. I'm not royal. I'm half-foreign.'

'You're perfect,' he said again, nipping the sensitive flesh beneath her ear.

This time, hearing the love in his words, she dared to believe.

'That's why I cancelled the wedding arrangements. I realised last night I couldn't take you as my wife in some second-rate ceremony. I want the world to know when I make you my bride.' His breath was warm on her skin. 'It will take longer to arrange, but we're having the biggest wedding Qusay has ever seen.'

'But you can't. The constitution…' Her words petered out under the sheer weight of sensual pleasure as he massaged her breasts and kissed her bare shoulders.

'The constitution will be changed. If Qusay wants me as King, then you will be my Queen. I met with Akmal today to make my ultimatum, and believe me…' he paused on a chuckle '…I made my point forcefully. Arrangements are being made as we speak.' He nuzzled her neck. 'Now, open your eyes, *habibti*.'

Annalisa lifted heavy lids, attuned now to the telltale heat of his body behind hers and his rigid arousal pressing against her. She saw their reflection. The knowing gleam in her lover's bright gaze: his hands roving her body, almost bare but for the stunning, regal jewels. Then his hand dipped low.

'I want you to watch,' he whispered, 'as I make love to my fiancée.'

The wedding celebrations had taken seven days.

As Tahir had promised, they'd been the most lavish Qusay

had seen. Partly because he'd ensured all Qusanis were welcome to attend the entertainments, and partly because it had been a joint celebration.

On the fifth day his coronation had taken place.

Now he stood, a sea breeze rippling the magnificent embroidered cloak that hung from his shoulders, the unfamiliar weight of the royal black and gold *igal* encircling the fine white cloth of his headdress. At his side the King's Sword lay heavy against his thigh. An ancient symbol of the wealth and power of Qusay's ruler, its scabbard was encrusted with gems. Its hilt, weighted with emeralds the size of pigeon's eggs, belied the fact that the blade was sharp enough to wreak justice on any who threatened the King or his country.

He felt the weight of expectation and responsibility on him, but he carried it easily, confident now that he'd done the right thing in accepting the kingship.

Music swelled on the late-afternoon air and the hum of voices. The perfume of fragrant spices from elaborate braziers mixed with the scent of yet more roast meats being prepared.

Tahir drew a deep breath and surveyed the gathering. Throngs of people laughing and chattering, some beneath open-sided tents lined with carpets and padded seating. Others strolling in the gardens or watching the horse-racing down on the white sand beach. Pennants fluttered, jewels flashed, silks swirled.

Yet among the throng one person caught and held his attention. His heart swelled with that unfamiliar emotion he realised now was love.

Annalisa. His bride. His queen. His love.

Her smile had been radiant all day, first with her cousins, who'd been genuinely happy for her, and now with his family.

'You've got that look on your face again, Tahir,' came a deep voice beside him. 'Didn't you know a king is supposed to look solemn and regal?'

Tahir's lips twitched and he turned to his brother Rafiq, looking debonair in a dark suit. 'Much you'd know about it. You were never King.'

Rafiq shrugged. 'What can I say? I had a better offer.' His eyes strayed to the cluster of beautiful women just metres away.

'You were saying? About that look?' Tahir laughed. It was a sound he'd become gradually used to these past few months, as his world had filled with a warmth and happiness he'd never take for granted.

'Oh, don't pay any attention to him,' said Kareef as he strolled up to join them, a glint of humour in his pale blue eyes. 'You know he's got it bad. Can't keep his eyes off his wife.'

'Which makes four of us, and you wouldn't want it any other way.' Their cousin Zafir came to stand on Tahir's other side. He raised a hand and the sun glinted off his sapphire ring. He gestured towards the cluster of women in the royal tent. 'We've been lucky, all of us.'

There was a murmur of assent from deep voices.

Tahir scanned the group. Zafir's Layla, dripping sapphires and dressed in regal finery, yet with a smile as warm as the sun. Rafiq's Serah, with her quiet beauty and gentle nature, now laughing with her childhood friend Jasmine, Kareef's lovely wife.

And his mother was there, looking happier than he'd ever seen her, matriarch of a growing family. For at their centre sat the most beautiful of them all: his Annalisa, cradling Jasmine and Kareef's tiny adopted daughter.

At the sight of his wife holding the infant so tenderly heat roared through him, a proud possessiveness he felt whenever he thought of the child she carried. Beneath her exquisite dress of silver her once-flat belly had begun to swell with the weight of their child.

He longed to reach out and stroke that satiny flesh with his palm, reacquaint himself with each luscious curve and line of her body. They hadn't shared a bed in seven nights, mindful for once of tradition. But tonight...

As if reading his thoughts, Annalisa lifted her head and met his gaze head-on. A delicate blush stained her cheeks and her lips parted in unconscious invitation.

Tahir almost groaned aloud.

He wanted to stride over, slip the dress from her shoulders and make love to her as she wore nothing but the emerald and diamond collar. As he had the day he'd first put it on her. An image of Annalisa naked but for the gems filled his mind. Pliant and sexy under his questing hands, soft and welcoming against his hard flesh. A shudder of pure need racked him.

Saying something to the other women, Annalisa passed the baby over and rose, a shimmering vision in her wedding dress. Late sun caught the golden lights in her hair as she walked towards him. Her gown sparkled with embroidered gems. Her jewelled chandelier earrings swayed against her pale neck, accentuating its slender curve.

Slowly she approached. Their gazes meshed.

He heard voices beside him and realised his companions were moving away, leaving him alone with his bride. His family showed the good sense to know when a man needed to be alone with his wife.

Then she was before him. Velvet eyes gazed up with a stunned delight he knew matched his own expression.

'You look like an impatient bridegroom,' she said, her voice husky.

'I am.' He claimed her, wrapping his hand around hers and drawing her close. 'I want you so badly it hurts to breathe.'

Her lips curved in an enchanting smile, even as her eyes gleamed with excitement. 'Then perhaps we should leave everyone to their celebrations, so I can…tend your hurts.'

Tahir sucked in a deep breath at the image her words conjured.

'Soon,' he promised, 'when I'm capable of walking.' He pulled her to him and turned her round so she stood, like him, looking out over the colourful scene. She fitted against his body, into his arms, as if made for him.

'No regrets about becoming my Queen?'

'Of course not.' She shook her head and the delicate scent of cinnamon and wild honey teased his nostrils.

Beneath the finery she was still the woman he'd met in the desert. Capable, loving, wonderful. His arms closed round her tenderly.

'I love you,' he whispered against her hair.

'And I love you, Tahir. Always.' She wrapped her hands over his encompassing arms and sank against him.

He and Annalisa would be together for the rest of their lives.

He'd never known such happiness.

When five o'clock hits, what happens after hours...?

Feel the sizzle and anticipation of falling in love across the boardroom table with these seductive workplace romances!

Now available at
www.millsandboon.co.uk

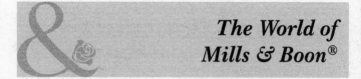